ALEXANDER
HALL OF THE GODS

A Star Publish LLC Book
http://starpublish.com

Mesquite, Nevada and St. Croix USVI

ALEXANDER
HALL OF THE GODS

By

G. M. Masterson

Alexander: Hall of the Gods

ISBN: 1-932993-79-7
ISBN 13: 978-1-932993-79-0
Library of Congress Number
LCCN:2007927937

Edited by Janet Elaine Smith
Cover Art by Robert Olsen and Kate Chesterton
Cover Design by Star Publish LLC
Interior Design by Mystique Design

Published in 2007 by Star Publish LLC
Printed in the United States of America

My thanks to
Robert Olsen, Kate Chesterton, and Kristie Leigh Maguire
for the cover design and layout for this book.

AUTHOR'S NOTE

This book was inspired by a true story and exciting recent discoveries in the fields of parapsychology and archaeology.

At the dawning of the twenty-first century a microchip driven super-civilisation hurtles towards an abyss of its own making. Has it all happened before, in the distant mists of time?

G.M. Masterson

Hieroglyphs discovered by Victorian archaeologists in an ancient Egyptian temple.

CHAPTER 1
NORTHGATE HALL

The plateau was silent after a powerful desert storm. Violent winds had scoured the sand from a massive slab, which now lay exposed. A single hieroglyph stood out starkly, etched deep into the stone.

"What do you make of it, Salim?" muttered an Englishman as he examined the ancient carving with his intense blue eyes.

"There is no mistaking it, Baron. It is the Eye of Horus, a symbol of protection—a warning," replied Salim. "I have a bad feeling about this. We should not disturb what lies below."

"You people are so superstitious," growled the baron. "This is the twentieth century, man! We have entered many tombs and hidden chambers. Whatever is down below us has been buried for thousands of years. Order the men to lift the slab!"

Lingering momentarily, Salim's eyes beseeched the baron to change his mind, but the Englishman's face was set like granite. Reluctantly, the Egyptian departed to do his employer's bidding. Back in his tent, the baron continued to ponder the hieroglyph, but the heat made him drowsy. His head slumped forward. An hour passed and it was hotter still. Awakening with a start, he felt the perspiration oozing from his skin. Salim burst in. "We have moved the stone!" he said, panting.

Stepping out of the shade of the canvas, the Englishman and his assistant walked into the burning light. The huge slab stood ominously in the distance, lifted intact and supported by a row of heavy wooden staves. With the slab removed, two steps cut into solid bedrock were visible. Below the steps lay grey-gold sand and rubble. Eyes narrowing, the baron inspected the site. "This is obviously the entrance to an underground chamber. Get the men to dig!" he commanded.

Drinking deeply from a water bottle, the baron returned to the tent. A sturdy journal, faced in red buffalo hide, lay on a battered wooden desk. The book was magnificently bound, tough, and built to endure the test of time. The baron kept a separate journal for each of his expeditions. They stood testament to his excavations and many discoveries. Opening the journal, he began the job of transcribing the hieroglyph and associated notes onto a fresh vellum page.

It was late in the evening when Salim returned. "With your permission, Baron, the men would like to retire for the night," he said, tired and drained from the long day's heat.

"By all means," responded the baron, "but we will start again at first light. Tell them to serve the meal as soon as it is ready. An excellent day's work, Salim, my friend. An excellent day's work!"

It was a blessed relief when the sun sank below the horizon and the sky grew black. Fed and rested in the cool of night, the men were up early, as directed by the baron, and the digging began again in earnest. Five days of hard labour followed. It was early evening on the sixth day when the rubble had been fully cleared. Making his way down the stone stairway, the baron entered the passage—a passage that had been hacked millennia ago, through solid limestone. Pausing in the darkness, he called out, "Salim, bring me a torch." Bursting into flame, the torch filled the passage with dancing yellow light. Ahead of him, the baron could see the entrance to the tomb. "Bring the torch closer," he commanded as he reached the end of the passage. "There are definitely no hieroglyphs, but the entrance to the tomb will be behind these blocking stones," he muttered.

Looking reassuringly at his assistant, the baron said with steady confidence, "Take heart, Salim. The eye cannot harm us. It is just a symbol from a long dead religion. Break down the wall!"

Salim looked at the Englishman, his eyes widening with fear. "Let us turn back now, Baron Northgate, before it is too late. I am not a coward, but something is not right in this place. We should leave now!" he pleaded.

At heart, the baron was an atheist and he despised the superstitions and simpering fears of the lower orders. He regarded the Egyptian closely. Salim was tall and skinny, with thinning black hair, a smooth narrow face, and a short broad nose. Small black eyes peered from behind a pair of round-rimmed spectacles.

"Salim, you surprise me," the baron replied, "surely we are rational men of science, not to be swayed from our task by primitive superstition. This could be a significant discovery! Tell the men to break through to the tomb. I will brook no procrastination." Walking briskly, the baron made his way up the passageway and back out into the desert. Soon, the crash of iron against stone could be heard, echoing from below.

As the sun began to sink, the scent of burning tobacco drifted into the air. Inhaling deeply from a Cuban cigar, the baron began to smile. This was a moment to savour and the excitement was mounting. Although a man of average stature, the baron's face was broad and strong, its strength accentuated by a thick black mutton-chop moustache. Every inch an aristocrat, he was confident, articulate, and impervious to criticism. During the depressing gloom of British winters, he amused himself in exotic lands, searching for lost treasures. The remainder of the year was spent running his estate and business empire. Algernon Northgate was a very rich man, but a man easily bored and always ready for a new challenge.

Salim emerged from the passage. The dust was making him cough, and his eyes were watering. Squinting at the baron through the grime-coated lenses of his glasses, he spluttered, "We have broken through, Baron Northgate!"

"Marvellous!" shouted the baron, grabbing a torch and descending rapidly into the passage. Dust was heavy in the air as he pushed his way past the diggers and thrust himself through a large, gaping hole. Standing stock-still, his eyes began to scan the chamber. Walls painted and carved with elaborate hieroglyphs and portraits of men and beasts danced in the light of the flames.

"No one is to enter!" he yelled suddenly. "Keep the diggers back!"

ഇ൏

It was the year nineteen hundred and two. Rain pattered gently off the enormous bay window of the library at Northgate Hall. The library was an impressive room, with huge bookcases extending a full fifteen feet above the floor. The bookcases housed a vast array of literary and scientific works, including the journals of Baron Algernon Northgate.

The baron sat at a large desk, with his latest journal open. Sinking back into a big leather chair, he closed his eyes. Nothing dramatic had happened when he had entered the tomb, he recalled. Indeed, the few artefacts he had found had been modest and represented the basic paraphernalia of death in the Egyptian New Kingdom; or at least that is what he had led Salim to believe. He had, in fact, found something—something of profound significance that he had long been searching for. But that would have to remain a secret, one of his many secrets. The tale that he related to the authorities in Egypt was that the most notable find was the two mummies in their stone sarcophagi, and the sad story told by the hieroglyphs painted on the walls of the tomb. The bodies were of a mother and her young daughter. The woman had been the wife of a courtier during the reign of Tutankhamen. One terrible day there had been a boating accident on the Nile and her daughter and husband were drowned. A single body was recovered from the water – that of her daughter. The mother, driven to total despair, killed herself. Mother and daughter were buried in the chamber. Well, that is the story that the hieroglyphs told.

The journey home had been uneventful. The baron was glad to be back in the freshness of a late English spring. The mummies and artefacts would arrive tomorrow. As was his custom, he would display the mummies for friends and relatives before donating them to a museum or selling them. They would not remain at Northgate Hall for long. His wife and daughter were none too comfortable with dead bodies lying around the place, even if they were embalmed and three thousand years old.

Northgate Hall had been the ancestral home of the Northgates for the best part of three hundred years. The Hall was approached by a long tree-lined carriage drive. It was a very large and imposing building, standing thirty metres at the gable, and constructed of meticulously cut Cotswold stone. In keeping with the architectural style of the time, the vast house had an impressive series of tall chimneys with multiple smoke stacks. It was extended forward at either end into two large wings. A more recent structure that had been designed in the style of the main building, but smaller in stature, had been added to the east wing; this was used as a museum by the current Baron Northgate. To those viewing Northgate Hall for the first time, the whole effect was impressive, if not a little daunting.

It was late morning of the following day before the clatter of hooves could be heard on the driveway. Peering out from an upstairs window, the baroness's deep blue eyes registered her husband standing below, ready to greet the approaching wagons. Her slender body was dressed for riding. She was a dazzlingly beautiful woman, with long luxuriant flaxen hair. Strikingly sensuous, she had the look of a goddess, with her high cheekbones, full lips and small aquiline nose.

"More corpses, no doubt," she sighed in mild exasperation. "Algernon is still a boy at heart. He loves to collect dead things to shock and amaze his friends."

The unloading of the wagons went smoothly. The four stocky removal men had had plenty of experience moving artefacts to and from Northgate Hall. As always, they were very keen and helpful; the baron was a very generous tipper. The two sarcophagi were wheeled into the museum on big trolleys and positioned to take centre stage in the Egyptian room. "The grand unveiling," as the baron liked to call the lifting of the sarcophagi lids, would take place in the evening, after dinner. Friends and family had been invited to view the explorer's latest finds. Dinner came and went and a small crowd had gathered in the Egyptian room. Arriving in full black tie eveningwear, the baron took up his position in front of his audience. Clearing his throat, he began to relate the story behind the discovery of the two mummies. As soon as he had finished speaking, four men who worked for the Northgate Estate took their cue and stepped forward. Crowbars in hand, they began to prise the lids off the sarcophagi, which had been elaborately carved and painted in the likenesses of a beautiful young woman and a small girl, both dressed in the costumes of the period. With a great deal of shuffling and grunting, the heavy stone lids were lifted and moved to one side.

Now the mummies lay exposed in their wooden coffins—the body of an adult with arms crossed on its breast, tightly bound by ancient wrappings, and the body of a small child similarly bound with arms crossed. In the light of the chandeliers, the larger of the two mummies looked faintly terrifying. Mummies were, after all, bodies that had been preserved from decay: bandaged sculptures of death.

Continuing with his tale, the baron told the faces gathered before him, now staring with a mixture of curiosity and concentration, about the hieroglyphs that he had found on the walls of the lost tomb. He told them of the tragedy that they depicted, of the death of a child, the loss of a husband and the inconsolable grief of a mother, a grief that led to a self-inflicted death. When he had finished his rendition, the baron invited everyone to come and take a closer look at the mummies. With growing excitement, the gathered assembly moved slowly forward towards the sarcophagi. Some, who had never seen a mummified body before, lingered at the rear. Slowly, the mummies were surrounded by people. They gazed at the bodies lying before them, stiff and bound in bandages.

By its nature, a mummy was a mystery, a human being that had once walked and breathed in the distant mists of time, still intact, but mercifully hidden by its wrappings. It never failed to chill, this vision of the ancient Egyptian dead. Christopher, the young son of Baron Northgate, reached out to touch the adult mummy, but recoiled in sudden fright. There was something deeply unsettling about the body before him. He stared at the bandaged face — narrow, gaunt and almost menacing.

ꕥ

Lucy, the baron's daughter, rose early the next morning. The little girl, now ten years old, had inherited her mother's good looks and blond hair. Her eyes, however, were a striking opal-green. Lucy had been very tired the night before and had gone to bed early, missing the viewing in the museum. Looking out of her bedroom window, she could see that one of the wagons had returned and men were loading a sarcophagus. "Damnation!" she bellowed. Although none too keen on mummies, she had wanted to see the child. "Too late now! They'll be gone by the time I'm dressed," she muttered dejectedly.

The morning sun came in shafts through the ornate windows of the Egyptian room as Lucy skipped in. Her father had told her that the big mummy had been removed and was being shipped to a museum, but the mummy of the child would stay at Northgate Hall for a while. Lucy was keen to look at it. She had never seen a baby mummy before. *Surely a baby mummy could not be scary*, she thought.

Approaching the sarcophagus, the little girl peered in. The bandaged body was small, about a metre long. Her father had described it to her as looking rather endearing, but she could not see that. She stared at the sad creature. The nose and eye sockets were clearly visible, moulded by the bandages. She shuddered to think what lay under those bandages. In the British Museum in London there was a mummy that had had its bandages removed. It looked so horribly ugly, all brown and shrivelled with a terrifying staring face. Lucy gazed more intently at the grim little figure in the linen wrappings. Suddenly, she shivered. It almost felt that the dead thing was looking back at her from beneath its bandages.

Is it still alive? she wondered. "No! Don't be silly!" she shouted, trying to reassure herself, but that did not stop the icy fear that was starting to seep through her. She could feel its eyes staring at her, burning into her.

The museum was deathly quiet except for the stark cawing of distant crows. Lucy looked again at the mummy, lying in its coffin. What a strange little creature it was. She drew closer to the thing. "Was it breathing?" she gasped. Heart trembling, she backed away from the sarcophagus, a sense of panic growing within her. Turning, she started to run—run as fast as her legs could carry her.

The arrival of the mummies marked a grim new beginning for Northgate Hall. The warm and friendly atmosphere of the great old house grew chilled, dark, and brooding. The terrible fear did not leave Lucy, and with each passing day she became more nervous and withdrawn. At night, in her dreams, the horrible little mummy began to stalk her through the dark corridors of the enormous house.

Baron Northgate had inspected the mummy closely. He had lifted the ancient body from the sarcophagus. It was bone dry and very stiff. *There is no possibility that this thing could have moved,* he concluded. *How ridiculous! The poor bandaged creature has been dead for thousands of years!*

The servants became increasingly uneasy. Shadows were reported lurking in corners and creeping down the passageways. In the dead of night, strange noises and whisperings were heard. A feeling of dark unease pervaded the house, and the children became so nervous that they had to be dragged to their bedchambers. One bleak night the baron returned from a short business trip to find the butler waiting for him in the vast hallway. Standing there as dignified and imperturbable as ever, he addressed his master. "The baroness and the children are no longer in residence, sir. They left for London yesterday."

The baron regarded the butler coldly. "Did the baroness give a reason for her departure?" he asked.

"No, Baron," replied the butler. "She merely stated that you should make all haste to London."

ꕥ

The baroness looked sadly at her husband, tears streaming down her pallid face. "Northgate Hall has become haunted, Algernon," she sobbed. "Why did you bring those accursed corpses to our home? The dead should be left to rest in peace and not torn from the cradle of their graves to provide amusement for curious fools! Our daughter is like a shadow now, and Christopher clings to me in a perpetual state of fear. Even the servants have started handing in their notices. It is too much, Algernon. It is too much. I will never set foot in that house again."

It was clear to the baron that his wife was too upset to reason with, but he knew in his heart that he could never leave Northgate Hall. The Hall was his ancestral home. He was born and had lived his entire life in that house. It was the home of his father and his father's father. In all, seventeen generations of his family had lived on the Northgate Estate before him. Was he to be dispossessed by ghosts? Was he to be driven out like a coward from his own home?

"There has to be a rational explanation for all of this," he had said to his wife as he departed for the Hall. She had pleaded with him to stay with her at their London residence in Regents Park and sell the estate, but alas, to no avail. That was the last she ever saw of her husband.

The baron had promised his wife that he would get to the bottom of things and rejoin her at the weekend, but he disappeared not long after returning to the ancient house. The police, called in by the butler, made a thorough search of the Hall and grounds, but no trace of the baron was ever found. The mummy too had mysteriously vanished and the story created quite a stir in the national newspapers. Vowing never again to set foot in Northgate Hall, the baroness dismissed the remaining staff, sold off the estate and had the house and grounds sealed. A trust fund was established so that the perimeter wall and gates could be kept in a state of good repair. Northgate Hall was left abandoned – a tomb for her dear lost Algernon.

CHAPTER 2
THE TEMPESTUOUS FELLOW

ꙮ

"Is it O.K. to have a look around?" enquired an attractive young American tourist, her perfect white teeth gleaming through a very winning smile. John, the head porter, was already putty in her hands. In the distance, proceeding down the quad towards the Porter's Lodge, a voice could be heard. Like muted thunder it approached, deep and resonant.

Wow! thought the girl tourist on hearing his voice. *What a hunk that guy must be! I have to get a look at him. He must be huge!*

A small man, by modern standards, flipped his mobile phone shut as he approached the lodge. At first glace he looked to be around forty-five years old, but at closer examination he was probably a good seven years younger than the tanned and weather-beaten face suggested. His hair was black and somewhat unruly, with a few strands of grey at the temples. Bushy eyebrows arched over strong steady grey eyes, and a straight but fairly broad nose dropped towards firm lips and a good square chin. Had it not been for the clean shave, tweed sports jacket, sharply pressed trousers and polished brown shoes, this man would have looked like a very unlikely Oxford Don.

The American deflected her beautiful eyes from the porter and stared in the direction of the voice. She was keen to inspect its mighty owner, but to her disappointment all she saw was a relatively small man approaching rapidly, with strong confident strides. *There's no way that's the guy with the voice.*

As the man strode by he boomed, "All right, John. I'm taking the afternoon off. Must dash!"

The porter averted his gaze from the dazzling young American and replied, "Well, for some, Dr. Malone!"

The girl looked on in amazement. "What a voice," she sighed.

"Yes!" laughed the porter. "Dr. Malone is one of our more characterful Fellows!"

ℌ

Dr. Frank Malone arrived had arrived at Lady Margaret Hall in 1990, as a lecturer in political science, and later as a Tutorial Fellow. Although teaching politics paid Dr. Malone's bills, the research and study of Egyptology, Parapsychology and the Occult were his all-consuming passion—other than fine alcoholic beverages, that is.

Frank Malone leapt into the well-upholstered leather seat of his aging Volvo Estate. This was a butch no-nonsense car for men, or at least that was what he thought. It had big steel bumpers, front and rear, not the flimsy plastic affairs that adorned modern cars. The gas-guzzling three-litre V6 version that he possessed was a cheap buy, second-hand. That had been a major consideration for the Irishman, who spent most of his cash on his extracurricular activities. Gunning the engine of the big Volvo, he moved off, down Norham Gardens. The University Parks were on his left as he drove away from the college, hidden for the most part by imposing redbrick Victorian houses. The parks were a favourite haunt of the Oxford academic, where he liked to sit on a bench, smoking cigarettes while he watched the world go by.

At the bottom of the road, Frank pointed the Volvo to the right. Many of the LMH Fellows turned right onto the Banbury Road at the end of Norham Gardens and headed for North Oxford, home of the rich and those favoured by the University. Truth be known, the University owned half of Oxford, or at least that was what he thought. The Volvo proceeded up Banbury Road, past the neat rows of shops, and on towards the Summertown roundabout.

Although he had been at LMH for over a decade now, a Professorial Chair at Oxford still eluded him. He was well regarded as a talented teacher, but his academic efforts in the field of politics left something to be desired. Unfortunately for his career, Frank devoted the bulk of his research time to more exotic material than politics had to offer. His volcanic temper and somewhat irreverent nature had not helped matters either. By way of some consolation, he had managed to wangle a Visiting Professorship at a small university up north. But in Oxford he was known as plain old Dr. Malone.

Frank's car traversed the Summertown roundabout and headed further north towards Kidlington. Kidlington, although essentially a suburb of Oxford, was considered a separate village, divorced from the city by a small stretch of fields and a golf course. It was in Kidlington that Frank resided in a modest semi-detached house with a neglected garden. The old lady living next door had dropped dead without warning, and her house had recently been sold by a cash-strapped relative. Frank was keen to inspect his new neighbours. He was told that they would be moving in today. The estate agents had been very evasive, even shifty, when questioned, so he was pretty much in the dark and not a little apprehensive. He hoped and prayed that at the very least they would be quiet.

Frank Malone originally hailed from Dublin, where he had had a distinguished career at Trinity College before snapping up a golden opportunity to lecture at Oxford. He loved the Irish style of driving, which was rapid, flamboyant and edgy. Dangerous at times, maybe, but always decisive – or at least that was what he thought. In England he found driving so sterile, with cameras and speed humps everywhere, and women drivers were the bitter end. Most were timid, indecisive, and had the Visio spatial awareness of zombies. Some of them were so insecure that, given half a chance, they would drive on the pavement. That was his view, anyway, and he did not keep it a secret in the senior common room amongst his male colleagues. Frank was something of a dinosaur in the modern world.

The big Volvo approached the Kidlington roundabout. A little absentmindedly, the Irishman slowed the car and entered the inside lane of the roundabout. Unfortunately, he did not register the large red bus in the lane next to his until it suddenly sliced across his path, forcing him to swerve to the left and mount a grass verge. Almost losing control, he slammed on the brakes. The heavy Volvo skidded violently, finally screeching to a halt within inches of destroying a parked car in a side road that was close to the roundabout.

Unlike most of us, who would have been shocked into a state of numbed paralysis by such a close shave with disaster, Frank sprang immediately into action. Roaring expletives like molten rocks from an exploding volcano, he took off in hot pursuit of the bus, ramming his car back over the grass verge and onto Kidlington Road. The red bus was unloading passengers as he drew up directly behind it. Springing out of the Volvo like a panther, he ran for the open door of the bus. Amazed onlookers gawped as the angry Irishman stormed up the steps and zeroed in on the driver.

Before he could roar out a word with his mighty voice, the driver was up and looming over him with a menacing glower. In momentary surprise, Frank took a faltering step backwards and lost his footing. Toppling out of the bus, he fell in a seamless dive, like a bird being shot from the sky.

Landing hard on his back, the impact thumped the wind from his lungs.

Almost laughing, the driver turned to the passengers and said, "Careful on those steps; they can be a bit slippery."

Frank lay spread-eagled and stunned as the bus eased back onto the road. A single sentence was running over and over in his head. *The bus driver was a woman...a woman!"*

The face of an old man suddenly appeared above him. "Are you all right, son?" he asked. The sight of the old man snapped the stricken academic back to his senses. New words were taking birth in his brain—words like *fiasco, idiot, scandal, career-prospects*—bringing the College into disrepute! The old man helped him to his feet. Staggering as quickly as he could to his car, Frank Malone made a rapid exit from the scene of his embarrassment.

CHAPTER 3
HEARTBREAKER

It's another beautiful day for May, and quite hot with it, thought Rosie as she worked her way through the breakfast dishes. *Global warming seems to be coming home to roost, but we might as well make the best of it!* she mused cheerfully.

Number 13 Arcadia Drive was an unassuming 1930s semi-detached, with bay windows and a neat square of front lawn. It was home to Rosie, her husband Jim, and Alexander. Arcadia Drive would have been a pretty humdrum piece of suburbia, had it not been for the fact that it was situated on the slope of a very steep hill in High Wycombe. The hill was called "the heartbreaker" in cycling circles. It was so steep that the houses appeared to stack one on top of the other, steadily climbing their way into the heavens. A cyclist had to be very fit to make it to the summit unscathed, for lesser mortals getting to the top was a pretty arduous experience.

At the bottom of Heartbreaker Hill, the High Wycombe Hornets Cycle Club were beginning their ascent. As usual, Mick Tomlinson had taken the lead with Pat O'Toole some ways behind him. The puffing and gasping intensified as the ten cyclists, clad in skin-tight Lycra, stood out of the saddle, their bronzed, muscular legs pumping the pedals.

It was not far into the climb when the burn began to intensify and the legs of some of the lesser members of the pack started to ache. Suddenly, a boy appeared on an ordinary-looking street bike and began to pass them, one by one. Here were all these powerful athletes, looking like professionals in their cycling suits and riding state-of-the-art light alloy bikes, and an eleven-year-old-boy was breezing by them. Wearing a navy blue AC/DC T-shirt and jeans, and sporting an unruly mop of corn blond hair, the boy was cutting through them like a hot knife through butter.

Each cyclist gaped with a mixture of disgust and amazement as the boy wafted by, whistling. He started to close in on O'Toole, who, sensing an impending assault began to pump the pedals for all he was worth. Furiously sucking in air with each rasping breath, he increased his speed.

"I'm number two in this club and that's the way it's going to stay!" he cursed. "Nobody's going to pass me on this hill."

The boy in blue drew level, winked cheekily, and powered ahead. O'Toole's jaw fell in amazement. "That's not possible!" he gasped, totally loosing control of his bike and crashing into a grass embankment on the side of the road.

The boy rode on. The lead cyclist was in his sights now, and he was closing fast. But in an instant, just as he entered the killing zone, the young assailant suddenly swerved right into a side road, his quarry of no further interest. Further down the hill, the vanquished cyclists, all of whom had stopped to check on their fallen comrade, breathed a collective sigh of relief. The honour of the club had been badly dented, but at least some dignity had been preserved, but just barely! Who in the name of hell was that boy?

Rosie heard the squeal of brakes through the kitchen window. *Alexander!* she thought. Into the kitchen burst the blond-haired boy. "Any milk, Mum?" he asked, grinning broadly.

ഩ൭

It was because of Alexander that Rosie and her boyfriend Jim had married nine years earlier. They were happy as they were, without forms, certificates and ceremonies, but then along came the boy with the golden hair. One summer afternoon, while riding their Hondas up on Turville Heath, they banked to take a right-hand bend, and there he was. Naked and smiling, he was sitting there by the side of the road. Completely taken aback, they hit the brakes.

As they approached the little boy, he looked directly at them and spoke. "My name is Alexander," he said, with disarming cuteness. He was a handsome little fellow, with deep blue eyes and a wide friendly smile. Rosie and Jim stared in amazement as the child, who could not have been more than two years of age, continued to speak with an assured fluency.

"I am all alone. My mummy has gone away… Can you help me?"

With that, the boy's happy demeanour melted away and tears began to roll down his little cheeks.

Jim removed his leather jacket and wrapped the boy in it. Rosie stayed to comfort the lost little fellow while her boyfriend went to find a telephone. The police arrived and took Alexander away. Nobody ever managed to trace the boy's parents, or where he came from. He had a hazy memory of his mother, and nothing more. Sadly, nobody ever came forward, and no child was reported missing in the county.

It was six months later when the adoption papers came through. The biker pair had been smitten by Alexander. They had tried so hard for a child of their own, but without success. No medical explanation could be found. How Rosie's heart had ached for a helpless loving little person to cuddle and play with, to care for and protect. There had been a lot of interest in the little blond charmer from prospective adoptee parents, but Alexander wanted Rosie as his new mother and Jim as his father, and that was that. They smartened up their act, became respectable citizens in the eyes of the adoption agency, and won through as Alexander's new family.

What a remarkable boy Alexander had proven to be. Although he was courageous and at times reckless in nature, he was sensitive and well-meaning. It was not long before it was discovered that he had a truly exceptional mind and he was fast-tracked through school. At age eleven he was already in the lower sixth form at St. Martin's Grammar School, with the University of Oxford firmly in his sights. Many a gifted child was deliberately held back at school, due to the psychological impact of being a high profile student. There were jealous jibes and bullies to contend with. There was the social displacement and the sheer impact of being in a class where everyone was older, bigger and more streetwise than you were. For those with the money, there were special schools and academies for the super intelligent, but not for Alexander.

While Alexander wanted for nothing of significance, his father Jim was a car mechanic and a special school was out of the question. The boy was strong, with a quick-witted sense of humour, so what would have been psychological trauma to many a child was water off a duck's back to him. Alexander was tall for his age, with an athletic build. His thick blond hair was quite striking, set against his evenly-pigmented skin and piercing blue eyes. He had a good firm jaw and a powerful mouth. There was no question about it—Alexander was a handsome young man. Next September he would be in his final year of the sixth form, and he was proud of it. At age thirteen, he was going to Oxford, and that was that. Deep inside, he hoped that he could make some sort of a meaningful contribution in this troubled modern world.

After finishing his milk, Alexander went to the garage to tinker with his bike. It may have looked like an ordinary bike, but it was not what it seemed. The frame had been adapted to carry the latest lightweight, high-power batteries. These fed a compact electric motor that had been integrated into the rear wheel of the bike. A dynamo that had been incorporated into the front wheel charged the batteries. This kicked into action when the bike was being peddled, or when it was freewheeling down hills. Alexander, with the help of his father and a local factory that made solar panels, had inserted an array of circular mini solar panels into the main cross member of the bike frame. It was essentially a scaled up version of the system used to charge solar-powered watches and helped keep the batteries juiced up and ready for action. The weight of the bike was reduced to compensate for the batteries and motor by the use of light alloy metals for the frame, wheels, pedals and gears. Jim had helped a lot with the construction. When the batteries were fully charged, Alexander had plenty of power on tap for blasting up hills and past unsuspecting cyclists. This did not come cheap, though, and was paid for with paper rounds, washing cars and so forth.

CHAPTER 4
THE NEW NEIGHBOUR

Frank poured himself an extremely large twelve-year-old malt whisky, which had been skilfully created by a small but venerated distillery in the Scottish Highlands. He collapsed onto the green leather couch in his study. The single academic had no need of a dining room; cooking was a mere inconvenience. Lunch was seldom eaten and dinner was taken in College, or in the many pubs that he frequented. He was also partial to Indian takeaways.

The study was crammed with books that bulged from wall-to-wall bookcases, or were piled in stacks on the floor. There were a wide range of manuscripts on the occult and parapsychology, archaeology, the Egyptian and other ancient civilisations. Positioned close to the window was a posh mahogany desk, its top surfaced in leather, and a comfortable deeply padded office chair. The desk was kept neat and clutter free and was home to a laptop computer.

In contrast to the study, the living room was maintained in pristine condition. The walls were adorned with strategically placed abstract art pictures – spectacular blobs, fusions and explosions of multicoloured paint mounted on art gallery-white walls. Centrepiece in the room was a marble fireplace, with a real flame-effect gas fire that Frank had recently had installed. Expensive double-glazed French doors led to the less- than-well-manicured rear garden. A light blue leather settee and easy chair stood on a dense pale cream carpet. In the far corner of the room was a forty-two inch liquid crystal TV set, connected up to an expensive Swedish sound system. This was Frank's chill-out den. It was here that he liked to drink whisky and watch the news, documentaries, and perhaps somewhat surprisingly, action adventure movies.

The whisky started to kick in and Frank felt his frayed nerves beginning to mellow. "What in the name of God are they feeding them on these days?" he fumed with considerable exasperation, recalling the size of the female bus driver. It was her sheer physicality that had made him lose his footing, and subsequently his dignity. "In my days in Dublin I was a fairly average sort of bloke, but now many a school kid is taller than me!" he cursed. "There must be growth hormones everywhere—in the water, in the vegetables, in the meat. Where's it all going to end? When people are the size of bloody dinosaurs, no doubt!"

The sudden sound of a powerful turbine-like roar jolted him from his ravings. There was no mistaking that sound. It was the engine of a big Japanese motorbike. His heart sank. As the peeved Irishman peered out of the front window, an athletic figure, clad in tight black leather and stylish biker's boots, kicked the support stand out and dismounted from a big silver Suzuki. A red crash helmet with a tinted visor hid the identity of the rider, who proceeded to the door of the adjoining house and disappeared inside. The veins on Frank's neck started to swell as his face flushed with fury.

Bloody marvellous! He began to swear out loud. He had never been in the Navy, but many a sailor would have been impressed by his repertoire. Finally cursing himself to a standstill, he finished with, "Bikers! They are all trouble. If there's noise next door—if they start playing that fecking awful rock music—I'm not going to stand for it! There'll be hell to pay, and make no mistake!"

Frank missed the arrival of the removal van and the movement of furniture and packing boxes that followed.

He was busy downing whisky, with his headphones on, as Irish ballads soothed his troubled mind. Eventually, he dozed off, awakening to silence in the small hours of the morning. Dejectedly, he slumped off to bed.

The clattering of the alarm clock awoke him as usual at 7.00 a.m. With bloodshot eyes and a throbbing brain, he staggered to the open widow and stuck his head out for some fresh morning air. To his surprise, there was no motorbike parked in the driveway of his new neighbour. In its place was a gleaming Audi A3 with pale lilac metallic paintwork.

Humm, thought Frank, somewhat bemused.

An hour and three strong cups of coffee later, the Irish academic had completed his ablutions and his brain cells were coming back online. Just as well, as he had two lectures and a tutorial session to get through. A final check in the mirror revealed a white shirt, pale blue tie, black sports jacket and grey slacks. His bleary red eyes were a dead giveaway to the heavy night before, though.

Oops. Better hit the eye drops when I get into College. He was no stranger to eye drops.

The latch on the front door turned and Frank strode out into a pleasant May morning. Reaching the Volvo, his head turned instinctively. Gazing back at him was the owner of the immaculate Audi.

"Good morning," said a somewhat high-pitched well-spoken voice. "The name's Mervin Peak. I'm your new neighbour."

Frank could not disguise the look of relief that was spreading across his face, as he stared over the waist-high ornamental wall separating the front gardens of the two houses. A slender man in his mid-forties, wearing a very sharp pinstriped navy-blue suit and handmade black shoes smiled over at him. His neatly-groomed grey hair was set off nicely by an expensive looking suntan.

"Pleased to meet you," responded the Irishman in his rich velvety voice. "The name's Frank."

The new neighbour was not a little impressed. *What a wonderful manly voice you have,* he thought, smiling into Frank's eyes.

Alarm bells started ringing in the Irishman's head. *Better tread carefully here*! "Grand to meet you. Must dash now. Catch you later," he said, disappearing swiftly into his Volvo.

Moments later, he made his getaway. "I don't care what side this bloke's bread is buttered on, so long as he's quiet, but I'll not be calling around to borrow a cup of sugar any time soon! A bit too friendly for my liking!" he rumbled. "I wonder what happened to that bike. Mr. Peak does not look like a biker, so the motorbike must belong to a friend of his."

CHAPTER 5
A NIGHT TO REMEMBER

It had been a long day for Frank and he yawned deeply as he swung the Volvo into his driveway. There was just time to have a nap, freshen up and catch a bus back into Oxford. Tonight he was dining in the Hall at Christ Church College, as the guest of Professor Anita Gupta. They had met by accident a couple of years earlier in the Bodleian Library. Dr. Gupta was a Professor of Experimental Psychology and a Fellow of Christ Church College. Although gaining increasing respectability in academic circles, parapsychology was still a sideline activity at the University, but it was an area in which Professor Gupta had a keen interest. They were both scanning the same bookshelf for the same book at the same time, but the Irishman reached for it first. As there was only one copy, this inevitably led to a conversation. Frank was very good at conversations and their relationship blossomed from there. It was a platonic friendship, based on their mutual interest in the paranormal.

The wine and port flowed very freely at dinners in the Hall, so Frank, as always, caught the bus or took a taxi into town. Feeling refreshed after his nap, he strode out of the house, in a black suit, light blue shirt, and navy blue tie. He had timed it well, and the bus pulled in shortly after he had arrived at the bus stop. Glancing at his watch—an old leather-strapped Rolex that he brought out for special occasions—he boarded the bus. Lifting his head to pay his fare, he came to an abrupt halt at the sight of the driver. It was her! It was the woman who had run him off the road at the Kidlington roundabout. In a heartbeat, the Irishman flipped from a convivial academic to a raging bull.

"By all the saints! It's you!" he roared, his eyes bulging from their sockets. "You almost killed me last week, you stupid cow! Who the hell taught you to drive? A blind drunk, by the looks of it! You're bloody useless. You're a menace on the roads! What have you got to say to that, you incompetent idiot? I'm going to get you sacked! What have you got to say to that?"

The male voice in full flight can be quite intimidating, but Frank's voice was no ordinary male voice. When he let rip with those tumultuous tonsils it was like being caught in an explosion, like being hit by some sort of sonic weapon. But as quickly as his temper had flared, it subsided. He surveyed, somewhat wistfully, the aftermath of his verbal tsunami. Wide eyes and gaping jaws greeted his gaze. The driver was in a state of suspended animation, staring at the diminutive Irishman in shock and amazement. She was no shrinking violet, this bus driver, but the verbal onslaught had come so suddenly, so powerfully, and so violently that it literally stunned her into paralysis. She was a tough lady, standing six feet tall and weighing in at one hundred and eighty pounds. She had only recently joined the bus company. Before that, she had been a truck driver. The other drivers in the company called her "Butch." Not a woman to be trifled with was Butch. But there she was, sitting like a startled child, reduced to silence by the verbal onslaught of the angry Irishman.

Rationality restored, Frank decided to make a hasty withdrawal before the situation deteriorated any further. Spinning seamlessly on his leather-soled shoes, he made a rapid, but dignified, departure from the bus. It was a considerable improvement on the exit that he had executed on his previous appearance on this bus, and he felt good.

Justice had been dispensed. Strutting back down the road to his house, he looked like a cock on parade. Tapping his mobile open, he ordered a taxi. A curt female voice told him it would take twenty minutes to arrive. That was plenty of time for a couple of congratulatory whiskies. All in all, he figured that despite the disruption, he would still make his dinner date on time.

As Frank approached his residence, he caught sight of his new neighbour, caressing his pretty little Audi with soapsuds and a sponge. *Your man is obviously one of those fastidious drivers. A bit too fastidious for my liking*! But it was too late to take avoiding action. He had been spotted.

"Hiya. How are yeew?" purred the neighbour.

There's just a bit too much of a feminine lilt in that voice, thought Frank. Frank was a man's man; he liked his steak bloody. "Grand," he replied politely. "That car of yours looks well taken care of. More than I can say for mine!"

Mervin smiled. "Yes, I have only had it a couple of months and we are still in the 'young and in-love' stage of our relationship."

Frank chuckled. "Alas, I cannot say the same for myself. My car and I are just distant acquaintances these days! I can't even remember when I last had it serviced, never mind washed!" After a short pause he added, "Anyway, must dash—late for an appointment." With that he headed rapidly for his front door, disappeared inside and poured himself a double scotch.

༻༺

It was just before six-thirty in the evening when Dr. Malone stepped from his taxi, paid the driver, and walked through the gates of Christ Church College. The foundation stone of this magnificent College was laid in 1525, but the College was not completed until 1532. It was originally called King Henry VIII College, but that name lasted a mere thirteen years. The adjacent cathedral subsequently became part of the College, which was then renamed Christ Church College.

Frank entered the quad and followed the path around the pond. The centrepiece of this elegant water feature was a statue of a naked Apollo in full flight. "He must be the God of streaking," grinned the Irishman, remembering a recent incident involving a drunken student at Lady Margaret Hall. He took the path towards Tom Tower. Normally, he walked straight through the arch under the tower without a second glance, but this evening, in the setting sunlight, he stopped to admire the imposing structure. It was surprisingly massive for a College tower. Looking up, he estimated that the tower must be pushing two hundred feet high. Like many people of his generation, even scientists, he could never get an accurate sense of proportion or perspective using the dreaded metric system. He either used, or had to convert everything back to good old imperial units.

Walking to within a few feet of the tower, he stared straight up. The sheer height of the structure was quite surprising and he started to feel a little giddy. *I wouldn't fancy having to do maintenance work on that tower. It's a long way down!* Shuddering at the very thought, he moved quickly through the archway. Reaching the Hall, he walked inside. The Hall never failed to impress him. It was one hundred and fifteen feet long and forty feet wide. The ceiling, which was made from richly ornamented oak beams, was a massive fifty feet high. High up on the mighty stone block walls were a series of large, arched ornate windows. Below the windows the walls were clad in a beautiful and ancient wood, adorned with imposing portraits of former College masters, benefactors, and long departed royalty. Taking pride of place at the end of the Hall, below a magnificent stained glass window, was the big man himself: Henry VIII. Christ Church Hall was undoubtedly the finest dining room of its kind in the world, or at least that was what Frank thought.

A series of polished wooden tables, arranged in parallel lines, stretched the length of the Hall. Under the portrait of England's largest ever king there was a raised platform, boarded by three steps. Here the tables ran transversely across the Hall. This was "High Table," where the great and the good of the College sat together with their honoured guests. Frank fell into the latter category of honoured guest and was thus elevated from the common throng of students and research graduates on the lower tables.

The Hall was filling fast as he approached High Table. He could see his Indian friend already seated, with a space reserved for him next to her.

"Hello, Professor Gupta," he said, in mock deference.

"Good evening, Dr. Malone," replied Anita Gupta, returning the compliment. She smiled up at him through voluptuous lips, adorned to considerable effect with red lipstick. Her eyes were large and beautiful, and she had a pretty little nose. She wore her black glossy hair long. It seemed to shimmer in the light of the table lamps.

"You are looking lovely, as always," continued Frank.

She smiled again, but her eyes narrowed in concentration. "Grab a chair, Frank. I have something very interesting to discuss with you," she said. Chairs were one of the perks of sitting at High Table. Dinners on the lower tables had to make do with long wooden benches. Frank took his seat next to the attractive Indian academic. The tables were neatly laid out for the impending meal; the bottles of red wine were already in position on the High Table and breathing nicely. He quickly noted that tonight's wine was a smooth full-bodied California Merlot, which he had encountered on more than one occasion. His mouth watered at the thought of red meat on the menu. Turning his head, he looked at his companion full on. "I am all ears," he said.

"It all started back in the 1970s at Kingston, a provincial university in the United States," began Anita. "The original concept for an extraordinary project, known as the Global

Mind Project, was developed at Kingston by Professor Gilbert Finley. You have probably heard of him. He has an impressive track record in the application of rigorously applied scientific techniques to the investigation of paranormal phenomena."

Frank nodded at the Indian professor, who was now fully focused on her story.

"Professor Finley has studied many aspects of the paranormal, including telepathy, telekinesis, and extra-sensory perception, using state of the art scientific technology. One of the machines that he uses is a small black box called a Random Generator (RG). It is essentially a small computer that generates random numbers. There are only two numbers involved: a one and a zero. These numbers are produced randomly, like tossing a coin."

The scent of the first of the dinner courses was wafting into the Hall. Frank's stomach began to rumble, and he was ready for a glass of wine. The last of the diners were now taking their seats. His heart sank slightly as he registered a portly man with a flushed red face who had just taken up a position opposite the nearest wine bottle. *Your man over there will be giving me some serious competition for the wine tonight,* he thought.

"I can see your attention wandering to the wine!" scolded Professor Gupta. Resuming her story, she said, "Stay with me, Frank. It gets more interesting. The team at Kingston developed software to convert the number readout into a graph. Because the number generation is purely random, the printout is a straight line, running parallel to the x-axis; in other words, the data is represented by a flat line. Any deviation from this random number generation shows up as a spike on the graph. In the early experiments, the power of the human mind was investigated, using the black boxes. The results were quite startling. It was found that many people could actually affect the readout from the box and produce spikes in the graph. Using the analogy of tossing a coin, test subjects appeared to be able to make the machine toss more heads than tails. The scientists agreed that this should not have happened. There was no known law of physics to account for it, and yet statistical analysis indicated that the effect was real."

Frank found this fascinating, and he gave Anita his full attention. A sudden interruption by the College chaplain, who stood up to deliver a short rendition in Latin, returned his mind to his rumbling stomach and thoughts of food. As soon as the chaplain had finished, a team of waiters and waitresses appeared, carrying steaming bowls of soup.

"I will continue after we have our soup," said Anita, whose gastric juices were also on the rise. The soup duly arrived and proved to be very tasty. It was cream of mushroom, made with plump fresh aromatic mushrooms. Making short work of his bowl, Frank started to eye up the wine. Nobody was ready to make the first move on this occasion, so he decided it best to wait for the serving staff. In any event, the story was compelling listening.

"How did you find the soup?" he asked, dabbing his lips with a serviette.

"Splendid," replied Anita, as she finished her last spoonful. "Anyway, to continue the story, the tests have been repeated many times and the effects on the black box are very real. Indeed, they were so real that the project has continued. It is now headed by a Dr. Preston, who is also based at Kingston. The work was extended to groups of test subjects focusing collectively on the black box. The results were even more dramatic, and large shifts in the shape of the graph were produced. With the advent of the Internet, it was possible to interconnect black boxes around the world. Dr. Preston connected up forty or so of the random event generators in different countries. This had the effect of massively boosting data generating capacity. There were no test subjects involved. The boxes were just left to run. Feedback to a central computer at Kingston generated the expected flat line on the graph. As I mentioned, this had been seen in previous experiments involving single black boxes, where no test subjects were involved. In 1997, early in the month of September, something sensational took place. There was a huge shift in the number-generation sequence of the interconnected black boxes, resulting in a massive spike in the graph. The scientists did not have to look far to find an explanation. The date was the 6th of September, the day of the funeral of poor Princess Dianna, so tragically killed in a car crash in Paris. It is estimated that a billion people around the world watched her funeral in Westminster Abbey. It was an intensely emotional event."

Frank nodded solemnly in agreement.

"The investigators at Kingston felt confident that the two events must be connected," continued Anita. "It looked like the black boxes had been affected by the collective emotions of millions of people watching the funeral around the globe."

"Wine with your dinner, sir?" said a voice in Frank's ear. It was a waitress holding a bottle of the Merlot, cocked and ready for pouring. The Irish academic was now so engrossed in the story that this sudden interruption was almost irritating—but not quite! "Sure. Pour away, me darlin," he said and smiled. Wine glasses filled, the beef arrived, accompanied by plates of miscellaneous vegetables.

"Enjoy your wine," grinned Anita, "I will save the finale for the cheese and coffee."

Thinking strategically, Frank downed his wine in three large, but smoothly executed gulps. With this manoeuvre he managed to outflank his rival on the opposite side of the table, who was only halfway through his first glass. Deftly securing the wine bottle designated for his section of the table, he filled his glass. With a sigh of satisfaction, he set to work on the beef. Three glasses of wine and a crème Brule later, Frank was ready for the final instalment.

"So, Dr. Malone," winked Anita, "I see that you are suitably refreshed." She was feeling quite mellow herself, after a large glass of wine. Being a Hindu, she had had to skip the beef in favour of tangy cheese pasta, which was the alternative choice on the menu that evening.

"So, finally," she said, "to the end of my tale. Exactly how emotions could influence the black boxes was not clear to the Kingston team. In 1998 they presented their findings for the first time to the scientific community. Nobody could come up with a rational explanation for the results of their studies, but a great deal of interest was stimulated. This led to the inception of the Global Mind Project, which now involves around seventy black boxes in forty or so countries. Many eminent researchers have joined the project. Some of the findings have proven very exciting and extremely thought-provoking. The boxes appear to be able to detect major global events as they happen. For example, the Russian tragedy involving the sinking of the Kursk submarine, the NATO bombing of Yugoslavia, the invasion of Iraq, and major events such as New Year's Eve celebrations. However, the appalling events of September the 11th, 2001, when two passenger jets exploded into the Twin Towers, annihilating thousands of innocent people, pushed things to another level. As the world watched the horror unfold in New York on live TV, the black boxes went crazy. But the amazing thing was that not only had the boxes registered the attacks as they were taking place, they had detected them about five hours before they actually began. So before the hijacked aircraft had even left the ground, the RG machines had picked up the attack on the New York skyscrapers. Astoundingly, it appeared that the Kingston scientists had created a machine that could look into the future!"

Frank interrupted the Indian professor again, an incredulous look on his face. "But surely that is not possible. No machine can see into the future! It must have been some sort of fluke."

Looking back at Frank, a little smirk of satisfaction spread across her lips. She certainly had him hooked now. "Yes," she agreed, "a lot of people thought just that. But then it happened a second time. In late December, 2004, the black boxes went wild again. About nine hours later, a powerful earthquake beneath the Indian Ocean generated the giant waves that ravaged the islands and coasts of South East Asia, killing over two hundred thousand poor souls. It was now clear that the black boxes were peering into the future, and the more terrible that future was, the further they could see.

"But surely this evidence is inconclusive," said Frank, scratching his chin in disbelief. "We live on a pretty catastrophic planet. Maybe it is all just pure coincidence."

Professor Gupta took a sip of coffee and continued. "Sure, Frank, you have a point. However, the scientists involved in the project say that rigorous analysis of their findings indicate that it is highly unlikely that the link between the black box readouts and these terrible events can be explained by pure coincidence. The scientists claim that the probability of getting these results by chance is one million-to-one against. Those are very long odds indeed against it all being a series of flukes. Still, many scientists remain sceptical."

"What about the laws of physics?" asked Frank. "Do they support the theory that it is possible to see into the future?"

"Well, let's put it this way," said Anita. "There is nothing in the laws of physics to preclude that possibility. In theory, time could flow backwards as well as forwards, much like the ebb and flow of an ocean tide. This may be the key to foretelling the future. We may remember the past as the future!"

"But surely there is no evidence to support this?" said Frank, plucking perplexedly at his right eyebrow.

Anita frowned at the Irishman. "Come on, Frank. You cannot be serious!" she exclaimed. There is a huge body of literature on telepathy and precognition. There has been some very high quality work carried out, using brain scanners and other high tech equipment that clearly shows that some individuals can see into the future. Surely you remember the work carried out using pictures. Individual subjects were shown a series of pictures, and changes in brain wave patterns and body metabolism were detected as the pictures were viewed. The more shocking or provocative the picture was, the greater the changes in the body that were detected. But the fascinating thing was that with pictures that depicted very strong subject matter, changes in brain wave patterns, for example, occurred before the subjects were shown the picture. In other words, a part of their consciousness appeared to be looking into the future."

The port arrived. Frank fingered his glass pensively. "So from what you have said, Anita, it would appear that the only way those massive shifts in the RG data output could have occurred is if they were affected by some sort of mass thought process."

Anita nodded in agreement. "Exactly, Frank! Perhaps the most exciting finding is not so much that the black boxes are able to see into the future, but that for the first time we appear to have evidence that there is some sort of mass consciousness; that at a deeper mental level we may all be connected."

Frank added, "The mystics have being saying this for millennia, but nobody has ever demonstrated it using modern science. I am truly impressed." Taking a sip of his port, he grinned at his beautiful companion. "So let me guess—they have asked you to join the project."

Anita nodded. "That is correct, Dr. Malone! They want to expand the number of black box sites around the world. But to maintain a high profile of credibility, only established scientists with the appropriate facilities and experience are being invited to participate."

Frank congratulated his friend and indicated his willingness to act as a sounding board for ideas and data interpretation, should the need arise. But at this juncture, in his private thoughts, he could not really see the point, unless the black box technology itself was moved to a higher level. At the moment, all they had was a spike in a graph, and that told them nothing about the nature of the future that the black boxes were detecting. Still, the philosophical implications were very intriguing. Great things can grow from small beginnings!

Professor Gupta rose from her chair. She was quite small in stature, about five foot four in her shoes, but perfectly proportioned and in great condition for a woman of forty. She wore an elegant pin-striped jacket and matching skirt, her brown skin radiant against the navy blue of the fabric. Smiling, she said her farewells, with the promise of a telephone call as soon as the RG machine arrived from the US. Her husband was due to pick her up. His car was by now, more than likely, outside the main gate on double yellow lines.

Frank smiled his goodbyes and sighed quietly as Anita Gupta turned and walked away. *If only she was not married, with children to boot. She is so beautiful, and we have so much in common.* But what could he do? Love and romance were seldom on the agenda in his rather turbulent existence.

Anita had left her port untouched. He dutifully quaffed it. A shame to waste good port, you know. *Well, that was definitely an evening to remember,* he thought, as he rang to check on the taxi he had ordered earlier. There was time enough to hunt down another port before it arrived!

It was a clear night, illuminated by a white glowing moon, when a rather tipsy Frank Malone paid his dues to the taxi driver and headed towards his front door, with plans for a hot drink before retiring to bed.

CHAPTER 6
A NASTY SURPRISE

Frank's fingers searched his jacket pockets for the ring of keys that would open, among other things, the door to his house. He felt very mellow now, with a tinge of euphoria – the sort of euphoria that alcohol can bring to the seasoned drinker. He knew that his boozing was slowly killing him, but what the hell, it made him feel good. Who wants to live forever, sipping herbal tea and nibbling organic vegetables? That was his life-view anyway.

A knife blade glinted in the moonlight. Engrossed in finding his elusive keys, Frank did not notice the two black shapes moving stealthily towards him from the rear. In seconds they were upon him, and before he could register the slightest sound, his left arm was grabbed from behind and rammed up his back. His throat felt the sharp coldness of the steel blade.

"Make a sound and you're dead," growled a rough London voice.

The Irishman remained surprisingly relaxed, given the dramatic deterioration of his circumstances. The alcohol definitely helped, and he did not panic. His assailants were two men, dressed in black biker leathers, their faces masked by balaclavas. There was a sharp ripping sound as one of the men pulled duct tape from a roll. Frank was gagged and his hands were taped together at the wrist. A powerful arm spun him around and pushed him forward as a white van drew up. Before he knew it, he was face down in the back of the vehicle, with the knifeman sitting sentinel.

"Move and I'll gut you," he was told as the van sped into the night.

The sickening gravity of his perilous predicament began to seep slowly through his brain. His mind began to race.

ഗ്രൂ

It seemed like an eternity in the back of that van, crashing and rattling his brain. The smell of exhaust fumes filled his nostrils and made him feel dizzy. And then, as he was starting to lose consciousness, the commotion ceased and there was silence. The van had stopped. By now his head was splitting and he was close to vomiting. Everything started to spin, and he desperately focused all of his willpower onto hanging onto the contents of his stomach. With his mouth taped shut, vomiting could well prove lethal.

The rear doors of the van burst open and the Irishman was dragged into the open air. It was a clear night and getting quite cold. Frank could hear the hoot of a big owl somewhere in the distance. Visibility was good in the hard white light of the moon, and after the acrid fumes of the van, the fresh air felt like nectar. He could see three of them now, all dressed in black leather, their faces hidden by balaclavas. Two of them approached him from the front of the van.

"It's time to die, little man," said one of the men, his voice cold and cruel. Frank's heart began to pound and nausea was replaced by cold fear.

"So this is it," he cursed silently. "The ignominious demise of Dr. Frank Malone; consigned to an unmarked grave, in some forgotten wood!"

"Tie the little twat to that tree over there!" barked the man with the knife.

His two associates pushed Frank to the tree, shoved him to the ground, and duct-taped him to the trunk.

"Nobody will find you here, little man," mocked one of the figures in black. "Not for days, or even weeks. You should've kept that big foul mouth of yours shut! Now you're going to pay, you arrogant little bastard!"

As they walked away, leaving him to his fate, they began to laugh. Suddenly, the man with the knife turned and in a seamless movement launched the deadly blade. With a sickening thud the knife hit its target. The Irishman's head fell forward; his mind plunged into a void of darkness.

ꟷ

Coming to with a start, his eyes adjusted to the light. He realised that it must be morning. His head felt fine and there was no trace of the nausea that he had felt earlier. Indeed, there was no hint of pain at all. The knife must have missed its target. Even more amazingly, his bonds had been mysteriously cut. Staggering unsteadily to his feet, he surveyed his surroundings. He was in a wooded area. The trees were mainly maples, decked with fresh green leaves, and the sun was shining through in patches where the tree cover was less dense. In the distance, through the woods, he could see what looked like a gravel driveway.

That's lucky. There must be a house close by. I can get a drink and find out where I am from there. Reaching the driveway, he could see a house about sixty metres ahead. He began to walk down the driveway towards it, his shoes crunching on the gravel as he went. It was a beautiful Georgian manor house, clad in limestone, with leaded sash windows. There was a large, impressive hardwood front door, with a big gleaming brass knocker. As he neared the house, the wooded area gave way to green lawns, with beds of spring flowers and attractive shrubs. Close to the house was a big magnolia tree, its spellbinding white-pink flowers in full bloom. He estimated that the house was set in an acre or so of gardens, surrounded on all sides by woodland.

Mounting the two large granite steps below the door, the Irishman rapped the knocker hard, the sound reverberating through the hallway. After a wait of a minute or so, it was clear that nobody was coming. Gripping the knocker, he banged harder. Again, there was no response. He looked at his watch. It was twenty past eight. *If anybody was home, they ought to be up by now.* Given his current predicament, he decided to investigate further and made his way to the back of the house. A gentle breeze carried the scents of the garden, along with the sounds of bumblebees, busy with their morning labours. *What an enchanting place.* At the back of the house there was a raised terrace with a carved stone balustrade. Traversing the terrace, he reached a pair of large French doors that opened centrally onto the terrace. The curtains were drawn back. Pressing his nose to the window, he peered in. The room looked large and sumptuously appointed. It was tastefully decorated in sympathy with the period of the house. *This must be the drawing room,* he guessed. There were many beautiful objects in the room, but one thing in particular drew his attention. It was a magnificent chess set, displayed on a small highly polished mahogany table that sat close to the windows. The pieces were large, at least eight inches in height, and intricately carved from what looked like ivory. *That set looks like a collectors item and is no doubt worth a fortune,* he drooled. The black and the white pieces were lined up at opposite ends of the board, ready for battle.

A sudden thunderclap exploded in his brain. Sharp, pounding pain followed. Opening his throbbing eyes, he looked at the morning. It was a very different morning to the one he had experienced moments earlier. His body was cold and stiff and bound to a tree. He had a thumping headache, worse than any hangover he could remember; he was too stunned even to swear. "I must have been dreaming," he groaned. "The exhaust fumes from that clapped out old van must have knocked me out. Those lunatics could have killed me!" And then he remembered the knife. Fortunately, it was not sticking out of his back.

It must be embedded in the tree. That probably means they did not mean to kill me – just scare me witless!

Frank swallowed. His throat was as dry as sand paper and his clothes were cold and damp from the morning dew. "Those bastards were just trying to frighten me!" he fumed. "They probably think this whole thing is a huge joke. Well, Frank Malone doesn't scare easily, and we will see who is laughing when I'm finished. I'll find you, and you'll pay for this…you bunch of cunts. And I know where to start looking!"

His temper had reached meltdown and he started struggling and ranging against his bonds. The duct tape was very strong indeed and would not give way to his mounting fury. His hands were tied in front of him, but his legs were free. He was secured to the tree by tape, wound around his body at both the waist and thorax. The tape binding his upper body prevented him from moving his arms.

He stopped to catch his breath. *Think man, think. Get a grip. For the love of God, stay calm.* The rage was building again, but then it came to him. *The knife! Where is the knife? They could have killed me with that knife, but that was obviously not their intention!* Bending his legs as much as he could, he began to push upwards. His body moved about five centimetres, then stopped abruptly. The tape had hit an obstruction. "With a bit of luck that is the knife!" he gasped. Fortunately, his assumption was correct. Digging his heels into the springy woodland turf, he jigged his body up and down. Slowly, the knife began slicing through the tape that was binding his upper body. Then, after a couple of minutes of effort, there was a pinging sound and the tape broke away from the tree. His arms and upper body were free, but his hands were still tied and he remained bound to the trunk by the lower ring of tape. He pushed again with every ounce of strength left in his legs, but to no avail.

"The tape must be snagged on something!" he cursed. Taking another breather, he looked around. The morning was misty and grey and everything was dripping with dew. The wood seemed denser than in his dream and there was a pervading sense of emptiness. He could feel the duct tape tight around his mouth. Lucky his nose was not blocked! His anger returned. *They are going to pay for this. Those bastards! I'm going to nail that bus driver. It was that bitch who was behind all this, I'm sure of that.*

Frank had more mobility in his movements now, and he began to flail around like a raging little bull. The tape around his waist loosened, but would not give way. "Come on, boy"! he roared to himself. "Use your brain!" Then he remembered his days on the school rugby team, playing as a fly half. "If you can't go through it, go around it!" That was his motto, and at his size, he used to spend a lot of time going around things, particularly large rugby players. Swivelling his legs sideways, he began to push again. The tape was now sufficiently slack to allow him to start edging around the tree. Five minutes later he could see the knife, firmly embedded in the trunk.

Whoever threw that was a pro. He stretched his arms up and cut through the bindings to his wrists. At last his hands were free! Ripping the tape from his mouth, he took a deep breath and bellowed. The sonic blasts from his huge vocal cords punched through the woods, throwing the nearby wildlife into disarray. Birds screeched their danger calls and small rodents scurried for cover. Nothing like that had ever been heard before in these woods; there was a monster on the loose! God, it was good to get those tonsils working again! The dishevelled looking Irishman grabbed the hilt of the knife and yanked it up and down until it popped from the trunk. Slicing through the last of his bonds, he broke lose.

After venting his emotions through a volley of swearwords, he started to make his way through the trees. He was curious to see if his dreamscape vision matched the reality of this misty morning, and headed in the direction of the driveway that he had walked down in his dream. To his surprise, the drive was actually there, exactly where he had encountered it in his subconscious, but it looked very different. Now there were only patches of grey gravel interspersed between large clumps of weeds and couch grass. Blocking the way in places, there were walls of brambles and nettles; nature was making good progress in reclaiming this once elegant driveway. Trees seemed to be encroaching everywhere, so much so, that he could only discern the roof of a house in the distance.

This is turning into a very bizarre adventure, he thought, as he gingerly pushed his way through the nettles and brambles towards the house.

CHAPTER 7
RAPTORS

Saturday morning at last! thought Alexander, back from his paper round and ready for some action. The route he had was tough, due to the extremely steep terrain. Anyone crazy enough to take the paper round on dropped it within a week. It was just too much like hard work, dealing with the hill. As a result, Alexander had the market cornered. He had negotiated double pay for doing the paper round. The newsagent had had little choice. Otherwise he would have had to deliver the papers himself by van; which worked out a lot more expensive in time and diesel than paying Alexander. Of course it was a breeze for the boy on his electric bike, but his employer did not know that and he marvelled at the boy's stamina.

Alexander had a lot going for him. He was good looking, athletic, and exceptionally clever. But in a sense, being brainy was his undoing. In the eyes of his peers, who referred to him as "the blond swot," he was something of a freak. "An eleven-year-old in the lower sixth form – weird!" It was no surprise, then, that he moved in a limited social circle. Indeed, there was only one person who would hang out with him, and he was something of an outcast too. Billy Jones was his name. He was "fondly" known as "Fat Boy" or "Fatty Jones" among the local children.

Now that Alexander was a sixth-former, it was becoming increasingly difficult for his parents to restrict his movements, but they were uncomfortable with him straying too far from home. Many parents of boys that age could say the same thing, but these days it was no easy matter to exert control. Modern technology gave youngsters access to just about anything, and many were cynical and world-wise by the time they hit their teens. With Alexander, however, it was not like that. He respected his parents. After all, it was he who had chosen them.

Of late, Rosie was experiencing a growing sense of unease. She could not put a finger on what was causing it. It seemed to permeate through her from deep inside, from a subconscious level. But what could she do? She could not rationalise this slow creeping fear; it was just there.

Draining his cup of tea, Alexander smiled across the breakfast table at Rosie. "I'm going to be out for a while today, Mum," he said casually.

"What are you up to?" asked Rosie, with a slight hint of tension in her voice.

"I'm going riding," he said, as he beamed another disarming smile at her.

"Well, this time make sure you wear your helmet and get back here in time for dinner. And take your mobile with you too," she said, adding, "Is that mate of yours going with you?"

Twenty minutes later, two riders sped down Heartbreaker Hill. "How are you finding the modifications to your bike?" shouted Alexander.

"Fantastic! Thanks, mate," roared Fat Boy Jones with devilish enthusiasm. "They don't know what's hit them when I flash past them on this hill. It's brilliant! The flying fat boy! I leave most of them for dead. You should see the looks on their faces. Priceless!"

❧

"Yeeeeeeess!" yelled Alexander, punching the air in triumph. The boys had stopped their bikes in front of a pair of massive wrought iron gates that hung from enormous stone pillars. The bars of the gates were rusted from long neglect, but they still looked strong. Secured firmly to the gates was a big board that read in dark red letters: DANGER. KEEP OUT. TRESPASSERS WILL BE PROSECUTED. There was something menacing about those gates. They stood like sinister sentinels; guardians of a place of dark secrets, a realm long abandoned by the living.

"Are you up for it?" exclaimed Alexander. "This has to be an abandoned mansion!"

As Billy Jones stared at the gates, a sudden coldness crept over him. Trepidation seeped slowly into the pit of his stomach, but he was determined not to look scared. "How are we going to get past those gates?" he asked in an even voice.

Alexander was also looking at the gates, but without any hint of fear. His quest had begun, and he was consumed by an ever-growing hunger for the truth. He felt that it would only be when he had unravelled the mystery behind the disappearance of his parents that he could begin to glimpse the path of his true destiny. Maybe this house held a clue. "Now that we know where we are," he said, "we can track around the perimeter wall until we find a way in."

They had found the place by accident after taking a small side road in order to relieve their bladders, and in the process had stumbled across the gates. The wall was an impressive thirty-centimetre thick structure made from granite stones. It stood about three metres high and was topped with broken glass. The stone barrier looked like it had been permanently maintained in a good state of repair, with the obvious intention of keeping the curious and the foolhardy out. Vegetation close to the wall was mainly long grass and weeds. *This must be cut periodically,* thought Alexander, as there appeared to be no trees or shrubs within four metres of the wall—a wall that seemed to stretch for miles.

"Whoever built this must have been filthy rich," remarked Billy Jones, surveying the magnitude of the construction.

"Indeed," said Alexander, "This must be the boundary wall to the grounds of a mansion."

Pushing their bikes, the boys began to walk along the perimeter of the wall. They passed through a couple of fields set over for cattle grazing, then into a copse of trees. The trees had been kept well back from the wall.

"This doesn't look too promising, mate; maybe we should come back with a rope ladder," said Jonesy, half wishing that the mission would be abandoned.

"I'd hoped we would find a tree closer to the wall," muttered Alexander, deep in thought. Turning to his friend, his eyes burning, he added, "There's nothing for it; we'll have to use the grappling iron. Let's continue our walk until we spot some trees on the other side of the wall. Hopefully, some of them will be nearer."

A bemused look crept across his companion's face. "How will that help us? What good's a tree that we can't get at, due to this whacking great wall being in the way?"

Alexander looked at his friend and winked. "Dude, a tree will be more use to us on the way out than on the way in," he said.

Reaching the boundary of the copse, the companions walked into a ploughed field. Then, by a stroke of luck, they came across an ancient maple with a sturdy branch that overhung the wall by two metres or so.

"Perfect!" exclaimed Alexander.

"But it's on the other side of the wall," responded Billy Jones, still none the wiser.

"Did you bring the blanket?" asked Alexander, who had propped his bike against the wall and was rummaging through one of his saddlebags. His hand located what he was looking for and he pulled it out. It was a sturdy nylon rope, attached to a metal bar about twenty centimetres in length.

"What's that, mate?" asked young Jones, who was in the process of extracting a dark blue blanket from his backpack.

Alexander grinned as he pressed the bottom end of the metal bar. Four equidistant prongs shot out. "It's a high tensile light alloy compactable grappling hook. Made it myself," he said proudly.

"That figures," responded Jonesy.

Alexander threw the grappling hook at the branch. Two of the prongs bit into the wood. "Lets do it, dude!" he yelled, grabbing a small hammer from a saddlebag. The rope was hanging about twenty centimetres from the wall. He pushed the handle of the hammer through his belt and began to climb the rope, using the frame of his bike to help him on his way. He was a strong and agile boy. The stones in the wall were rough-cut, so he had plenty of footholds to help him in his ascent. He reached the branch, which was about half a metre above the top of the wall. Carefully, he swung his feet onto the wall, placing them between the razor glass. Then, using both his legs and his arms, he clambered onto the branch. Lying belly down, he produced the hammer and started to smash the jagged glass down into harmless stumps. When he had made a large enough patch of demolished glass, he ordered Jonesy to toss the blanket up to him.

Placing the blanket carefully so it overlapped the top of the wall on either side, he looked down at his companion. "Now it's your turn," he said, the excitement mounting in his voice.

Billy Jones was a little daunted by the sight of the rope dangling before him. Climbing did not feature on his résumé. Alexander dropped his legs to either side of the branch and sat up. Swinging a leg over the branch, he slid himself carefully onto the wall. Lying on the blanket, his arms dangling down, he motioned to his friend to start climbing. Jones stretched up his arms and grabbed the rope with both hands. Hauling himself about a metre up the rope, he swayed a little unsteadily, his feet supported by the crossbar of the bike.

"Take a few breaths," called Alexander to his friend. "Now pull yourself up a little at a time and use your feet to find footholds in the wall."

Jonesy, panting heavily, clambered slowly upward until Alexander grabbed the top of his jacket and tugged hard. This stabilised his companion, who was starting to sway on the rope.

"Make sure you find good foot grips on the wall," grunted Alexander, struggling with the weight of his fellow climber. Jonsey heaved again and eventually managed to scramble onto the top of the wall. A few minutes later, both boys had climbed down through the branches of the tree and were standing in the mysterious grounds beyond the wall.

"Well, at least it will be easier getting back!" gasped a still panting Billy Jones.

ꙮ

The boys were in a wood. Many of the trees looked mature and massive. *In former times this must have been the arboretum of the great house, now overgrown and neglected,* thought Alexander. There was no beauty here, just a strange cold silence. Ancient branches reached over their heads like giant gnarled fingers from wizened old hands. Above, the sky was slowly darkening with heavy grey clouds and the air was growing cooler as a breeze picked up, rustling dried leaves through the undergrowth.

"This place is starting to give me the creeps," said Jonesy.

"Yes," agreed Alexander, "it's a weird place. Shall we turn back? I will leave it up to you."

With no tangible danger in sight at this point, Jonesy said bravely, "Let's soldier on, mate!"

Alexander dropped the blanket as a marker at the base of the tree that they had climbed down. "OK. Let's try and find the house," he said calmly.

A savage scream smashed through the air. "What the hell was that?" hissed Jonesy, who was starting to shake.

Like a great computer, Alexander's brain started searching through its memory banks. Every single thing that he had ever seen, read, or experienced was stored there, never to be forgotten. "Sounds like the hunting cry of an owl," he whispered. "It sounds like a very big owl. Strange that it should be flying in daylight—very strange indeed."

The boys ventured cautiously through the trees. As they moved forward, the woods began to thin out, eventually opening up onto rough grassland. In places, wizened trees extended their lifeless branches like the arms of dead men, stiff with rigor mortis. "This must've once been part of the gardens of the great house, now the realm of grazing goats," muttered Alexander.

From out of nowhere, a violent wind began to blow. The trees behind them creaked and moaned as a howling gale battered against their faces. Bang! The mighty roar of thunder ripped the air. In a blinding flash, a massive lightening bolt hurtled down from the angry clouds, exploding into the trees. The noise almost burst their ears with its ferocity. In amongst the stricken trees, tongues of blue-red flame flashed and crackled, devouring the living wood.

Suddenly, Alexander's head was drawn skywards. High above them, two dark shapes were circling. Billy Jones noticed them too. Curiosity overtook fear.

"What do you think they are?" he muttered.

"They're probably raptors gliding on a thermal air current, but it is difficult to tell because they're so high up," responded Alexander.

"I thought raptors were some sort of dinosaur," continued Jonesy.

"Well, they where originally, but they evolved into birds. Raptors are birds of prey," said Alexander, still staring upward.

The wind dropped away as quickly as it had begun.

"We should get out of here now," pressed Jonesy. "This place is starting to scare me."

Ignoring him, Alexander continued to stare into the heavens. The birds were dropping rapidly from the sky, and he was fascinated by them. Spiralling closer with each passing second, their shapes were now clearly visible.

"They look like eagles," gasped Billy Jones, "and they're coming our way!"

Alexander was gazing intensely at the rapidly approaching birds. "They're much bigger than eagles," he said in a detached analytical tone. The birds were almost upon them now, their massive talons extended for attack.

"They mean to kill us!" roared Jonesy. "Run! Run for your life!" With that, he turned and fled. For a large boy, he ran with surprising speed. Heart thumping violently in his chest, he headed for the shelter of the trees. His legs were wobbly with fear, but he was pumping them for all he was worth. Alexander followed close behind him. The two boys ran flat out, not daring to look behind them. Their breath was coming in deep rasping, desperate gasps as they reached the cover of the woods. Crashing blindly through the foliage, all logic was banished by the terror of pursuit. Alexander watched in horror as Jonesy lost his footing and fell headlong, his head bouncing off the leafy turf.

There's nothing for it but to stop, he thought, determined to help his friend. Struggling to his feet, Jonesy stumbled forward, fell again, recovered, and ran on. As he reached a small gully, he lost his balance again and collapsed, rolling over the soft woodland floor. Facedown, he lay there, winded and helpless. Alexander reached his friend. He knew they had to keep moving at all costs. The birds were eagle owls, but much bigger than any he had ever seen before. He estimated their wingspan at four metres. These raptors could pluck a sheep from the ground and carry it off to a grizzly fate. Although the birds looked like vicious killers, it was strange that they were attacking humans.

Billy Jones's head was spinning and his breath came in rasping gasps. A wave of dizziness and nausea swept over him as the birds dived upon his back. He could feel their weight pinning him to the ground and compressing his chest. Searing pain shot through him, as powerful talons bit into his stricken body, holding him in an iron grip—the grip of death. Using their terrible beaks, the raptors sliced through the boy's jacket and shirt and tore at his plump back. Agony raged through him like a burning fire. His shrill screams reverberated through the trees, as chunks of bloody flesh were ripped from his body. One of the ghastly birds reached for the poor boy's neck, and using its razor mouth like a lethal dagger, severed the carotid artery. Spurting out in a sickening fountain, blood splattered onto the ground and formed into dark, dreadful puddles.

Alexander stood, frozen, paralysed by utter horror. There was nothing he could do. It had all happened so fast. But the sight of the spurting blood as his friend was slowly torn apart was now too much for him, and he turned his head from the ghastly carnage. In that instant, his mind was freed from its horrified stupor and he started to run. He ran, hearing nothing but the sound of his breath coming in rapid, bellowing gasps. There was no sensation of desperate panic. It was more a kind of intense excitement, almost exhilaration, that he felt as he fled through the trees. He could not believe that those terrible raptors would catch him and end his life here in this abandoned wood. A perverse gratitude gripped him. It was his companion that was being shredded to pieces and not him. Reaching the tree marked by the blue blanket, Alexander knew his friend was dead by now for sure. There was nothing he could do. He had to escape. He had to get over that wall fast and find sanctuary from this accursed place.

But it was too late! Above him on the wall perched one of the giant eagle owls, his friend's blood dripping from its beak. The enormous bird stared down at him with large unblinking eyes; the ruthless eyes of a merciless killer. Swinging around in desperation, the boy sought any means of escape, but alas the game was over and he had lost. The other bird stood facing him, huge and ruthless, its feathers splattered red. A fearsome shriek came from its bloodied mouth; the clarion call of death.

Alexander knew that he had only moments to live, that his life was all but over. His legs began to shudder. He felt the furious pumping of his heart as it forced the blood through his veins. The shock and horror of what he had just witnessed turned fear to an uncontrollable terror. Opening his mouth, he screamed a hopeless scream.

CHAPTER 8
THUNDERSTRUCK

ꟷ

Frank could see the house now, as he continued to pick his way through the weeds and brambles. Surprisingly, it looked like the house that he had seen in his dream. As he got closer, he sensed that something dark and sad had happened here. The house stood empty and derelict, its large front door still in place, but scarred and battered. "No point in knocking," he said and sighed.

There's at least a decade of neglect here, he thought, as his eyes surveyed the garden. It had a wild desolation about it; the lawn had long since disappeared under weeds and sapling trees and there were nasty, barbed brambles everywhere. With a sinking heart he turned to walk away, but a strange curiosity gripped him. *I wonder what happened to that chess set*? He decided to make his way to the back of the house and do a little exploring. Had he actually seen into the past in his dream? Things were getting interesting.

Arriving at the rear of this once elegant building, he was not entirely unscathed. His right hand was throbbing with nettle stings, and brambles had gashed his ankles in places. Amazingly, the terrace was exactly as it had appeared in the dream, except that it was strewn with large pieces of stone and rubble. It looked like a massive explosion had ripped a large gaping hole in what he guessed had been the drawing room. After gazing in disbelief for a couple of minutes, he made his way across the terrace and looked through the shattered wall. The room was a scene of black destruction. *Nothing that was in here could have survived. I pray to God that nobody was killed in the explosion.*

He looked around the room at the charred remains. The smell of destruction still lingered. There was nothing recognisable in the room, just blackened debris. Many of the floorboards had been burnt through, leaving gaping black holes. It would be dangerous to venture far into the room, but he had an impetuous and reckless streak. He stepped into the room, treading gingerly on what remained of the floor. He had only gone a few paces when there was a loud crack and the floorboards gave way. Suddenly he was falling, dropping into blackness. Hitting the ground, he landed heavily on his side, the impact punching the air out of his body and leaving him momentarily stunned and senseless.

Gulping air back into his lungs and coughing furiously, the Irishman struggled to his feet.

"Nothing broken," he rumbled, his voice sounding hollow. *Must have fallen through to the cellar,* he thought. *Bloody idiot!* Luckily, the charcoaled debris had broken his fall. As his vision started to adjust to the darkness, he could see shafts of light penetrating the chamber from the shattered floor overhead. A strange eeriness began to tingle up his spine. "Not a good place to linger!" he grunted. Slowly, he edged his feet along the cellar floor. The smell of dank burnt air was oppressive and his back ached from the fall. His head was throbbing again. All in all, he was not a happy man.

"Bugger this!" he yelled suddenly, close to another eruption. Striding forth into the darkness, he was determined to find a rapid exit from the charcoal pit. Ten metres ahead, the light was stronger.

That must be the stairwell to the cellar, he reasoned. Unfortunately, he did not get very far before snagging his right foot and sprawling headfirst into the black dust and debris that lay inches thick on the stone floor. Shaking with rage, he lay there with his face immersed in soot. Just as his fury hit the point of no return, he felt something with his left hand. Struggling to his feet, he grasped an object, which, although layered with grime, felt cylindrical. Pushing it into his jacket pocket, he moved forward more cautiously.

ℰ𝒪𝒞ℛ

The morning clouds were starting to clear and the birds were chirping cheerily as they went about their business. Suddenly, a horrible black thing stuck its head out of a ground-floor window in the old house and roared. The shrill screeches of alarmed birds rang out as they headed for cover. The monster was back!

Pushing his way through the shattered window, Frank Malone climbed out of the ravaged house. Black and furious, he stormed his way through the undergrowth, ran through the woods, and found himself in a small lane.

"Where the bloody hell am I?" he fumed. Nobody was around to ask, so he headed left up the lane. There were no houses in sight, just woodland. Soon he arrived at a junction with a larger tarmac road. It looked like he was on some sort of Common. Turning to the left again, he began to follow the road. A car approached and he waved furiously, trying to flag it down. Swerving past him, the car accelerated away. The look of horror on the woman driver's face shook the Irishman from his fury. It was comical. Inspecting himself more closely, he could see that he was covered from head to foot in black grime, like a refugee from a coal mine. He laughed as he forged on down the road. In the distance he could see a majestic rolling green hill, topped by a mighty oak tree and a white windmill.

"This must be Turville Heath," he muttered, as he grabbed his mobile phone. Fortunately, it was still working, and he punched in the number for directory enquiries. Moments later he had the number for the local taxi company.

Lucky he had spotted that white windmill. There was only one windmill like that in these parts. Ten minutes later a red Peugeot 407 drew up.

"Are you the bloke that ordered the taxi?" enquired the grey, balding middle-aged driver, his face crinkled by countless disappointments.

"Too bloody right," replied Frank, as he reached for the rear passenger door.

"Well, I'm sorry mate, no can do!" said the taxi driver in a tone of mild disgust. "You're filthy, mate, and I'm not having you mess up the upholstery. I've a living to make, you know!" And with that he gunned his engine, turned full circle and was off, leaving Frank open-mouthed by the roadside. The eruption was not long coming. Tearing after the taxi, the furious Irishman waved his fists and roared curses.

Five minutes later, the red mist had cleared and he panted to a halt close to the village. He needed a drink—a very large strong drink—and woe betides anyone who got in his way!

CHAPTER 9
THE BLACK CASTLE

ꟸ

The giant eagle owls came at Alexander from both sides. Instinctively, the boy put his arms to his face and braced himself for the attack. He felt the grip of the merciless claws and a terrible shaking. Death was certain.

ꟸ

Rosie sat in her kitchen, nursing a cup of coffee. She looked over at her husband Jim, an oak of a man who stood six feet two inches in his socks and weighed a good two hundred and thirty pounds. Jim was one of those men who were just naturally big-boned and powerful. His large square face wore a thick black moustache. In his leather biker's jacket he could have easily been taken for a Harley Davidson riding Hell's Angel. But beneath that somewhat intimidating exterior there lived a sensitive and gentle soul. Jim was surprisingly soft-spoken for such a big man.

"Darling," said Rosie, with a hint of worry in her voice, "could you check on Alexander?"

Jim nodded and went to look for the boy.

ꟸ

In a rush of blinding light it was all over, and Alexander found himself in his bed. Jim's face came into focus, and in that instant he knew that it had all been a terrible dream—a ghastly nightmare.

"Steady," said Jim, looking very concerned. "Are you all right, son?"

Still in shock, Alexander gazed wide-eyed at him. "Thank God, Thank God," he sighed. "Jonesy is not dead! It was just a dream, a horrible dream!"

Looking steadily at his adopted son, Jim said softly, "Sounds like you've had a bad nightmare, son. Time to get up! Let's get a move on. You're late for breakfast."

With that, the big man left Alexander's bedroom. Falling back on his pillow, the shaken boy stared at the ceiling. That was the worst nightmare that he had ever had. He began to run the events of the previous day through his mind. It had been a nice day out on Turville Heath. The two of them had had a great lunch; that was pretty much guaranteed when you were with Jonesy. Then they had dozed off under a tree. When they woke up, there were only a couple of hours left for exploring. They had to be back home by dinnertime. It was either that or end up grounded by Rosie. Riding around the area, they had found nothing of interest. All the houses they had encountered were too modern, too small, or too well-maintained to be the house that Alexander was looking for. There were also lots of trees, making things difficult.

Maybe they had got closer than Alexander had thought. Maybe this dream was some kind of sinister warning. If it was, it had worked. It would be a long time before he would go looking for that house again. He was scared—very scared.

ꕥ

Jim backed the family car out of the driveway and parked it on the street in readiness for the trip to Oxford. Alexander had been invited for a tour of Lady Margaret Hall. An interview would follow in December. He would also have to take one of the College's entrance exams. For many prospective students wishing to study at the College, entrance exams had been scrapped some years previously, but Alexander was a special case. Because of his tender age, the College had decided to evaluate him very carefully. If he made it through the selection process, he would be one of the youngest students ever to attend the great and ancient University of Oxford.

Being a mechanic, Jim knew his cars. In his view, for the money, you could not buy better than Japanese. He had owned a string of Japanese cars and they had all run as smoothly as Swiss clocks. All in all, Jim had found Mitsubishis to be the most reliable. Mitsubishi also made aeroplanes and definitely knew more than most about reliability. Let's face it, it's one thing having a car breaking down on a road, but you cannot have an aeroplane conking out in mid-air! Planes had to be reliable, and that philosophy was carried through into their car manufacturing. Jim was currently running a metallic dark red Mitsubishi Gallant hatchback. It was fuel-efficient and drove superbly. The car was eight years old now, but still looked great, due to its galvanised body and regularly waxed paintwork.

Jim gave the windscreen a quick rubdown. He wanted the car to look good for the day out in Oxford. Inside the house he could hear raised voices.

"I'll bet they are arguing about wardrobe," chuckled Jim.

Sure enough, the verbal fencing was underway.

"Alexander, for goodness sake!" said Rosie in a loud stern voice. "You can't go to Oxford University dressed like that. You look like a roadie for a rock group. I know you love that Australian band. I like them too, but Lady Margaret Hall is no place for an AC/DC T-shirt! Not on a day like today."

Alexander stood in the kitchen, dressed in jeans and his navy blue T-shirt, a look of resignation on his face. Rosie did not come on all heavy like this very often, but when she did, you had better take notice! She was a big woman, and not to be trifled with on those rare occasions when she felt that she had to lay down the law. Still, Alexander was angling for some sort of compromise.

"But Mum!" he protested, "I look like a kid when I wear a shirt and tie, and all dolled up in a suit I look like a choirboy. Who invented those stupid ties, anyway? Dr. Malone will take one look at me and say, 'We can't let that boy into Oxford. He is too young and innocent. Come back in five years, young man, when you have grown up.' That's what he'll say!"

A compromise was reached. *The boy does have a point,* thought Rosie, after digesting the logic of his words. "All right," she said, in a more conciliatory tone. "You can wear a plain black T-shirt, navy blue slacks and your black sports jacket. That's as far as I am prepared to go, young man."

❧

Back in Oxford, a bruised, but hosed-down Dr. Frank Malone was sitting pensively in his College "rooms." The Fellows of the Oxford Colleges all had rooms, which varied in size and magnificence depending on the College. Tutorials were a key facet of education at Oxford, and they took place in the rooms. The rooms were also used as offices, and if space permitted, places to entertain guests and visitors. In Frank's case, he had a single room, but it was quite spacious and well lit by a very large and imposing window. Indeed, imposing windows were a feature of this beautiful red brick Victorian-built College, set in superb grounds that ran down to the river Cherwell. The gardens of Lady Margaret Hall were considered amongst the finest in Oxford.

"If it wasn't for these wretched end-of-term tutorials, I could have taken a few days off sick," grumbled a disgruntled Dr. Malone, the horrors of the last two days still vivid in his mind. The police had been informed, but without a registration number for the van in which he was abducted, Frank did not hold out much hope of the culprits being brought to justice. He would have to take matters into his own hands. Nobody was going to try and put the wind up him and get away with it. Then his mind turned to Alexander.

I will have to meet this wonder boy that they are all talking about. They want me to take him under my wing if he gets in. Well, we'll have to see about that. I'm not the most patient guy on the planet, just the one with the most time on his hands. Well, at least that's what the principal seems to think! Then the thought of a few medicinal brandies from his "entertainments cabinet" cheered him a little.

ᘓᘐ

They were all in the car now—Jim in his births-deaths-and-marriages suit, Rosie in her multifunctional loose-fitting black dress, and Alexander, looking like a trendy American newscaster—in miniature.

"A little soothing music for the journey," suggested Jim.

"No thanks!" was Alexander's instant response. "I'm too young to appreciate classical music."

Jim grinned. "What would 'sir' like to listen to," he laughed, knowing full well what was coming next.

"A little rock, my good fellow," yelled Alexander, from the back seat of the car. Rosie nodded in approval, and Jim hit a knob on the in-car stereo unit. Those wild boys from Australia sprang into action and "Stiff Upper Lip" burst from the speakers. Raised voices were now required for any further conversation.

"It surprises me," said Rosie, looking back at Alexander, "that you're so into those older rock bands, like AC/DC, Metallica and Judas Priest."

The power of the music had already gripped Alexander, who was now shaking his head. Slowly, Rosie's face registered in his faraway gaze. "Sorry, Mum. What was that?" He smiled, refocusing his eyes. Rosie raised her voice a notch.

"Why do you like bands like AC/DC so much? Surely that's music for old rockers like me and your dad."

Alexander shrugged his shoulders. "Well, Mum," he answered, "I've grown up listening to you play that sort of music. Anyway, bands as good as that still have a big following. There are loads of kids my age who like them. This Hip Pop stuff does nothing for me, but hey, each to his own! Anyway, as you're always pointing out, I'm only eleven and I have a lot of growing up to do yet."

Rosie smiled and said, "Yes, son, but don't grow up too fast!"

The car sped down the M40 motorway and turned off for Oxford at Junction 8. The rock music was still going at full tilt as they drove through Headington and down the hill into central Oxford. As they crossed Magdalen Bridge, the architecture suddenly changed and the resplendent tower of Magdalen College came into view. They were now in the land of dreaming spires. These days, regular traffic was prevented from driving down the High Street during the day and was diverted down Long Wall Street. This tactic is supposed to reduce air pollution in the city centre. Many would say that was questionable, but it has helped protect the stonework of the ancient buildings from corrosive car fumes.

Driving down Long Wall Street and on into South Parks Road, they passed the high stone walls of Magdalen College, the nineteen sixties architectural abomination known as the Zoology Department, the magnificent Radcliff Science Library and the majestic red brick of Keble College, to mention but a few of the interesting sights on their route through the golden centre of Oxford. Finally, the Mitsubishi Gallant followed the perimeter of the University Parks and Jim hunted for a parking spot close to Lady Margaret Hall

The family checked in at the Porters Lodge. They were met by a plump young woman, bubbling with enthusiasm, who said she was in her third year and studying Classics. Her name was Brenda. After the introductions, Brenda guided the Strongsons into the Front Quad.

"We will start the tour here," she said, looking directly at Alexander. There was already a buzz going around the College that a super-intelligent young boy had applied to become an undergraduate. It was obvious from her expression that she was quite impressed with Alexander's good looks.

Brenda launched into her routine. "Lady Margaret Hall was named after Lady Margaret Beaufort, the mother of King Henry VII, a generous benefactor to the Oxford and Cambridge Colleges. These days the College is generally referred to as 'LMH.' LMH has had a profound impact on the University by opening it up to women. The first female students arrived in October, 1879. They were pioneers who played a pivotal role in freeing women from the bondage of a male-dominated society. Many significant things have been achieved by the ladies of LMH over the decades. One hundred years after its founding, its pioneering mission completed, LMH became co-educational."

Alexander's attention was drawn by the architecture of the Quad. Looking around, he asked if the College had been built in one go, or had evolved over time. Brenda acknowledged his question, and continued.

"The original site of the College was a Victorian building, essentially a large house, called Old-Old Hall. You passed it on the right, just before you came through the main entrance. A little later, a second house was built next to the first, and it was called New-Old Hall." Rosie chuckled at this.

"Sounds a bit eccentric," she smirked.

"Yes," agreed Brenda. "That's Oxford for you!"

She continued. "Wordsworth, the first of four buildings for LMH, designed by Reginald Blomfield, was opened in 1869. You can see it there, at the far end of the Quad, on your right. The Talbot building was completed in 1910. It was named after the founder of LMH: Edward Talbot. You can see the building straight ahead. It is the centrepiece of the Quad, and for many years served as the main entrance to the College."

Brenda paused for a moment while her guests inspected the imposing building at the far end of the Quad. It was built in the Greco-Roman style, from red brick and ornate limestone. The entrance to the Talbot building was bordered by five long, curved stone steps. Above the steps was an elegant porch with a domed roof, supported by pillars.

"So the Quad was built in stages over time. When was it finally completed?" asked Alexander.

"I believe the building work was finished in the mid 1960s," replied Brenda. "That's when the library on your left, and the Wolfson West building, containing the new main entrance, and Porter's Lodge were built."

Jim's face registered a little surprise. "That's pretty recent," he said. "They did a good job. All the buildings blend very well together, and the bricks match perfectly."

Brenda smiled. "Yes, we like to think so," she said, looking up at Jim.

There followed a quick tour of the Talbot building, with its wood-panelled walls, main lecture hall and the original College dining room. The library was visited, and then the party were guided back outside and into the Quad. Alexander looked around him again. "The whole effect—the quadrangle, the red brick and the arches—reminds me of a Roman palace," he said.

Brenda, who was now pointing her charges in the direction of Centenary Gate, nodded in agreement. "Quite a few people have said that," she replied. "The whole place has a very unique atmosphere."

"Centenary Gate" was a rather grand name for a passageway between Eleanor Lodge and the Wordsworth building. It led out into the College gardens.

"Wow!" gasped Rosie as the gardens came into view. "The grounds are truly stunning. So many beautiful trees! The stands of wild grasses and flowers look absolutely amazing."

Walking down a gravel path to the side of the Wordsworth building, they entered the Sunken Garden. Even Jim, who was not a great gardening buff, just a humble mower of lawns, was impressed by the enormous copper beach tree, which took centre stage in this part of the College grounds, its iridescent copper red leaves dancing in the breeze.

The plump undergraduate looked at her watch. Fifteen minutes to go before the meeting with Dr. Malone. "The College is very close to the river, and punting is a favoured activity of the students in the summertime," she said, setting off down a gravel path to the right. Jim recalled a few interesting punting experiences that he had had whilst courting Rosie. The last time he had tried it was when he hired a punt from Folly Bridge, back in the early 1990s. It looks easy enough, does punting, but disaster is only a heartbeat away; a long narrow boat and a very long pole are not easy bedfellows. Steering the punt is tricky. It is an art that needs to be mastered patiently. Balancing precariously whilst endeavouring to propel the craft forward and trying to look cool and in control into the bargain is a risky business for the novice. Something's got to give. In Jim's case, he ended up soaked before he was even in open water. He still remembered the embarrassment of his fall from grace vividly. After guiding Rosie to her seat at the front of the punt, he had proceeded to step majestically aboard to take command at the helm, only to lose his footing and find himself chest-deep in the murky water, much to the amusement of a passing punt full of sneering schoolboys.

The group made their way to the river through a trellised walkway, decked with climbing plants that had grown to form an enchanting green tunnel, splashed with white and pink flowers. The tunnel ended in a path that traced its way along the edge of a narrow canal. To the other side of the canal was the University Parks, a favourite haunt of Dr. Frank Malone. The canal served as a mooring for the punts and fed directly into the glimmering grey-green waters of the Cherwell. On the far bank of the river was a pretty meadow, dotted with ancient trees.

"This is truly lovely," sighed Rosie.

"Any chance of a cup of tea, luv?" enquired Jim.

"Sure," said Brenda. "There will be tea and biscuits when you meet Dr. Malone. Let's finish our tour by visiting the student accommodation at the Deneke building, and also take a look at the Chapel."

ꕥ

Frank Malone's powerful and resonant oration, well lubricated by his "medicinal" brandies, rolled down the Quad. Jim almost laughed out loud as he caught sight of the strutting academic, dwarfed by two gangling male youths who were earnestly hanging onto his every word.

So that's Dr Malone, thought Alexander. *Looks like an interesting sort of dude. With a voice like that he'd make an awesome lead singer in a rock band.*

Frank eyed them up as he approached. Quickly dispatching the youths, he introduced himself and guided them in the direction of his rooms.

"Please make yourselves comfortable and help yourselves to the tea and biscuits," gestured Frank in full performance mode as he took up position in an easy chair opposite a large couch. Students generally sat on the couch during tutorials, but it also doubled as Frank's bed when he needed a nap, or when he had had one drink too many after an evening in the senior common room. Alexander and family made themselves at home on the couch.

"It's grand to meet you. This must be himself—your gifted son, Alexander," said Frank.

Normally, Alexander would have blushed a little at a compliment like that, but his attention was elsewhere. An object standing eight inches tall glistened on the academic's big wooden desk. It was a piece from a chess set, a very expensive chess set. "That's an impressive looking chess piece you have there, Dr. Malone," said Alexander.

"We are here to talk about you," retorted the Irish academic, "but as you mention it, there is an interesting story behind that black castle, or 'rook,' as it is called, but I will tell you about it on another occasion, when we have more time." Frank was keen to get this chore over with and head for home.

As Alexander recalled later, the conversation went well and Dr. Malone, although a little overpowering, seemed like a decent bloke. He even said he could find a friend to put him up during the weekdays while he was studying—if he made it through the College selection procedure, that is. It was made clear to Alexander that he would have to go home to his parents on the weekends and during holidays; the College would expect that. Dr. Malone wished him the best of luck and said he hoped to see him again.

ꙮ

Spring turned to summer, and it got hot. The patch of lawn outside Number 13 Arcadia Drive, once plump and green, turned shrivelled and brown. England's green, pleasant land fell under the full glare of the summer sun. The novelty of cloudless blue skies soon started to wear thin as the hosepipe and sprinkler bans kicked in and dry and dusty became the order of the day. Alexander's thoughts turned to global warming. When he was not messing around on his bike with Jonesy, he was researching everything he could about the factors contributing to climate change and how these changes could impact on the planet.

Winter eventually arrived and Alexander found himself confronted by the entrance exam for LMH. His interview had gone smoothly and the Selection Panel seemed very sympathetic. If he got through the entrance exam, logistics would be the main concern— who would keep an eye on him, where he would live, and that sort of thing. In many ways, Alexander felt that the key question that the Interview Board asked was, "Why do you want to study Politics and Economics at Lady Margaret Hall, and why at such a young age?" They seemed satisfied with his answer. His Head Teacher, in close consultation with his parents, had made extensive enquiries. LMH seemed to be the best College to fulfil his needs and requirements. The College was the right size and had a very friendly and welcoming atmosphere. LMH was not hidebound in pomp and tradition. It had wonderful grounds for a young boy to relax and play in, and the University Parks were right next door. Alexander told the panel that school was no longer a challenge for him. He also told them that he had a tremendous interest in how the modern world worked, and that most things in life were ultimately governed by politics and economics. This particular degree course would give him an immense insight on how to move forward with his life and ambitions.

Let's face it, there is a lot at stake here, thought Alexander. There were about ten candidates sitting in a classroom at his school, most of them looking a little nervous. The classroom was being used for the University of Oxford entrance exams. Many of the Oxford Colleges still required applicants to take an examination for certain subjects, such as mathematics.

He felt a little hard done by being the only applicant in the country asked to take an exam for the Politics and Economics course at LMH. But he had to face the fact that since he was so young, he would have to walk the extra mile. The clock at the front of the room struck eleven a.m., and the Deputy Head instructed the assembled applicants to turn over their examination papers and begin the test. A tingle ran down Alexander's fingers as he gripped his pen and read through the questions. In this exam, there was more of an emphasis on essays than is the case with school A level exams, where these days there was a high proportion of multiple-choice questions. Questions on the College entrance exams tended to be more general, and were a broader exploration of a candidate's knowledge and abilities than the school exams.

Alexander's approach to exams was to deal with the easiest and most appealing questions first, then move onto the other more problematical questions. One question shone out, and he decided to tackle it first. It read, "Discuss a phenomenon or event that is likely to have a significant global impact. Express a personal view on the likely response of world governments." Global Warming was a phenomenon that Alexander was now regarding with growing concern. His pen began to race across the paper.

When the essay was completed, the boy lifted his pen, troubled by the words he had just written. The future looked very bleak indeed. He had had many bits of information on Global Warming stored in his brain, but this was the first time that he had put them together and written them down on paper as a coherent whole. However, as disturbing as things were, Alexander had to press on. He had an exam to pass.

CHAPTER 10
THE FRESHER

ഇര

As expected, the following summer Alexander passed his A levels with top grades in five AS subjects. Because the interview and the entrance exam had also gone very well, the boy was now on his way to Oxford. There was still the problem of the fees, but like any other student these days, he would get a loan from the government.

Professor Gupta's BMW drew up to the main entrance of LMH. It was autumn now and the trees in Norham Gardens were tinged with subtle hues of yellow and red. Alexander leapt out of the car, keen to launch into Fresher's Week. He had hit gold with her. Frank Malone had put in a good word for him, and Anita was happy to take the boy in as a lodger. Being a psychologist, she thought it would be quite intriguing to have a hyper-intelligent child to study at close quarters. She also missed her twin sons, who were away studying at other universities. It would be nice to have a boy around the house. Like many Indians, she was very family-orientated.

Alexander waved to Anita a little tentatively as he disappeared through the arch of the main entrance and made his way to the Porters Lodge. Fresher's week was a whirlwind of activities that helped get the new intake of undergraduates up and running. There were orientation lectures to let the wide-eyed teenagers, freshly escaped from the confines of school, know where the main lecture theatres were located, the identity of their lecturers and tutors, the books they would need to buy, and so on. There were talks by students about their take on college life, joining the students' union, and the vast array of clubs on offer. And then there was lots of drinking and getting to know people. It was all a bit of a shock to the system for a boy who had only recently arrived at his thirteenth birthday. Alexander was disorientated and a little depressed, waking up in a strange room every morning, with no Rosie to call him down for breakfast.

It was not long before the boy felt isolated and ignored by his fellow Freshers, who regarded him as a kid who should still be in school—a babe in the woods, a child to be avoided in case he became needy and clingy. Alexander was counting the days until he could go back home at the weekend and hug his mum and fall blissfully asleep in the comforting familiarity of his own bedroom.

Frank Malone had been asked to keep a close eye on Alexander, particularly during his first year. He had requested Brenda, the student who had shown Alexander around the college, to keep a discrete watch over the boy whenever possible. It was the third day after Alexander's arrival at LMH when Frank spotted him walking across the Quad. Opening his window, he shouted down to the blond-haired boy, his voice reverberating like a summons from the thunder god.

"How are you, young man?" the academic called out, as Alexander walked through the door. "Congratulations! A tremendous achievement to secure a place at Oxford! Welcome aboard."

The boy looked back at him. "It's great to be here, sir," he replied enthusiastically, "but I'm still learning the ropes."

Swivelling in his comfortable leather office chair, Frank pointed to the couch. "Take a seat," he said, studying

Alexander closely. "The first couple of weeks are the trickiest; after that, things should start falling into place."

"Excuse me for saying this, Dr Malone," said the boy, "but for a Dubliner, you don't sound that Irish."

"Well, there are all sorts of accents in Ireland." Frank laughed. "My father was a geologist working in the oil industry, and we travelled a lot when I was young. I guess that must have blunted the Celtic lilt—that and all the years in England. But make no mistake, by temperament, I'm every inch a hot blooded Irishman, so you had best behave yourself, young man."

Alexander and Frank, who was the boy's main tutor, chatted for about half an hour about background reading and timetables for tutorials. As Frank was about to show him to the door, he could not help but notice him staring at an object on his desk: the black castle.

"Ah yes," sighed Frank. "I promised to tell you about that rook the last time you were here." Rising from his chair, he made for his entertainments cabinet, an ornate rosewood piece of furniture. He opened the drop-down front, revealing an impressive array of whisky and brandy bottles. There were also bottles of sherry and port, designated for guests. Frank poured himself a large whisky and returned to his desk. He gestured to Alexander to sit down again.

"Sorry, you're too young for one of these, and anyway, it is purely for medicinal purposes. The story I am about to tell you still makes my blood boil," he said, taking a large swig from the Waterford crystal whisky glass that he had lifted to his lips. Alexander said nothing; he was looking with piercing intensity at the black castle on the desk.

The Irishman took another slurp of whisky and settled back in his chair. His gaze fell on the boy, who had a curious look of concentration on his young face. It was almost as if he had been mesmerised by the gleaming chess piece. Clearing his mighty throat, Frank commenced the tale of his bizarre adventure—the abduction, the escape, and the strange discovery of an old abandoned house. To spare his embarrassment, he omitted the bit about falling through the floorboards and ending up black as the ace of spades. He finished with, "So there you have it, boyo. I saw the chess set in my dream, and then when I woke up I found by accident a chess piece that was identical to those I had encountered in the dreamscape; a strange experience, to say the least!"

Alexander looked pale now, almost as if he was in shock. "It sounds like the house— the house I remember from when I was a baby," he murmured in a far away voice.

Eyebrows rising, Frank said, "I thought you came from High Wycombe? The house I found was on Turville Heath."

Responding to the searching gaze of the Irish academic in a slightly faltering voice, Alexander said, "Very few people know this, Dr. Malone, and I hope that you will keep it to yourself, but I was adopted at the age of two. Rosie and Jim found me by a roadside on Turville Heath. I could remember nothing except my mother's face, but more recently I've been having memories of the house where I was born. This is very odd, because I've a photographic memory. The house you describe matches the one I remember exactly. I have been looking for it for over a year now. I would be in your debt if you could kindly show me the location of this abandoned house."

Frank was very moved by the way the boy had taken him into his confidence with such a deeply personal secret. He too was an orphan, albeit at the age of twenty. His parents and sister had been killed in a gas explosion at the family home in Dublin. A deep sense of loneliness had pervaded him ever since. Even now, so many years later, he felt their loss profoundly, but at least he had many fond memories of his family. Alexander, on the other hand, had been torn from his mother and father at a very early age. The boy had now reached early adolescence and was searching for a greater understanding of himself. To achieve this, he felt that he needed to find out where he had come from. He desperately needed to discover his true identity—the names of his parents, the face of the woman who bore him, and the history of his family. He was a gifted child, and now he wanted to know if there was any meaning, any significance behind his exceptional intellect, or was he just another freak of nature?

Frank smiled reassuringly at the boy. "The best thing would be if I drove you out there one weekend," he said. "The house is dangerous, as I know to my cost, but you can certainly take a look at it from the outside."

Alexander beamed at the Irishman. "That would be great, Dr. Malone," he gushed excitedly. "When do you think we could go?"

Frank finished off the dregs of his whisky and winked. "Let's give it a month or so, until you are more settled in here. Now be off with you, young man. I'm sure you have plenty to do."

Alexander, although a little disappointed that he would have to wait so long, thanked the Irish academic profusely for his kindness and made for the door. Just as his hand reached the knob, Frank called him back. "You seem very fond of the black chess piece," he grinned, his teeth betraying a weakness for cigarettes. "The blasted thing is starting to irritate me," he rumbled. "Too many bad memories! Why not take it off my hands?"

Alexander's eyes lit up. "Wow!" he blurted. "Thanks, sir! The chess piece looks so familiar to me. It may help jog my memory. Thank you!" Lifting the black castle from the desk, the boy smiled and offered another "thank you" as he departed.

ꙮ

Bicycles are the primary form of transport for students the world over, and Alexander was no exception. He had purchased himself a rather sorry looking second-hand boneshaker, but it was good enough to get him around the city, or back to his digs in North Oxford. Bike crime was rife in Oxford, and no bike was safe from the chain cutters. The more knackered looking the bike, however, the better the chances were that it would still be where you left it, when you returned. It was early evening and already getting dark when Alexander mounted his bike and pedalled towards his new place of residence. He was getting more used to things now. In his final year at LMH, he thought it would be great to live in at the college and get the full-on LMH experience: a bedroom-study in the Quad, dinners in the dining hall, visits to the junior common room on a regular basis, tennis and evening strolls through the grounds, even swims in the Cherwell.

Alexander's brakes squealed to a halt outside the house of the Indian psychologist. It was very imposing for a semi-detached house, extending over four stories. Anita Gupta had bought it when she moved to Oxford in the mid-eighties with her husband Ravinda, who was a Consultant Radiation Oncologist. Now the house was a prime piece of North Oxford real estate, and worth a fortune. He had his own key to the front door, and he let himself into the spacious hallway. It was lit during the day by a symphony of multicoloured lights from the intricate stained glass windows in the doorframe. Removing his shoes, the boy ran up the stairs, which were covered in plush light green carpet. There were two floors above the ground floor. The first had four bedrooms and a family bathroom, and the second two bedrooms, a shower room, an office and a TV/ music room. Alexander's new room was one of the guest bedrooms at the top of the house, on the third floor. It had a comfortable single bed, easy chair, modern storage cabinets and built-in wardrobes. He had exclusive use of the office, with its Internet-connected computer, printer and photocopier. He also had the TV room to himself, as the Gupta boys were away at college.

The rich aromatic scents of dinner percolated their way from the kitchen into the adjoining dining room. The dining room was quite imposing, with its high ceiling and big

French windows opening onto a long leafy garden. This was laid to lawn, with beds of mature shrubs. The centrepiece in the room was a large mahogany dining table, set for the evening meal. A deep, resonating clang sounded in the hallway and carried all the way to the top floor of the house—the sound of the dinner gong. Alexander was developing quite a taste for home-cooked Indian cuisine. Ravinda, or Ravi, as his wife called him, helped bring in the large bowls of hot food from the kitchen and position them on the dining room table. Anita was a very accomplished cook when she had the time. It was one of those fortunate evenings when she had prepared a very delicious looking meal of curried chick peas, spinach-paneer and lady fingers (an Indian vegetable), along with rice and parathas. There was also a fresh vegetable salad. No meat was used in the cooking, because like many Indians, the Guptas generally preferred vegetarian food.

Alexander arrived at the table, washed and ready to go. Ravi had taken up the position at the head of the table and was spooning the various dishes into small bowls. Anita came in with serviettes. This was Alexander's third evening meal with the Guptas, and they were getting to know each other quite well.

"How was your day, Alexander?" asked Ravi.

The boy looked at him through his radiant blue eyes. Ravi was a well-fed looking middle-aged man; a little chubby around the cheeks, with the beginnings of a pot belly. His hair was luxuriant black, and dense stubble was starting to peek through the brown skin of his face. He wore a closely clipped moustache and had a calm commanding sort of personality, typical of many medical doctors.

"Actually, today was quite incredible," he answered, with considerable enthusiasm. "I had a meeting with Dr. Malone. There was a chess piece—a black castle—on his desk that I've found strangely fascinating every time I have encountered it. I seem to recognise it from somewhere deep in my mind. Today, Dr. Malone told me the story of how he found it."

He paused and looked at Anita. "You and your husband have probably heard the story before."

Anita looked back at him, her smile revealing perfect pearl-white teeth. "Yes, Alexander, we have heard the story," she replied. "I found it very interesting. Looking at it from a parapsychology point of view, the dreamscape visions of the house matched very closely to the real house that Frank discovered in the morning when he woke up in the wood. It appeared that he was having some sort of psychic vision of the house as it had looked many years ago, before it was abandoned. The discovery of the chess piece also supports the hypothesis that Frank's dream was a psychic vision of the past."

Ravi passed around glasses of water and the meal began. Alexander looked on in admiration at the Gupta's skilful handling of the parathas. The paratha was like a pancake of unleavened bread. Small pieces are broken off and used to scoop or wrap around food, dependent on the consistency. Try as he may, Alexander could not master the art, and soon resorted to a spoon to deliver the tasty food to his mouth, munching separately on the parathas. Everybody was hungry after the long workday, and the meal passed in relative silence. When it was over and appetites satiated, Alexander produced the rook from a pocket in his fleece jacket and placed it on the table.

"Dr. Malone very kindly gave this to me and said that I could keep it. He told me it still gave him bad memories," said the boy, trying to stifle a belch.

"I don't blame him," said Anita. "The kidnapping that he had to endure was a terrible ordeal. It seems that he must have annoyed somebody, and they took revenge by trying to scare him witless."

"Frank can be his own worst enemy at times," added Ravi. "He has a terrible temper and it gets him into trouble."

Anita studied the glistening chess piece. She picked it up and rolled it about in her fingers. "It is very large and heavy for a chess piece, but beautiful, none-the-less. The original chess set must have looked very impressive," she said. Placing it back on the table, she asked Alexander if she could borrow it. She was going to give a tutorial on dreams tomorrow, and it would make a very interesting exhibit for the students. Alexander kindly agreed to lend it to her. Ravi suggested that they have their coffee in the lounge.

Alexander settled into a comfortable armchair, close to the large Italian marble fireplace, and stared at the flames that were flickering warmly in the hearth. Ravi arrived with a tray of coffee in mugs. Continuing the conversation where it had left off in the dining room, Anita asked, "So, Alexander, you feel that you remember seeing the chess piece at some point in the past, before Frank discovered it?"

"Yes," responded Alexander. "It seems strangely familiar." He did not wish to develop this thread of the conversation any further, as he may be forced to admit that he was an orphan.

Ravi saved the day by chipping in with, "Maybe it is something you remember from a past life. Do you believe in reincarnation, Alexander?"

The boy stared into his half-full coffee mug. "It's an interesting theory," he replied diplomatically. "My parents are not religious and God doesn't crop up in the conversation... I've never really thought about it, to be quite honest."

Ravi went onto say, "We are Hindus and the philosophy of reincarnation is an integral part of our religion. The Buddhists also believe in reincarnation. Life has a lot more sense and purpose to it if you believe that existence is a journey that involves many lives and deaths. These are necessary for the progressive evolution of our consciousness."

Alexander's thoughts turned to death. "So what do you think happens when you die?" he asked, looking more closely at Anita than Ravi. He knew that Anita had a strong interest in parapsychology.

"Well," said Anita, her eyes sparkling with enthusiasm, "looking at it from a scientific perspective, death remains a mystery. There are no instruments that can reliably detect anything resembling a spirit or a soul. Parapsychologists and paranormal investigators, or ghost hunters, often use small portable instruments that can pick up changes in electromagnetic fields. In places that are believed to be haunted, the meters on these instruments can go off-the-scale, and room temperatures can drop dramatically, so it is possible to measure changes in the environment in locations that are reputed to be haunted. However, because these changes cannot be linked to visual sightings, video, or camera images, it remains an area of debate as to the underlying causes behind these physically detectable changes."

If it had not been for the terrible nightmare that he had experienced the previous year, he would have been very sceptical about phenomena that science could not clearly detect, measure, and identify. There was also the strange dream of Dr. Malone to contend with. So all in all, he had become more open-minded about the paranormal. "It is clear that science still has a long way to go before machines and instruments can be developed that are sensitive enough to make definitive explorations in the realms of parapsychology and the occult," he said.

"That's true," replied Anita, "but of late, some progress appears to have been made." She then went on to relate to Alexander the story that she had told Frank Malone about the black boxes. He listened in complete silence until she had finished.

"Wow!" he exclaimed. "That is a very exciting study! Perhaps for the first time you appear to have clear evidence that a physical instrument can be affected by mind power. But more exciting still, the black boxes appear to be interacting with some sort of collective mind. If there is a collective mind, then every human being on the planet is interconnected through this mind. If this mind could be consciously tuned in to, untold knowledge could be accessed and revealed. Taking things up to another level, if there are other intelligent life forms in the Universe—and there could be billions—then they would also have collective minds. But what if all of the collective minds were connected? We would then have a Universal mind. Perhaps that could be what man calls God! If that mind could be contacted, the knowledge attainable would be beyond comprehension. A person with such knowledge would have the power to change the world—for good or bad. All that power invested in one individual would be a frightening thought!"

"That's very impressive reasoning," said Anita, her eyes shining.

Ravi nodded in agreement. "In all the religious traditions there are Masters," he said. "It is believed by the faithful that these Masters have attained free access to the Universal mind, or the mind of God. These Masters are reputed to have tremendous powers. To give you an example, just look at all the miracles that Jesus performed: raising the dead, curing the sick and feeding the five thousand with a few loaves and fishes. The Masters are teachers of humanity, and through their oneness with the mind of God, they act as His representatives on Earth. Their job is to guide the human race and move it forward."

Alexander's mind was leaping further ahead. "If it is possible to convincingly prove, using valid and irrefutable scientific techniques, that the collective human mind really exists," he mused aloud, "then that would have tremendous implications in relation to human consciousness and the perception of God. If the collective mind of the human race exists, then it must have had a beginning. The same would hold true for the collective minds of other intelligent beings in the Universe. The question is, what existed before the advent of the first intelligent, self-aware beings in the Universe? Is God the collective minds of all the self-aware creatures in the Universe, or is the God consciousness something beyond that. Was there a God-mind before the

Universe came into existence, or is it merely the product of the mental evolution of sentient beings on different planets?"

"Those are very weighty thoughts," interjected Ravi. "More coffee, anyone?" There were no takers. "Looking at it from a philosophical perspective," Ravi added, "all the major religions agree that there is one God or an all pervading 'Universal Consciousness.' The great Masters, who it is believed have free access to the Mind of God, all say the same thing. The Universe came into being as an act of creation by God. They say that God has always existed, and was a fully self-aware consciousness before the Universe came into being. Indeed, they say that the complex organisation of the Universe, long before life existed on the planets, did not come into being as a result of a series of chaotic events. There is an intelligent plan behind it all: God's plan."

Alexander finished the remains of his coffee. "Philosophy and religion are fascinating subjects," he said. "I'll have to study them. Up until now, science and the physical world have been my main interests, but now I can see how science can open new doors to realms beyond the gross physical. The concept of God, however, remains a mystery to me. I prefer solid evidence, rather than faith in other people's words."

He looked over at Anita, who was sitting next to her husband on a comfortable four-seater settee. "Do you think I could visit your laboratories sometime?" he asked. "It would be great to have a look at the black box, and the work that is being carried out with the other black boxes around the world."

"It would be a pleasure, Alexander," said Anita. "We will agree on a time when you are more settled." Inwardly, she was pleased with the way the conversation had gone. The mind of the boy was starting to expand its horizons beyond the realms of the physical.

Later, as Alexander settled himself for sleep, he felt a little concerned that he had parted company with the gift from Dr. Malone. He had not yet had a chance to study the chess piece closely, and he was growing uneasy that it might not be entirely safe in the hands of Anita Gupta; she could lose it or misplace it.

ꕥ

Morning came and Alexander arrived in the kitchen to be greeted by the perplexed face of the Indian academic. "I'm terribly sorry, Alexander," she said apologetically, "but I can't find that chess piece of yours anywhere. I left it on the kitchen table last night, and now it's nowhere to be seen. I have searched the kitchen, lounge and dining room."

Fury rose rapidly in the boy. The chess piece could be a key – the only link to the memories that had been obliterated from his mind. He wanted to dance up and down, yelling, "I knew you would loose it, you stupid woman! Idiot! Idiot! Idiot!" But then a thought suddenly entered his head. "Has Lucy been in here this morning?" he asked, as calmly as he could, his rage seething.

"Yes," said Anita, still flustered. "I always feed her before I go to work."

Alexander made for the kitchen door. "I'll bet the dog's got it," he yelled, as he sprinted towards the garden.

The dog, a golden retriever, was munching on something. To his horror, as he got closer, he could see that it had the chess piece in its mouth. Reaching the startled animal, it dropped the chess piece and looked at him quizzically. Grabbing it, he frantically inspected it for damage. To his horror, he saw that the outer surface was mangled with tooth marks, and a piece of the base had been chewed away; but the damage was only superficial. It was clear that the black ivory-like material was only a veneer and underneath it was glistening silver metal. Exposed at the base of the chess piece was an embossed eye in the style of an Egyptian hieroglyph. As he stared at the ancient image, a cold shiver ran through him.

CHAPTER 11
THE QUEST BEGINS

ꕥ

The green Land Rover Discovery pushed its way slowly through the tangles of brambles, its big tyres scrunching the gravel. It drew to a halt in front of a Georgian manor house clad in limestone, with large leaded sash windows—now cracked or smashed. "Here we are, young man; this is the house... What do you make of it?" asked the Irishman, looking over at his young companion. Staring wide-eyed at the deserted house, a tear trickled down one of the boy's cheeks.

It was November now. Frank had borrowed the Land Rover off a friend of his who worked as a grounds-man at the University Parks. Negotiating the gardens of this derelict house in a rugged, go-anywhere, four-wheel drive vehicle was a much better option than trying to hack through the undergrowth on foot. "Let's get out, son, and have a look around," said Frank, oblivious to the boy's deep emotion.

The forgotten garden lay dull and misty in the thin morning light, and the raucous cries of rocks echoed through the woods. Jumping from the jeep, Alexander looked around him. He knew instantly that the house had once been his home, but the garden was unrecognisable—sad and desolate. *What happened to this place?* he wondered. Frank grabbed a big hand scythe from the back of the vehicle.

"This will take care of the nasty stuff," he said, grinning at Alexander. "Let's make our way to the back of the house."

A couple of minutes later, they had hacked their way to the rear of the building, and they walked across the terrace. It was just as Frank remembered it, littered with shattered blocks of masonry and rubble. Alexander gasped when he saw the large hole in the drawing room wall.

"What do you think could have caused this, Dr. Malone?" he asked.

"Could have been a gas explosion," answered Frank, wincing at the memory of his family tragedy in Ireland.

Peering through the hole, the boy surveyed the damage. "I don't think so," he muttered. "The upper floor above this room is still intact. A gas explosion radiates in all directions from its point of origin. If it was powerful enough to blow a huge hole in the wall, it would have blown out the ceiling and probably part of the roof. I've always had a strong fascination with lightening. This could have been caused by a massive thunderbolt, or multiple lightening bolt strikes."

Frank was sceptical, but Alexander was insistent. "Such strikes on houses are rare, especially in this country, but they do happen. I've seen photographs of buildings that have been extensively damaged by lightening. Anyway, now that I know the location of the house I can check the local authority and newspaper records. There must be an accident report somewhere."

"So," asked Frank, looking at the shattered floorboards that marked the spot where he had fallen into the cellar, "does the place seem familiar to you?"

Alexander was inspecting every inch of the burnt out room very carefully. "Thanks again for bring me here, Dr. Malone," he responded. "I'm in no doubt that this derelict house was once my home."

"Jeeze! That's amazing!" exclaimed Frank, his voice echoing loudly through the blackened shell that was once a room. "Do you remember anything else now?"

"No," said the boy, his sadness obvious. "There's nothing in this room but unrecognisable burnt debris."

And a lingering sense of death! thought Frank, but he did not say anything.

Alexander turned to the Irishman, with pleading eyes. "I need to see more of the house, Dr. Malone," he blurted. "Better with you than by myself! I have come this far; there is no turning back for me. There's a terrible longing inside of me that is growing more intense with each passing day. I have to find out who my real parents were and what became of them. I can have no real peace until I discover the truth."

Both of them were equally surprised by the passion that drove these words. They had welled up from somewhere deep inside the boy. Frank knew only too well the dreadful, lingering loneliness and the painful sense of loss that still haunted him, even to this day.

"Well, what do you propose we do, boyo?" he asked, looking kindly at Alexander. "You do realise that if anything untoward were to happen to you, the principal would have my head on a plate."

Alexander's head moved slowly, as his eyes searched for a relatively safe point of entry into the house. He was about to tell the Irish academic that under the circumstances they should leave, when a long submerged memory surfaced in his mind. "Dr. Malone," he said, "I think I know where there's a key." The boy walked briskly across the terrace and made his way to the front of the house. Frank followed in silence. Reaching the now dirty and discoloured dark grey granite steps below the front door, Alexander dropped to his knees and began to feel along the right hand flank of the top step.

"Ah ha!" he exclaimed, and pulled out an object coated in earth and grime. It was a large key! "I found it in a concealed groove, just under the lip of the step. It must've been the emergency key!" he said triumphantly.

Frank walked to the Land Rover and returned with a rag and a can of WD40. "Let's clean it up," he said. The anticipation was growing in both of them.

The boy set to work cleaning the key, while Frank put the nozzle of the can next to the keyhole and pressed until the internal mechanism of the lock was liberally soaked with the WD40. The key cleaned up well; there was no rust, as the metal had been galvanised. Frank sprayed the lock again.

"OK. Let's give it a try," he said to Alexander, who was poised with the key.

Hand slightly trembling, the boy inserted the key into the lock. He gripped it hard and twisted, but it would not turn. Producing a screwdriver, Frank inserted the shaft through the metal loop at the end of the key. Using the screwdriver as a lever, he pushed hard. Slowly, the key began to turn—then there was a clunk. The lock was opened.

"Now try the door handle," said Frank, retreating down the steps. Alexander grabbed the corroded brass doorknob with both hands, but it was stuck fast. The Irishman returned with a massive wrench from the toolbox at the back of the Land Rover. A little spraying and heaving later, and the knob turned, but the door would not open.

"It may be bolted from the inside," rumbled Frank.

"That's unlikely," replied Alexander. "Front doors are usually only bolted from the inside when people are at home."

"All right," said Frank, "It's probably stuck in the lintel. Stand back, young man." And with that, he charged at the door, shoulder on. The door burst open and in he went. Alexander stood there, momentarily stunned. The door had given way quite easily and Frank's charge propelled him forward with such force that he lost his footing and fell. Flipped onto his back, he slid along the floor.

The boy entered the house, his heart beating faster. At last he was home! Frank was not a happy man. Sitting up, his face crimson red with fury, molten magma began to surge through his veins; the eruption was not long in following. "That's the second fecking time that's happened!" he roared. His voice blasted through the house like an explosion. It was only the face of the boy in the doorway that stopped him from unleashing a volley of profanities.

"Lucky I brought the hip flask!" he muttered, reaching into an inside jacket pocket.

After assisting the stricken Irishman to his feet, Alexander helped dust him down. His slide along the floor had cut a track through the thick dust, revealing a beautiful white marble floor.

"The owners of this house must have been quite wealthy," concluded Frank, as he stood admiring the grandeur of the hall. The magnificence of the old mahogany staircase still shone through the grime of neglect. "OK," he said, taking another fortifying swig from his hip flask, "let's stick together and move through the house room by room. If any room looks unsafe, we will not enter. Agreed?"

Alexander nodded his head and they began the quest.

"We'll start with the ground floor," said Frank. "Let's skip the cellar. I can testify that there is nothing down there but soot and charcoal!"

The hall was very spacious, with the staircase centrally placed within it. There were large solid wood-panelled doors to either side of the stairwell, all closed. They started on the right side of the hallway. The first door creaked open to reveal an empty room with a high ornately plastered ceiling. The air was cold and damp, with a lingering musty odour. Everything had been stripped from the room except the imposing white marble fireplace. At the front of the room there was a big casement window, its glass dull and layered with grime. Some of the panes were cracked or smashed.

"I think this may have been the sitting room," muttered Alexander sadly.

"Nothing in here, son," said Frank, his voice booming in the hollow emptiness of the room.

They worked their way through all the rooms on the ground floor: the ravaged drawing room, the morning room, the dining room, the study, the kitchen and scullery. The rooms were stripped of everything except their peeling wallpaper and fireplaces. A chilly, musty desolation pervaded everything.

Teacher and pupil mounted the staircase, leaving foot tracks in the dust. It was the same story upstairs. All the rooms were empty, save one.

"This was once a library," said Alexander, remembering the rows of books and stacks of papers. All that now remained were a couple of large, empty oak bookcases. Something drew the boy into the room. Frank remained in the doorway, looking aimlessly on. As far as he was concerned, the search had been fruitless and it was time to leave. Inspecting the room carefully, Alexander could see nothing of interest. With a sinking heart he turned to leave, but something caught his eye. Protruding from the back of one of the bookcases was a yellowed piece of plastic. It looked like nothing, but Alexander felt a sudden compulsion—almost as if he were being pushed by some unseen force—to investigate further. Walking over to the bookcase, he found it surprisingly heavy, but managed to heave it a few centimetres forward. A large pouch fell to the ground.

ഇര

It was noon when Frank dropped Alexander back at Arcadia Drive. "Let me know if you come up with anything interesting," was Frank's parting comment as he drew away in the Land Rover. Alexander dashed indoors. He could not wait to come to serious grips with the contents of the pouch, and he ran straight to his bedroom. The plastic tore as he ripped it open. It was filled with old newspaper clippings. At last it looked like he may have some kind of a lead, a glimmer of hope.

CHAPTER 12
CLUES EMERGE

It was the evening of the following Monday, and Alexander was seated in his office. He was getting quite used to his well-appointed surroundings, and considered himself very fortunate. He had heard some real horror stories about the state of the digs that some of his fellow students, who were not boarding in the colleges, were living in. And here he was, sitting in a plush house, with his own fully-equipped state-of-the-art office.

He had spent the weekend reading through the newspaper clippings and thinking about their contents. Every detail was locked into his photographic memory. On the workbench, next to one of the computer screens, a cylindrical object glistened. Picking it up, he examined it closely. A short time ago it had been an expensive looking chess piece. Now it was stripped bare of its thin black veneer. While it still had the basic profile of a chess piece, there were significant changes. At the top of the piece there were four rectangular prongs. On the roof of the castle turret there were three, equally-spaced circular indentations of differing size and depth. Most intriguingly, ringing the base of the castle were a series of embossed letters.

This is indeed a peculiar object, thought Alexander, placing it back on the bench. He had decided that the best way to organise his thoughts and analyse all the material that he had so far unearthed was to write a series of reports. The first would be on the discovery of his lost home, the second on the newspaper clippings, and the third on the chess piece. He had written the first report over the weekend. Tonight he would work on the second report. From now on, anything related to his search for his lost identity and Northgate Hall would be written direct to a memory stick, and not to the computer hard drive. The keyboard began to click rapidly as he punched out the sentences. It took a couple of hours to work through everything.

REPORT 2

NEWSPAPER CLIPPINGS FOUND AT THE MANOR HOUSE TURVILLE HEATH

A search of the derelict house on Turville Heath, Bucks, revealed a plastic pouch containing a series of newspaper clippings. The pouch was the only item recovered from the house.

The newspaper clippings were photocopies taken from articles published in the late 19th and early 20th centuries. They were in good condition. The fact that the photocopies had been made using regular 80 gm white paper, and not thermal paper, indicated that they were probably made within the last 20 years.

The newspaper articles were all on a single subject—a wealthy aristocrat and landowner who disappeared mysteriously in 1902. His name was Baron Algernon Northgate. Most of the articles came from local newspapers and related to the barons generous support of a number of local and national charities, his donation of ancient artefacts to museums around the country, and lectures and exhibitions on his archaeological work in the Middle East, and Egypt in particular. An article that struck me strongly, for some reason, was on a spectacular garden that the baron had installed in the grounds of Northgate Hall. The work commenced in 1897 and took four years to complete. It was called "The Egyptian Garden" and was one of a number of beautiful gardens at Northgate Hall. Centre stage in this amazing garden was a gigantic obelisk, which the article stated was four hundred and fifty feet high. It was one of the tallest freestanding structures in the country at that time. In actual fact, it was not a real Egyptian obelisk cut from a single slab of stone, but rather a massive tower, built in the shape of an obelisk and skilfully faced in granite to make it look like it was carved from a single block. The obelisk was approached by a long walkway that was made from enormous stone slabs.

The final news articles, and here there was extensive national press coverage, were on the subject of the baron's sudden disappearance in November 1902. There were all sorts of speculations: kidnap, murder, and a strange Egyptian curse. The baroness refused to be interviewed, except by the police. It appears she paid generously for the silence of the servants, but some information leaked out. The police investigations at the Hall went on for a number of months, but not a trace of the baron was ever found. The disappearance of one of England's wealthiest noblemen remains a mystery to this day. My Internet searches have come up with nothing new so far.

There were a number of photographs of the obelisk. One was taken from the far end of the walkway, so that the entire obelisk filled the frame. Another showed a sunken stone stairwell that led to a cast iron door. Behind the door lay a stairway that ran all the way to the top of the obelisk, where there was a viewing deck carefully concealed within the structure. There was a close-up shot of the top of the obelisk, which tapered to a point in the shape of a pyramid. Having examined this photograph closely with a magnifying glass, it is clear that at least in one of the faces of the pyramid—or "pyramidion," as it is called—there was carved an Egyptian hieroglyph: a large eye.

In conclusion, it is evident that at some point, between ten and twenty years ago, someone at the abandoned house on Turville Heath had an interest in Baron Northgate and his stately home. It is clear now that two lines of investigation will need to be pursued. I need to find out as much as I can about the abandoned house, and the fate of its owners—they could be my parents—and I need to establish if they were connected in any way to the Northgate family or the Northgate Estate. I also need to discover the location of Northgate Hall.

When he had finished typing out the report, Alexander returned his attention to the metal object standing on the workbench. There was no mistaking the words etched around the bottom section of the object: THE EYE OF THE QUEEN HOLDS THE KEY

Well, it's in English, he thought. *It could be in code, it could be a riddle, or it could a literal statement of fact. If it were literal fact, then the queen would not be a human being, but some type of object. If the eye were conventionally shaped, then it would have to be a pretty strange key that would fit into an eye.*

He put the metal object back on the bench and looked at it from a distance. *The object itself could be some sort of key,* he reasoned. *It was circular and could fit into the iris of a very large eye.* Picking up a magnifying glass, Alexander examined the object minutely. On its base he could now discern some tiny writing, which was difficult to see with the naked human eye. The letters read "NORTHGATE HALL."

"Ah ha!" he exclaimed. "The chess piece is connected to Northgate Hall!"

In a flash, he remembered the eye—the eye on the obelisk! *But an obelisk is a slab of stone, not a queen,* he thought, a little miffed. He returned to the computer, logged onto the Internet, and initiated a search on the subject of obelisks. An hour later, he continued with his report.

Egyptian obelisks originated from the granite quarries of Aswan. The term "Obelisk" is derived from the Greek word "Obeliskos." It is a stone that is frequently monolithic, has a quadrangular base, is mounted vertically and terminates with a pointed tip. Obelisks were positioned in the centre of large open spaces in the temples of the solar god Ra.

Many obelisks were taken from Egypt over the years by invaders and foreign powers. The Roman Emperors brought numerous of these structures to Rome, a city which now has 13 obelisks (including the Vatican). When the Roman Empire was in decline, the obelisks gradually collapsed and remained buried in the ground until the Renaissance, when they were restored to their former glory.

The two most famous obelisks were made by the Pharaoh Thutmose III in 1468 B.C. and were originally sited in the Temple of the Sun in Heliopolis. Queen Cleopatra had the obelisks moved to her palace at the city of Alexandria, and as a result, they have come to be known as "Cleopatra's Needles." One of these obelisks now resides in New York, and the other on the Victoria Embankment on the banks of the River Thames. It stands about 21 metres tall and weighs nearly 200 tons.

Alexander lifted his head from the keyboard. The words "Cleopatra's Needle" were ringing in his brain. *This could be the connection that I'm looking for. Cleopatra was a queen. The obelisk replica at Northgate Hall could have been inspired by*

Cleopatra's Needle in London. Such being the case, the obelisk would be the needle of the queen.

Then the words "eye of the needle" entered his mind. He got up and paced the room. *The eye on the obelisk could be the eye mentioned in the inscription on the chess piece. Such being the case, it could be considered as the eye of the needle, Cleopatra's Needle. It may well be that the inscription was referring to the eye on the Northgate Hall obelisk. If this were true, then the chess piece could be a key that slots into the eye on the obelisk at Northgate Hall!*

Alexander returned to his chair in front of the computer screen. *Who would be crazy enough to lock something away at the top of a four hundred and fifty foot obelisk,* he wondered, chuckling to himself. Then Indiana Jones sprang into his mind. *That's the sort of thing he would do if he wanted to keep something extremely valuable secure. Not many people would think of looking at the top of a huge obelisk, never mind have the guts to climb the pyramidion and risk a sheer drop of over four hundred feet to certain death. Come to think of it, by all accounts Baron Northgate was quite an adventurer. In some circles, he would even have been called a tomb-raider, much like Indiana Jones. It is not beyond the realm of possibility that he hid something up there. But why leave clues? Maybe it was some sort of test, some sort of initiation for someone that he hoped would succeed him if he died suddenly. Only somebody brave and relatively intelligent could retrieve his hidden treasure.*

"But that is all speculation," he said and sighed. "I need to find Northgate Hall!"

Alexander included his reasoning in the report and finished for the night. The following morning he could not settle to the thought of a day filled with lectures; he had too many important things to do. Anyway, he had studying down to a fine art now, or at least the type of study needed to pass exams. With his photographic memory, anything that he read was instantly memorised, word for word. At school, anything said by the teachers in class was remembered effortlessly. When the exams finally came, he was more than ready. At University, a great deal more self-motivation was required, and he had to start thinking a lot more for himself. This was where the tutorials came in very handy. He could bounce ideas around and get a lot of feedback from the tutor and his fellow students. With a brain like Alexander's, though, a few missed lectures were neither here nor there.

It was evening on the following day and he was back in his office, doing his best to review his labours of the day. He had skipped lectures that morning and headed straight for The British Library in London. Here he had secured a workstation in the Newspaper Reading Room, and had accessed the Twentieth Century Master File. His major objective had been to find out what he could about the explosion at the Manor House on Turville Heath. He arrived back in North Oxford at about seven in the evening, and battling with some very strong emotions, set to work on the Internet.

Four articles had surfaced on the abandoned house—two in local papers and two in the nationals. The best and most comprehensive of the various articles was in the *Times*. It was dated 30th November, 1997.

THE NORTHGATE CURSE?

A freak storm that struck Buckinghamshire last August had resulted in the accidental deaths of three people, all from the same family, was the conclusion reached in a coroner's report published this week. The three unfortunate victims were father and mother, James and Elizabeth Northgate, and their young son. The bodies of the adults were burnt beyond recognition. The body of the child was believed to have been completely incinerated. Identification was made, using dental records. The forensic studies indicated that death was most probably due to a freak lightening strike.

Lightening strikes occur frequently, but deaths due to direct hits are relatively rare in the British Isles.

Eyewitnesses from Turville, a small village situated on Turville Heath close to High Wycombe, reported seeing a series of massive lightening bolts in the vicinity of Turville Grange on the day of the tragedy. The bodies of the Northgates were discovered by the housekeeper, who had been out shopping at the time of the accident.

Baron James Northgate came from one of the country's wealthiest dynasties. Locals claim that the family has been cursed. Our enquiries suggest that the curse began with the mysterious disappearance of Algernon Northgate in 1902. He was last sighted in the vicinity of his ancestral mansion, Northgate Hall. An extensive police investigation was eventually wound up, with no trace of the baron ever being found. It was rumoured that the trouble started at the Hall when two Egyptian mummies where displayed there in 1902. It is believed that the tomb, from which the mummies were taken, close to the Giza peninsula in Egypt, was protected by an ancient curse. This curse appears to have taken root in the Northgate family. All the male offspring who were direct descendants of Baron Algernon Northgate died prematurely. Debate still rages as to the veracity of tomb curses. The most famous of these is the curse of Tutankhamen.

Tears were streaming down Alexander's face as he reread the article. At last he had found his parents, and they had been destroyed in the very spot in which he had been standing only a few days previous. Many questions raced through his brain. Did their deaths have a rational physical explanation? How did he survive, while his parents were killed? Could he ever prove that he was a Northgate and claim his inheritance? Was there really a curse, and was he marked for death? One thing he knew for sure, if there was a curse, he would have to get to the bottom of it. His life would depend on it. In due course, he knew he would have to track down any relatives who had descended from Algernon Northgate. He also desperately wanted to see photographs of his mother and father. But first things first, he had to find Northgate Hall.

The results of his Internet query to the Ordinance Survey had come through. Somebody at the Historical Mapping Archive had emailed him the location of Northgate Hall.

CHAPTER 13
THE ABYSS

Frank Malone pulled deeply on a freshly lit cigarette and exhaled a satisfying stream of smoke. It was his first cigarette of the day. His teaching duties were finally over, and he was sitting on his favourite bench in the University Parks, well wrapped against the chill winter air. The bench overlooked a pond with a small central island on which grew a pretty little tree. This was where the Irish academic did some of his best thinking.

It was fascinating, he thought, *that conversation with young Strongson.* Earlier in the day, after a tutorial in his rooms, Alexander had updated him on the contents of the plastic pouch and the results of the subsequent detective work that he had carried out. The boy had seemed very animated, if not a little upset. Who wouldn't be, at finding out that your parents had been burnt to death, that the family that you came from could be cursed, and that you were probably the next on the list!

This is turning into the most interesting paranormal adventure that I have ever been involved in, he thought, as he took another drag from his cigarette. *From what the boy has discovered, it would appear that my experience at that derelict old house was more than a dream. It was as if somebody was trying to communicate with me, trying to give me a message from beyond the grave. The key image in the dream was the chess set. Finding that chess piece in the house was no accident. There are forces at work here. We now know that the chess piece is some kind of a key. If the curse is real, it may be the only thing standing between Alexander and an early death.*

ꟈ

Time flashed by, as it does in this modern hurried world, and the weekend came around again. The wind was blowing gently from the south, making it very mild for November.

"Take the next right, Dr. Malone," said Alexander, as the big Volvo sped up the A413 in the direction of Winslow. "The house is close to the village of Aylesforde."

Turning, the car headed down a narrow tarmac country lane until it reached the village, with its old red brick high street and ancient Saxon stone church. "Carry on through the village and take the first right," said Alexander, his stomach starting to tense a little. Reaching the right hand turn, Frank nursed the big car carefully down an even narrower lane.

"About four hundred metres down here, again on the right, there should be a driveway. This runs for about one hundred metres to the perimeter wall of the house," continued Alexander. Frank noticed that the pitch of the boy's voice has gone up a little. With the car slowed to a crawl, teacher and student scanned the road ahead carefully for signs of a driveway. They were now in an area of dense woodland. Driving on for a mile or so, they could find no evidence of the elusive driveway.

"We must have overshot," muttered Alexander, staring intensely at the map.

"Let's do this scientifically," rumbled Frank, not the most patient of men. Turning the car, he returned to the top of the lane at considerably greater speed than he had driven down it. "Right," he growled. It was still a good-natured growl, but Alexander knew it was time to get his act together. "On the map, estimate the distance that the driveway should be from our present position. Do it in miles, not that metric nonsense!"

Producing a small transparent Perspex ruler, the boy placed it on the map. It was an Ordinance Survey map, and very accurate. "The driveway is about a quarter of a mile ahead," he said, without a moment's hesitation. Frank noted the reading on the car's odometer, and off they went.

"This should be the spot," said Frank, drawing the Volvo to a halt. "Let's get out and do some exploring." A few minutes passed and there was no obvious evidence of a driveway. It was approaching noon now and getting close to Frank's traditional Saturday lunchtime. This consisted of a couple of pints of premium ale, and more often than not a Ploughman's.

"Maybe we should make enquiries at the local pub," he chirped, already visualising his first weekend gulp of frothy ale.

"Forgive me for making so bold, sir," responded Alexander, determined to head the thirsty academic off at the pass, "but the perimeter wall should only be a short walk through the trees. Once we have located it, it should be easy enough to find the main gates and the remnants of the driveway."

Frank looked a little disgruntled, but he could not argue with the boy's logic. Inspecting Alexander more closely now, it was clear that he had come well equipped. He was wearing a bright blue jacket—the sort that climbers use, and expensive boots. He also had a bulging haversack with him.

"This is merely an exploratory mission," boomed the Irishman with his commanding tonsils. "We are not here to take risks. Is that understood, young man?"

Alexander nodded with sincere intensity.

The unlikely duo set off into the woods, a pleasant enough walk through mature birches, maples and occasional oak trees, now stripped of most of their leaves. Strangely, as they ventured further into the woods, the deciduous trees were gradually replaced by big evergreens, mainly Douglas Firs.

"These pine trees have been deliberately planted as a screen," ventured Alexander.

"You are probably right, son," agreed Frank. "It does look like very deliberate planting. These trees are huge and would act as a very effective all-year-round curtain, deflecting the eyes of curious passers-by."

The two marched on, the air growing still and cold in the shade of the trees. Suddenly, a wall loomed before them, and with it, memories of the terrible dream. A cold trepidation came over the boy as a vision of those vile killer owls returned. But nothing now would deflect him from his quest. Something deep inside him was driving him forward; even the risk of death could not stop him now.

The massive granite wall, topped with menacing broken glass, towered above them, just like in the dream. "There is obvious evidence of regular maintenance work here," commented Frank. "The cement pointing is in good condition, and the trees have been kept back a good twenty feet from the wall."

The vegetation on which they stood consisted of a tangle of weeds and grass that had been trodden down to form a track, running along the edge of the wall. Alexander started to head down the track to the left, and Frank followed. It did not take long before they found a pair of huge gates. The gates were constructed from thick metal bars, with no signs of rusting. These metal sentinels were just as forbidding as he remembered them in his nightmare. Secured firmly to the gates was a large plastic warning sign that read in big dark red letters "DANGER. KEEP OUT. TRESPASSES WILL BE PROSECUTED." In smaller, navy blue letters underneath were the words, "Protected by Sector Security. Guard dogs in use."

Alexander read the sign slowly, out loud, mentally comparing it with the one that he had seen in his dream. It was identical, except that there was no mention of the security patrol in his dream. He found this encouraging. The dreamscape was not totally identical in every detail to the reality before him. There was little chance that they would be attacked by giant man-eating eagle owls! Or, at least that was what he hoped.

The words "guard dogs" were not music to Frank's ears. A concerned look stole over his face as he turned to the boy. "The concept of large-fanged Alsatians, or worse, roaming the grounds does not appeal to me. We need to rethink this one, boyo," he rumbled.

Peering through the gates, all Alexander could see was trees. There were large clumps of brambles and nettles running up to the gates, and beyond them a dense wood. "I don't think that the grounds of the house are patrolled, Dr. Malone," he replied. "It's clear that they have been left unattended for many, many years. There would be little point in patrolling the outside perimeter with dogs. I think it is just a bluff. It's a good bet that the wall is merely inspected periodically for maintenance purposes. The track has probably been made by locals walking their dogs."

A faint smile stole across the Irishman's face. "You don't miss a trick, do you? Very well! Let's fetch the ladders. But by the saints in heaven, I'll have your guts for garters if you're wrong!"

Frank and Alexander traced their way through the trees and back to the car. They returned to the gates with two lightweight, foldable aluminium ladders. One of the ladders was positioned so they could climb up the gates, and the other so they could climb down the other side. In no time, they were in the grounds of Northgate Hall. The ladder used to climb in from the outside was retrieved and employed to flatten a path through the brambles. There was little foliage beyond the brambles, due to the dense tree cover. Hiding their ladders, the duo ventured into the trees. After a couple of minutes of walking, the trees began to thin out. In this part of the grounds the trees looked ancient, exotic and huge. Many were not native species. "This must have been the arboretum," muttered Alexander, trying to quell the terrible memories of the eagle owls. There was a strange beauty here, wild and forgotten.

The man and the boy ventured on. After about one hundred metres, the woods began to thin out as it opened up onto rough grassland.

"This must have been part of the gardens to the great house," said Frank.

"Look at all those goats," said Alexander. "They must be wild. Their grazing is keeping the trees at bay in this area."

As they got closer, the goats began to scatter. Clumpy irregular grass, interspersed with weeds and thistles, rolled gently down into a shallow valley; in the distance stood a vast house. As they moved forward, Frank noticed that Alexander kept glancing skyward, anxious, and a little agitated. "Looks like you're expecting something to drop out of the sky," chuckled Frank, a little insensitively. "Vampire bats, is it? Is an attack imminent?" As they walked further, Northgate Hall came clearly into view.

There was an eerie, menacing strangeness about the old mansion, a dank crypt-like grimness. Northgate Hall was a solidly-built house, and even after one hundred years of neglect, the basic structure was still intact. The roof was holed in places, primarily where chimney pots had collapsed from the stacks and crashed through the thick slates. Many of the roof gutters had corroded and fallen away, and there were large patches of dampness on the walls. Most of the windows on the upper floor were badly discoloured with years of grime, but were still intact; the windows on the ground and second floors had been bricked up. As if guarded by some unseen force, the house looked untouched from the time that it had been sealed. Oddly, there were no trees growing close to the house, just burnt stumps.

"I made it clear," growled Frank, "that the house is strictly off limits. It is far larger than I'd imagined, and it looks like a death trap. Only qualified building professionals should venture in there, and even then I would warrant that it would be extremely risky. If you ask me, the whole place should be levelled to the ground. It looks like a giant neglected tomb."

Alexander stood, staring at the house as if mesmerised by the place. This is very, very, weird. I've never seen this house, yet it seems so familiar. I feel a very deep connection with this house. It's almost overwhelming.

The Irishman's powerful voice punched through his thoughts. "Do I make myself clear, Alexander"" he boomed.

"Sorry, Dr. Malone," responded the boy. "I was miles away... Of course I'll keep well clear of the house. It's the obelisk that we have come to see."

Averting his gaze from the boy, Frank looked about him for signs of the mighty tower. Nothing tall was visible through the trees.

"According to the map, Dr. Malone, the obelisk is situated behind the house. The ground slopes quite sharply into a sunken garden, which was called 'The Egyptian Garden,' when the house was occupied."

Frank's stomach started to rumble. "Let's get on with this," he grumbled. "Time is marching by." He still had hopes of reaching a pub before last orders. Skirting around the house, the man and the boy made their way down what had once been a series of beautiful terraced lawns, now wild with overgrown grass and spiked weeds. In the distance, the obelisk was now visible, hulking over the tree line.

"That fecking thing is enormous," gasped Frank. "I guess it is not visible from the road because it is down in this dip and the grounds are shielded by very tall trees."

Having reached the bottom of the embankment, they made their way through a set of trees, and there it stood, vast and magnificent. The huge granite slabs that ringed the base of the structure were still intact and had kept the trees at bay for about ten metres around the obelisk.

Standing close to the obelisk now, it was a breathtaking sight. "Remind me again, Alexander," mumbled Frank. "How high is this thing?"

The boy had produced a pair of high-power binoculars, which he was aiming at the top of the tower. Without moving the binoculars, he responded, "It's well over one hundred metres. The old newspaper articles put the height at four hundred and fifty feet."

Frank walked to within a metre of the obelisk and looked up. "It looks taller than that," he hissed. "It seems to go on forever." He remembered Tom Tower at Christ Church College, and how high that had seemed. This mighty beast dwarfed Tom Tower. He felt dizzy as he looked up, and cold spasms of fear began to run up and down his legs. The sky was cloudless, and the granite stone of the enormous tower looked like a stark grey road, running into a bottomless blue abyss. His legs started to quiver; he began to imagine that at any moment he would be ripped from the earth and hurtled into space. He closed his eyes and staggered back. For the first time in his life, he knew, without a shadow of a doubt, that he had no head for heights. There was no way that he was going up that tower.

Putting down the binoculars, Alexander made for the stairwell. His heart sank as he reached the position were it should have been. It had been filled with concrete. There was no way into the obelisk from here. He turned to Frank, who looked a little pale and rather pensive. "Rosie has made us a little picnic, Dr. Malone," he said, reaching into his backpack. He withdrew a large plastic re-sealable box containing beef and mustard sandwiches, salad, pound cake and custard rice. There was also coffee in a thermos. Frank turned his back on the dreadful obelisk, found a seat on an old fallen tree trunk, and began to demolish his portion of the picnic. So keen was he to keep the obelisk out of view that he did not notice Alexander slip away.

Sometime later, his hunger satiated, the Irishman turned his head toward the tower, expecting to see the boy eating, but he was nowhere to be seen. *The little divil cannot have gone far,* he thought, springing to his feet. *The entrance to the obelisk is sealed, so there is no danger of me having to follow him up there.*

He traced his way around the base of the obelisk. There was no sign of Alexander. Then to his right, close to the edge of the granite slabs, he noticed what looked like a large earth mound, covered in weeds. Walking over to the mound, he began to inspect it more carefully. To his amazement, when he got up close, he could see that it was a big stone sphinx, now colonised by nature. He began to move around the sphinx, which was sitting on a raised stone platform about six feet high. A sudden pulse of horror cursed through him. To the rear of the sphinx, a big slab of stone had been pushed forward to reveal a gaping black hole.

"Alexander!" roared Frank. "Where the hell are you?"

The dead in their graves would have heard those words blasting forth, but there was no response from Alexander. Frank continued to examine the sphinx. The slab of stone was a concealed door. A patch of lichen and moss had been stripped away to reveal polished granite. Close to the edge of the stone door, and about two thirds of the way up, was a small circular hole. In a flash, the Irishman figured that Alexander had used the chess piece as some sort of key.

Venturing inside the base of the sphinx, he clicked on his torch. The light beam danced off glistening black metal, attached to the back of the slab, obviously some kind of locking mechanism. A similar material had been used for the casters and running rails, allowing the slab to be slid open and closed. There were no signs of corrosion on the metal. Frank returned to the open air. Spotting the binoculars that were lying close by, he grabbed hold of them. Forcing himself to look up at the terrifying tower, a paralysing numbness seized him. He could see a tiny figure clinging to the pyramidion. Aiming the binoculars, he focused the lenses. It was harrowingly clear now. Alexander was climbing the obelisk!

A sudden hot fury burnt at his fear. "You stupid little bastard!" he roared. "You're going to get yourself killed!" Alexander could not have failed to hear his voice, but he continued to climb. "Ignore me, will you, you little cunt!" bellowed the Irishman. His temper had reached the point of no return now. Turning the air blue with swearing, he was spitting fire, all logic banished! Storming back to the sphinx, he disappeared inside.

A force was driving the boy forward. He could not stop himself. The sphinx had drawn his attention the second they had reached the obelisk. He had left Frank to his meal while he examined it more closely. Something had clicked deep in the core of his consciousness. Instinctively, he had stripped down a section of the stone slab with a chisel from his haversack to reveal the keyhole. The chess piece had fit perfectly. Twisting it to the right, he had heard a hollow clunk. Pushing on it, the slab had slid forward. The stone plinth supporting the body of the sphinx was hollow. Withdrawing a torch from his backpack, he had discovered a line of descending steps at the far end of the plinth. Following the steps down, he had found himself in a brick-lined tunnel. This ran in two directions: left and right. Without hesitation, he had turned right and moved swiftly through the blackness. It had not taken him long before he encountered more steps that appeared to be ascending into the obelisk. After he had climbed the steps for three or four metres, they had swung hard right and ended abruptly in a stone panel. The torch had revealed another locking mechanism with a lever attached.

Pressing the lever, he had pulled and the panel had creaked back, letting him through into a small chamber. In one of the walls he had seen a big rusted metal door. *This must have been the main entrance to the obelisk before it was cemented in,* reasoned Alexander. He guessed that the tunnel that he had just emerged from, if followed in the opposite direction, would lead to the house. It was some sort of secret passage. Playing the torch light around the chamber, the beam had illuminated a vast stone staircase that spiralled upwards.

ജര

Cursing with every breath, the Irishman pounded up the stone steps. Panting and gasping, he reached the top of the tower and burst out onto the viewing platform. Blind fury still had hold of him and he was oblivious to any danger. The platform was bounded by a solid stone balustrade, about a metre and a half high. At the four corners of the platform were stout square pillars, rising from the floor to a height of about two and a half metres. The floor of the platform was about two metres wide on all four sides, and abutted the walls of the central core of the obelisk, which supported the pyramidion. The walls of the central core were faced in a black marble-like stone, so that when the obelisk was viewed from the ground, the viewing platform was effectively invisible to the naked eye. Walking rapidly around the platform, he looked for a way up to the pyramidion. There was no door, or steps, nor anything obvious that could help him. Recalling the position of the face of the pyramidion that the boy was climbing, he rushed to the corresponding side of the platform.

The air was warm and tranquil for November. A new burst of anger gripped the Irishman. That stupid boy was on the verge of getting himself killed. The idiot was going to fall to his death on his favourite day of the week when he should have been safely down at the pub enjoying the crack. With hot blood pounding through his veins, he grabbed the outside edge of the pillar and sprang onto the balustrade. When he was this mad there was no fear, just hot molten rage. As his grip tightened, he noticed a deep vertical groove that had been cut close to the edge of the pillar. Grasping this with his left hand, he swung his body out so he could inspect the outside of the pillar. There were a series of large grooved steps cut into the stone. It was effectively a ladder, but a ladder hewn only for the very brave. One wrong move and he would be cast into a long, screamingly horrible death plunge.

Swivelling around and still gripping the pillar with his left hand, Frank placed his right foot into the first groove. He grabbed a groove higher up with his right hand, as if he were climbing a ladder. Conditions were harsh at this exposed height and not much would grow in the grooves of the steps, other than lichen and an odd clump of moss. Fortunately, the weather had been dry for days so he could get a good strong grip. He began to climb the steps. Clinging to the stone face, with the enormous drop gapping below him, he did not look down—only up. There was a parapet at the base of the pyramidion, about twenty centimetres wide. At this height, twenty centimetres was not very wide, but wide enough for a hero or a madman. Without hesitation, he eased his way onto the parapet. With his body pressed against the sloping wall of the pyramidion, he craned his neck.

"Alexander!! You stupid boy!" he thundered. "There'll be hell to pay for this! Climb back down now, before you get us both killed!"

The boy ignored him, seemingly impervious to his calls. The pyramidion measured about forty feet from the parapet to the tip of the obelisk. There were a series of smaller steps cut into its face. The steps were offset from each other and had to be climbed in a somewhat spread-eagled fashion. At the centre of the face, a massive eye had been carved. Frank recognised it immediately as resembling the eye of the Egyptian god Horus, or the "All Seeing Eye of Providence," so bizarrely printed on American one dollar bills.

Alexander was totally focused on the task at hand. Something beyond him had driven him up here, and now there was no turning back. He had climbed the steps as far as he could. It was a real stretch to reach the iris of the gigantic eye, but he had done it. With his left arm almost fully extended, he had located a raised, centrally-situated disk. It was made of the shiny black metal he had encountered earlier. He guessed that it might be some sort of protective cap. Carefully placing the key in a jacket pocket, he located his chisel. Pressing it against the cap, the tip dug in under the lip. He twisted the chisel. The cap did not budge. He repeated this manoeuvre, and on the third attempt there was a "pop" and the metal disk sprang off. Bouncing down the face of the pyramidion, it fell into the depths below. The boy had uncovered a circular hole in the iris. Inserting the chess piece key, he pushed it carefully into the hole, rotating it left and right until he felt the indentations in the top of the key engage with what he assumed were studs. He turned the key, slowly, clockwise, and heard a faint "clunk" as the prongs of the key engaged with what he guessed was a cylindrical barrel within the hole. The key would turn no further clockwise, so he tried using it as a lever. He pushed and pulled, but to no avail.

Frank roared again, but this time with less ferocity. His rage was slipping away. In its place, creeping slowly but surely through him, was cold terror. Looming above the crazy boy, he could see the blue abyss. There was no comforting ceiling of dense fluffy clouds, just a terrible chasm of infinite space. His world was starting to flip, and he felt that terrifying giddiness that height can induce. And then the horror came over him like a flood. Every muscle in his arms and legs locked. He was clinging to the stone face for dear life now. He could not move. His mind raced in pure panic. Was he upside down, about to fall into the endless sky, or was he right side up, teetering on the brink of a four-hundred-foot drop onto solid granite slabs? Closing his eyes, he prayed. Above him, Alexander started to turn the key anticlockwise. After it had travelled one hundred and eighty degrees, there was a tinny sounding "click." The boy could not make this out. Had it come from the mechanism within the hole, or from the key itself?

He repeated the procedure, pressing and pushing the key in all directions. His arms and legs were starting to ache, and he was getting frustrated. In a moment of sudden impatience, he gave the key an almighty tug. In that instant, the shaft of the key separated effortlessly from the base. The hard tug on the key, coupled with its sudden fracturing, sent the boy reeling backwards with such force that he lost his footing. Still clutching the shaft of the key, he slid helplessly down the face of the pyramidion. The petrified Irishman, his eyes scrunched shut, did not see Alexander dropping towards him. There was a sudden terrible "thud" as the boy crashed into him, the force of his body pushing him outwards. Falling from the parapet, he hurtled into the abyss.

CHAPTER 14
PARTING OF THE WAYS

ຣ໑ෆ

The only thing that saved Alexander from certain death was Frank Malone. It was his body that broke his fall and stopped him from crashing to the ground. He stood there, stunned, but still clutching the key shaft in his hand. A sudden bellow wrenched him back to his senses.

"Idiot boy! You have not quite killed me yet! When I get my hands on you, I'm going to break your bloody neck!"

Easing himself from the stonework, Alexander looked down. He could see fingers desperately clinging to the parapet. "Dr. Malone!" he gasped. "You're still alive!"

"Just wait till I get my hands on you, little bleeder!" raged the Irishman. "I'll rip your innards out!"

These threats were music to the boy's ears. It was fury that was keeping Dr. Malone alive. Shoving the object that had nearly killed the two of them into his pocket, he moved as rapidly as he could to the point where the pillar was situated. Without hesitating at the sight of the terrible endlessly drop below him, he scrambled down the steps in the pillar until he was level with the stricken Irishman. Anger ebbed out of him now. The pain and shock of the boy hitting him had thrown him into an instant fury, forcing him to open his eyes and lash out with his arms. He had grabbed hold of the parapet in a nick of time, but now the pain was burning through him. His fingers ached unbearably, and his grip was beginning to loosen. And then he heard the little voice singing in his head.

"Let go. Let go. Release the pain. Death is not so terrible. Set yourself free. Death is the sweetest peace. Let go! Let go!" And then, with awful inevitability, the pain became unbearable and he gave up the fight. As he began to fall, he knew that death was certain.

Hurling himself forward, with his left arm extended, Alexander hit the Irishman in the small of the back, pushing his body forward. Crashing onto the balustrade, he came to rest with his legs dangling over the abyss. The force of the charge sent a searing pain through Alexander's left shoulder as he was thrown back by the impact. It was nothing short of a miracle that he did not fall to his doom, but somehow he had managed to hang onto the steps with his right hand and foot. Gasping desperately, he flung himself over the balustrade, rose rapidly to his feet, and dragged his tutor to safety. Lying there, with frantic staring eyes, the Irishman mumbled, "Jesus, Mary and Joseph! You brave stupid little bastard!"

Although numbed by shock, Alexander was ecstatic. He had scaled the first hurdle. He had passed the test. Sometime later, Frank, who was now staring blankly and trembling, hissed, "Drink, drink... For God's sake, get me a bloody drink!"

ഊ

Four days later, back in his rooms at LMH, Frank Malone sat impassively at his desk. Standing opposite him was Alexander, his left arm supported in a sling.

"How is your shoulder?" asked Frank, now his normal composed and confident self.

"It's still very sore, Dr. Malone," replied Alexander, "but Dr. Gupta has checked me out and assures me that nothing is broken, only sprained."

A faint smile crossed the Irishman's face. "Grand, grand... Glad to hear that," he said. Then his eyes narrowed and his face became set as hard as stone. Alexander braced himself for a verbal onslaught, but it never came. Frank fixed the boy with a penetrating and unblinking gaze. "You almost caused my death, and yet I owe you my life. You are a very gifted and clever young man, but at the same time, you are reckless and foolhardy. You have an obsession that threatens to destroy you. It appears to be an obsession that nobody can control, least of all you. I urge you to speak to Anita Gupta about your thoughts and fears. Perhaps she can help you. I had considered contacting your parents, but it is clear now that you are beyond their control. It would do more harm than good, the worry that it would cause them. You believe you are battling for your very survival. While I am open minded enough not to discount the possibility of a family curse out of hand, I am sorry to inform you that I will lend you no further assistance. You have persistently ignored my guidance and advice, and you almost got me killed. Most likely, I will have nightmares for years to come. From now on, ours will be a strictly teacher and student relationship. Outside of tutorials and lectures, I will have no further contact with you. Good afternoon, young man."

The force and power of the Irishman's countenance left the boy speechless. He stood there silently for a few moments, his eyes pleading. Tears trickled down his face as he turned to depart. He knew he had gone too far, but now there was no turning back.

ꙮ

Placing the headphones on his ears, Alexander lay back on his bed. AC/DC thundered into his brain. The force and raw energy of this band never failed to lift his spirits and galvanise his determination, particularly at times like this; times when he felt that he stood alone against the world. But this was worse, much worse. Here he was, just a boy, faced with some unseen assassin, some dark thing that was biding its time—a monstrous entity that would one day hunt him down and kill him. Lying there, he let the music roar through him.

Later, he turned his mind to the chess piece. What a fascinating object it was. Now that the top of the chess piece had been removed, it looked more like a small candlestick than anything else. Inside the shaft was what appeared to be a layer of cotton padding. This protected a glass vial that contained a dark, transparent-looking liquid. Alexander guessed that this was some kind of acid—part of a security device. Wrapped around the vial was a piece of parchment. The head of the chess piece had probably contained some type of mechanism for breaking the vial, should anybody have guessed its true purpose and attempted to pry it open.

Alexander had carefully removed the parchment, which he had kept hidden under a couple of heavy books. Retrieving it, he studied it again. Scribed in what looked like black fountain pen ink was a hand-written message. It read as follows:

The year is 1902. I must congratulate you on your cleverness, resourcefulness, and courage. The very fact that you are reading this message means that I am dead, that I have died suddenly and unexpectedly. I am the guardian of a great treasure. The nature of that treasure I cannot reveal to you at this time. You need to prove yourself worthy. If Northgate Hall has fallen, all is lost. If the Hall still stands then enter the library. Your quest begins there. The key is not yet spent.

Algernon Northgate

CHAPTER 15
THE LADY DETECTIVE

Livonia Sloan, Fellow of LMH and lecturer in Ancient History, rose suddenly and walked rapidly to the door of her office, pushing it tightly closed. "Malone's having another one of his raving sessions," she said and sighed.

Frank Malone did not deal with his personal mail at home. As far as he was concerned, home was a place for doing interesting things. Mundane paperwork, particularly post in official looking envelopes, was dealt with at work. A letter lying in front of him on his desk had triggered his incandescent temper into overload.

"How dare they say it was my fault? Fecking cheek!" he fumed. "She was to blame, not me! There is no excuse for the way she cut me up on that roundabout. It was criminally irresponsible driving, plain and simple!"

His complaint to the bus company had finally been dealt with, after a string of letters and delays. It was clear that they were not prepared to sack that "idiot driver"; they even had the cheek to blame him. The volume of his voice cranked even higher as he blurted, "You have not heard the last from Frank Malone, not by a long chalk!"

Grabbing the yellow pages, he began to search for private detectives. "The police are no bloody good!" he raged. "I will have to get this job done myself! Nobody abducts me and gets away with it. Those idiots almost killed me! Payback is coming, lady. One way or another, payback is coming."

He found what he was looking for under "Detective Agencies." There were more than he had expected. Quite a few of the companies were international and pretty sophisticated. They did all sorts of work, both commercial and private. Picking up the telephone, he started with the first agency in the directory. The conversation did not last long.

"How much?" gasped the Irishman. "And then there are expenses and equipment charges on top of that?"

After ten phone conversations along similar lines, he was about to give up when a tiny little box caught his eye. It read, "Zoe Watts: Private Eye. THE AFFORDABLE DETECTIVE."

"That looks more hopeful," he muttered, as he dialled the number. An answering machine picked up. He rang off without leaving a message. *Must be very small-time if she hasn't even got an assistant. I'll try a few more numbers later.*

ꕥ

A fly that had doggedly survived the ravages of winter buzzed in through a slightly open window. Navigating over a pale pink fluffy carpet, it alighted on a pretty floral duvet. Launching itself back into the air, it landed on a naked shoulder-blade protruding from the duvet. Skin twitched. Half yawning, half groaning, a woman began to stir. Reaching for an alarm clock, her bleary eyes registered that it was 10 a.m.

Time to get up, she thought reluctantly. It had been a very late night and she had earned those extra three hours of sleep. Kicking off the duvet, she sprang out of the bed, pulled on a warm, woollen dressing gown and headed for a strong cup of coffee. A little later, as the caffeine began to kick in, she ambled into her office. Like millions these days, she worked from home. The advent of the Internet and mobile phones made it an easy, even attractive option for self-employed one-man bands. The answering machine was flashing. Pressing "playback," all she got was the sound of somebody ringing off. Dialling 1471, she retrieved the caller's number and pressed the "ring-back" button.

"Malone," came the blunt response.

Not a man in a good mood, she thought.

"Zoe Watts returning your call," she said.

"Ah, yes," replied Frank, a little surprised. "I did ring earlier, but I wanted to speak to a person, not an answering machine."

"Sorry about that," said the female private detective. "I work very irregular hours; it's the nature of the job. Actually, I give my clients another number where they can reach me 24/7."

Frank had made some more enquiries since ringing her earlier. It was now very clear that it was a very expensive business, hiring your own detective. He came straight to the point.

"How much do you charge?"

"I like to keep things simple," said Zoe. "I charge the same rate for all my services: missing persons, marital issues, surveillance and so on. I charge extra if specialist equipment is involved, mind you."

The rate that she quoted was a lot less than the big companies, so Frank decided that it was worth a face-to-face meeting to discuss his problem. "Can we meet up?" he asked. "A quiet pub would suit me better than an office."

"How does the Star in Stanton Saint John sound? Tonight at 6.30?" came the response.

"See you there," Frank answered.

ꕥ

The Irishman liked old English pubs; they had plenty of ancient wood, exposed roof beams and big fireplaces. He knew the Star well. It had a good menu and a very nice beer garden.

Punctual as ever, he arrived exactly at 6.30 p.m. There was no sign of Miss Watts, so he ordered himself a pint and sat down in a secluded, but comfortable corner. The beer was halfway down the glass when a woman walked in. She looked quite striking, with her short sweptback blond hair, white even skin and pretty grey-green eyes. Frank watched her carefully. She was wearing skin-tight black jeans, spike-heeled boots and a stylish blue leather jacket over a white blouse. Moving with a lithe sensuality, she approached the Irishman; at this early hour he was the only person in the bar.

"Hi," she said. "Zoe Watts."

Frank stood up to greet her. She was taller than him in her heels.

"Can I get you something to wet your whistle?" he asked.

"No," she said firmly. "I'll get them in. Looks like you're drinking bitter... same again?"

Frank was never one to turn down a free drink.

The barman flinched, suddenly startled from his evening newspaper. Turning his head, he looked through to the lounge bar.

"Oí," said the woman again. "Two pints of 6X."

The voice was surprisingly gruff and there was no mistaking the Liverpool lilt.

She's not bad looking, thought the barman, as he filled the glasses, *but with a voice like that, definitely not to be trifled with.*

Zoe Watts was a master of voices. It was something that she had worked hard at—a skill that came in very handy in her line of work. Born in Toxteth, a deprived area of Liverpool, the rough lilt had stayed with her, even though she had lived down south for many years. She had mastered it now, though, and could be anything she wanted to be, from a princess to a Scottish charwoman. Currently, with Frank Malone, she was being a middle England professional.

Carefully depositing the brimming glasses, she sat down opposite Frank. The Irishman was quietly impressed.

Lord love us! She drinks pints, he thought.

As she smiled over at him, two lines deepened on either side of her mouth. They were faint, except when she smiled. Her nose was straight, but feminine, and her eyebrows dark and neatly plucked.

"Let's get down to business," she said, dispensing with any further pleasantries. "What can I help you with?"

ഇര

About half an hour later, the detective got up to leave. "So it's agreed," she said, handing him her card. "I start in two weeks' time. After five working days on the job we will review progress and take it from there. Remember, two days cash in advance, no cheques. You can drop it at my home address tomorrow."

Frank flashed her a brief smile. "Sure I can't get you another beer?"

"No thanks, Dr. Malone," came the quick reply. "I've a lot of work to get through tonight."

An unusual lady, thought Frank, as she glided majestically out of the bar. *I hope she has not bitten off more than she can chew; these people are dangerous.*

CHAPTER 16
DARK SHADOWS

෴

Frank Malone's nerves were still on edge as he slammed the door of his Volvo and walked quickly towards his house. He needed a large scotch; his narrow escape from the jaws of death still weighed heavily on his mind. He had been forced to face a mind- warping terror head on, and every time he closed his eyes he had visions of the huge obelisk towering menacingly above him. When he finally went to sleep, he found himself hanging by his fingertips off the top of that massive tower, the terrible unbearable pain searing through his arms and hands. The horrible chasm yawned below him as he finally lost control and released his grip. There was no shoulder charge, no Alexander to save him, and he plunged at stomach-churning speed to a screaming death, but at the final moment of impact, his eyes burst open and he found himself lying in a cold sweat.

He felt drained and exhausted as he switched off the table lamp by the side of his bed and closed his eyes. Night after turbulent night had taken their toll. Nestling his head on the pillows, he fell into a restless sleep. At times mumbling incoherently, he tossed and turned, trying to escape the nightmare of the tower. The night was deathly still when he awoke suddenly, stunned and disorientated, not quite knowing where he was, but the certainty of his old familiar surroundings quickly returned.

The moon shone brightly through the window, bathing the room in its pale light. Instinctively, he lay very still, wondering why he had awoken so suddenly from a peaceful interlude in his troubled dreamscape. The silence seemed to grow; his heart-beat quickened, a sense of unease rising in him. A sudden sound punctured the stillness. It came so sharp and fast that it made him jump. Sitting bolt upright now, his heart began to pound; his warm, familiar house was suddenly eerie.

That was a creak. He tried to rationalise it. *Probably just a floorboard contracting.* Holding his breath, he strained his hearing. There was nothing, just the gentle ticking of a clock. Heartbeat slowing, his eyelids began to droop as he sank back onto his pillow. Then he heard it again, but this time twice! Heart racing now, he clicked on the table lamp. It sounded like somebody was in the hall. It sounded like somebody was walking stealthily up the stairs!

Frank reached for the metal baseball bat that he kept under the bed for occasions such as this. "OK, baby, let's dance," he growled, as he leapt out of bed and switched on the light. Holding the bat firmly, he bounded to the bedroom door, but as he touched the knob, he hesitated, a wave of apprehension sweeping over him. Clutching the cold metal, he eased the door open and walked onto the landing. Shafts of light from the bedroom penetrated the darkness, but it was dark, very dark out there.

Cautiously, listening intently and hardly breathing, he ventured forward in search of the light switch. Down below him in the stairwell there was silence—a thick, almost tangible silence. The hair on his body started to stand erect. He could sense something moving towards him—a black menacing presence—but there was nothing visible, only dark shadows. A sudden coldness crept over his skin and he began to shiver. There was something there, but he could not see it. Forcing himself to continue, he trembled and groped his way along the wall. He felt it clearly now, the presence of hatred and malevolence—of evil. Hand shaking violently, he reached for the light switch. Thank God! Light flooded the hall and he charged forward, furiously waving his baseball bat.

"Bring it on!" he roared, as he marched down the stairs, swinging the bat wildly. Angry now, he was ready to fight, but there was nothing there. The house was empty, cloaked in the sharp coldness of a winter's night. He checked all of the rooms; the doors were locked and the windows were firmly secured. When he had satisfied himself that no one was there, nothing physical at any rate, he returned to his bedroom. Everything seemed as it should be. He cursed aloud. "It was all in your imagination," he muttered. "You're a bloody nervous wreck. For God's sake, get some sleep!" Swallowing two sleeping pills, he returned his head to the pillow. Slowly, he drifted into blackness.

The terrible ringing hit his ears. It was 7:00 a.m. and still dark. Hitting the alarm-off button on the clock, he rose wearily from his bed. His nerves were still on edge as he stumbled towards the bathroom.

A long hot shower will help.

As the hot water cascaded over him, he found it soothing; so soothing that it was a good ten minutes before he stepped out of the shower. The windows, shaving and vanity mirrors were all steamed up from the onslaught of the hot water. Eyesight blurred by the vapour, he fumbled for his bath towel. Its dry, warm softness felt good. Rubbing the water from his face and eyes, he started to towel down his chest, and then it hit him like a thunderbolt! The colour drained rapidly from him as he gazed in disbelief. Staring back at him from the vanity mirror was an eye. After what seemed like an eternity, he shivered, and then grew angry. "Jeeze! How the hell did that get there?" he bellowed. Moving closer, he studied the eye carefully. It was drawn in an Egyptian style that he had seen before. It looked like the eye on the obelisk! Staggering back in dismay, it was clear to him now. The encounter on the stairs last night had been no flight of fancy. It was real. The thing from Northgate

Hall had tracked him down. It had traced out the eye on his mirror with a long dead finger. Was it a warning, or was it the mark of death? He had to know.

ഌ

A plump, white-haired lady with an angelic face and large, friendly hazel eyes opened the door to her terraced house in Jericho. She regarded the man standing before her with concern, for he looked deeply troubled.

"Frank," she said in a soft welcoming voice. "I was not expecting you until tomorrow evening. You look quite rundown, even peaky."

Staring at her with hunted eyes, the Irishman said, "I'm sorry, Margaret. I tried ringing earlier, but kept getting the answering machine. This matter is too delicate for an answering machine. I thought I would call around on the off chance that you had returned home."

Margaret Maguire was a clairvoyant medium whom Frank had known for some time. He was a regular at the spiritualist meetings she held in her house. These were small, private gatherings for trusted friends and people who were genuinely seeking contact with departed loved ones. She was the only link Frank had with his long departed family. He trusted her implicitly.

By profession, Margaret had been a schoolteacher. She was now retired and was living on a good pension. Spiritualism was her major interest these days. She had been gifted with the second-sight since childhood, but had kept it hidden for many years. Her family had been staunch Christians, and they considered clairvoyance to be the work of the devil. Now, in these more enlightened times, she openly used her extraordinary abilities for the good of those who came to her, seeking help.

"Please come in and make yourself at home," she said, leading the way into the lounge. Frank opened a large brown envelope that he had been clutching, and withdrew a photograph. "This is a digital image of something I found on my bathroom mirror this morning," he blurted, still trying to come to terms with what he had experienced.

Taking the photograph from him, Margaret studied it closely. "Interesting," she murmured. "It looks like it was traced out by a finger when the glass was dry, and was later picked out by the condensing steam. A finger would leave a thin deposit of grease on the surface of the glass, and this would be enough to prevent the adhesion of condensing water droplets. A clever way to leave a message!"

Lifting her gaze, she looked hard at Frank. "You are certain that it was not drawn by a friend or visitor, only to be revealed at a later time by the steam?" she asked.

His face flushed slightly. "I am certain," he rumbled. "I take it from that comment that you are not picking anything up from the image?"

Margaret's face softened. "I will need to touch the mirror, Frank, but you know that already," she said.

He smiled. "Well, I had to show you the photograph to convince you, even to convince myself, that this is real."

They walked out to the car, which was parked directly outside the house. Margaret settled herself into the passenger seat next to Frank.

"This is the first time that I have been in your car," she said, examining the interior. "'Solid' is the word that comes to mind. It all looks a bit old fashioned, but well put together. And these padded leather seats are sublimely comfortable."

"Yes," responded the Irishman. "It's an older model, but still rock steady. Volvo makes the best car seats in the world. No other car manufacturer, including the premium German car makers, design seats that can hold a candle to Volvo seats." At least, that was what he thought.

On the drive to Kidlington, Frank related the strange events that had befallen him since his abduction—the finding of the chess piece, and the old newspaper clippings, his brush with death on the obelisk, and the terrible visitation of the night before. The concern on Margaret's face grew as Frank told her about the Northgate curse.

"Yes," she nodded, "I have heard of something similar happening to a wealthy family in Ireland, although it was not as extreme as this Northgate phenomenon sounds. The dead should remain buried and not be put on display for amusement and entertainment. It is a form of desecration, and it can have serious consequences. The dead are best left to rest in peace."

Turning the key, the Irishman pushed the front door open. As soon as Margaret entered the hall, she sensed something. "I can feel residual energy here," she said, gravely. She began to climb the stairs. "Yes, a spirit entity has been here recently," she continued. Walking across the landing, she came to a sudden halt. "The psychic odour is bad here. This is a vengeful spirit. It is evil," she murmured.

Margaret entered the bathroom, closely followed by Frank. The condensation had gone now and nothing was visible on the mirrors. Walking straight for the vanity mirror, the old lady touched it. As if hit by an electric shock, she was jolted backwards! Frank caught her just in time. She recovered quickly.

"Are you all right?" he asked. "Let's get you to a chair."

"No," replied Margaret firmly. "Let's get you to a chair and a stiff drink," she said. "I'm afraid you're going to need it!"

CHAPTER 17
RETURN TO NORTHGATE HALL

It was noon on a Wednesday in early December, and the air was raw as Alexander made his way across the Chapel Quad. High above, a lone hawk circled in a leaden sky. Entering the chapel, he could see a figure kneeling in silent prayer. Turning suddenly, it looked towards him and beckoned him to its side.

"You wanted to see me, Dr. Malone?" asked Alexander, a little hesitantly.

"Yes, son," whispered the Irishman.

"Pray with me for a while."

The boy was a stranger to prayer. Indeed, he had never prayed since the day he was born. But matters of late had opened his mind to the possibility of consciousness beyond death. Kneeling silently beside the Irishman, he folded his hands, but he did not pray. He was eager to know why his tutor had sent for him. Surely this meeting could not be related to his studies. What else could it be about?

Ten minutes later, Frank was back at his desk and Alexander was sitting there, facing him. The Irishman's persona exuded an air of resignation as he spoke. "We both appear to be sailing in the same boat now, young man," he sighed. "There's no point in beating about the bush. The situation appears to be quite grave. A friend of mine who is a clairvoyant has advised me that there is an unquiet spirit abroad—a ruthless entity that has a vendetta against the Northgate family. It has killed, and it means to kill again. It means to kill you; that is your fate as a Northgate. The entity is bent on destroying the Northgate dynasty. It entered my home two nights ago and left me a message. Clearly I too have been marked for death."

Alexander sat completely motionless except for his eyes, which moved rapidly as he desperately wracked his brain for answers.

"Have you anything to say, young man?" asked Frank, his tone surprisingly gentle. "You have got me into this mess. Have you had any bright ideas since we last talked on this subject?"

The boy looked pale now and deeply troubled. "I'm sorry, sir," he squeaked, the sudden tension getting the better of his vocal cords. Coughing to clear his throat, he continued. "Up until now, I was not entirely certain that this entity was real. My mind is still having difficulty accepting it. I have searched in vain for surviving descendants of Baron Algernon Northgate. It appears that I'm the last. If the curse is real, then time is running out. The baron's dynasty is on the verge of extinction."

Pausing, he cleared his throat again. "Forgive me for asking this," he said, "but was there any evidence that the so-called entity was present in your house?"

Frank had been expecting this question, and quickly produced the photograph.

"There's no mistaking it. This is the eye of Horus, the eye that is carved on the obelisk at Northgate Hall!" gasped Alexander.

ഌര

Saturday arrived and the unlikely duo found themselves standing once again outside the forbidding gates of Northgate Hall. Frank stared pensively through the iron bars. "I'm still questioning my sanity for agreeing to this," he rumbled. His voice was far too powerful to betray fear. This was true, even when he was genuinely scared; currently, he was just apprehensive. "We could do with help on this one, but I daren't get anyone else involved for fear that they too will end up marked for death. It is down to you and me, Alexander, to sort this mess out. Still, we need to be as careful as we possibly can."

Turning to the boy, he handed him a beaded necklace from which hung a small crucifix. "Take these rosary beads," he said. "They've been blessed. We need to protect ourselves from evil. Given the short notice, it is the best that I could come up with."

Alexander looked sceptically at the beads, but took them to humour the Irishman.

"From what I have been able to discover," he said, placing the rosary beads around his neck, "the entity appears to kill by using electricity. In the middle of a thunderstorm we would be in mortal danger, but not otherwise. The thing appears to have the power to target lightening bolts at living matter."

Frank stared at him, with raised eyebrows. "I've heard of spirits hurling spoons and the like, but not lightening bolts!"

Alexander looked at the Irishman square in the eyes. "This is no ordinary spirit, Dr. Malone," he said.

As on their previous visit to Northgate Hall, they negotiated the gates with ease and set off towards the house. The bleak winter's morning hung heavy and dark as they made their way through the woods; eventually, the big house loomed into view. It stood there in the grey gloom, desolate and menacing. Staring with unblinking eyes, Frank sensed something vile about it, like a decaying corpse. It was as if it was waiting for them—evil, but patient.

"Maybe there's a way into this awful mausoleum from here," sighed Frank.

"Not much chance of that, Dr. Malone. The first two stories are entirely bricked up," responded Alexander.

Groaning, the Irishman reached for his hip flask, and unscrewing the top, took a long swig. Whatever was in there was very strong, and he grimaced as he swallowed. "That's better," he hissed. "Only for emergencies, this stuff! Distilled from Irish potatoes!"

Frank knew there was no option but to return to the dreaded obelisk. There was a very good chance that the tunnel that they had found previously would lead to the house. He would have to bite the bullet and confront that terrifying tower once more. With Alexander leading the way, they moved forward towards the obelisk. "I would rather suck a thunderbolt than climb up there again," cursed the Irishman. As the massive structure towered into view, he was at odds to understand why anybody would build such a thing. It must have cost a king's ransom. What was the point? Maybe it was just meant to be the biggest folly in England; the baron was both wealthy and a tad eccentric. Stumbling from time to time, Frank walked with his eyes half closed; he could not bear to look up. The horrible memories came flooding back.

"Let's get into that bloody tunnel fast," he growled, shielding the obelisk from view with one of his hands.

Alexander struggled unsuccessfully to suppress a smirk at the sight of the terrified Irishman, but fortunately he was too preoccupied to notice. The ravaged sphinx stood as they had left it, with the concealed door still open. Armed with large heavy-duty torches, the man and the boy stepped inside. Both carried backpacks, stuffed with equipment. Soon they were in the tunnel and took the left spur in the direction of the old house. The light beams from their torches bounced off the arched brick walls, casting eerie shadows. Beyond the reach of the beams lay a heavy blackness. Walking forward, the sense of unease was slowly growing.

Moving more cautiously now, the blackness felt suffocating in the cold, unnerving silence. A sudden gasp exploded into the air and echoed down the tunnel. Something cold and wet had hit Alexander on the forehead and the shock had forced the air from his lungs. Frank aimed his torch upward. Droplets of water were budding from the roof and slowly dripping onto the stone slabs below.

"Are you OK?" asked Frank, his voice echoing hollowly in the void of the tunnel.

The boy nodded sharply, his nerve shaken. The black silence was smothering now, but still they pressed on. Dank air began to linger in their nostrils and cling to their skin. There was a growing sense of something, of something disquieting, of unseen hands grabbing at them through the shadows. A voice in Alexander's head screamed "Turn back, turn back! Run now and save yourself. It is hopeless. Turn back!" But still, he walked forward. It was life or death now. There was no turning back.

The boy looked at his watch. "We've been walking for about five minutes now," he muttered, trying to visualise their location relative to the house. Frank aimed his torch straight ahead. The beam of light picked out something in the distance. As they moved closer, it was clear that they were reaching the end of the tunnel. It looked like they were approaching an opening. At last the tunnel led them through, into a small chamber.

Frank's heavy sigh reverberated off the stonework. "It's a relief to have that out of the way!" he said, reaching for his hip flask. He felt that he definitely needed a top up before facing the next leg of the mission. As he gulped another swig of the burning liquid, Alexander inspected the chamber with his torch. Straight ahead was what looked like a heavy oak door. It was barely discernable under the dust and cobwebs, but it was definitely some kind of door.

"That must be the way into Northgate Hall," mumbled Frank, reluctant to cross the threshold of the forbidding house.

"There is no obvious handle or lock," responded Alexander, brushing the grime from the edges of the door and searching with his hands.

"Let's try pushing it," suggested Frank.

They braced themselves and then pressed hard, first on the right side of the door and then on the left. The oak barrier did not budge.

"It may be stuck," said Frank.

"Time for the crow bars!" said Alexander, with boyish enthusiasm.

They both delved into their backpacks and produced sturdy steel levers. Setting to work on the right edge of the door, Frank levered from above and Alexander from below. It was not long before the wood gave a reluctant creak and the door groaned slowly forward.

"Right," said Frank. "Put your back into it and push with everything you've got."

Straining and blowing, they moved the heavy door far enough forward so they could both squeeze through the gap. The moment of truth had arrived. Panting from the exertion, the Irishman eased his way into the cold black void. The boy was right behind him. Nervously, they pointed the torches into the chilling emptiness. They were in a large, rough-bricked chamber with dark brooding alcoves. Above their heads were heavy wooden crossbeams, festooned with dusty cobwebs that hung like ghastly shrouds. Scattered haphazardly was what looked like discarded furniture, layered in thick dust. Frank turned to examine the opening through which they had just emerged. It was a massive wine rack.

How ingenious! Hiding a secret door in a wine rack. Looking more closely, he could see that the racks were still well stocked. His eyes lit up as he rubbed the dust from one of the bottles. "Wow!" he gasped, "This is vintage stuff! One hundred and thirty year old Napoleon brandy! There is probably a king's ransom worth of booze in here!" Cleaning the dust off the bottle, he pushed it into his backpack. *If I die today, I'm going out in grand style!*

Alexander's torch picked out a stone staircase on the far side of the chamber. "We're obviously in the cellar," he said to his companion. "We should move as quickly as we can to find the library." He pulled out a compass and a set of surveyor's drawings. These had been photocopied in sections onto A4 paper sheets that had subsequently been stapled together.

"Impressive," murmured Frank.

"It took a bit of doing," grinned Alexander, "but where there's a will, there's a way... At the top of those steps there should be a corridor. We need to turn left, walk down to the end of the passage, then follow it right until we come to the library."

There was something protruding from Frank's hefty rucksack. He tugged on it and out came a baseball bat. "Let's do it!" he growled, waving the bat.

Silhouetted in the torch beams, their footfalls sent little clouds of dust billowing into the air as they climbed the steps. Approaching the top of the stairs, it was clear that the cellar door was half open. Moving past the door, they bore left into the corridor. The sense of mustiness, of a lingering mouldy dampness, was even stronger here. It was penetratingly cold and deathly silent. The silence seemed to leer at them, daring them to move deeper into the blackness. Even in its heyday, when the house was filled with light and life, this corridor would have appeared stark, with its flagstone floor and bare plaster walls, but now it looked completely desolate. Clumps of plaster lay strewn across the floor and large patches of ugly mould grew in the dampness of the walls.

"This must have been a service corridor used by the servants," whispered Alexander, reluctant to break the silence and warn anything lurking within that they had entered the house. Standing side-by-side, they moved briskly down the passageway. It was not a place to linger. The torch beams traced the way forward in the blackness. Reaching the end of the passageway, they bore hard right into a wider and grander corridor. This serviced the east wing of the house and had many alcoves along the right-hand sidewall. These had once been windows. They were now bricked in so nothing could penetrate, not even a glimmer of light.

As they progressed down the passageway, they passed a number of doors on the left. Alexander ignored these. "We are looking for a set of double doors," he whispered. Walking carefully along the debris-littered floor, they eventually found what they were looking for. The doors were tall and impressive, powdered grey by a century of dust. Frank pushed at one of the doors. Creaking stiffly, it jerked stubbornly forward. Cautiously, they entered a vast room. The stillness and the brooding shadows beyond the torch beams were even more unnerving than in the dank corridors. It was as if the room itself was watching and waiting. The very air reeked of malice.

Bravely and undaunted, the man and the boy began to explore the library. Remnants of books lay scattered across the dusty floor, nibbled to pieces by rats. Many of the books on the higher shelves were still in place, but they were contorted and discoloured with dampness, and speckled with mould. "It's hopeless," said Frank. "These books are damaged beyond recognition."

Oblivious to his tutor's dejection, the boy walked carefully down the rows of bookcases, plying his torch over each self. After what seemed like an eternity to the exasperated Irishman, Alexander reached the last bookcase on the left-hand side of the library, close to the huge bay windows. The topmost shelf was completely bare, except for one dust-laden book, lying on its side. Frank moved close to the boy and aimed his torch at the book. Without uttering a word, Alexander put down his torch and began to climb the bookcase. Grabbing the book, he clambered back down in a cloud of dust. They both began to cough as the dust hit their lungs. Amazingly, the book was still completely intact. The buffalo hide cover and vellum pages had stood the test of time.

When the dust was rubbed from the book, it was clear that it was a journal. Frank lifted the cover. "It's handwritten, and difficult to read," he said, handing the journal to the boy. Alexander's young eyes were still razor sharp. "Looks like it was written in 1885. The first page is titled, 'Journal 1, 1885/6, Algernon Northgate'."

The boy flicked through the pages, his disappointment growing as he studied their contents. "It's basically a travel log of the Middle East. Looks like the baron was getting to know the area and making contacts in various cities before beginning his explorations. I would guess that there are a whole series of these journals. The question is, where are they?" he asked, his voice betraying his frustration.

Frank walked over to the bookcases and began to examine them closely. "It's not uncommon for grand libraries in stately homes to have a hidden chamber," he muttered as he inspected the woodwork. "They were used to keep valuable or sensitive books out of the reach of servants, or even family members." He started to prod the backs of the bookcases with the end of his baseball bat. Each impact produced a dull, muted thud. He tested all the bookcases on the left side of the library. "Sounds like solid wall behind this lot," he muttered. Moving over to the opposite wall, on the right side of the library, he started again. It was the same dull sound every time. Finally, he reached the last of the bookcases, banging the bat harder in frustration. The thud had a hollow sound. "This is it!" he shouted in triumph, his powerful voice reverberating around the room like a foghorn.

Alexander grimaced. *Whatever lurks within these walls will know that we are here now, for sure! But then again, the entity is probably already watching, biding it's time and waiting to strike.*

Frank handed Alexander his torch and began to search the bookcase for a hidden catch, button, or lever. He continued for a few minutes until he had to withdraw, sneezing and covered in dust. "There is no sign of anything, just smooth wood," he gasped, trying to clear the dust from his lungs.

Alexander continued to study the bookcase. There was a stretch of about thirty centimetres of wall between the end of the bookcase and the adjacent wall, which housed a big bay window. *I'll bet there is a very good chance that this last section of bookcase is some sort of secret panel that swings out. More than likely, it swings from left to right. That way, you could easily slip behind the bookcase using the gap to conceal your movements. But how to open it? Time is running out. There is a good chance that things could start getting nasty around here anytime soon!*

Frank returned to the bookcase and leaned heavily against the side end panel as he reached for his hip flask. A sudden creak broke the silence. "Where the hell did that come from?" gasped the startled Irishman.

Alexander waved the torches rapidly around the room. Nothing was caught in the beams, just the desolate vastness of the mighty room. He trained the torches back on the bookcase. Frank had stepped back a few paces and was examining the side panel.

"Yes," he rumbled, "it has definitely moved!" Grabbing the panel with both hands, he pushed hard. "It seems to be hinged," he grunted, as he continued to push. The panel had moved in an arch of about ten centimetres, but it would budge no further. "So what do we do next, brain box?" he asked, panting slightly, but with a wry smile on his face.

"A hundred years ago, this last section of bookcase would have probably popped out towards us," said Alexander, grinning. "I'll bet it's stuck. Let's set to work with the crowbars!"

Frank decided to hold the torches and let the boy loose with one of the crowbars. Alexander set about his task with relish. He drove the sharp end of the crowbar into the back of the side panel, where it abutted the wall. A chunk of plaster fell away as he pushed on the crowbar. With a loud grating noise, the end of the bookcase juddered forward.

"I think we're in!" exclaimed Alexander.

Placing the torches on the floor, Frank went to the boy's assistance. They slid their fingers behind the back end of the bookcase, where it had been separated from the wall, and tugged. The whole thing hinged open like a door. Collecting their torches, they walked into what was clearly a concealed room. It was windowless and narrow, but ran the entire length of the library. The torchlight revealed that they had entered through a doorway in a wall that had been deliberately concealed by the end bookcase. On the wall opposite them was mounted a set of five large book cabinets, faced in glass. Beyond the cabinets were a number of objects that were covered by dustsheets. Dust was far less of a problem in this room. It had probably remained sealed since the house was abandoned. Three of the cabinets were filled with books, and two of them were empty. The books had survived the rigors of time far better than the books in the main library, although the growth of mould was still evident. Sliding back the glass panel of the first cabinet, Frank began to examine the books. Alexander showed no interest in the contents of the cabinets and made his way further up the room towards the objects covered by the dustsheets. As the boy approached them, he could see that there were three of them. Slowly and carefully, he removed the sheets, trying to displace as little dust as possible. His lungs were really starting to suffer now in the stale air.

Revealed underneath the sheets were two small barrels and a sturdy wooden trunk. Burying the crowbar into the lid of the first barrel, Alexander yanked it off. Reaching a hand inside, he withdrew a package. It was wrapped in muslin that had been impregnated with an oily wax-like substance. With the packaging removed, a red leather-faced book was revealed; the missing journals of Baron Algernon Northgate had been found! Alexander wasted no time in removing all the journals, wrappings in tact, and placing them in three piles. He counted sixteen journals in all. Next, he turned his attention to the trunk. It was not locked. Lifting the lid, he found more muslin-wrapped packages. Removing the wrapping from the first package, he discovered a leather-bound ledger, which appeared to have been used for keeping the estate accounts. He worked his way through another six packages, only to find more accounts ledgers. Two packages remained. One proved to be an inventory of household contents, and the other an inventory of the artefacts held in the Northgate Hall Museum. This was one of the books he had been looking for.

Alexander returned to his companion, who was still enthralled by the books in the cabinets. Tapping him on the arm, he said, "Dr. Malone, I've found the journals and the museum inventory. I feel that we should leave now."

Reluctantly, Frank turned his attention to the boy. "There's a small fortune worth of first editions here, as well as extremely rare books on metaphysics and archaeology. I need time to work my way through this collection. It's an absolute goldmine!"

The beam on one of the torches began to dim. "Damn!" hissed Frank "The batteries are running low! Better put the replacements in." With that he broke from the cabinets, took off his backpack, and retrieved a new set of batteries. Alexander needed no encouragement to do the same. With the torches recharged, Frank returned to the cabinets. Looking at the boy, he barked, "I know we need to retrieve the journals, but I am taking one of these books as a souvenir." With that he grabbed a book, and could not resist a second one.

"How are we going to carry all this?" groaned Alexander.

"Not to worry, son," responded the academic, cheerily.

The man and the boy emerged from the secret room, with backpacks bulging. They had had to leave most of their equipment behind, including blankets, axes, ropes and a first-aid kit, to make room for the journals, books and the ledger in their backpacks.

"OK," said Frank, "Let's get out of here as quickly, but carefully, as we can."

Walking briskly across the library, they headed for the double doors. The excitement and fascination of their discoveries in the hidden room was fading fast. A sense of tension was growing in them. They could both feel it unmistakably now. Something was watching them in the blackness. They reached the corridor. It was deathly cold, a supernatural cold that pierced through them like freezing knives.

"Take it steady, son," said the Irishman. "Walk quickly, but don't run."

The silence was heavy now, pressing against them, and the darkness ahead was threatening. Moving down the corridor, they began to retrace their steps to the cellar. The cold grew even more intense, and they could see their breath condensing into clouds as the torch beams scanned along the passageway. A dreadful strangeness hung in the dank air. They reached the servants' passageway.

The blackness beckoned. A dark instinct, bourn of intense anxiety, started to surface in their minds; an urge to run blindly like hunted animals from an unseen predator that was closing in. "Steady," growled Frank, gripping his baseball bat. "Keep calm. We're approaching the cellar door now."

Reaching the door, they hurried down the steps, panting and glancing fearfully in all directions. With thumping hearts, they scrambled through the opening in the wine rack, and made rapidly for the tunnel. "We are almost out!" gasped Frank, marching ahead. And then there was total blackness; the torch beams had been snuffed out like candles!

A sudden, horrible screech punctured their ears! Intense pain ripped through the boy as two icy claws bite into his shoulders. Unable to move, a numbing coldness surged through his veins. As the grip of the terrible talons tightened, his mind moved beyond shock to a paralysing uncontrollable terror.

CHAPTER 18
THE QUEST CONTINUES

ജ്ഞ

Summoning every atom of will power he possessed, Alexander forced his right hand towards the crucifix, and in that instant a blinding light burst through the blackness. As his vision cleared, he could see Frank standing there, holding a burning flare. Slapping the boy hard across both cheeks, he dragged him forward. As the boy staggered, his senses began to return, and anger welled up within him.

"Don't look at me like that!" roared the Irishman. "For the love of God, run for your life!"

ജ്ഞ

Fifteen minutes later, they were sitting in the Volvo. "Sorry I had to slap you, Alexander," said Frank, as he pointed the speeding car back in the direction of High Wycombe. "It was the only way I could bring you back to your senses."

The boy looked straight ahead, still in shock. "That's OK," he mumbled. "I fear that I would never have left Northgate Hall alive if it had not been for you. Where did you get that flare from?"

The Irishman gave a sly smile. "I had three of them in my pocket for emergencies," he said. "It's well documented that spirits can drain the power from batteries. I had the flares to protect us, in the event of the torches dying. The thing in the house used the energy in the torches to attack you. There was not enough power there to kill you directly, only to stun you, to shock you. Maybe the mental shock would have killed you if I had not been there. Who knows? It was a good job, mind you, that the heavy clouds that we saw earlier in the day had cleared. If the entity had had thunderclouds at its disposal, we could have been reduced to ashes out in the open. That thing could scare a man to death, but it failed with us. We have faced it and survived! It will bide its time now. Stay well away from thunderstorms, that's my advice to you, young man!"

ꙮ

Later that evening, Frank sat in his study, inspecting the journals they had retrieved from the house. He nursed a glass of very fine spirits, the best by far that he had ever tasted. *A glass of this nectar is probably worth more than my car, but I've earned it,* he thought, smirking with satisfaction. It was the brandy from the wine cellar at Northgate Hall.

He had agreed with Alexander that for the moment, his house was the best place to keep the journals. If the entity came back looking for them, he felt that he was better equipped to deal with it than the boy, who seemed to know next to nothing about the paranormal or the occult. He had given Alexander a key so he could come and go as he pleased. These were desperate times, and a boy with a key to his home was the least of his worries.

ꙮ

Standing in the Gupta's garage, Alexander surveyed his electric bike. Rosie had questioned why he wanted to risk bringing it to Oxford, where it could easily be stolen. He had assured her that he needed the bike to get him to and from Kidlington, where he would be using his tutor's private library for a research project; his regular old banger of a bike would still be employed to get him around Oxford. She seemed to think that that was reasonable, and they had brought the bike up in the car on the previous evening.

He was still shaken from his terrifying adventure in Northgate Hall, but he had disguised it well when he got back home to Arcadia Drive, mainly by spending a lot of time in his room. Frank had let him keep the ledger, which he had been reading very carefully. He had not mentioned to his tutor the awful dream he had had the year before about the man-eating eagle owls. In the dark of the tunnel, he had been convinced that he was being attacked by one of those dreadful creatures, and that he was going to be torn to pieces. The entity could get inside people's heads; that much was clear now. It played on its victims worst fears, and that was where its power lay. He had survived its head-on attack, and now he was determined to vanquish it. Next time he would be ready. Without a lightening bolt, it could not kill him. He would watch the weather closely. He would find a way to avenge his family. He would learn what he needed to learn and he would drive it from Northgate Hall, and ultimately from his life.

Lectures were out of the question now. He had no time for them. In any event, he had already read and memorised all of his course books for the entire year. Tutorials would be another matter, though. He had to keep his masters at LMH happy. He could not afford to get kicked out. He needed Dr. Frank Malone, and above all, he needed those journals.

Wrapped up well against the cold, Alexander mounted his electric bike and headed out of Oxford. The bike could easily do 40 miles per hour when peddled hard, but Alexander tended to cruise at 20 miles per hour. It was easier on the eyeballs, particularly at this time of the year. Approaching Frank's house, he could see the big Volvo in the driveway. To be polite, even though he had a key now, he knocked hard on the front door. There was no reply.

I hope everything's all right, he thought, a little anxiously. *Let's face it, these aren't normal times!* He knocked again, but there was no reply. Inserting his key, he unlocked the door and cautiously pushed it open. The house was quiet. There was no sign of movement. He entered the hall. "Dr. Malone," he called, nervously. There was no reply, only silence. *I'd better check this out,* he thought reluctantly. All the doors on the ground floor were closed. Walking over to one of the doors he turned the knob and pushed it open. The lounge was empty. *Nice decor.*

"Dr. Malone," he called again. There was only silence. He checked the kitchen and then the study. Nothing. *Everything's surprisingly neat, except for the study.* Mounting the stairs, his heart beat faster. He reached the landing. "Dr. Malone, are you there?" he called, his voice echoing in the hallway.

The thing has been here once before. Perhaps it returned! Dr. Malone could be lying stiff and blue with wide staring eyes. Maybe the thing was waiting for him, determined to prevent him from reading those journals. And then the anger grew within him. "I will not bow to you!" he shouted, as he burst the doors open, one by one. There was nothing, nothing except fastidiously made beds and a pristine bathroom. He blew a deep sigh of relief. *Dr. Malone's a very tidy man,* he thought, as he descended the stairs.

In the study, Alexander found the journals stacked in two neat piles on the floor, close to the desk. The red leather covers showed various changes in pigmentation. Much of this would have been due to exposure of the leather to sunlight when they stood on a bookcase, or had lain on a desk in the great library at Northgate Hall. *They must have originally been kept in the main library, and not in the concealed room,* he reasoned. *It was a good bet that the Baron had hidden them just before his mysterious disappearance. They probably contained information that the baron did not want to fall into the wrong hands.*

He had decided that the first thing that he would do was to read all the journals from cover to cover. With his amazing photographic memory, he could remember every last word of the text from every single journal. He would then write a summary report. This would be useful in their investigations. He totalled up the journals. There were indeed sixteen of them, just as he had counted before in the hidden room. They had been stacked in chronological order. He picked up the first journal. It was the one that he had discovered in the main library. It was hardly surprising that it was in the worst condition of all of the journals, but it was still readable. It felt weird, picking up and opening the ancient journal. *There's something bizarrely familiar about this.* Sitting at Frank's desk, Alexander dredged his memory. There was nothing he could put his finger on, but he could not shake the feeling. It was strange. The boy could read about three times faster than the average person. He began to read the journal dated 1885/6, his eyes moving like scanners across the pages.

CHAPTER 19
TERMINATOR

ꕥ

A tall figure walked out of the Oxford bus depot and onto the Cowley Road. It was "Butch," the female bus driver. Her blond hair was tied back tightly into a ponytail and she was still wearing her driver's uniform. She stopped at a bus stop close by. Shortly after, a smaller woman with long mousy brown hair and spectacles joined her. She was wearing a denim jacket and baggy jeans. A red bus pulled up, and the door hissed open. Mounting the steps, Butch muttered a brief "hello" to the driver and took a seat at the front of the bus. The slightly scruffy looking woman with the spectacles followed her in, paid for her ticket, and moved farther back into the bus.

In the centre of town, the big woman stepped off the bus. Walking briskly, she headed in the direction of Broad Street. Someway behind, the woman with the glasses was following her, weaving carefully between shoppers and plodding tourists. People on the pavement started to thin out as Butch reached the end of Broad Street. Turning left, she began to walk down Parks Road. The woman with the mousy hair continued to follow. The shops had petered out, to be replaced by high resplendent walls that concealed the manicured grounds of a number of the colleges The pavements were virtually deserted now. If the bus driver turned her head she might see the woman tracking her, might remember her from the bus stop. Mousy hair crossed to the other side of the road; there was a line of neatly planted trees she could use for cover.

Butch picked up her pace as she started to pass the striking red brickwork of Keble College. The woman in the denim jacket followed stealthily, a little distance behind. They reached the Science Library and the museums. It was a good bet now that the target was making for the University Parks. Sure enough, Butch entered the parks and headed up a gravel path towards a man sitting on a bench. The woman following stepped off the path and casually strode across the grass, working her way into a position where she could discretely view the man's face. A concealed camera began to record digital images. Without exchanging even a glance with the man, the big bus driver sat down on the far end of the bench. She lit up a cigarette, inhaled deeply, stood up and left. As soon as she had departed, the man moved to where she had been sitting and picked something up. It was a brown envelope.

A brief smile of satisfaction stole across the face of the woman with the mousy hair. Turning her head, she started to track her new target—the man on the bench. Reaching the gravel path, she felt a sudden thud against her left thigh. Focusing intently on the bench, she had failed to spot the little girl directly in front of her. Looking down, she could see the child sitting forlornly in the gravel. Two hefty looking women approached rapidly.

The little girl, standing now, was sizing up the situation. Anger and concern in her mother's eyes, panic in the stranger's. *Sweeties*, she thought. Drawing in a deep lungful of air, she began to howl. "Did you see that?" said the mother, grabbing hold of mousy hair's arm. "This bitch deliberately knocked over my little girl. Let's do her!"

The mother's friend—they both looked working-class—rounded on mousy hair. She had to think fast or she would lose the target—or worse still, her cover would be blown. Dropping her head, she began to shake. "I'm terribly sorry," she whimpered. "It was an accident. I wasn't looking where I was going." She started to sob.

The mother released her grip.

It's working, thought mousy hair. "They've just told me I've got cancer," she blubbered.

In that instant, anger melted into surprise and the two women stood there, open- mouthed, caught between guilt and sympathy. Mousy hair slipped swiftly away. Clever as she had been, though, it was too late. The target was gone.

ஐ

Zoe Watts sat in her dressing room, combing her hair. Lifting her head, she looked at her reflection in the mirror. She was totally bald, her skull shaved smooth. This was the way she liked herself best, swept clean of pretence—hard and uncompromising. She was the master of many roles, but this was her favourite, the role that she could seldom play: herself. Carefully, she positioned the blond wig that she had been combing and pressed it to her scalp, the tape gripping tightly. Smiling at her reflection in the mirror, she said, "Welcome back, Zoe Watts, private eye."

Displayed on a mannequin head amongst other wigs was the mousy brown one that she had just peeled from her head. Back in her office, Zoe fired up a computer and began downloading images from the concealed camera. "Let's see what we can find out about these two characters," she murmured as an image of Butch and her male companion came up on the screen. "No beauty, that's for sure," she said, looking at Butch.

The man was more interesting. His hair was black and closely cropped, and he had dense facial stubble. Set in a powerful square face, his small grey eyes looked cold and ruthless.

"I'll bet he's got history," said Zoe with satisfaction, as she drafted out an email to her brother.

ஐ

It was very early morning on the following day, and Hiddington Thame station was only lightly sprinkled with passengers. A thunderous roar shook the station as an express train blasted through. In a streaking flash it had been and gone. An old man in a long grubby coat, leaning heavily on a walking cane, shuffled along platform two. He wore a grey cloth cap, pulled down low, and his head was stooped. Slowly, he approached a man further down the platform. The man looked like a strutting young city gent in an expensive pinstriped suit and shining handmade shoes. Carrying a black leather briefcase, his attention was directed to a light pink newspaper that he held, partly folded.

A new message flashed onto the overhead platform display: NEXT TRAIN APPROACHING. Soon, there was no mistaking the formidable sound of the speeding express. The old man drew level with the city gent. The train screamed through. Turning, the old man began to retrace his steps. Nobody seemed to notice that there was one less person standing on platform two—not the two old ladies busy gabbing, not the pretty young girl half dosing on a plastic bench, or the labourer studying the sports pages of his paper.

The old man walked slowly out of the station and into the car park. Eventually, he reached the top of the ramp and shuffled out onto the open road. It was a rural location, mainly fields and hedgerows. As the old man moved out of sight of the station, a Yamaha trail bike drew up and the rider threw him a helmet. Lifting his visor, he asked the old man casually, "How'd it go?"

"Perfect," replied the old man, equally casually. "One hard prod in the small of the back and he was a goner, smashed like a bug on a windscreen."

With his helmet secured, the old man, suddenly agile, mounted the motorbike.

ꕥ

The following morning, Zoe checked her emails. Her brother had replied. There was nothing on the woman, but the man did indeed have a history. A former Marine commando, he had been sentenced to five years in prison for grievous bodily harm. He had almost beaten a man to death in a bar fight. After getting out of prison, he had lived for a number of years in Bristol, and then he disappeared off the radar. He was currently listed on the police computer as being "of no fixed address." Not good news. Still, she had his name now: Douglas Flint.

It was handy, having a big brother on the police force. Based on Merseyside, he was now a Chief Inspector. In his view, they were both fighting crime, so he would bend the rules and help her out when he could. She was ex-police herself, having served seven years as a beat constable in Birkenhead. In many ways it had been a great job, but in the end, bureaucracy and paperwork had gotten the better of her, and she had resigned. She worked for a private security firm for a while, and then moved down south to take up a job with one of the larger private detective agencies. Again, there was too much paperwork and not enough action, so eventually she set up her own business. In her view, that was the best decision she had ever made. She was the boss now, and if she took risks, it was her decision, not some plonker in an office. Zoe Watts was a woman who liked danger, and she was not afraid of violence.

CHAPTER 20
THE HIDDEN CHAMBER

ﻉ

Alexander had left Kidlington at 6:00 p.m, without encountering Dr. Malone. The boy assumed that he was staying over late in Oxford, and that alcohol would be involved. Things had been pretty traumatic of late. He really could not see what Frank Malone found so fascinating about the stuff. It must be slowly killing him by now. But that was the way of things at College. Everybody seemed to drink. The whole social life of the students revolved around booze and parties. He had begun to resent alcohol. He was too young even to have a choice about whether to drink or not. Because they would not allow him near alcohol, he was excluded from everything. He had no friends, and he sat alone in lectures. He was some sort of geeky child freak that everybody tried to avoid. Often, of late, he wished that he was just a normal boy, still in school and looking forward to the Christmas holidays. In the strange world that he inhabited, Frank Malone was the nearest thing he had to a friend.

Anita commented over dinner, not for the first time, that they seemed to be seeing less and less of him. *Little does she know that she will be seeing nothing of me at all, if I do not get to the bottom of the mystery of Northgate Hall!*

The computer in the Gupta's top floor office burst into life. Alexander had decided to do two things: he would type out the journals, one by one, exactly as they were written, page for page, and as he progressed he would build up his summary report. There could be coded messages in the text of the journals, hence the need to type them out word for word. He set to work; his fingers danced furiously over the keyboard for about four hours. It would soon be the end of term, the Gupta boys would be back, and he would have to go home to High Wycombe. By the time he had finished for the night, he had transposed two of the six journals (word for word) that he had read earlier, and he had made a start on his summary report. It dealt with the first six journals and made interesting reading.

NORTHGATE HALL
JOURNALS OF BARON ALGERNON NORTHGATE

SUMMARY REPORT

Sixteen journals were retrieved from Northgate Hall. One of the journals was found in the main library and the other fifteen journals were discovered in a concealed room that connected with the library. It is of interest to note that a seventeenth journal, that would have been dated 1901/2, was missing.

Journal 1

In the first journal, dated 1885/6, Baron Algernon Northgate began his narrative with some very personal notes about his disillusion with the Christian conception of God. He did not tell his wife about his loss of faith, but he did inform her of his initiation into the Brotherhood of Freemasons. According to the baron, she just thought the Masons were a silly club for men who were still boys at heart. That suited him fine.

The baron registered his surprise in his journal as to how many men of wealth and influence were in the Brotherhood. Many of the key players in the French Revolution and the American War of Independence had Masonic connections. Even kings and some American presidents had numbered amongst the ranks of the Brotherhood. Now that he was initiated, he saw anew many famous monuments. They were monuments to Freemason symbolism and they adorned many of the capital cities of the Western World.

The Freemasons could trace their origins to a culture and philosophy that had its roots in ancient Egypt. This amazed Baron Northgate. As time went by, the baron became familiar with the symbols, rituals and ideology of the Brotherhood. He considered himself a man of science, a man of objective and rational thought. The baron began to wonder if there was not a civilisation far older and more advanced than Egypt's; a civilisation that was alluded to in the symbols and myths of the Egyptians. And then he heard of the "Hall of Records." He delved and he probed within the ranks of the Brotherhood, but learnt very little. Fuelled by the wall of silence, his determination to get to the truth grew into a passion.

The baron had tired of symbols, myths and rituals, be they Christian or Mason; except for one. It was rumoured that there were hidden chambers in Egypt that contained the secrets of an ancient and mighty race. If the legend was true, their scientific knowledge far outstripped that of the Western World in the 19th century. If this hidden knowledge existed, he was determined to find it. He would dedicate his life to it. If he found it, he knew he could shake the Old World Order to its core. He could usher in a new age of scientific enlightenment. That would be his legacy to the Northgate dynasty and to England.

Much of the rest of the first journal deals with the baron's preparations for his quest. He carried out extensive research work in libraries and museums around the country. He talked to scholars and Egyptologists, and he tracked down and purchased rare and ancient books. Eventually, a picture began to emerge. In 590 B.C. the Greek politician Solon visited the Egyptian administrative capital, Sais. There he was told a story of a highly advanced ancient civilisation that suddenly disappeared, due to a titanic natural catastrophe. Three generations later, his cousin Critias told the famous Greek philosopher Plato the tale. Plato gave the story to the world in two great works entitled "Timaeus" and "Critias." These two books are known as the earliest written references to the lost civilisation of Atlantis. According to the dates given by Plato, Atlantis was wiped off the face of the earth about 12,000 years ago. But there is evidence that remnants of the Atlantean civilisation survived.

The baron was much taken by a book written by a contemporary of his, Ignatius Donnelly. The book had the title "Atlantis and the Antediluvian World." In his book, first published in 1882, Donnelly pointed out the cultural and linguistic similarities between ancient Egypt and the ancient civilisations of South America. Both built pyramids, both embalmed their dead, both had a highly developed astronomy. To account for such similarities, the author postulated that an ancient culture, which originated in Atlantis, was carried eastward and westward by survivors of the doomed continent. To the baron, the theory had a compelling appeal.

Inspired by this rather tenuous evidence of a lost civilisation, the baron travelled to Egypt.

On this occasion, he took his wife with him. He spent three months visiting cities and historical sites in that ancient country. His wife did not take too well to the heat and contracted dysentery on a number of occasions. She left for England early. In those days, their love was still young and fresh, and the baron missed her. At first he pined for her, and his loneliness grew more intense with each passing day. But then he met Sir Anthony Burrows in the bar of the Windsor in Cairo. Sir Anthony had made his fortune in coal and had retired at the age of fifty-six. Now divorced, he spent much of the year in Egypt, digging for the "lost treasures of the ancients," as he liked to put it. Sir Anthony invited the baron to join him on one of his digs on the Giza peninsula, and things moved on from there. The baron stayed with the dig for a month. He learnt much and made some useful contacts.

There is no mention in any of the journals that I have read so far of the baron's life in England. The journals deal exclusively with his expeditions overseas, primarily in Egypt.

Journals 2-6

Journals 2-6 were dated 1886/7, 1887/8, 1888/9, 1889/90 and 1890/1, respectively. Journals 2-5 dealt with expeditions to Egypt. The baron started to co-finance digs with Sir Anthony Burrows. He brought many interesting artefacts back to England, including the occasional mummy.

Of the initial six journals, journal 6 proved to be the most interesting. In this journal, the baron indicated that he had now gained sufficient experience to organise his own digs. There is, however, no mention of a dig in journal 6. It deals exclusively with the baron's travels in the Middle East, tracking down rare manuscripts and ancient texts. The baron devoted a great deal of time over the initial six years of his expeditions in the Middle East to learning how to read and interpret hieroglyphs. The baron's findings from his research work are detailed below.

For centuries, people have been searching for a secret chamber that is believed to be hidden somewhere under the Giza peninsula. These days, noted the baron, Egyptologists ridicule the notion that such a chamber exists. He remained unconvinced by their arguments. In England, he talked with an eminent scholar who told him of a book called the "Korea Kosmou," a first-century manuscript belonging to a collection known as the "Hermetic Books." In this book, the Egyptian goddess Isis tells her son, Horus, that another god called Thoth (known to the Greeks as Hermes), inscribed the "great mysteries of the heavens" in sacred books, which he hid somewhere in Egypt. Thoth prophesised that, in the distant future, these books would be discovered by men referred to as the "worthy."

The scholar also mentioned the writings of ancient authors and historians. The work of the first-century Roman historian Pliny indicated that deep below the Sphinx is concealed the tomb of a ruler named Harmakhis that contained great treasure. The fourth-century Roman historian Ammianus Marcellinus wrote about the existence of subterranean vaults that led to the interior of the Great Pyramid. Iamblichus, a fourth-century scholar from Alexandria, recorded that ancient texts from Sumerian cylinder seals indicated that a secret entrance to the Sphinx was hidden under the sand. Interestingly, they describe the Sphinx as having the head of a lion. Herodotus, who visited Giza in the middle of the fifth century B.C., said that Egyptian priests recited to him their long-held tradition of the construction of underground chambers by the original architects of Memphis (Giza). These ancient writings, therefore, suggested that there were tunnels and secret chambers below the Giza plateau.

For some time now it appeared that the baron had lost his faith in God completely and had become an atheist. Looking at things with his "rational scientific mind," he considered the whole concept of gods, or divine super beings, as an illogical and superstitious mythology. To him, a far more rational explanation was that so-called gods were flesh and blood beings from an advanced civilisation who merely appeared god-like to the primitive cultures that they interacted with.

A German philologist he had met in Cairo brought an old papyrus to the baron's attention. It was called the "Westcar Papyrus," and was named after the Englishman who discovered it in 1824. It was believed to be over 3500 years old. The German afforded the baron with a translation. In the text the Pharaoh Khufu discussed a secret chamber of hidden knowledge. After reading this, the baron became convinced that a lost Hall of Records was not a myth, but an historical reality. At that point, he now fully believed that there was indeed a secret chamber that contained an ancient knowledge—a knowledge created by men, not gods.

The baron also indicated that he had come to learn that the Sphinx was referred to as "Aker," the guardian to the entrance of the Underworld, in a number of tomb paintings. An ancient book was written about the Sphinx, called the "Book of Aker." The baron commented that the Egyptologists believed that these texts were mythological and that they were essentially funerary works. They disputed that the texts could be literal references to a secret chamber under the Sphinx. Again, the baron did not hold with their views. He noted that there was more evidence suggesting the presence of a chamber under the Sphinx. A stone stela had been placed on the body of the Sphinx, between its front legs, by the Pharaoh Thutmose IV. On this stela, the Sphinx was depicted as sitting on top of a pedestal with a door underneath. This could have been the entrance to a chamber, or temple, under the Sphinx.

Towards the end of journal 6, the baron recorded his first meeting with Salim Hassan. The baron referred to Mr. Hassan as "Salim." The Egyptian engineer was brought to the baron's attention by Sir Anthony Burrows. Mr. Hassan had studied and worked in England for about eight years and spoke fluent English. Returning home, he developed a profound interest in Egyptology and had made quite a name for himself on a number of prominent digs. In addition to his extensive knowledge of the Giza plateau, Salim had a reputation as a very reliable and discrete man. Apparently the baron paid very generously for the Egyptian's discretion. He took him into his employ at three times the going rate. Even at this early stage, the baron had decided that there would be times when his excavations would have to be carried out in absolute secrecy.

CHAPTER 21
TEA AND FRUIT CAKE

ꕥ

There was no escaping the tutorial in the rooms of Dr. Frank Malone. Perched on the edge of the couch, with his notebook cradled on his knees, Alexander had his pen poised to record the next significant utterance. To his left was John, a tall, earnest, spotty young man, and to his right was Michiko, a small but very attractive Japanese girl, with beautifully painted toenails. To Alexander's mind, now occupied by far weightier matters than politics and economics, the tutorial seemed to drag on endlessly. The boy noticed that the Irish academic's eyes wandered frequently to the pert little feet of the Japanese girl, beautifully displayed in her pretty open-fronted high-heeled shoes.

I'll bet he's wondering why she is wearing those stupid shoes in this freezing weather, thought the boy, with the disarming logic of a child.

The tutorial finally drew to a close and Alexander's companions departed. "Right," said Frank enthusiastically, "you can put your bike in the back of the car, and we will head over to my place. There is much to talk about... I left a message with Anita to say that I would feed you tonight. How does pizza sound?"

ꕥ

Later, after they had wiped the residue of the delicious, but greasy meal from their mouths and where sipping Frank's full-bodied Irish tea, they got down to business.

"Thanks for updating me on your progress in the car on the way over," said Frank, settling into one of his comfortable leather chairs in the lounge. The journals had been stacked neatly into piles on the coffee table. "With one thing and another," continued the Irishman, "I have not had much of a chance to look through Baron Northgate's journals. It's a task that I was saving for the weekend." He took another swig of the dark steaming tea. Alexander sat close by on the settee, his eyes scanning the stacks of journals.

"Dr. Malone," responded Alexander, "as I mentioned, I've got as far as journal 6. It would appear that the baron's primary objective in visiting Egypt was to search for the lost Hall of Records. This he believed was hidden somewhere close to the pyramids on the Giza plateau. The baron was convinced that the ancient Egyptians had knowledge of an earlier, highly advanced civilisation, which had disappeared from the face of the earth. Based on what I would consider rather thin evidence, the baron was of the opinion that information relating to the identity, culture and scientific knowledge of this mysterious civilisation was stored in the lost Egyptian Hall of Records."

Alexander took another slug of the Irishman's tea. *Boy, is this strong*! He could feel the caffeine coursing through his veins. "Is there any convincing evidence that civilisation is a lot older than the mainstream archaeologists would have us believe?" he asked

Looking over at Alexander, Frank grinned. He was now hankering for a cigarette; he never lit one in the house, as he did most of his smoking outdoors. Smoking relaxed him and helped him concentrate. It was a stupid habit, he knew, but he was hooked. For the moment, he decided to resist the temptation.

"Well," he said, "I've read extensively in this area. At the end of the day, it is a matter of interpretation and belief.

But when you put the various strands of evidence together, it makes for interesting reading, to say the least. Mainstream Egyptology would have us believe that the Sphinx was built at the same time as the pyramids on the Giza plateau. At first they thought that it was Khafre that built the Sphinx, but it became clear, using sophisticated image analysis software, that the face of the monument did not match with known images of this pharaoh. There was a much better match for his father, the Pharaoh Khufu, although even here it is far from perfect. But just because the Sphinx has the face of a pharaoh does not necessarily mean that that pharaoh built it. The head is out of proportion in relation to the rest of the body. Its relatively small size suggests that it may have been carved from something that existed before it. It has been postulated by some that the Sphinx originally had on its shoulders the head of a lion, and not the head of a man. Relatively recently, a number of geologists who have considerable experience in the area of weather erosion have concluded that the limestone from which the Sphinx was carved has been subjected to the effects of heavy rainfall. Weather patterns that could have produced the characteristic gullies and grooves in the limestone have not been prevalent in Egypt for at least seven to eight thousand years. This strongly suggested that the Sphinx is considerably older than the pyramids. If this were true, then a major revision of current Egyptology would be required. Needless to say, there is not a great deal of enthusiasm for the findings of these geologists among orthodox Egyptologists."

Alexander stood up suddenly, indicating that he needed the bathroom. The tea was playing havoc with his bladder. Frank, never slow to miss an opportunity, nipped outside for a quick cigarette. A little later, they resumed the conversation.

"Another thing," said Frank, "ancient Egyptian astronomy and mathematics were impressive, even by modern standards. Moreover, the knowledge base for these sciences appears to have been complete from the very beginning of detectable Egyptian civilisation. Furthermore, there appears to have been no progressive evolution of the sciences over the centuries. Take the Great Pyramid, for example. It was believed to have been built about five thousand years ago, and the second and third Pyramids not long after that. Nothing the Egyptians did in later dynasties came close to these three pyramids. That is recognised by mainstream Egyptology, and raises many interesting questions."

Alexander nodded his head in agreement. "Many questions," he said, "but no definitive answers."

The Irishman sighed. He was dealing with a very sceptical young man. "True," he agreed, "but it makes it easier to see where ideas about an advanced civilisation predating the ancient Egyptian civilisation come from. And now, finally, hard evidence is starting to appear. A short time ago, two sunken cities were discovered in the Bay of Bengal, off the coast of the Indian subcontinent. The larger of the two cities stretches for eight kilometres and is of considerable sophistication. Some of the artefacts that have recently been retrieved from the city have been dated at over ten thousand years old. So, young man, solid evidence is starting to emerge that human civilisation is indeed far older than had been suspected. At the end of the last Ice Age, when sea levels rose dramatically, it now appears that these highly advanced civilisations were wiped from the face of the Earth. Much of the surviving evidence lies under the sea, and very excitingly, it is now starting to be rediscovered."

"Something of greater concern to me at the moment, Dr. Malone," said the boy, his face becoming graver, "is the continued existence of consciousness after death. As you know, I prefer clear proof to theories and beliefs. Whatever it was that attacked me in the tunnel was very real, and yet it had no body."

Frank did his best to suppress a shudder at the memory of the dreadful event. "Yes, it was definitely real," he agreed. "I heard that terrible shriek and the torches had fresh batteries; they were both drained of all power instantaneously. And of course, there was that awful eye on my bathroom mirror. We are definitely dealing with some kind of spirit entity here."

The boy, in pure exasperation, blurted, "But why is it trying to systematically annihilate my entire family? What have we done to deserve such an appalling fate? You'd have thought that it would have been satisfied by killing the baron. He was the one that violated its tomb."

Frank grimaced. "It's a mystery to be sure," he said. "I've never encountered anything like it before. But the thing is very real and it means to kill me, as well as you. We need to get to the bottom of this. We need to try and find the cause of its relentless fury, and as we both agree, the best place to start is with the journals."

Frank rose from his chair and sighed heavily. "We need to work our way through those journals as quickly as possible," he said.

Before he could start his next sentence, Alexander interjected with, "Would it be OK if I took the remaining ten journals back to the Gupta's? I'm a fast reader, as you know."

The Irishman's face stiffened. "It's still risky, you know," he rumbled. "Get a good night's sleep and come back here early tomorrow. I will call in sick and help you as best I can. It's nine o'clock now. Have an early night and we will get cracking first thing tomorrow. Now, let's be getting you home, young man."

CHAPTER 22
THE FIRKIN

ꟗ

For fieldwork, Zoe generally wore black training shoes. Having to move fast and unexpectedly was part of the job – no place for pointed heels. The trainers matched perfectly with her black leather trousers, dark red T-shirt and navy blue leather jacket. Tonight, she wore her hair straight, long and blond.

Finding out were Butch lived had been easy. Zoe talked to a lot of people and had many contacts. She got Butch's real name from a friendly bus driver she knew, and she found her address on the Oxford register of electors. Ann Crouch lived in a surprisingly upmarket neighbourhood. She had a flat in an imposing Edwardian house on a quiet North Oxford side road.

The private detective sat in her Mini-Cooper with the engine off, waiting for something to happen. *I'll stick with Butch,* she thought. *Ann Crouch – what a boring name. Even the bus drivers called her Butch. Impressive flat for a bus driver!* Losing sight of Mr. Flint in the parks had been a bad break. She would have to track Butch for the moment.

Tonight her luck was in. The big woman suddenly appeared, wearing black leathers. A silver motorbike stood close by, parked in the street. Mounting it, Butch dropped a black crash helmet over her head and cranked the engine.

"Game on," smiled Zoe.

The motorbike took off, but Zoe's car remained stationary. Pressing a button on the dashboard, a satellite navigation screen flashed on. This was no ordinary system; it doubled as a GPS tracking device and had cost a fortune to install, but if you followed people for a living, it was money well spent. She had guessed right. Butch was probably a biker, and the only motorbike close to her flat had been the big Triumph. Earlier, Zoe had attached an electronic transmitter unit to it; small, unobtrusive and magnetic, it was easy to conceal.

Zoe started up the Mini and was soon driving up the Banbury Road, following the progress of the flashing blue dot on the digital map display. It was clear that Butch was heading towards Kidlington. A short time later, the Mini drew to a halt in the car parks of the Firkin pub, just off the A34. She had seen the insides of many of the pubs around Oxford, but mostly when on the job and in disguise. The Firkin, she knew, was popular with gay women. Entering the lounge, she registered Butch sitting close to the bar and reading a newspaper. Zoe ordered herself a cranberry juice and took a seat at the far side of the lounge. She seldom drank alcohol while working.

It was an atmospheric pub, with its old flagstone floor, ancient oak tables and expensively upholstered red leather furniture. Being midweek and fairly early, the place was pretty quiet. A couple of old male regulars haunted the bar and a number of couples, mainly female, were dotted about. Tonight, Zoe was playing the part of estate agent Stephanie Jones. Half an hour passed and nothing much happened. Then, as she stifled a yawn, a woman walked in. Her hair, bleached blond, was closely cropped, and she wore no makeup. She looked like a farm labourer, in boots, work jeans and a thick, dark green fleece. Ordering a pint of bitter, she turned, scanning the room. Taking a large gulp from her glass, she made straight for the attractive woman with the long blond hair and lovely green eyes.

"Wrong disguise for a pub like this," cursed Zoe.

"Hi," said the big woman in the fleece. "Mind if I join you?"

Still in character, Zoe replied politely, "No offence, but I am expecting somebody soon. Business dinner, you know."

"Maybe see you later," winked fleece woman, moving to another table.

Time passed by and a few more drinkers entered the pub. Butch started on her second pint and struck up a conversation with fleece woman. Zoe was getting a little bored now. She went up to the bar and ordered herself another cranberry juice.

"No sign of your dinner date," shouted fleece woman from across the bar. Butch looked over and regarded the blond estate agent closely.

Damn, thought Zoe, *this isn't going well.*

"Must have got lost," she shrugged.

"Why not join us?" said fleece woman.

"Maybe a little later, if they don't show up," Zoe said and smiled.

It was time to leave, she knew, but preferably without blowing her cover. Returning to her seat, she began to sip her drink. Soon the two burley women were deep in conversation and Zoe took her chance. Moving swiftly, she was soon in the car park. It was dark now and nobody was about. Making her way towards the Mini, she searched a jacket pocket for her keys. As far as Zoe was concerned, handbags were an accident waiting to happen. She only used them when she absolutely had too.

Registering the sound of crunching gravel, Zoe spun around. Fleece woman was running towards her. *Not enough time to get into the car; anyway, can't have her seeing it.* Turning quickly, she waited for her admirer, with open arms. As they embraced, Zoe kissed the big woman full on the lips; then pushed her away provocatively and smiled. That moment of surprise was all she needed. Firing off a rapid straight-armed punch, karate style, she hit fleece woman hard in the solar plexus. The force of the punch drove the air from the big woman's lungs. Doubling up in agony, she fell to the ground, moaning. By the time she had staggered to her feet, Zoe was gone.

ꕥ

Frank Malone opened up the large brown envelope at home. He had guessed what it was. Sure enough, it was a progress report from Zoe Watts. "Not a lot of information for a week's wages," he grumbled. "Still, she got me a few names and an address."

He studied the photographs. *Nasty looking piece of work, that bloke. Could easily be a killer*. Then he chuckled. "Butch—great name—suits her perfectly, that bus driver."

Late in the evening, the telephone rang. It was Zoe Watts. "Did you get a chance to read the report?" she asked.

"Yes," responded Frank. "I see you've made some progress."

"But nothing much the last three days," said Zoe. "Butch, at least so far, appears to lead a surprisingly quiet life."

"So it would appear," responded Frank.

"I never rip off my clients," said Zoe. "Every day I draw a blank it costs you money... I suggest we suspend operations until I can get a line on Douglas Flint."

Frank was quite frustrated, but he did not like the look of Douglas Flint. He had a gut feeling that the man was a killer. For all her bravado, Zoe Watts was a woman, and he would never forgive himself if anything bad happened to her. He quite fancied her, actually. There was also the danger that Flint could find out that Frank was having him followed. Better to let sleeping dogs lie.

"I've changed my mind," he said. "Let's call it a day on this one—too much time and money. Forgetting about the matter is a much cheaper option."

"But not necessarily the best," said Zoe. "I'm sure those two are up to no good. That brown envelop pretty much confirms it."

"Well, my decision's final," said Frank emphatically

"As you wish," responded Zoe, rather disappointedly.

"What about meeting up again in the Star?" asked Frank hopefully. "I can pay you the rest of the money and buy you dinner."

"No thanks," said Zoe, without an explanation. "Just post me a cheque when you receive the invoice."

"No problem," said Frank, hanging up.

ꙮ

A sign on an unassuming single-story building in a side street off the Cowley Road stood out boldly. Written in large bold green letters were the words, "SHAMROCK CLUB," and in smaller letters, "Irish Guinness." To the uninitiated, that did not mean much, but if you were a lover of the black nectar, it meant a very great deal indeed. Irish Guinness was a different animal to the stuff brewed in England. It had a lot to do with the water. The Dublin brewery used crystal pure water, tinged with Irish magic. The English just used water. Nobody knew better than the Irish how easily Guinness bruised. It was a delicate masterpiece and had to be handled with care and respect. You could not just squirt it into a glass. It took patience—a minimum of two minutes to pour a pint. Guinness was an art form, not just a mere stout.

Inside the club, a red-haired, freckled barman placed a pint of Guinness in front of a woman with grey-green eyes. "Ta Pat," came the gruff voiced reply.

A small elderly man with a flushed face and a thick head of grey hair sauntered into the bar, which was empty except for the figure dressed in navy blue and wearing a black baseball cap.

"Hello, Kathleen!" he shouted.

Looking up from her paper, Kathleen smiled. "What's yer poison, Jim?" she asked with a strong Liverpudlian accent.

"The usual, thanks; God bless ya," came the reply.

The barman needed no further instruction and a pint of Irish bitter duly appeared on the bar. The Shamrock Club was one of the very few places that Zoe Watts removed the final mask. Real name, Kathleen Dolan, she was a working class girl brought up the hard way. Her fight had started the day she was born, and she had grown to like violence. But she had joined the club for the Guinness, not particularly for the wild company. Few women ever set foot in the Shamrock Club, so she could relax and be herself without fear of recognition. The male members were tight-lipped. What happened in the club stayed in the club. If a fight broke out—and with a clientele dominated by Irish ex-pats and exiles from Liverpool, it did happen—it was allowed to run its course. But when they started breaking the furniture, a pickaxe handle from behind the bar soon quietened things down.

Kathleen was just another drinker now, but it had not always been like that. There had been jibes and veiled insults to start with. One night a big drunken idiot went too far and tried to grope her. A quick snap punch to the throat and it was all over. She was respected after that.

Lifting her head from the paper, Kathleen took a thoughtful sip of Guinness. *Interesting article. Murder or suicide? The police were saying probably suicide, but they were still trying to trace a mysterious old man. He hadn't bought a ticket and just appeared on the platform around the time the death had occurred. Apparently the surveillance camera had conked out. The guy who died was a businessman, due in court on fraud charges. Just jumped in front of an express train – hell of a mess afterwards. They were leaning towards suicide. Bollocks – it was a professional hit.*

CHAPTER 23
AN AMAZING DISCOVERY

ꕤ

It was Saturday evening and Alexander's head was spinning. In the past two days he had read through all the remaining journals. He lay back in an easy chair in Frank Malone's lounge and closed his tired eyes. Term was drawing to a close and the long Christmas break was a luxury that he could no longer afford. He had learnt a great deal over the past week, but it was now clear that he had to locate the missing journal at all costs. He was convinced that it held the master key to the terrible mystery. Frank sat close by. He had read through what he considered the more pertinent of the journals, and he had been amazed by what he had read. If what was written was true, the baron had made a number of discoveries that would have created quite a stir in the realms of Egyptology, if they had been revealed to the world.

Their next course of action would need thinking through very carefully. The Irishman picked up a neatly typed report. *It will be interesting to learn what the boy makes of all this,* he thought, as he began to study the document.

Journal 7

In journal 7, which was written in 1891/2, the baron details his preparations for his first dig. In his own mind, he was convinced that many great secrets lay buried underneath the Giza plateau. From the evidence that he had been able to acquire, albeit fairly scant, the Sphinx seemed to be the best place to begin his search for the hidden Hall of Records. The days were long gone when he could just start digging close to such a famous monument as the Sphinx. He needed permission from the Egyptian Authorities, a "Firman," as it was called. Salim had been instructed to start working on this.

The idea was not to dig too close to the Sphinx, even if permission were granted. This would attract too much unwelcome attention. The baron noted that others had tried to break into, and excavate under the Sphinx earlier in the century. None had been successful. One of the problems was the many thousands of tons of sand that had accumulated in the Sphinx enclosure, and now covered much of the body of the mighty statue.

The baron recorded his surprise as to how strong Freemasonry was in Egypt, now a modern Muslim country. Salim had informed the baron that he himself was a member of the Brotherhood. The baron was, of course, fully aware that at the highest levels of the Order there was a secret knowledge relating to the monuments on the Giza plateau, not least of all, the Sphinx. Salim indicated that he had some high-level contacts and would make some enquiries.

The baron recalled his intense excitement when Salim informed him that he had had a meeting with a gentleman who said he had access to an ancient plan diagram of the Sphinx. The baron wanted to buy this immediately and asked Salim to get hold of it. Money was no object. He was immensely disappointed to learn that the diagram was not for sale at any price. Further negotiations ensued and Salim was eventually able to secure a hand-drawn copy of the papyrus. There was no way of knowing if this was an accurate copy, or even if the original was genuine, but they both agreed that it was better than nothing, and a good place to start.

When the baron eventually got his hands on the sketch, he was quite impressed. It had been carefully drawn, rather than hastily scribbled. He questioned Salim further about its likely authenticity. As the baron was also a Freemason, Salim told him more than he would otherwise have done. Apparently the origin of the papyrus was mysterious. It was displayed very carefully under glass in a secret room in a Freemasons lodge in Cairo. The room was used for initiation into the highest levels of the Brotherhood. Apparently, such initiations had their origins in secret chambers on the Giza plateau. The baron warned Salim that from now on, their work would have to take place in complete secrecy.

The first thing that the baron noticed was that the Sphinx, as depicted in the drawing, was much larger than the monument on the Giza plateau in the nineteenth century. This shrinking effect was due to the progressive accumulation of sand in the Sphinx enclosure. According to the plan, the Sphinx sat on top of a chamber, hollowed out of the limestone. Directly in front of the Sphinx was a large temple. The baron noted that in his era there was just sand in front of the Sphinx. If the temple had existed, it had been buried At the rear of the temple was a concealed entrance that led through to the chamber under the Sphinx. In the baron's view, this was probably a secret door that could only be opened by the priests of the temple.

The entrance to the chamber was about thirty feet below the front paws of the Sphinx and was accessed by a flight of steps. What a magnificent sight this mighty monument and its temples must have looked in the Old Kingdom, before it was forgotten and buried by the desert. It was no wonder that the entrance to the Sphinx had lain undiscovered for millennia. Over forty feet of sand and rubble had concealed it.

Beyond the entrance lay a chamber that was about sixty feet long and at least ten feet high. It had been carved through the limestone bedrock that was underlying the Sphinx. At the end of the chamber was a tunnel that led to a second chamber below the hind flanks of the monument. This chamber was about thirty feet in length. At the end of this chamber was another tunnel. Underneath the cross-sectional diagram of the Sphinx was a second diagram, which was an overhead view of the plateau. This showed a maze of intersecting passageways and chambers, leading from the rear of the Sphinx that ultimately connected with the Third, Second and Great Pyramids.

It was a number of days before the baron and Salim came up with a plan. Subject to permission from the authorities, they would carry out a series of shallow excavations close to the Temple of the Sphinx. This was an ancient building, situated to the left of, and about four hundred feet from the front of the Sphinx. The plan of the Sphinx and surrounding area clearly indicated an underground passage running from the rear right hand corner of the Sphinx Temple for about 700 feet. It intersected a common passageway that lay close to the underground chamber at the rear of the Sphinx. From there, access could be gained to the labyrinth, or the underbelly of the Sphinx itself.

The story that they would tell the authorities was that they were searching for artefacts that would hopefully give new insights into the purpose and history of the Sphinx monument. The Sphinx Temple seemed a logical place to start. The real objective, which the baron wanted to keep secret at all costs, was to locate the tunnel at the back of the Sphinx temple and use this to penetrate into the Sphinx itself, but this would obviously take a great deal of time and thought to bring to fruition. Permission was granted for them to commence the dig. They were true to their word and confined their activities to superficial excavations, but the stage was now set.

Journal 8

In journal 8, dated 1892/3, the baron returned to the Giza peninsula. It soon became clear that there would be no easy, but more importantly, discrete way of locating the tunnel from the temple. Deeper excavations revealed that below the desert sand there was a bed of solid limestone. Even if they knew the exact location of the tunnel, it could take years to chisel discretely through the rock and locate the hidden passageway. Both Salim and the baron reluctantly concluded that they would have to find another way. The baron returned to England early, leaving Salim to continue with his enquiries.

Journal 9

In journal 9, dated 1893/4, the baron embarked on his next journey to the Giza peninsula, with considerable excitement. Salim had located an ancient church in the old district of Cairo. In the basement of that church was an entrance to an underground river. With all speed, the baron made for the church. The entrance to the hidden river was a closely guarded secret. It was by pure chance that he met a Coptic priest who told him of the river. In return for a very generous donation to the church maintenance fund, and an assurance to keep the location confidential, the priest revealed that the entrance to the river was in the crypt of his church.

The baron recorded that he entered the crypt with a pounding heart. The priest guided them to an old iron gate, about seven feet high and four feet wide. Beyond the gate, they found themselves in a tunnel that had been carved through the bedrock. Salim questioned the priest about the origins of the tunnel and what he knew of the river beyond. The priest said that he knew very little. The tunnel and the river had been there since ancient times. He also said that he had had no interest in exploring the river, but his predecessor at the church had told him that it eventually opened into an underground lake.

After thirty feet or so, they came to the river. They were in a shallow cavern, and the river flowed slowly past them into the darkness beyond the light of the priest's lantern. The river was about three feet below them and could be reached by steps cut into the rock. The priest told them that over the centuries the level of the river had been slowly rising. He said that they had come at an opportune moment, because it was only a matter of time before the river inundated the crypt, sealing the entrance to the underground lake.

It took a couple of weeks to prepare for their exploration of the underground river. They needed two sturdy canoes, photographic equipment, lanterns, ropes, excavation tools, a tent and supplies. The baron decided that Salim alone would accompany him on this expedition. He was the only one that he could trust, if he could really trust anyone, that is. A few eyebrows were raised when the equipment was delivered outside the church. The priest helped them get the canoes and equipment onto the mooring and into the river. He pointed them left, telling them that the river eventually disappeared under a rock outcrop in the other direction.

Setting off, the baron took the lead. The canoes moved with the current and made good progress. The baron inspected the banks of the river carefully. It appeared that the steps that they had used to reach the water were the only entry point onto this mysterious river. After thirty minutes or so, the waterway opened abruptly into a large underground lake. They found themselves floating in a vast cavern. The amazing thing was that they had no more need of the lanterns. Ahead of them, the cavern was illuminated, as if by moonlight. Salim began to shout and point. In the distance, they could see a shoreline of golden sand. They both gasped in astonishment at the sight before them. It was an ancient underground city.

As the canoes got closer, the baron could discern the layout of the city. It appeared to be meticulously planned on a grid system similar to a modern American city. They beached the canoes on the shore and were soon walking on the stone roadways of the lost city. The only sound was the gentle lapping of the water on the shoreline. The baron's thermometer registered a temperature of 68^0 F. He noted that this was a good deal cooler than the surface temperature at this time of the year, and would have been an excellent place to live during the scorching Egyptian summer months. The buildings were in surprisingly good condition. Most were a single story high with flat roofs. The baron selected one such dwelling and indicated to Salim that they would set up camp there.

When all of the equipment was unloaded and they had refreshed themselves, they began to explore the city. Their findings have been very briefly summarised below. Although an ancient city, it was of incredible sophistication. There were a number of structures that looked like temples, built using enormous limestone blocks. There were stables, workshops, other unidentifiable buildings and even a palace. They discovered a complex drainage system of hydraulic underground waterways. Amazingly, some of the more elaborate buildings had sit-down toilets, constructed of a marble-like stone. Salim estimated that the city could have supported a population of up to ten thousand people.

It became evident that the light that illuminated the city was emanating from transparent spherical crystalline globes embedded in the walls and the roof of the cavern. The globes were about the size of footballs. The baron was utterly amazed. In all his days, he had never seen anything like this. This was far beyond any technology that he knew of in the Western World. Lights that had probably been burning for thousands of years seemed an impossibility Many of the globes were covered in dust, noted the baron. He guessed that when they were first installed, it would have been as bright as daylight in that cavern. The baron could hardly contain his excitement. Already, they had made the discovery of the century, and they had hardly started.

The baron and his assistant spent the rest of the season travelling to and from the hidden city. They drafted detailed maps of the layout and took photographs of the buildings. It was evident that the city had lain deserted for a very long time. It must have been visited over the generations by people who were told of its location, for there were no remaining artefacts other than broken pottery. According to Salim, the pottery fragments appeared to date from the Old Kingdom. There were hieroglyphs and wall paintings in the temples and palace. The baron, who indicated that they would be subjected to careful study when he returned to England, photographed all of them.

Journal 10

The baron detailed his findings from the hieroglyphs and wall paintings in Journal 10, dated 1894/5. He also talked of another incredible discovery. Only the baron and Salim had access to the photographs of the lost city. The baron knew that it would probably be many years before he was ready to face the world with his discoveries. Hieroglyphs from one of the temples clearly indicated that the city was very, very old. Even in the Old Kingdom, it was viewed as ancient. It was considered a sacred city, a city which only the "Worthy" could inhabit. The city was refurbished by one of the early pharaohs, but the baron does not mention his name. It was inhabited by priests and initiates.

From time to time, the pharaohs themselves would visit and live there for a while on spiritual retreat. This discovery alone could have made the baron world famous, but he had far greater ambitions. He knew now that he would have to bind Salim closely to him. He would reward the Egyptian extremely handsomely for his silence.

The months went by and they continued their meticulous study of the city. One day, as the season was drawing to a close and the baron's thoughts were turning to his return trip to England, he heard a yell from Salim. Sprinting to an adjoining room in a temple that they were exploring, he found Salim clutching a glistening spherical object. His assistant indicated that he had found it by chance when he had tripped over a small pile of rubble. On clambering to his feet, he found the object lying right in front of him. They cleaned the dust off it to reveal a beautiful crystalline ball about the size of a grapefruit. At the centre of the crystal was a tablet, inscribed with a series of exquisitely etched miniature hieroglyphs. They would need a magnifying glass to read the tablet. Naturally, the baron took charge of the crystal. Salim knew that he would never see it again.

Journal 11

In Journal 11, dated 1895/6, the baron indicated that his discoveries in the cavern were momentous, and that from now on he would use separate journals (with blue covers) to record artefacts or knowledge that he wished to keep highly secret. The baron recorded that he was able to translate the hieroglyphs that were etched into the core of the crystal. How on earth anybody, let alone a so-called mechanically primitive civilisation, could achieve such a feat was beyond him. The translation of the message in the crystal was so earth shattering that the baron wrote it down in the first of the blue journals. His business concluded on the Northgate Estate, he headed back to the hidden city with all due haste. The rest of the journal is blank.

Journal 12

In Journal 12, dated 1896/97, the baron recorded that he was only briefly in Egypt, and that he had left his trusted assistant to handle a series of digs. The locations of the excavations were indicated, but nothing of relevance to the lost Hall of Records appeared to have been discovered.

Journals 13-16

Journals 13-16, dated 1897/98, 1898/99, 1899/1900 and 1900/01, are along a similar theme. Salim was deployed to handle the continued digging activity. The baron spent much of his time in England, supervising the construction of his giant obelisk.

Conclusion

The baron's primary objective in visiting Egypt was to search for lost knowledge relating to a highly advanced civilisation that predated the ancient Egyptian civilisation. He hoped to make discoveries that would change the course of history and immortalise the Northgate name. A major breakthrough in his investigations came with the discovery of the hidden underground city. It is probable that the message etched into the mysterious crystal gave him some critical information in relation to his quest for the hidden Hall of Records. Much of his findings beyond journal 10 were probably recorded in the blue journals. To progress any further in our own investigations we must, at all costs, locate these journals.

CHAPTER 24
THE MUMMY

ဢ

The Irishman stood, glowering at the boy. "I want you to promise me," he said sternly, "that you will not return to that house over the Christmas holidays."

Alexander looked at him with wide innocent eyes. "I'd hoped," he said rather dejectedly, "that we could go back to Northgate Hall together to retrieve the blue journals. We can make no further progress without those journals."

The Irishman was unmoved. He dropped his voice an octave and spoke like low rumbling thunder. "We both need a break. The nervous strain of these past months has been too much. It's important that we take some time out to clear our heads. Trust me, Alexander, this is the best way forward." Pausing momentarily, he looked at the boy with stern unblinking eyes and then said, "That is my final word on the subject. Come to my house at the beginning of the new term. Now promise me, boy!"

Dropping his eyes, Alexander sighed. "After what happened the last time, I would be too scared to venture back there alone," he muttered. Then suddenly, his face brightened. "Thank you, Dr. Malone, for all your help and support. I got you into this mess, so the least I can do is let you have your holiday in peace." With that, he said farewell.

Alexander could hear the sound of his reverberating footsteps as he ran down the icy black tunnel. *It wasn't a lie,* he thought. *I was scared then, but now something is driving me with irresistible force; like an addiction. I can't control it. I have to get those journals. If the thing attacks me I'm ready this time; I have protection.*

His mind was surprisingly calm. It had taken him two weeks to prepare for this trip, but now he was ready. He had told his parents that he was spending the day in the library, which was true, in a bizarre sort of a way. It was no great effort to cycle to Northgate Hall on his electric bike—just cold. He climbed the gate with relative ease, using his grappling hook and a blanket, and made his way to the house. He knew the route to the library now and had no intention of lingering in the passageways. There was no alternative. He had to search the library and the secret room from top to bottom. In the boy's mind, finding the missing journals was literally a matter of life or death.

As Alexander moved into the cellar, his courage began to fail him slightly. Pressing on his I-Pod, AC/DC exploded into his ears. Pulses of energy and aggression began to course through him as the music took hold of his mind. Inspired by newly-found bravery, he forged forward. Sprinting up the stairs, he ran down the corridors towards the library. Panting heavily, he reached the enormous room and pushed the stiff old doors together until they were tightly closed behind him. Retrieving a hammer from the pile of tools that they had discarded on their previous visit to the library, he knocked a series of door wedges under the doors to seal them shut. Next, he removed a necklace of garlic and hung it over both door handles. He also tied together the handles with a sturdy piece of rope, further increasing the security of the doors. The garlic was to ward off the evil entity. His researches had indicated that numerous herbs could help in repelling evil spirits, and that garlic was one of the most effective. While he was sceptical about this, he was prepared to try anything.

Alexander was a brave boy. Not many grown men, never mind boys, would entertain doing battle alone with an evil entity in the blackness of a menacing old house. But Alexander felt that he was marked for death and his only hope was to fight. Not only that, he had gotten someone else involved as well, and condemned them to death in the process. To defeat this thing, he had to find out what was driving its relentless rage—a rage so terrible that it would soon obliterate the entire Northgate family from the face of the Earth. He needed to find those blue journals at all costs, and he had no choice but to do it alone.

His task completed, he moved swiftly towards the secret room where they had found the red journals. It was the most logical place to start the search for the blue journals. The music gave him comfort in the eerie black silence as he stood in front of the glass-faced book cabinets.

Suddenly the boy started in shock. Something had brushed against his forehead! His gaze shot upward. The large, ugly spider that had collided with him was retreating hastily up a silken thread, back to its lair in the cobwebs above; the loathsome creature was just as startled as the boy. Shivering now, he felt that familiar sense of unease growing in the pit of his stomach. Reluctantly, he switched off his I-Pod. At first he could hear nothing, only the terrible menacing silence of Northgate Hall. Then the air became suddenly disturbed. Outside, he could hear the wind blowing. Soon it was coming in powerful gusts, growing in ferocity with every second. The old house began to creak as the wind, now a roaring tempest, blasted against it, howling and moaning down the massive chimneys.

"Great!" he hissed, "I'm trapped! There's no way I can leave the house in this storm, not without running a gauntlet of lightening bolts!" He tried to focus his attention on the book cabinets. Sliding back one of the glass doors on the first cabinet, he began to scan the books. There was no sign of any journals, blue or otherwise. Slowly and carefully, he worked his way through the other book cabinets. As he was reaching the end of the final row of ancient looking books, he stiffened suddenly. Through the terrible cries of the wind he could hear a sound—an unmistakable sound. He stood there, hoping against hope that the wind was causing it, but no! The sound was getting louder and it was coming down the passageway towards the library. It was the sound of heavy footsteps thudding against the old oak floor—slow and deliberate, almost mechanical. Petrified, the boy knew that he was cornered now, cornered like a rat with nowhere to run. He had prepared himself the best that he could for the onslaught of a spirit, an entity without a body whose main weapon was fear, but this was different. Whatever was out there sounded solid—as solid as stone.

Alexander slipped back silently into the main library, desperate to track the source of the sounds. He could hear them with horrifying clarity now. The lumbering footsteps came to a halt outside the big wooden doors, which now seemed flimsy. For what appeared like an unbearable eternity, there was silence. Moving closer to the doors, he strained his ears to pick up the slightest noise, but all he could hear was the crying of the wind. *There has to be another way out of here!* he thought frantically.

As he turned to make his way back to the secret room, he heard a new sound, faint at first, but then louder. It was the sound of fingers scratching and searching the doors! As he froze in horror, there came an even worse sound. It was the sound of laughter—a manic, mocking laughter. He turned to run.

A massive bang crashed through the air and the doors shook violently, then all fell silent except for the horrible howling of the wind. Alexander began to tremble. His nerves were at the razor's edge now, strung so taut that he felt like his brain would explode. Another sickening bang ripped through the air and an ironclad fist exploded through one of the door panels, showering splinters over the petrified boy. Blow after shattering blow rained down on the doors. Then, with a groan, one of the doors shuddered violently and gave way, toppling forward, its hinges wrenched from the lintel.

With wild, bulging eyes, Alexander stared in utter disbelief. There before him stood a hulking metal clad monster. It towered above him like a horrible iron vulture. The breastplate was rusted in places, but solid. Underneath the breastplate and enveloping the exposed areas of the upper body was dull grey chain mail. Even in this moment of mortal danger, Alexander's vast brain was analysing the armour. It was state-of-the-art fifteenth century, with faulds and tassets protecting the abdomen, lower back and hips; cuisses, poleyns and greaves protecting the legs; and sabatons shielding the feet. The metal was still solid. Motionless now, the monster loomed above the petrified child like a giant bird of prey.

Suddenly, the suit of armour lurched forwards, its metal feet rising slowly and then crashing down. It carried no weapon, but its mailed knuckles were studded with spikes. Slowly, one of its arms began to rise, its huge fist clenched in readiness to crush the boy's skull. Alexander could feel the hatred, the malevolence in the thing as it moved towards him.

All rational thought was banished now. His mind was lost to fear. An awful icy nausea rose up inside him. He had reached the borders of madness, the point at which sanity can snap in an onslaught of horror, or the body bereft of reason takes flight in blind screaming panic. The deadly fist flew past him, its metal spikes grazing his forehead. As the monster steadied itself for the fatal blow, stinging pain returned the boy to his senses and anger welled up inside him. Turning, he fled from the lumbering beast.

The library was lit by one of the two lanterns that he had brought with him. They were Victorian diving lanterns, a much safer bet than the battery powered torches that they had used the last time. He made for the hidden room, where the second lantern was burning. The floor shook as the metal thing thundered after him. Grabbing the bookcase door, he pulled it shut behind him. His mind was racing now. There was another explosion as an iron fist crashed through the wood. Cowering, Alexander cursed his own stupidity. His fate was sealed. There was nowhere else to run.

The wind howled and wailed, as if in lament for the boy's impending death. A second blow crashed through the bookcase. In desperation, and trembling violently, he grabbed one of the crowbars that they had discarded on their previous visit and smashed the glass doors of the first book cabinet. Desperately, he threw the books from the shelves as a third blow shattered another hole in the secret door. Using the crowbar, he levered with all his might. The book cabinet came away easily from the wall. At first he tugged it, and then he pushed it towards the remnants of the door. Blow after blow fell on the door; it was being systematically demolished, section by section. Soon all that would lie between the boy and certain death was the empty book cabinet.

Instinctively, Alexander searched the exposed wall for a concealed door. His heart leapt as his desperate fingers met a small circular hole similar to the one that he had found in the pedestal of the sphinx. Pushing with all his might against the wall, he failed to budge it. The key was useless now, but he still had the stem with him. Pulling it from his pocket in wild panic, he inserted it into the hole. Behind him, the book cabinet started to move. It was being pushed slowly to one side, as if the monster was toying with its helpless victim, feeding on the terror of his screeching mind. Frantically, Alexander started to turn the stem of the key to and fro in some crazy hope that something would happen. Suddenly, there was a crunching sound as the glass vial within the stem shattered.

A vile, horrible hollow laugh echoed in his ears as the cabinet inched slowly forward. The iron-clad thing was closing in for its bloody feast, and then a clunking sound came from behind the wall. Alexander's razor brain immediately registered that a corrosive fluid must have been released from the glass vial and deactivated a locking mechanism behind the wall. He steadied himself for a shoulder charge at the wall, but in that instant a metal hand gripped him from behind and lifted him effortlessly off the floor. In screaming panic, his fingers searched through one of his pockets.

The creature laughed again as it wrapped an enormous arm around the boy's chest, intent on crushing the life from him. Seconds from death, and with violent pain shooting through his chest, Alexander raised his right arm and fired at the iron assassin. In his hand he held a spray bottle filled with sacred Ganges water and extracts of lavender, heather, garlic, angelica and agrimony. These plants were used to ward off evil spirits, and they saved Alexander's life.

Recoiling from the spray, the monster dropped the boy. Spinning around in a fury, Alexander sprayed directly into the helmet of the leviathan. Clutching desperately at its head, it crashed to its knees. Tearing open the visor of its helmet, Alexander fired into the black void with savage ferocity. Collapsing, the thing lay still, a motionless pile of metal.

Straining every muscle fibre to the limit, Alexander pushed against the stonework of the wall. The concealed door moved slowly forward. Grabbing the lantern, he squeezed through the gap in the wall, and taking no chances, heaved the stone door closed behind him. The door had a different locking mechanism to the hidden doors that he had encountered previously. A heavy lever had been propped up in the locked position by a small piece of wood, now burnt away by the acid in the vial. This mechanism had been designed so the wood could be dislodged by acid or a sharp poke with a rod from the other side of the door. With the wood removed, the lever would fall by its own weight into the open position.

The problem that faced Alexander now was how to relock the door, just in case the armoured beast was revived by the terrible entity. Fortunately, there was a big metal hook secured to the door, about ten centimetres above the lever.

This was obviously a design feature that allowed the door to be permanently locked by looping a piece of rope around the lever and tying it off at the hook. He found some string in one of his pockets. That would do the job nicely.

With the door secured, the boy flopped to the floor. That had been the worst ordeal of his life, even worse than his brush with death at the obelisk. His chest was sore and his head was throbbing. He needed time to think. Pulling out a bottle of energy drink from his rucksack, he used it to wash down some painkillers. Some time later, his head began to clear.

The wind vanished as suddenly as it had arisen. Sitting there in the uneasy silence, Alexander surveyed his surroundings. The air was musty and stale, like the air in an ancient crypt. In the light of the lantern, it was clear that he was in a small antechamber. Abutting the wall in front of him, he could see another glass-faced cabinet.

The aches in his body began to subside under the influence of the painkillers, and he decided it was time to move again; this was no place to linger. Getting up a little unsteadily, he took hold of the lantern and walked towards the cabinet. *This is obviously were the most sensitive books were kept,* he thought as he slid the grimy glass door open. Curious as he was, there was no time to waste. He picked his way through the moulding volumes. There was no sign of the missing red journal, but on the bottom shelf he discovered a dusty package. Grabbing it, he ripped off the cloth wrapping. To his intense relief and satisfaction he found two books; they were clearly journals. Although discoloured, it was evident as he peered closely at them in the yellow lantern light, that their covers were originally blue.

With the journals securely stowed in his backpack, Alexander began to move forward. Ahead of him a stone stairway was visible, leading downwards. Swivelling around, he shone the lantern in the opposite direction. On the wall directly in front of him, he could see another locking mechanism. It was similar to the one that he had just encountered. The lever was secured in the raised position by a piece of rope. Walking over to it, he tugged at the rope. It slipped away easily from the shiny black metal and the lever dropped down. Tugging at the lever, the stone door slid towards him with surprisingly little effort. Through the opening, he could see a curved stonewall. This was obviously a tower. Tentatively, he ventured forward, but came to a sudden halt as he noticed a big oak door to his right. The door was ajar.

This must lead directly into the house. It's too risky to proceed in this direction. I need to find the safest way out of this place. I'll return another time with Dr. Malone.

Alexander retraced his steps and firmly locked the stone doorway behind him. Moving towards the stairway, he descended cautiously. The steps ended in another small chamber. The light from the lantern picked out a locking mechanism in one of the walls. *The house is riddled with secret doors and passages. Many must date back to the Elizabethan era but others are the work of the baron.*

He guessed that this concealed door would lead into an underground tunnel, which would eventually feed into the big stone chamber that they had encountered on their first visit to Northgate Hall. A deep sigh echoed hollowly off the stone. He had found a quick way out of the accursed house. Levering open the door, he stepped into a dank tunnel that was lined with dust-laden cobwebs. The tunnel only ran in one direction, so there was no decision to be made here. Moving as rapidly as he could, he ventured forward into the darkness. After a short while, a stairway leading upward appeared out of the blackness. Approaching it, he could see that the tunnel turned hard left. He decided to investigate the steps in the hope that this would be the quickest way out into the daylight.

ꙮ

The forgotten gardens lay drab and misty under a grey sky, swollen with rain clouds. High above, the old house stood glowering in the gloom. Suddenly, a stone slab at the base of the enormous terrace below the house was pushed aside and a blond head peered out. Sucking fresh air into his lungs, Alexander crawled through the opening and into the blessed light of day.

"Yesss!" he hissed, punching at the sky. Soon he would be home free, or at least that was what he thought. Looking around him, everything seemed still and strangely silent. There was not even a hint of a breeze, but the clouds hung heavy and menacing above him. The stillness unnerved him. Tugging up his hood, he took a deep breath and started to move around the side of the house. The stillness grew more sinister.

Picking his way through the tangled mess of the grounds, he headed towards the relative safety of the woods. A sense of unease started to seep into him again and his flesh grew colder. Fine drizzly rain began to fall as the light of the day slowly faded. Alexander looked at his watch. It was 3.30 p.m. He picked up his pace, but then a sudden urge made him stop and look back. The house stood, lonely and desolate, its stonework shining in the gentle rain. *It's just a house, built by men, from rock, bricks, wood and glass. It is the home of my ancestors – once a warm and beautiful home, now made cold and terrible by the dreadful thing that dwells within.*

Wiping the rain from his eyes, he turned and hurried on. His flesh grew colder still, and then he heard it! A quiet mocking whisper drifted through the still air.

"Alexander! Alexander!" it called.

Heart pounding in his ears, the boy began to run. The sky grew darker, and in the distance a slow, dull rumble rolled across the clouds.

"That sounds like thunder!" he gasped as he reached the tree line.

"Alexander! Alexander!" called the ghastly voice.

His breath was coming hard and fast now, but the big gates were in sight. Suddenly, he started violently, as an almighty thunderclap blasted from the clouds. Missing him by inches, a massive lightening bolt exploded into a tree, shattering it to pieces. Thrown off his feet, Alexander lay stunned in a pile of broken and smouldering wood. Quickly regaining his senses, he crawled forward, desperately trying to reach the gates.

At last he could feel the cold metal in his hands; he was almost free! Hauling himself to his feet, he gathered himself for the climb, but then he heard it again.

"Alexander! Alexander!" called the vaporous voice.

Knowing there was nothing for it, he turned to face the thing. The sky roared with savage ferocity and another lightening bolt thundered towards him. Instinctively, he dived forward as a powerful explosion blew the gates to fragments. Staggering frantically to his feet, he searched the sky for the next attack. He was fortunate indeed not to have been impaled by the shattered iron.

A mocking, horrible laugh pierced though him. Dropping his gaze, Alexander stared through the trees in front of him. An uncontrollable spasm of terror shot through him as the terrible vision approached. Pushing through the undergrowth, the creature moved relentlessly towards him. The boy's legs trembled so violently now that he feared that they would give way.

In a heartbeat, the mummy stood directly before him, its head bent forward. The terrible bandaged corpse was looking at him, regarding him like some insect ready for crushing. Legs buckling, Alexander fell to his knees. Slowly, awfully, the bandage concealing the mummy's head began to unravel, as if being peeled away by some unseen hand. The ancient wrapping rose above the mummy like a vast uncoiling tapeworm. At first it was only the tangled black hair that was visible, springing out from under the bandage. Then the forehead was exposed – brown and vitrified. And then the vast black unblinking eyes were unveiled. They stared remorselessly at the trembling boy, spearing him with hatred. Slowly, the bandage unravelled from the shrunken nose and the vile mouth. The hideous thing was grinning at him, black lips parted from rotting teeth, and skin drawn tight over a terrifying scull-like face. Slowly, the corpse leant forward and a bony, bandaged hand grasped at the stricken boy. Recoiling suddenly in utter horror, blind panic drove him to his feet. Turning, he ran, as a blood-curdling shriek burst through his ears. Crashing wildly through the trees beyond the broken gates, he could hear the pounding steps of the mummy close behind him.

The rain fell heavier now, blurring his vision, and low lying branches clawed at him as he fled. With lungs close to exploding, he fought his way through the last of the tangled barriers and out onto the road. As he stood there, desperately sucking in oxygen, the thing came at him again, its gnarled fingers clawing at his face. Too stunned to think, he fell backwards. Leaning over him, the mummy's horrible hands reached for his throat. But at the instant of certain death, Alexander grasped the handle of the cricket bat. Dragging it from the rucksack, he swung it hard and fast, smashing through the right leg of the creature. Springing to his feet as the mummy fell, he aimed another swift blow at its head. As the bat hit home, the terrible thing burst into dust.

"Just another one of your tricks!" spat the boy, still gasping.

CHAPTER 25
UNDER THE PAW

Ꟊ

The feeling of euphoria died the moment Alexander arrived back home. He felt drained; his nerves badly frayed by an experience that would have driven many a sane man mad. The stress proved too much for his immune system and the following morning he did not make it out of bed. Influenza had gripped him. The nights did not come easy. His sleep was fitful, restless. He sweated and tossed violently, trying to escape the shadows that haunted him. At every turn there was a feeling of dread and foreboding, a sense of the dark thing watching him, stalking him, waiting for its chance to finish him. And the memory of that terrible face, those awful staring eyes, and that hideous grin, pierced his troubled dreams.

It was a week before he had the strength to look at the journals. His body still felt heavy and drained, his mind stale and tired, and his nerves on edge, but he knew that he had to move on. The clock was ticking and the new term was drawing closer. He had to get to the bottom of those journals before Dr. Malone returned. After forcing down some breakfast, he set to work on the first of the two journals. The style of writing was different from that in the red journals. The words flowed seamlessly, like the narrative of a story. It was strange, reading those words, almost like he had once been there and the words were reminding him of forgotten memories. Pictures flooded his mind.

ꙮ

The year was 1896. The baron had set up camp in the underground city and had made the preparations for further exploration. Salim took up position at the front of one of the canoes, with the baron behind him.

"So," said the Egyptian, the pitch of his voice betraying his excitement, "the moment of truth is upon us, Baron. The final goal is at last in sight."

The baron shifted a little uneasily. "I am not so sure, Salim," he replied. "Giza is very reluctant to give up its secrets. This is a dangerous quest and we will need to tread carefully. Men have died and will continue to die in this mysterious place."

He scratched a match and the flame bit into the end of a fresh cigar. "Let us proceed as planned," he continued.

Cutting the surface of the lake, the paddles propelled them forward. The baron studied the compass needle closely. They were heading in the direction of the monuments on the Giza peninsula. As they moved deeper into void of the cavern, the light that illuminated the underground city slowly dimmed. The message engraved in the crystal was clear; the underworld was a reality, not a myth. It was the hidden realm beneath the Giza peninsula. They were floating in this underworld, and soon they hoped to find the second entrance to this mysterious place—the entrance guarded by the Sphinx. If they could find this entrance, they firmly believed that they would be able to penetrate the fabled underbelly of the Sphinx.

Eventually, the cavern began to narrow, tapering into a tunnel that had been carved through the rock by water erosion over countless millennia. The tunnel was about thirty feet wide, but its roof was only about five feet above the water line.

"I fear that the water level has been rising over the years," muttered Salim. "I would warrant that in ancient times it would have been possible to navigate a large barge or boat through here."

They entered the tunnel. At times they had to duck their heads, as great chunks of jagged rock protruding from the roof leapt into the lantern light. After about thirty minutes the tunnel widened into a second cavern, somewhat smaller than the first. To their left and about fifty feet away they could make out the outline of the cavern wall. Pointing the canoe in that direction, they started to follow the perimeter of the cavern. It did not take long before a hole in the rock-face appeared in the distance. They had found it!

Drawing closer, they could see a stone jetty, mainly submerged. Soon they had moored the canoe and were scrambling unsteadily onto the last remaining step above the waterline. Ahead of them was a tunnel, rising gently upwards. Pensive, even apprehensive, they stood peering into the darkness. The baron felt suddenly nervous, like the first time he had set eyes on the magnificent woman who was destined to become his wife. He was wonderstruck and tongue-tied when she had walked into the ballroom. It took every ounce of courage that he possessed to approach her for a dance, so smitten was he by her beauty and so terrified of rejection. As he stood facing the tunnel, he felt much the same now. All his hard work, hopes and dreams were centred on this moment. He stood on the threshold of what could be the greatest discovery ever to be made in the field of archaeology, and he could feel himself shaking.

"Salim, this is it!" he said, turning to his companion. "At the end of this tunnel we may find immortality! But let us proceed with all due care. There may be sentinels laying in wait for the careless and unwary."

Inching their way forward, they inspected the walls of the tunnel closely in the muted light of the lanterns. It was clear that the tunnel had been rough hewn from the living rock. Salim estimated the passageway to be about twenty feet wide by about twelve feet high.

The pharaoh, his guards, chariots, wagons or a multitude of priests could have passed down here with ease, thought the baron.

They picked up their pace. It was clear that there were no obstacles or booby traps, and there were no hieroglyphs to study—just rough-cut walls. The tunnel levelled off and they walked out into a large chamber that ran at right angles to the tunnel.

"This is it!" gasped the baron. "Light more lanterns so we can see the scale of this amazing place!" he commanded.

Salim made numerous trips to the canoe to retrieve equipment, without any help from the baron. The veneer of equality and civility had been wiped away. Like a voracious raptor, the English aristocrat began to devour the chamber, inch by inch, with his eyes. Salim set up two lines of lanterns, six on either side of the chamber. It was a large rectangular room, carved into the limestone, around thirty feet wide, ten feet high and fifty feet long. At the far end was a tunnel, about seven feet high and six feet wide, sloping downward. Salim saw it first, when he was positioning the lanterns. He called out excitedly, pointing its location to the baron, who was at the other end of the chamber. As soon as the baron saw it, he rushed across the sand strewn granite block floor, lantern in hand. Without a word to Salim, he entered the tunnel and disappeared into the blackness. Salim grabbed a lantern and was preparing to follow when he heard the furious curses reverberating off the stone.

The baron burst out of the tunnel, his face white with anger. "It's blocked!" he shouted, desecrating the silence with his furious voice. "It's full of bloody water! A cave-in we could have dealt with—but water!" His initial ecstasy, the sweet tasting wine of discovery, had been turned to vinegar.

The chamber was devoid of artefacts. The gateway to further chambers, and possibly the Giza labyrinth beyond, was protected by an impenetrable barrier. Salim stood in silence, patiently waiting for his employer's anger to subside. Reaching for his hip flask, the baron gulped a large mouthful of brandy. He paced the chamber, kicking at rubble and fragments of pottery. Eventually his anger subsided, and he returned to his inspection of the walls. If he had to, he would employ divers to explore the submerged tunnel, but then only the murder of everybody involved, including Salim, would protect the secrets of the Sphinx. Alas, he was an addict now. Like a hungry wolf, he could smell the scent of his quarry. In his heart he knew that he would stop at nothing to find, possess and control the fabled knowledge of the ancients.

There were a total of twelve square pillars in the chamber, all faced in red granite and carved with hieroglyphs. The walls of the chamber were finished with polished red granite and were carved with hieroglyphs and exquisite figures. Interspaced between the granite where expertly painted friezes depicting priests, priestesses, neophytes, gods, goddesses and animals. They were in a remarkable state of preservation. There was even a painting of an ancient temple.

The two explorers spent many weeks visiting the chamber, photographing and sketching the paintings and hieroglyphs. The material was eventually transferred to secure rooms that the baron had rented in Cairo. It was here that the Englishman and his assistant set to work, studying the secrets of the chamber.

"It appears obvious to me," grumbled the baron, "that the chamber has been cleared of all artefacts. This was either accomplished in ancient times, when the site was abandoned, or by visitors to the chamber at a later date. It is evident that we are not the first to view this hidden hall since the days of the pharaohs. Others must have entered the underground world of Giza from the crypt in the Coptic Church."

Salim regarded the aristocrat closely before replying. He had no wish to bear the brunt of another furious outburst.

Measuring his words carefully, he said, "What you say is true, Baron, but it is quite possible that the secret location of the chamber has again been buried. Even the priest who directed us to the underground river appeared to have no knowledge of the hidden city or the chamber."

The baron rose from his chair and paced the room. "You have a point there," he huffed.

"On a more positive note, Baron," continued the Egyptian, "I have developed the photographs and all the material is now in place for detailed study."

The baron returned to his chair. "Then let us begin," he said with a little more enthusiasm.

ꙮ

After a month of intense study, a fascinating picture began to emerge. Everything adorning the chamber dated to the Old Kingdom. The genealogy of the Giza plateau had been recorded in stone. In the time of Pharaoh Snefru and his son Khufu, the Sphinx, known as Aker, was already an ancient and neglected monument. Indeed, there were two of them. The second Sphinx stood at a location that Salim guessed was now the site of the Coptic Church. A restoration project on the Giza peninsula was initiated by Snefru and continued by Khufu and the later pharaohs of the fourth dynasty of the Old Kingdom. Unlike the first Sphinx, which had been carved from a living limestone outcrop, the second Sphinx had been sculptured from massive blocks of quarried rock. Eventually, it fell into decay and its stone had been plundered until nothing remained

The Sphinx on the Giza plateau, then known as Rostau, was cleared of sand and restored. As the restoration work was drawing to a close, six descending steps were discovered in a concealed chamber at the rear of the temple in front of the Sphinx. The steps led to a mighty brass door. When this was eventually opened, access was gained to the hidden chambers under the Sphinx and the ancient underground city.

When first discovered by Snefru, the walls of the chambers were devoid of decoration, but each chamber contained many metal tablets inscribed with hieroglyphs. While the priests had preserved a fragmented knowledge of the "First Time," or "Sep Tepi," as it was called, when they believed that the Egyptian culture had first come into being, the tablets contained detailed and priceless knowledge of astronomy, mathematics, music, architecture, geography, medicine and agriculture, all dating from Sep Tepi. This was a hall of records left by their ancestors, the secret hall that Snefru and his son Khufu had sought for many years.

The knowledge contained in these records proved to be invaluable to the Egyptians of the First Kingdom, and it powered their civilisation forward so that eventually it became the most advanced in the ancient world. The head of the Sphinx, originally that of a menacing lion, was re-carved in the likeness of an earlier Pharaoh shortly after the unification of Upper and Lower Egypt.

The Great Pyramid and its two sister pyramids were already ancient structures at the time of the Old Kingdom. The Great Pyramid was believed to have been built as an eternal monument in stone to, and a record of, the ancient knowledge. The dimensions and architecture of the Great Pyramid embodied a profound understanding of building, engineering, astronomy, geodesy, metrology, geometry and harmonics. The Great Pyramid was an immortal testament to the knowledge of a highly advanced civilisation that had an immense understanding, not only of the arts and sciences, but also of mysticism. It was built to be the greatest of all temples, the ultimate temple of spiritual initiation; or so thought the Egyptians who discovered the ancient records at the time of the Old Kingdom.

The Sphinx also became a temple of initiation and continued to be used as a hall of records were the tablets of knowledge were kept. Only priests, advanced initiates and the pharaohs, had access to the secret world below Giza. A series of tunnels connected the Sphinx with the pyramids. Due to massive construction and restoration projects, the Giza plateau increased in prominence as a sacred site of learning, initiation and spiritual enfoldment. The Sphinx was considered to symbolise the embodiment of the Sun God – Re-harakhty, in his manifestation as Horus of the Horizon. The Sphinx at Giza was viewed as one of the two Aker-lions that guarded the entrances to the Duat, or underworld.

The baron and Salim were greatly intrigued by a list that they found carved into one of the pillars in the chamber. First on the list was a succession of "Shemsu-hor," or "Followers of Horus," that spanned an amazing thirteen thousand five hundred years. There was then a gap until the Old Kingdom when the name Snefru appeared, followed by Khufu, Djedefre, Khafra, Menkaura and Shepseskaef. This was followed by another interval of over one thousand years until the New Kingdom, when the name Thutmose IV appeared, followed by Amonhotep III and Amonhotep IV (Akhenaton). It was here that the list ended. The two explorers debated this list for many hours and the conclusions that they reached were startling.

"Civilisation in the land of the Nile," said the baron, through the haze of his cigar smoke, "would appear to be far older than anyone has guessed."

Salim nodded. "There is an indeterminate interval, probably many thousands of years, between the Shemsu-hor and the Old Kingdom, when Snefru's name appears on the list. So we are talking about a civilisation that stretches back at least twenty thousand years from the present time, probably much further."

The baron blew a pungent cloud of tobacco smoke in the direction of his assistant. "But it was not continuous, that much is obvious. Any Egyptologist would tell you that the succession of Egyptian kings began about five thousand years ago. They would also say that much before that period there was no evidence of a high civilisation. Well, we have evidence now, Salim, my friend!" responded the baron. "It looks like the original great civilisation disappeared for some reason, perhaps due to some natural disaster."

"That is possible, Baron," said the Egyptian, exhaling the smoke from a Turkish cigarette. "Something that is also clear, Baron," he continued, "is that there are not that many pharaohs on the list. This would certainly suggest that the hidden chambers were not common knowledge amongst the Egyptian royal families."

"Very true," responded the baron. "All of the pharaohs on the list lived in eras of high significance. Snefru and the generations of his dynasty that followed appear to have been the discoverers and preservers of an ancient wisdom contained in the Hall of Records below the Giza plateau. They used this wisdom to propel Egypt to the forefront of all the civilisations in existence at that time. For reasons unclear, by the fifth dynasty of the Old Kingdom the Hall of Records appears to have been forgotten, lying buried in the sand. It was not until one thousand years later that the Hall of Records appears to have been rediscovered by Thutmose IV. Indeed, it was only about fifty years after that that Akhenaton came to the throne. It could be that the rediscovery of the ancient knowledge by his grandfather inspired Akhenaton to restore the original beliefs of the Old Kingdom. This, of course, proved a disaster. By this time the Egyptian nation was entrenched in the worship of the god Amun and many other gods. The worship of the original god, the so called 'sun god' Re or Ra, was by then a minority religion, mainly preserved by the priests in the Temple of Heliopolis. It was no surprise, then, that there was a massive backlash, and that the Egyptians tried to erase Akhenaton's name from history. But his memory would not die, and today many consider him the first champion of monotheism."

Salim smiled. "So you see, Baron," he said, "our labours have not been in vain. What we have discovered is of profound historical significance."

The baron's face hardened. "But where the hell are those metal tablets now?" he growled. "Are they submerged in water-filled chambers below Giza, or have they been stolen by ancient tomb robbers? Perhaps they reside in the vaults of a secret Brotherhood such as our own... The question is, Salim, where in the name of Hades do we go from here?"

Without hesitation, Salim interjected bravely. "I believe that for the moment, Baron, the best way forward would be to persist with our analysis of the material that we have gathered."

CHAPTER 26
THE HOUSE OF SOKAR

In an era when smoking was at best considered beneficial to the health and at worst an innocuous pastime, two men bellowed thin grey clouds of burnt tobacco into a shuttered room. Both were peering intently at a large black and white photograph. It was an image of one of the wall paintings from the secret chamber below the Sphinx. The painting depicted the Giza plateau at the time of the Old Kingdom. The Valley and Sphinx temples stood next to a giant lion. In the distance and to the right of the rear flanks of the lion lay three huge gleaming white pyramids, their summits crowned with magnificent gold capstones.

The text confirmed that the "Mound of Creation" was located in Rostau (Giza), but no specific location was given. The text also spoke of an ancient temple called the "House of Sokar." The authors of the text believed that the tablets of knowledge had been taken from the House of Sokar, which contained the original Hall of Records. They indicated that this temple had been destroyed in an earlier era and that the tablets had been moved to the secret chambers below Aker.

"That is very interesting," hummed the baron. "It appears that there was an earlier Hall of Records and that it was located below a temple on the Giza peninsula. I wonder who wrote this text?"

Salim looked at the Englishman and shrugged his shoulders. They moved onto another photograph, an image of an extensive temple complex that was identified as the House of Sokar. The temple, which was of cyclopean construction, was located within a double- walled enclosure. This was situated next to a hill, shaped like a large mound with steep slopes. At the centre of the temple there was a well that contained a spiral stairway within it. The stairway led to a tunnel that descended further into the bedrock. Eventually, the tunnel opened into an underground cavern and a lake. In the middle of the lake was an island, and below the island lay a complex of interconnected chambers. There was a total of fourteen of these chambers. The first chamber was connected via a tunnel to a ring of twelve chambers. These were all interconnected to a large chamber, located at the centre of the ring. Within this chamber there stood a large elongated egg-shaped object—a lingam—which could have been a stone or crystal. It was orange in colour and was surrounded by a ring of twelve smaller conical-shaped orange coloured stones or crystals. The text associated with this painting identified it as a depiction of the Fifth Division of the Duat-underworld—the House of Sokar. The lake, called "Netu," was long and narrow and was fed by the waters of a river named "the Nun." The hill next to the temple was identified as the "Primeval Mound: the Mound of First Creation." The long descending passageway, the gateway to the House of Sokar, was called the "Road of Rostau." The island in the lake was named the "Island of Sekri," and the lingam stone was identified as the "Benben stone"; it was described as emitting a radiance or fire.

The two men went on to discuss the other material they had collected. Much of it had to do with the worship of Atum, a more ancient name for the sun god, Re. It appeared that the chamber was used as a hall—a place of preparation for neophytes to the priesthood. For the highest and most advanced of the initiates, the ultimate destination was the Great Pyramid. Within the Kings' Chamber of the Great Pyramid there stood an empty, lidless sarcophagus. Lying silently within this granite box, the neophyte received the highest initiation, and subsequently, admittance into the priesthood of Atum and the Brotherhood of the Sphinx.

The following morning the baron informed Salim that for the moment their investigations below the Sphinx would have to come to an end; he needed to master the art of diving. The baron knew that this endeavour would take some time and would entail the purchase of cumbersome equipment from Europe. Starting forthwith, he asked Salim to assemble a team to search for the lost temple. If he could find the lost temple, he reasoned, it should hopefully mark the location of the House of Sokar. It was clear that something of immense power could be hidden there—perhaps an advanced technology. He would spare no expense to find it.

Turning to the Egyptian, the baron asked, with enquiring eyes, "So, Salim, what are your views on the House of Sokar? Do you think that the search will be a waste of time? Do you think that the temple ever really existed?"

Salim, who was a considerably more knowledgeable Egyptologist than his employer, replied, "Yes, Baron," nodding his head repeatedly to emphasise his agreement. "Standing between the forepaws of the Sphinx is the Dream Stele of Thutmose IV. While sheltering from the sun in the shadow of the Sphinx, a young prince fell asleep. The Sphinx, in the form of Hor-em-akhet, appeared before him in a dream. The god proclaimed that if the prince cleared the sand from his body, he would become the next pharaoh, even though he was not in direct line for the throne. The prince did as he was bidden by the Sphinx, and in due course he became Pharaoh Thutmose IV. A section of text in the stele described the area where the prince had fallen asleep as the Setepet, or the sanctuary of Hor-em-akhet, that was beside Sokar in Rostau. Thus, the stele tells the reader that the House of Sokar was located in a position that was close to the Sphinx. The stele goes on to suggest that the location is near the southern wall, known today as the 'Wall of the Crow.' It also mentions the goddess Sekhmet, who presides over the mountain, the splendid place of the beginning of time, also known as the hill of Sokar. There is a hill close to the Wall of the Crow. It is called 'Gebel Gibli' and could well be the hill of Sokar. In conclusion, Baron, it is possible that this hill could be the original Mound of Creation. This is the site where we should begin our search. Remnants of the temple of Sokar may still exist at the base of this hill."

"Then let us begin without delay," said the baron. "I will leave the arrangements to you, as I must return to England forthwith. The money is already in the account at our Cairo bank."

ꕤ

The baron returned to Egypt in 1897. Regular carefully-worded telegraphs kept him informed of the digs while he was in England. Salim had found numerous Ushabti figures that had been buried in pits, about ten feet deep. These had been discovered in the sandy plain below the rocky outcrop known as the Southern Hill at Giza, or Gebel Gibli. It was traditional for pilgrims in ancient Egypt to leave these figures close to sacred tombs and temples. Both the baron and Salim were encouraged by these finds, which led them to speculate that the Wall of the Crow could have served as a causeway that led to a temple, now destroyed; or if not a causeway, then it may have functioned as an enclosure wall for the Temple of Sokar. Salim decided to investigate the debris field at the end of the wall closest to the hill. The initial dig revealed large chunks of red granite, suggesting the former existence of an expensive structure in this vicinity.

ꕤ

The baron had not been idle in England. Money can open many doors. He had spent four months in Portsmouth, learning the basics of deep sea diving from a navy diver. He had also practiced free diving, without a suit or breathing apparatus. In Egypt, he would need both skills. For part of the time, his wife and children had stayed with him in the big house that he had rented close to the seafront. He loved his family dearly and they were the main reason he had returned to England. Indeed, if it had not been for his wife's fragility, where Egypt was concerned he would have set up a second home in Cairo, such was the magic of the country and the draw of its many mysteries.

One dazzlingly bright morning, the baron arrived to inspect the dig site. Salim's team was excavating the barren ground in twenty-foot square plots. When an excavation was completed, it was photographed and then re-covered with sand and rubble. This was a low profile operation and they were hiding their tracks. Standing over the latest excavation site, the skull of a fleshless corpse stared up at him, its bones yellow-grey in the dust. Spotting the baron, Salim walked over from the far end of the dig.

"You appear to have hit a burial site," commented the baron.

"Unfortunately, that is true," replied the Egyptian. "Looking at the ground, you would think that nothing had ever been here, but once you start exploring below the surface, it is a different matter entirely. This grave is not overspill from the Coptic cemetery; it is a Late Period burial. It is the fifth one that we have discovered in this area. Below the graves there is evidence of habitation. There was a village, or maybe a small town located here at one point."

"Have you any idea how old it could be?" asked the baron.

"The layout, construction methods and artefacts that we have found suggest The Old Kingdom," responded Salim.

It was growing hot, and perspiration was starting to ooze from the baron's forehead. Turning his gaze to the Egyptian, he said, "I will need your assistance in the caverns. I assume your excavation team can work unsupervised for a while?"

"Yes, they are an experienced team," said Salim, "but I will need to check on their progress every three days or so, given the sensitivity of the work."

ಖ೧ಡ

It took them awhile to transport the extra equipment to their base camp in the underground city. The equipment included heavy diving gear and a small boat, which had to be ferried into the underground realms in sections, using the canoes. The boat was subsequently assembled on the beach of the forgotten city. A bigger vessel than a canoe was required to provide a stable platform for the bulky pump needed to circulate the air in the diving suit.

Salim was pleased to be back in the caverns. He considered this work a breeze, compared with the dusty excavations in the sweltering desert sun. Now that they had the diving gear, things were a lot more exciting. When they had everything in place, they rested until the following morning. As they approached the boat, the baron rubbed his hands in anticipation.

"So, Salim," he said, "as we discussed, we will start our explorations with the chambers under the Sphinx. The water in the tunnel should be no barrier now!"

Sometime later, when they entered the chamber, it almost seemed familiar. They had spent so much time studying the photographs that the mystery was gone now, and a new adventure beckoned in the tunnels beyond. The baron could hardly contain his excitement as he struggled into the diving suit. The cumbersome thing was made of canvas and rubber, and was completely watertight. Lowering a big metal shoulder piece over the baron's head, Salim employed a spanner to clamp it securely to the suit, using twelve heavy-duty metal bolts. Finally, the big metal diving helmet, with reinforced glass portholes, was placed over the baron's head and screwed onto the shoulder piece, creating a watertight seal. Tubes were attached to the suit to allow for pressurisation and the circulation of fresh air. This was achieved by using a hand-powered force pump that Salim would operate. Communication would be via a time-honoured system of rope signals, which they had practiced repeatedly over the past few days.

When everything was finally in place, the baron lumbered forward, his heavy metal boots clattering against the stone floor of the tunnel. It did not take long to reach the water, which got progressively deeper as the tunnel began to descend. Soon the baron was entirely submerged in the water. Protected by the heavy diving suit, there was no sensation other than a drop in temperature, and the newfound ease with which he could move down the tunnel. His diving lantern helped guide the way through the inky blackness that now enveloped him like a shroud. Salim worked the handle of the air pump at an even rate, with one arm. The tubing and rope gradually played out. He kept a light grip on the rope so he could pick up the baron's signal when he reached the end of the tunnel.

The baron moved deeper into the flooded passageway. The water was clear of sediment and visibility was good. After travelling down the tunnel for a number of minutes, the baron found himself in a large chamber. He tugged sharply on the rope to indicate to Salim that he was now in the chamber. After receiving an acknowledging signal from his assistant, he moved left out of the tunnel and started to track along the walls. Rough-hewn from the bedrock, they were devoid of any markings. Approaching the end of the second wall, his lantern picked out a massive pile of rubble that blocked any further forward progress. His heart sank as he stood there, staring in disbelief.

"It is very clear now why the Hall of Records has remained hidden for so long!" he hissed. "There are obstacles and barriers at every step! It is as if the very gods of Egypt are barring the way!"

Tracing his way along the perimeter of the rubble field, his dismay grew increasingly intense. There was no way forward. The rubble blocked off the entire end of the chamber. Examining the rubble more closely, it was clear that this was no ordinary cave-in. It was fine-grade—a mix of small rocks and sand.

Emerging from the tunnel, the baron trudged towards Salim like an ungainly robot, dejected and wet. As the Egyptian lifted the heavy helmet from the baron's head, his exasperation was clear. "The chamber is blocked at the far end," he mumbled disconsolately. "At a guess, it is about thirty feet square."

Salim nodded. "Yes," he said cautiously, "that fits in with the plans that we were given. As you know, Baron, they indicate that the chamber was ventilated by a series of massive vertical airshafts, and that it was the intersection point of at least three tunnels running off in the direction of the pyramids. When the underground complex fell into disuse, sand and rubble must have been blown down the airshafts, eventually sealing off the tunnels."

Salim began to work on dismantling the next section of the suit.

"It would be impossible to remove the rubble without a massive engineering effort," sighed the baron. "For a start, the water would have to be pumped out of the chamber. That is just not possible at the moment. But I have not given up hope, my Egyptian friend. We will find another way!"

ꙮ

Returning to the surface, they found that the excavation team had uncovered further evidence of habitation running along the inner perimeter of the Wall of the Crow. While from an archaeological perspective this was very interesting, the odds were diminishing that they would be able to locate the lost Temple of Sokar. The latest excavation revealed the walls of an Old Kingdom bakery. It was beginning to look like they may be uncovering some type of complex, perhaps even a town that could have once housed and fed the work forces that renovated the pyramids. While all of their discoveries were fascinating and deeply significant to Salim, who was a true intellectual, the baron was growing increasingly frustrated; that was until he was struck by a flash of inspiration.

ꕤ

"Are you certain of those measurements?" asked the baron, who sat facing Salim in the boat.

"Yes, Baron," said the Egyptian, puffing and blowing with the effort of rowing his heavy companion across the waters of the cavern. "Gebel Gibli is located about half a mile due south of the Sphinx. We are most definitely heading in that direction."

If Gebel Gibli was indeed the Mound of Creation, had reasoned the baron, then the House of Sokar must be located underneath it. If they could not penetrate the House of Sokar from above, then they would find a way in from below. After about fifteen minutes, Salim could see the far wall of the cavern, and he informed the baron of this.

"I expected as much," said the Englishman. "I am hopeful that there is another cavern beyond this one. The question is, how do we find a way in?" They followed the wall of the cavern until they had travelled a full circle back to their original position. Other than the passageway from the cavern containing the underground city to the northwest, and the tunnel into the first of the chambers under the Sphinx, there were no openings in the solid rock walls. Lying on his stomach, and with Salim's assistance, the baron, now fully suited up, slid feet first into the water.

Dropping rapidly, his heavy metal boots thudded into the silt at the bottom of the lake. As he stood there at a depth of about forty feet below the surface, sediment billowed up around him. Fortunately, the floor of the lake was relatively even and he made his way slowly towards the wall. He signalled to Salim that he would track the perimeter to the right. As luck would have it, he did not have to walk too far before he discovered a large fissure in the rock. Rising about eight feet above the cavern floor at its highest point, the fissure was about five feet wide.

Ten minutes later, he signalled Salim to pull him to the surface. He motioned to his assistant to unscrew the lugs on the front porthole of the helmet and release the glass cover. "There is a fissure down there," he said. "Lower me back down and I will explore it." Five minutes passed and he surfaced again. "It narrows to nothing further in," he said dejectedly.

A number of hours later, after numerous dives, the baron indicated that he was exhausted, and they retired for the day. The two men spent the next five days exploring the wall, but without success. After he had broken the surface of the water for the last time, the baron reluctantly concluded that they would have to redouble their efforts on the plateau. He indicated to Salim that he would return to Cairo for a week to drown his sorrows.

Salim returned to the dig, but the baron did not return to Cairo. He had not been entirely truthful with his assistant. The fissure did indeed narrow for the last ten feet, but beyond the wall of the cavern there lay another lake. He knew that he could make it through the gap in the rock without his bulky diving suit. It would mean holding his breath, but he had been practicing that while submerged in his bath. He could now manage over two minutes, but that was while lying motionless. Ninety seconds was probably more realistic while swimming. He estimated that he should be able to dive down and swim through the fissure with ten seconds to spare. It was risky, but the stakes could not be higher, or at least, that was what he thought. They had marked the position of the fissure with a heavily chalked white arrow. He journeyed back to the location by canoe. Having hammered a large metal piton into the limestone of the cavern wall, he tethered the canoe to it. Sliding into the water, he took a mighty breath and disappeared below the surface.

CHAPTER 27
THE SECRETS OF SOKAR

ဢ

Lifting his head, Alexander yawned deeply. Tiredness had overcome him again. Lying back on his bed, he drifted to sleep, his breath becoming deep and heavy. A small clock ticked rhythmically on a bedside table. Time was running relentlessly on.

ဢ

Frank Malone gazed vacantly at the lights of Birmingham as the aircraft commenced its descent for landing. He visited his hometown of Dublin whenever he got the chance, which was usually two or three times a year. Dublin was where most of his friends lived; some he had known since his days at Trinity College. On this particular visit, he was like a man possessed, like a man that had been told that he only had a few months to live. Money was no object. He had stayed in one of Dublin's finest hotels and he had lived life to the fullest. He had dined at some of the best restaurants the city had to offer, and he had drunk Guinness and eighteen-year-old Scotch to his heart's content. He had spent his time singing and laughing in the pubs and at plays and concerts. Given what he had been through of late, stress relief was high on his agenda. But now it was time to return to the well-worn routine of college life in England. Or at least it used to be routine. Now, life seemed to grow more uncertain with each passing day. The Irishman was not looking forward to his return to Oxford, or his next meeting with the boy—that dreaded boy.

ꟗꟗ

Alexander opened the faded blue journal for the second time. Instantly absorbed by the handwritten narrative, his mind was transported back to 1897.

It was frightening, swimming through the fissure without the diving suit. The baron had a limited supply of air in his lungs and the craggy walls stretched endlessly before him. In seconds, he would reach the point of no return; he would have to swim further through the deadly water if he turned back than if he carried on forward. Bravely, perhaps foolishly, he swam on through the forbidding shadows cast by the light of the diving lantern. He felt the pressure build in his chest. It was death or victory now, he knew. With increasing desperation, he struggled forward. There was no end in sight and the pressure was getting worse. As his solar plexus began to spasm, his body screamed for oxygen—screamed like a mad man. He struggled on. Head pulsing, the screaming grew louder still. The terrible desire to suck in new air was overwhelming. He was swimming frantically now, his chest heaving violently.

At last, the end of the fissure came into view! Pushing through into the open water, he desperately sought the surface, but he could hold on no longer. Oxygen-starved lungs exploded, forcing the dead air from his body! A violent inhalation followed, but with nothing to spare, his head broke the surface, and it was air and not water that he drew into his ravenous lungs. Gasping furiously, he devoured oxygen in massive gulps.

The baron had the presence of mind to hold his position until he had recovered from the oxygen starvation. He had cut it very fine indeed and was thankful not to have joined the infamous ranks of dead tomb robbers. Gripping a small outcrop in the wall of the cavern, he steadied himself and inflated the rubber life jacket he was wearing. That made things a lot easier, as he was now floating effortlessly. He withdrew a piton from one of his pockets. As well as the lantern, he carried a tool belt around his waist. Removing a hammer, he drove the piton into the rock, securing a piece of white cloth to it to act as a marker; but he wondered if he would find the courage to make the return dive through that fissure.

A gut feeling prompted him to follow the wall to the left. Holding the lantern in his right hand, he moved cautiously forward. It was like floating in a void of blackness, silent except for the gentle lapping of the water against the rock. Time seemed to stand still; it was as if he was drifting in an endless chasm.

His luck was in for a change, and it was not long before the lantern picked out something up ahead. The water felt cold now and it made him shiver. As he moved closer, he could see that there was a grotto cut into the rock. It looked manmade. Soon a jetty and stone steps came into view. Reaching the steps, he clambered from the water, shivering. His shivering grew more intense and his heart began to race; he was onto something, at last—he was onto something big; he could feel it in his bones.

The grotto was about twenty feet wide and forty feet deep, its ceiling tapering gradually upwards to merge with the rock face. Turning, the baron looked out across the lake. His eyes were well adapted to the darkness now. Although the light cast by the lantern fell away sharply, he could discern a faint outline in the distance. It was an island of some sort.

"This must be it!" he shouted, his voice reverberating through the emptiness of the cavern and calling back to him through the silence.

The baron began to track the perimeter of the grotto. It was not long before he encountered the first passageway. It looked to be about seven feet high and six feet wide, and it ran in an easterly direction. He moved on until he reached a second tunnel. It was orientated to the south and descended rapidly into the bedrock. It had similar dimensions to the first tunnel. Finally, he discovered a third tunnel, running in a westerly direction. A massive granite slab blocked its entrance. As he examined the slab more closely, he cast his mind back to the ancient depictions of the "Road to Rostau." In the drawings on the walls of tombs and temples, the ceiling of the Road, or tunnel, was marked with a series of equidistant horizontal lines. *Could this have been a depiction of the security system?* he wondered *Could the lines in the pictures represent a series of suspended granite blocks interspersed in the limestone?* Such security devices, with stone doors suddenly dropping or sliding from the walls or ceilings of passageways, were not unknown in Egypt. Had tomb raiders gained unauthorised entry to this tunnel, triggering the release of a whole series of massive granite blocks? One thing was for sure; the tunnel was well and truly sealed now.

The baron decided to investigate the tunnel that descended to the south. If this was indeed the Road to Rostau in the House of Sokar, he could well be standing on the threshold of the fabled Hall of Records. Staring into the mouth of the tunnel, a terrible trepidation took hold of him. However rational a man thinks he is, there are many unlit fears lurking in the subconscious realms below the mind.

What if some terrible secret, some awful thing lurks below, something so horrible that it has been left hidden for eons? What if I am trapped or crushed by falling granite blocks? What if there is nothing but empty stone down there? Where would I go from here? How I wish I did not have to cross this daunting threshold alone.

He felt cold now and his head was throbbing. He knew that he could not face it, could not face the knowing. Perhaps foolishly, without checking for traps, he turned and walked briskly into the other tunnel. Glancing at the ceiling, he could see no evidence of granite blocks. The passageway had been rough hewn through the limestone wall of the cavern. With each step the sense of relief grew stronger.

It was difficult to judge how long he had been walking through the tunnel when it veered sharply to the right; he had left his timepiece in the canoe. The Englishman guessed that the passageway was following the contours of the other cavern. Sure enough, further on, the tunnel turned again sharply. Excitement was growing in him once more. If he could find a way out of this tunnel, there was a good chance that he would have discovered a far easier way into the mysterious cavern. Ahead of him now, he could see the end of the passageway. His heart leapt as the lantern revealed what he suspected could be a concealed door. As he got closer, he could see what looked like carved diorite protruding from the walls of the tunnel. There were eight squared-off sections of this dense black stone—four on either side. Each section had a deep groove cut in the top surface. Inserting a hand into one of the blocks of diorite, he tugged and it slid easily in its socket. It abutted a relatively smooth-faced slab of limestone that blocked the entrance to the tunnel. He reckoned that this had to be a concealed door. When the diorite beams were pulled out from their recesses in the rock they would very effectively bar the door. Strangely, the stone beams were all housed snugly in their recessed housings.

It appeared that the door had been left unlocked. More than likely, it was of the pivoted type, he guessed. Rubbing at the stone, he cleared away the dust. He could see now that the edges of the door had been cut unevenly, like a jigsaw piece, presumably to disguise it on the other side. He pushed at the stone cautiously with one of his feet. The door hinged slightly forward; the top had moved towards him and the bottom away from him. It was a classic hinging mechanism. *How amazing*! It still moved so easily after all these years; a superb piece of engineering. But then another thought struck him. Who was to say when the door was last opened! He stood to one side and pushed hard. Within seconds, the door had hinged fully open and he had moved into another passageway. He knew instantly where he was. It was the passageway that led from the cavern to the underbelly of the Sphinx!

ꙮ

The baron returned to Cairo. He needed time to prepare for what could be the final phase of his quest. From now on, he had decided that he would have to work alone. He communicated to his assistant that he had to return unexpectedly to England, and that he could be away for at least two months. Reluctantly, he moved to another considerably less luxurious hotel that was close to the Coptic Church. By now he had his own key to the crypt and could pretty much come and go as he pleased. The priest, a genuinely spiritual man, was glad of the extra revenue that the baron's frequent visits had brought him. The money went to many needy causes. The priest had no interest in the artefacts of the "pagan ancient Egyptians," and was unconcerned by the baron's activities. He saw plenty of equipment going into the crypt, but nothing much coming out. This fit with the story that they had told him about exploring underground waterways. They had failed to mention the hidden city to him.

And so it was, when everything had been prepared, that the baron returned to the caverns below Cairo. The base camp in the underground city had been restocked with provisions, and the baron had acquired the additional tools and equipment that he felt he might need. Making his way once more through the tunnel, he was soon standing in the grotto. From the wheelbarrow that he had brought with him, he slid out a sturdy iron pole from a stack of ten such poles that were secured with rope. Two additional lanterns burst to life, throwing their light into the darkness that surrounded him. There was now sufficient illumination to afford a very careful inspection of the entrance to the tunnel, perhaps the final section of the Road to Rostau.

Carefully, he brushed both walls for as far as he could reach, without stepping onto the floor of the tunnel. When the walls had been cleared of dust and cobwebs, two metal objects were clearly visible, glinting in the lantern light. They had been embedded in the walls, close to floor level, one on either side. Their edges had been fashioned to an irregular profile and their outer surface was flat and smooth. These were some sort of keys, he guessed. They probably functioned in one of two ways—they either activated, or deactivated security mechanisms within the tunnel. From past knowledge of such devices, detailed in archaeological texts, it was more likely that they deactivated the security system. But that begged the question as to why somebody would have effectively left the "key in the lock?"

Not wishing to take any more risks than he had to, he inspected the ceiling of the passageway. Sure enough, he could see the suspended granite blocks positioned at intervals of eight feet or so. The first was located immediately above the entrance to the tunnel. He was not going to take any chances. Taking the first of the iron poles, which was six feet ten inches in length, he placed it close to the wall under the first of the granite blocks. He secured it in position, using a wooden wedge, which he hammered between the pole and the surface of the granite block. So far so good! He repeated this manoeuvre on the other side of the tunnel. Nothing happened. The blocks remained static. Sometime later, the last of the poles was in place and he stood there, wondering what to do next.

About ten feet ahead of him, he could see that the tunnel turned sharply to the right. He could either return to base-camp for more poles or he could move deeper into the tunnel without protection. With two lanterns, one in each hand, he moved cautiously forward. Impatience had got the better of him. Reaching the turn in the tunnel, it was clear that it changed direction again, to run due north, about fifteen feet ahead of him. As he reached the section of the tunnel that descended to the north, the glint of metal again caught his eye. As before, two keys had been inserted in the locks. This gave him the confidence to move a little more rapidly. The tunnel dropped quite steeply now, and he guessed that it was now running under the bedrock of the lake.

A sudden noise ripped through the tunnel as the baron lost his footing! His right leg, followed swiftly by his left, disappeared from under him and he hit the floor with a heavy thud. Lying on his back, winded and dazed, he still clutched both lanterns. Slowly regaining his composure, he sat up. Ahead of him, he could see what looked like a metal bracelet, partially covered in dust. He guessed that he must have caught his right heel on it and slipped, knocking it further down the tunnel. Rising slowly to his feet, he carefully placed one of the lanterns on the sloping floor and picked up the bracelet. Examining it, he could see that it had fresh scratch marks on it. This was the culprit that had obviously caused him to fall. Interestingly, the bracelet was inscribed. Pushing it into a pocket, he decided to examine it later.

The baron progressed down the tunnel without further incident. Eventually, it levelled off and in the distance, about seventy feet ahead, he thought he saw a light. Turning out one of the lanterns, he could definitely make out light, and it was coming from a chamber. This was disconcerting, even frightening. Had somebody left, forgetting to turn out the light, or was somebody sitting there waiting for him? Light in a place like this! Gripping the handle of his revolver, he withdrew it from its shoulder holster and cocked the trigger. Fearfully, his limbs trembling, the tension almost unbearable, he moved forward. He felt as helpless as a child and terribly alone, but he would not turn back. Slowly and silently, except for the sound of his pounding heart, he moved towards the end of the tunnel. At last he reached the entrance to the chamber. Walking straight in, he was ready to shoot anything that moved; but there was nothing—only the stark stone of the rough-hewn walls. Looking up, he could see that the light was coming from the strange crystal globes that he had encountered previously in the underground city. The ceiling of the chamber was studded with them.

Ahead of him, he could see another tunnel of similar dimensions to the one that he had just walked through. Peering in, it was illuminated by the same dull grey-white light. Like the chamber, it had been carved directly out of the limestone bedrock without elaboration. He walked briskly down the tunnel, his gun still cocked and his lantern burning. Anticipation was slowly starting to replace his fear. Bursting into a second chamber, with his pistol cocked, he was jolted to a sudden halt. Legs buckling, he crashed to his knees, the lantern falling to the floor. He had found it—the hidden Hall! Like a dam breaking, tears burst from his eyes and he sobbed like a child.

Although smeared by the dust of time, the chamber was stunning, magnificent, breathtaking! It was not long before curiosity started to permeate the baron's turbulent emotions and he began to look around him. The walls of the chamber were faced in polished red granite; the ceiling was lined with enormous granite beams and the floor was made from green-white marble. This place had been built to withstand the ravages of time. There was no carving or ornamentation in the chamber, except for a massive door. The door had been moulded from a strange silver-yellow metal that glistened and shimmered. Now standing, he walked over to the door and touched its surface. It was silky smooth, so smooth, in fact, that not even dust could settle on it. Dominating the door was the embossed image of a giant lion. The door bore an inscription that was composed of a series of strange symbols; they were very distinct from the hieroglyphs of Egyptian writing. He had never seen their like before.

Behind the mighty door, which stood ajar, the baron could see shimmering light. Moving past the door, he entered another chamber. This chamber was about the same size as the previous chamber, which he had estimated to be about twenty-five feet square. The ceiling was again built of granite and was illuminated by the crystalline lights, but unlike the previous chamber, all the walls were lined with the mysterious silver-yellow metal. It was a spellbinding sight! The metal was covered from top to bottom with inscriptions in the strange script. Equally spaced and close to the far end of the chamber, opposite the door, were three lidless sarcophagi, carved from black granite.

Walking over to the sarcophagi, the baron looked into them, one by one. As he suspected, they were empty. They were all of identical dimensions. He estimated the sarcophagi to be about seven feet long, three feet wide and four feet high. He guessed that they once contained the metal tablets—the metal tablets that were spoken of in the hieroglyphs carved into the walls of the chamber under the Sphinx. The question that now came to his mind was, were the metal tablets a copy of the wall inscriptions he could see around him, or did they exclusively carry the ancient knowledge that he was seeking? His heart sank a little. He needed to find a way to decipher the wall inscriptions, but from where he currently stood, that would be no easy task.

In addition to the entrance that the baron had walked through, there were three openings in the chamber, one in each wall. On closer inspection, they all proved to be tunnels seven feet high and about four feet wide. He decided to investigate the left hand tunnel first. Floor, walls and ceiling were lined entirely in red granite. There were no inscriptions, or for that matter, crystal lights. The tunnel stretched for about thirty feet and ended in another chamber. Again, it was lined in metal and covered in inscriptions. As before, it contained the three empty sarcophagi. He repeated the procedure of taking the left hand tunnel of every chamber that he encountered. When he had finished his fascinating journey, he had passed through twelve metal-clad chambers in total, and he had travelled around in a full circle that ended where it had begun. In addition to the inscriptions, he had seen pictures, diagrams and schematics of strange machines. His head was spinning with it all. *Thank God for photography*. It would have taken years to sketch all this by hand.

Having discovered that the twelve chambers were arranged in a circle, it was evident that the other tunnels that he had not yet explored would all lead to a central point, presumably a central chamber. He decided to rest for a few moments. Gulping from his water bottle, he thought about lighting a cigar, but somehow in the ancient majesty of this temple of knowledge, that seemed almost like a desecration. Replacing his water bottle, he walked into one of the tunnels that he hoped would lead him to the central chamber: the epicentre of the Hall of Records.

CHAPTER 28
THE BEAUTIFUL WOMAN

The sun was high in a winter-blue sky as the big Volvo powered its way down the A40 towards Oxford. Frank had decided to avoid the motorway in favour of a more scenic route back to the city of dreaming spires. He had had a real scream of a time in Dublin, and he was in no hurry to face the relatively mundane realities of the new term at LMH.

Rounding a bend, he suddenly saw her! She was standing a short way ahead in the road, directly in his path. It was too late to brake, and he would have to turn the steering wheel violently to avoid hitting her. It was a life or death decision—carry straight on, or swerve the car out of control?

Time seemed to stand still as he stared in disbelief at the woman. She was beautiful, strikingly so. Her nose was well defined, but feminine, and her lips were full and red. A magnificent hat concealed her hair. It was similar to a top hat, but rimless and flared out more at the apex. The hat was a deep dark blue with an ornate bronze-coloured band around the middle. The bottom section of the hat was bright gold and seemed to shimmer. Around her slender neck she wore a dazzling necklace of sparkling multilayered gemstones. Dressed in thin ankle-length white muslin, the garment barely concealed her beautiful light-brown skin and the sensuous curves of her body. But it was her eyes that struck him more than anything. Accentuated with heavy eyeliner in the Egyptian style, they were large, black, almond-shaped and bewitching. They looked at him, almost seductively.

Both enchanted and horror struck, Frank stared at the vision of loveliness hurtling towards him. Tensing to swerve the car, something inside him hardened, and he drove straight on. Melting through the bonnet, the woman crashed straight into him. A searing coldness shot through him as her body merged with his. Desperately, as a terrible darkness descended, he grabbed at the rosary beads dangling on the dashboard and slammed on the brakes.

A sharp, piercing sound wrenched the Irishman back to consciousness. As his eyes flickered open, a huge shape careered, writhing and squealing, towards him. Clutching the rosary beads, he sat there, dazed. To his horror, he could see that his car was straddling both carriageways of the road, but miraculously, the engine was still running. The huge juggernaut was almost on him as he slammed the gears into reverse, shooting the Volvo backwards. The massive truck roared past, breaks screeching. It had missed him by inches.

Fortunately, there was a large grass verge next to the road and the car slid to a halt, suffering no damage. Sitting there shaking, Frank held the steering wheel in a white-knuckled grip. Nerves in tatters, he was tempted, there and then, to turn the big car around and hightail it back to Ireland—never to return.

❧

Alexander turned another page of the journal. The baron walked rapidly down the passageway, leading to what he hoped would be the central chamber of the complex. He glanced only briefly at the inscriptions and drawings etched into the shiny red granite. Unlike the other tunnels, this one was illuminated by the mysterious crystal lights, and it was about three times the length of the previous tunnels. Approaching the end of the tunnel, he could see that the way ahead was barred. The massive bulk of a shining metal door stood between him and whatever lay ahead. Brushing his hands gently over the surface of the door, he could perceive no obvious way of opening it other than by pressing against it. He decided not to risk it. It was clear that somebody had been here before him. Perhaps another door had been left open. He would try the other passages in hopes of gaining entry. Turning, he broke into a run. Five tunnels later, and now panting heavily, the baron approached another metal door. At first it looked closed, but something made him look more carefully. There was a gap between the door and the granite lintel. It was tiny, but perceptibly bigger than the minute gaps that he had seen when inspecting the other doors.

Cautiously, almost fearfully, he pushed gently at the shining metal. At this, the defining moment of his life, he had no wish to be trapped and buried for millennia, like some second-rate amateur. The door opened, moving effortlessly forward, and the baron stepped into the chamber. Instinctively, he swung around to check the rear of the door. A sturdy metal rod that would effectively bar the door from opening was raised in a vertical position. Glancing swiftly above him, he could see that there was a hole in the roof, about a foot square, and situated immediately above the door.

At a calculated guess, he thought, *a forced entry through the door would trigger the release of a torrent of water, guided through channels from the lake above. More than likely, there was a similar mechanism linked to all the other doors. Triggering one of the doors would probably open all of the floodgates simultaneously, submerging the entire complex in minutes. Without the benefit of sophisticated diving gear, a recent invention, the Hall of Records would become impenetrable to bandits and tomb robbers. Even a pharaoh would have been hard pressed to gain entry!*

Turning now to look at the chamber, the baron was surprised at what greeted his eyes. He was expecting a marble palace, but the chamber was stark, almost futuristic. It was about fifteen feet high and ended abruptly in a flat ceiling. Circular in shape, the chamber had a diameter of about forty feet. There was remarkably little dust. Stark white in colour, the walls were very smooth and felt odd to the touch, like ivory rather than stone. The floor of the chamber was joined seamlessly to the walls and appeared to have been constructed from the same material as the walls, although it was discoloured in places and had been dimpled to aid grip. Running around the chamber was a series of twelve sturdy equally-spaced columns, each positioned at a distance of four feet from the wall. They had a rounded profile and were made from the same strange metal as the wall panels and doors. It was only the columns that were engraved; the walls were completely unadorned. At the foot of each column, facing the centre of the room, was a metal pedestal.

Centrally positioned in the chamber were three white columns. Square in shape, they were four feet high and arranged in the form of a triangle. They supported a platform that was about four feet square and six inches thick. The platform looked like it was composed of the same material as the walls and floor, but had become blackened towards the centre. The baron's attention was drawn to an enormous yellow-brown metallic- looking rod that projected from the ceiling, immediately above the platform. Gleaming at the end of the rod was an amazing looking multifaceted red gemstone, bigger than a man's head. It was suspended about seven feet above the centre of the platform. Not far from the platform, lying on its side, was a large metal container made of a similar looking metal to the rod. The baron guessed that it had fallen from the platform and was perhaps used to support a stone or crystal, a very large stone or crystal. And this was all that appeared to be in the room.

With the euphoria of discovery starting to wane, the old familiar frustration began to seep back in to the baron. He had spent a king's ransom, he had surmounted many obstacles, and he had even risked death to stand here in this forgotten room. And what did he have for his troubles? A collection of incomprehensible inscriptions, a metal container and a gemstone! Where were all the magnificent technologies and the fantastic machines? Long gone, by the looks of things. He felt like a man in an empty shop, and he wished that he had Salim here to talk things through with. How the hell was he going to make sense of this lot? But then again, he knew that if Salim were here he may end up having to put a bullet through his skull! He could trust nobody with this, he knew, but where the hell did he go from here? There was nothing else for it, he knew. He would have to adopt the same painstaking approach that they had taken with the chamber under the Sphinx. *All very well, but I can't read the accursed language!*

Anger took hold of him and he made for the red gemstone with a chisel in his hand. Attacking it furiously, he rained down blow after blow. He even took a hammer to it, but to no avail. It did not budge; it was not even marked. Then he noticed a glinting coming from one of the pedestals. Looking closer, he could see that there was a single gem embedded centrally in the top face of each pedestal; the gems were all of different colours. Stripped of any academic dignity, the Englishman set about one of the gems with the chisel. As he tried to winkle it from its metal casing, it depressed suddenly in its housing. There was a clunking sound and the top of the pedestal popped up like a lid. With caution thrown to the winds, the baron ripped open the pedestal. Concealed inside was an exquisite transparent crystal that looked like quartz.

His frenzy somewhat appeased by finally finding something that he could hold in his hands, the baron examined the crystal. It was about five inches in diameter, and as he rotated it slowly in his hands, a single human eye came suddenly into view. Almost dropping the crystal in surprise, he could see that the eye had been exquisitely etched into its centre. His fingers began to tingle as he held the crystal. It seemed to buzz with a strange energy. Viewing the crystal from certain angles, the baron could discern thousands of tiny fracture lines inside it.

What on earth are these? he wondered. They did not appear natural; they looked patterned and deliberate. He felt a strange sensation on his skin, like a gently blowing breeze, and he became aware of sounds, like voices, talking in the distance. His attention was suddenly drawn to his wrist-compass; the needle was spinning! It was clear that what he held in his hands was an object of incredible technical sophistication. The question was, what in the name of heaven was it?

He guessed that the coloured gems were markers. There were twelve of the mysterious crystals in all—one inside each of the pedestals. He recorded their positions on a small notepad that he carried with him. Some time later, he started to chuckle as he pushed his wheelbarrow along the passageways. He was carrying twelve priceless crystals away from the fabled Hall of Records as casually as if they were a pile of turnips. They may as well have been turnips, for all the knowledge that Victorian science would be able to extract from them. But they were objects of profound beauty in their own right and a glittering testament to a lost race with an incredibly advanced civilisation. Panting, he reached the top of the final tunnel and walked out into the grotto.

A sudden impulse made the baron drop his tool belt and strip off his shirt and boots. Lighting one of the diving lanterns, he dived into the black water, bellowing with the shock of its coldness, but soon he felt invigorated as he swam towards the island. It was situated about three or four hundred feet from the grotto, difficult to estimate in the water. As he swam closer, he gasped in disbelief, for standing on the rocky island was a gleaming white pyramid with a yellow-bronze coloured capstone. The pyramid looked to be around forty feet high. A metal rod ran through the apex of the capstone and penetrated the roof of the cavern.

Eventually, the baron found a place on the shoreline where he could scramble up an outcrop of rock. He moved carefully, as the island was composed of pitted and irregular limestone. Reaching the pyramid, he could see that it had been built with fantastic precision; the joints between the limestone cladding blocks were almost imperceptible. Due to the presence of the rod at the top of the pyramid, he deduced that it must be connected in some way with the underground complex. This was a truly awe-inspiring structure and he could only imagine the staggering majesty of the pyramids on the Giza plateau before they had been stripped of their original white cladding blocks and their dazzling metal capstones.

A couple of minutes of close inspection revealed no discernable way into the pyramid. Before departing, he decided to explore the rest of the island. It was difficult to gauge its size in the dark, particularly as he had to step gingerly to avoid ripping open his feet, but it was a fair bet that it was pretty small. After he had walked seventy paces or so, the lantern light picked out another structure. Standing about thirty feet high and built from granite blocks was a step pyramid. There was a clear entrance to the structure, but it had been sealed. The cartouches were unmistakable. It was the final resting place of the Pharaoh Khufu. In Egyptology circles, this discovery alone would have made the baron immortal. But he knew, even as he stood there, that it was highly unlikely that he could ever reveal the location of Khufu's tomb to the world. He did, however, intend to enter the tomb at a later date. How could he resist? But for now he had more pressing things to deal with, not least of all deciphering the mysterious language. Indeed, all depended on that.

CHAPTER 29
A LUCKY BREAK

ꟊ

Frank Malone sat, clutching a very large glass of brandy with trembling hands. He was not sure how much more of this that he could take. *Who the hell was that woman?* he pondered. *She looked like an ancient Egyptian princess, or maybe a priestess. It was clear that she was dead, a spirit entity. There was no trace of a body on the road, and anyway, she had melted through the car! Was what happened a weird accident, or did she mean to kill me? The whole experience was horrible, but at the same time amazing. In the past, on ghost hunts I've seen the odd orb and mist, but nothing like this. The blessed woman looked as real as daylight and damned attractive with it! But let's get real here. There is no question that she intended to kill me. She tried to shock me into crashing the car. She must be the entity, the thing that hunts us! Once she was beautiful like that, but not today! Somewhere she lies withered and awful in a dark hidden place.*

ꟊ

Alexander continued to devour the journal. The baron had moved his photographic equipment into the chambers below the lake. He had decided to start with the central chamber and work out from there. Walking around the pillars, prior to photographing their inscriptions, he came across something that rooted him in his tracks. Soon he was laughing, and then he started to dance. Etched on one of the pillars was what looked like another Rosetta Stone! Well, it was a similar concept, anyway. There were lists of what appeared to be words of the ancient writing, and next to each word there was what looked like a hieroglyph. On closer inspection, he could see that they were not quite the classical hieroglyphs of the Egyptian language, but rather a representation of animals, household objects, and so on. Eventually, he figured, if enough of the words were connected with the objects, it should be possible to crack the code and decipher the language. He was not confident that he could do this alone, but he knew people who could do it for him, people that he could relay onto be silent at a price. He was in little doubt that the ancient Egyptians before him had deciphered the language.

The question that now nagged the baron was the nature of the inscriptions on the walls and pillars. Could it possibly be the ancient knowledge that he sought, or was that knowledge contained exclusively on the metal tablets spoken of in the chamber under the Sphinx? He even began to wonder if he had really discovered the hidden Hall of Records at all. Something was clear though; cipher keys had been inscribed on a metal pillar in the central chamber. This was the most secure part of the complex. Nobody could enter this room without the knowledge that unlocked the secret chambers. Why protect something to this degree if the inscriptions were inconsequential or trivial? His optimism growing, the baron began the laborious task of cataloguing and photographing everything in the chambers and tunnels.

❧

The months passed by and the baron found himself once more face-to-face with his assistant on the Giza plateau.

"Good to see you again, Baron Northgate," said the Egyptian, smiling broadly. "You received my telegrams and letters, I take it?"

The baron nodded. "Yes, Salim," he replied, "but I would like you to give me the key information again so that I can fill in a few gaps." The baron was a good liar.

"Well, as you instructed, Baron," said Salim, tensing a little, "we have continued our excavations in the region of the Southern Hill and the Wall of the Crow. We have excavated more pottery and tools, all dating from the Old Kingdom, and we have uncovered bakeries, and even a pillared hall containing benches; it was probably a dining hall. There appear to be two types of layout: one rather haphazard and the other extremely well organised with blocks of long galleries and straight roads based on a grid system. We have uncovered what appears to be a royal building in which we have found the insignias of the Pharaohs Khafre and Menkaure."

The baron frowned. "No signs of the ancient temple, it would seem?" he said.

"No, Baron," winced the Egyptian.

The Englishman continued, a little more good-humouredly. "So, Salim, you have confirmed that that there appears to have been a lot of activity in this area of the plateau in the Old Kingdom? Presumably, there was a great deal of building work going on, as we inferred the last time I was up here."

Salim raised his eyebrows. "That is true, Baron; the latest excavations confirm it. They appear to have been building temples and masteba."

A slight grin crept over the baron's face. "There was undoubtedly a lot of building going on at the time, but much of it was probably renovation work rather than new construction," he said. "Renovating those pyramids would have been an enormous task."

The Egyptian nodded his head. "Yes, Baron. If the hieroglyphs and paintings that we discovered are to be believed, the pyramids were probably the subject of a massive restoration project during the time of the 4th Dynasty," he said. "But I think that we would both agree that they were built by Egyptians, and not foreigners, albeit in an earlier era before some great calamity struck the Nile Valley."

Without responding, the baron handed Salim a piece of paper. Drawn upon it was a series of hieroglyphs and a translation written in English underneath. Salim scrutinised the paper. The words in English read, "Nesmut, Priestess of the Sphinx and Lover of the Aten." "Most interesting," he murmured. "If I may make so bold, Baron, where did you find this?"

The baron produced the bracelet that he had discovered in the tunnel leading to the underground chamber complex. Scrutinising the bracelet, the Egyptian said confidently, "Yes, this looks like New Kingdom jewellery." He handed it back to the baron.

"I found it in a pile of artefacts back in England," said the baron, less than truthfully. "I must have picked it up in the Sphinx chamber and then forgotten about it. Find out what you can about this woman, Salim."

The Egyptian was a little suspicious of this request, but did not question his employer. He was making an extremely good living out of the exploits of Baron Algernon Northgate. "I will do what I can, Baron," he said.

"It is important," responded the baron firmly. "Start your investigations with immediate effect. I will oversee the digging team in your absence."

ജ്ഞ

The baron stood on Gebel Gibli, surveying the plateau below. The view was magical. Spread out before him, he could see all nine pyramids, the Sphinx, and various temples and masteba. The Great Pyramid and its two sister pyramids were truly timeless masterpieces of architectural design. Many thousands of years old, they looked more modern, streamlined and purposeful than any other building that he could think of in his era. Were the pyramids really over-engineered stupendously extravagant tombs, or secret temples? Somehow, that concept did not ring true. There was no real evidence that conclusively demonstrated that the pyramids on the Giza plateau were designed, or ever even used, as the burial places of pharaohs. The baron wondered what these magnificent structures were originally built for. He hoped that the strange inscriptions in the chambers below the very area where he stood would throw new light on this age-old question.

The terrain on which the Englishman was standing was irregular and rugged. There were numerous chunks of exposed limestone in evidence. They appeared natural—part of the living bedrock. It was difficult to envisage that there could ever have been a great temple up here, but he was curious to know if the big metal rod that he had seen in the complex below the underground lake had originally penetrated the surface up here somewhere.

Thank God I discovered that underwater fissure, he thought, for it was becoming increasingly evident that they would never find a way into the hidden complex of chambers from the surface. Of course this was all to the good now. If his team came up empty-handed, then it was likely that other treasure hunters and archaeologists that followed them would suffer the same fate. The baron directed some of the members of the excavation team, all Egyptians, to explore the summit of the hill and see if they could find anything. There were deposits of sand and rubble in places that may have been concealing something.

ꟸ

Salim returned to the dig site a week later and handed the baron a handwritten report. "I have transcribed everything I could find out about the woman named Nesmut, Baron, including copies of the relevant hieroglyphs," he said. "She proved to be the wife of a prominent aristocrat in the court of Tutankhamen. There was a great deal of intrigue and murder around at that time. The country was still in turmoil after the reign of the Pharaoh Akhenaton, who was branded a heretic. His son, Tutankhamen, succeeded him as a child and was pretty much a puppet of the vizier Ay. When the young pharaoh reached early manhood and began to develop a mind of his own, he died suddenly, under mysterious circumstances. Ay succeeded him as pharaoh. It is possible that the powers that be at that time, and Ay is the prime suspect, fearing that Tutankhamen was on the verge of openly embracing the 'heresy' of his father's religion, murdered him to avert the country plunging back into chaos. It is clear from the inscription on the inside of the bracelet that Nesmut was a member of the 'heretic' religion—a priestess no less! The unfortunate woman died shortly after her husband. It was claimed that it was suicide, but of course it may have been murder."

Although the baron's face did not betray it, this was disturbing news.

Nesmut knew the location of the Hall of Records, he thought. *It looks like her final visit was a hurried one, which probably explained how she lost her bracelet. It was also a possible explanation for the absence of artefacts in the hidden chambers. It is lucky that she did not take the twelve crystals, or have the pillar that was inscribed with the cipher keys defaced. The woman must have been in a terrible rush, for she even left the "doors unlocked." Whatever she came to collect must have been of critical value to the old religion, and must have posed a tremendous danger if it had fallen into the wrong hands. It would appear that the artefact or artefacts were so important that the inscriptions and drawings in the tunnels and chambers were relatively trivial in comparison... It was possible that she was being hunted by the agents of Ay, and in desperation relocated the artefact or artefacts to a safer hiding place. It is possible that, fearing torture, she killed herself rather than risk the secrets of the hidden world below Giza falling into the wrong hands.*

CHAPTER 30
BACK IN OXFORD

ഗ്രാ

Alexander reached a big wooden door, bleached by decades of sunlight. He stood there, hesitating, almost in trepidation. This was his first tutorial of the new term. Now the moment of truth had arrived and he had to face Dr. Malone. How could he tell him that he had ignored his advice yet again, and that he had broken his promise? The contents of those two blue journals were nothing short of momentous. Indeed, he had summarised the journals in another report that highlighted the key issues and findings. It was vital that his friend and ally read this report, for the next course of action was far from clear. But how was he going to get him to read the report without invoking his anger yet again? Given the Irishman's volcanic nature, it was an anger that this time could destroy their alliance once and for all. Alexander tapped hesitantly on the door.

"Come in," boomed a mighty voice, without the slightest hint of humour.

As soon as the boy was through the door, the Irishman raised a hand. "Please take a seat," he rumbled. "Sit down and wait for the others. I can tell, just by looking at you, that you have something to say to me. Northgate Hall is involved, no doubt." Frank would never admit it out loud, but he half hoped that the boy had gone back to the house and found out something new that could help them. It was clear after his latest brush with death that things were starting to come to a head. "Meet me at the Porters Lodge at 5.00 p.m. sharp; we can catch up then," he added.

ꙮ

At 6.00 p.m. that evening, the man and the boy sat facing each other in Kidlington. Frank was on the phone, ordering an Indian takeaway. "Grand, that's sorted," he said, putting down the receiver. "Let's just briefly recap what you told me in the car on the way over. You broke your promise to me and returned to the house. Well, why am I not surprised? You found two more journals and managed to get out of that dreadful place without any real problems. Well, you are still alive and in one piece, so I can't argue with that. The thing from the house seems to have turned its affections in my direction instead."

"Well," butted in Alexander, with a newfound confidence bourn of the relief that their partnership was still in tact, "after what you've told me about that frightening incident with the woman and that truck, I think we can finally put a name and identity to the entity."

Frank looked at the boy a little sceptically. "We shall see, young man," he said. "Go and make us some coffee and I will get started on the report. Leave the journals here. It is best that we keep them all together. Anyway, I will need to read through them for myself."

ꙮ

The Oxford academic began to study the report. The first page was a brief summary of the first of the two blue journals. It focused on the access routes to the complex of chambers and tunnels under the Sphinx, and the metal-lined chambers located below the hidden lake. The summary also detailed the identity of the woman who was probably the last person to enter the chambers prior to the baron. The remainder of the report dealt with the second of the blue journals and read as follows:

Blue Journal 2

The journal was dated 1897 – (no end date was given). The photographs, sketches and notes that the baron made in the chambers of records were written up in this journal. The order of appearance of the information tracked the baron's progress through the twelve outer chambers, followed by the twelve tunnels that connected with the central chamber, and finally the central chamber itself. Entries in the journal related exclusively to science and technology. It is probable that, had he lived, the baron would have eventually recorded other aspects of the ancient civilisation such as religion, astronomy, agriculture, medicine and the arts. The information, as presented in this report, has been edited and reorganised into a more concise and logical sequence than it was written down in the journal. I have summarised the sections of text, rather than transcribed them word for word. As much of the technology would have been alien to the baron, I have reviewed the text in the light of our current knowledge, rather than from the perspective of a Victorian aristocrat. When time permits, both journals will be scanned and recorded in CD format. They will also be typed up, word for word.

It is evident that the baron found a way to translate the ancient language. No doubt he used the cipher key that was inscribed on one of the metal pillars in the central chamber. He may well have had help from a philologist, but no mention of it is made in the journal. The baron described the script used in the inscriptions on the walls and pillars in the chambers of records as cuneiform. It consisted of a series of strange looking wedge-shaped vertical, horizontal and triangular markings. The lines of writing were arranged with mathematical precision.

The names of places and objects written in the journal have to be taken at face value, for no indication was given as to how they were translated from the original language. Additionally, no mention is made of the assumptions and interpretations that were used. Verification and clarification can only be achieved when, and if, the original photographic plates are recovered. We have no way of knowing if this journal is a partial or complete overview of all the material. My guess is that the baron never got to complete the work, due most likely to his premature death. Ultimately, the material contained in this journal can only be authenticated by experts who have been able to gain access to the chambers of records themselves.

ENTRANCE PORTAL TO HALL OF RECORDS

The inscription on the metal door leading to the first chamber was translated as:

AZTLAN
EMPIRE OF LIGHT

The identification of the authors of the knowledge contained within the chambers of records was inscribed on one of the pillars in the central chamber, the most secure area of the complex.

CREATORS OF THE HALL OF RECORDS

The authors of the knowledge described themselves as the "Scribes of the Council of Elders." Their homeland was originally the great continent of Aztlan, which at the time that the records were written was the most powerful empire in the world. In those days, the land of Egypt was a colony of Aztlan named Osiris and was controlled by the Elders. They were called the Elders because they were the direct descendents of the original colonists. In Osiris, they were the racial elite. According to the baron, the Hall of Records was constructed well over eleven thousand years before his era. Unfortunately, no indication was given in the journal as to how he dated the chambers

The journal contained a sketch of a map of the world, and associated notes. All of the continents were in the same positions that they are in now, but their coastlines looked different. There was more land area than there is today, and massive icecaps covered huge tracts of the northern and southern hemispheres. Islands such as the Bahamas, Cuba and Malta were much larger than they are now. The map in the chamber appears to have been a map of the world before the end of the last Ice Age. At that time, sea levels were much lower than they are now, due to the enormous volumes of water trapped in the icecaps. The continent of Aztlan, as depicted on the map, is now called South America. It was divided into ten city-states, all governed by the primary city, which was called Azal. That city was located in a region of the continent that is now known as Bolivia.

Azal was shown on a schematic as being circular, with alternating bands of land and water. In all, there were three circular waterways surrounding the central circular zone of the city, with a band of land between each waterway. The walls of the city were faced with Orichalcum—a shimmering metal alloy of gold and copper.

Azal was known throughout the civilised world as the city of water and copper. In the ancient language of the Aztlaneans the word for water was “Atl.” and the word for copper was “Antis.” So Azal had the nickname “Atlantis.” If these records are to be believed, the original continent of Atlantis was actually South America, and the fabled island city existed in Bolivia, close to what was once a large inland sea.

PURPOSE OF THE HALL OF RECORDS

The astronomers of Aztlan detected an asteroid that was on a collision course with Earth. They predicted a period of five years before it struck. Being a highly advanced civilisation, they knew the implications of this terrible discovery. The Aztlaneans had an array of weapons that could fragment the asteroid, but not destroy it. It was already too close to the Earth. A super weapon had recently been invented that could vaporise metal and rock. If enough of these weapons could be deployed around the planet, the asteroid could be completely destroyed in the outer atmosphere by mighty death beams. There was, however, one problem: the Rama Empire. This was an impressive civilisation that was becoming an increasingly powerful rival to Aztlan and its wealth-generating colonies.

As it was, Aztlan and Rama were close to war. For many millennia, Aztlan had been a highly cultured and technologically advanced confederation of city-states, but in recent centuries, Rama had grown in power and their technological development was catching up fast with that of Aztlan. Some of the outer colonies were starting to fall under the influence of Rama’s power. Rather than share the technology of the new weapon with Rama and risk it being turned against them when the asteroid had been vaporised, it was decided that they would subdue the Kingdom of Rama. When Rama had been defeated, the new weapons could be deployed at critical locations around the globe without risk, or so the Aztlaneans mistakenly thought.

A terrible war ensued. The armies of Rama put up a ferocious resistance to the Aztlanean onslaught. There was massive destruction, and millions died on both sides. In short, the war had been a catastrophic miscalculation on the part of the Aztlaneans. Although Rama was eventually defeated, Aztlan was greatly weakened and it no longer had the resources to build enough of the death beams to ensure destruction of the asteroid. Indeed, those that they already possessed were destroyed or neutralised during the war. Fearing that their civilisation would be obliterated by the asteroid, the Aztlaneans decided to preserve their vast knowledge in sanctuaries, or chambers of records, that would be hidden in mountains or deep below the earth. The Giza chambers were part of these sanctuaries of knowledge.

SCIENCE AND TECHNOLOGY

The Aztlaneans had acquired extensive knowledge of the Earth's geodetic grid system and its effects on the human psyche. Large-standing stones, and eventually pyramids, were used to amplify the geodetic energies. They acted like enormously powerful spiritual boosters, allowing priests and scientists to attain amazing levels of awareness. The early pyramids were in effect psychic generators built over powerful geodetic centres of earth energies. They were machines that allowed the minds of mortal men to unite with the Universal Mind—the all-pervading consciousness of the cosmos.

It is clear that the Aztlaneans had attained a level of technological development far in advance of that in the

Victorian era. Indeed, in some respects their civilization appeared to be more advanced than our own in the 21st century.

BUILDING AND ARCHITECTURE

It is clear from the journal that the Aztlaneans were masters of stone. They had manufactured a chemical solution that could temporarily render limestone as soft as putty. This permitted stone blocks to be shaped and positioned with incredible precision. They also had a recipe for producing synthetic stone that was almost identical to high quality limestone. This could be handled like modern concrete. The Aztlaneans had invented highly sophisticated cutting and drilling tools. The baron believed that working examples of these tools had originally been left in the chambers of records below Giza. Indeed, the Aztlaneans had developed sonic technology to a very high level and used it to levitate massive stone blocks, weighing many hundreds of tons. They also used this technology as a highly destructive weapon. There were schematics of a machine that could be used to levitate rocks, but no details on the weapon.

Public buildings, monuments and temples were built, using huge blocks of interlinked stone. The construction techniques rendered these structures highly resistant to earthquakes. In the cities, space was not the issue that it is today. Buildings generally did not exceed five stories, although some of the public buildings had towers and domes of up to three hundred feet in height. Pyramids dotted the landscape and sometimes reached heights of around five hundred feet. Towns and cities were laid out on a grid system. Lakes, canals and vast parks were a feature of the larger cities. The Aztlaneans had developed highly sophisticated systems of dams, reservoirs, canals, aqueducts, drains, hydraulic underground waterways and sewers.

It was indicated in the chambers of records that the Great Pyramid at Giza was an exact duplicate of the largest of the pyramids built in Aztlan. These pyramids were constructed with specific functions in mind. The primary purpose of the Great Pyramid was not as a repository of knowledge; indeed, the architectural dimensions of the pyramid were formulated to maximise its power.

ENGINEERING

The Aztlaneans devised a complete scale of measurements based on the Earth's dimensions. Their primary unit of length was identical to the Egyptian cubit.

The baron indicated in the journal that a whole range of tools had been illustrated on the metal walls of the chambers of records. He believed that working examples of some of these tools would originally have been present in the chambers. There were tools and instruments for all sorts of purposes: astronomy, medicine, building, agriculture, etc. A technology that particularly captured the baron's imagination involved the use of sound.

Some of the machines that the Aztlaneans employed to work with stone involved the use of high frequency sound, or ultrasonics, as we call it today. Stone could be drilled and hollowed out using high-speed crystal-tipped drills. Ultrasound was used to vibrate these drills at extremely high frequencies. They could cut through the hardest types of stone with great precision and rapidity. At the other end of the spectrum, machines generating very low frequency, highly amplified sound waves were used to disintegrate rock by means of acoustic vibration. This technology was most frequently employed in the construction of tunnels and for mining.

An extremely advanced form of sympathetic vibratory physics appears to have been used to levitate massive stone slabs weighing many hundreds, if not thousands of tons. The process involved establishing the resonant frequency of the object to be moved. While no technical specifications were given in the journal, it was indicated that once the correct harmonics had been identified, a wall of sound was directed at the object to be lifted. This appears to have generated some sort of electromagnetic effect in the object itself, causing a powerful repulsive force with the ground on which it rested; this effect rendered the object temporarily weightless. Sonic technology made it possible to push or lift massively huge weights.

CRYSTALS

The Aztlaneans used crystals extensively. They possessed immense knowledge of crystal refraction, amplification and storage. The crystals used were natural forms, or they could be manufactured artificially. Some of the crystals were massive—anything up to 20 feet high and 7 feet in diameter. Crystals were utilised for different purposes, such as in medicine, communications, and power generation and transmission.

The various types of crystals received their power from a variety of sources, including the Sun and the Earth's electromagnetic and gravitational fields. Massive gems, called "Fire Crystals," functioned in receiving and broadcasting stations, while smaller crystals were used as receivers for large buildings, vehicles and homes. Energy could be used for various purposes. Electricity could be transmitted through the air using crystals, and sound and moving images could also be broadcast around the empire.

Crystals were used to store and process information, much as we use silicon in computers in the 21st century. My guess is that they had light-based computers, rather than the slower electronic computers that we still use. The baron, like the ancient Egyptians, would have had no conception of computers. I feel that there is a very good chance that details of Aztlanean computer technology are stored in one or more of the twelve crystals that the baron retrieved from the chambers of records.

POWER SYSTEMS

Electricity was as central to the technologies of the Aztlaneans, as it is today. A variety of ways to generate electricity was recorded in the chambers. With the exception of the production of simple batteries, however, detailed technical specifications were not given.

The Aztlaneans recognised that the Earth is a powerhouse of tremendous mechanical, thermal, electrical, and magnetic energy, each a source of sound. In other words, they knew that the energy locked up in the Earth generated sound waves. These sound waves were directly related to the particular vibration of the energy creating them and the material through which they passed.

It appears from what is written in the journal that the Aztlaneans developed a device that could respond to the Earth's sound vibrations to generate energy, or ultimately electricity. This device was a pyramid that contained specially constructed internal components. It was indicated in the chambers of records that the Great Pyramid was originally designed as just such a device. In other words, the Great Pyramid was a geo-mechanical power plant that responded sympathetically with the Earth's sound vibrations and converted that sound into electricity.

The reasons for the various structural anomalies in the Great Pyramid, so well known to Egyptologists, were inscribed by the Elders on a wall in the hidden chambers. These included explanations as to why the "ventilation shafts" of the Queen's Chamber, terminated before they reached the exterior of the pyramid and the strong sulphuric smell and salt deposits in this chamber; the function of the five spaced layers of massive granite beams located above the King's Chamber; and the presence of the well shaft at the entrance of the Grand Gallery.

It was indicated that the Great Pyramid of Giza was a power generator that directed an energy beam out of the southern ventilating shaft, which was actually a wave-guide. The massive dimensions of the pyramid, together with the precision of its construction, facilitated a coupling effect with the Earth. In essence, the pyramid was designed as a coupled oscillator that could resonate in harmony with the Earth. The vibration energy generated in the pyramid was translated, through a system of resonators, no longer present in the pyramid, in the Grand Gallery, into sound. The sonic tone, greatly amplified in the Grand Gallery, was projected through to the Antechamber, where it was purified. In other words, the Antechamber acted as an acoustic filter. The purified sound waves then entered the King's Chamber, causing the chamber and overlying granite beams to resonate at a precisely determined frequency. This produced an alternating compression and decompression effect in the quartz crystals that composed the granite. These hundreds of tons of microscopic quartz crystals created a powerful electromagnetic field, due to an effect known today as the "piezoelectric effect."

The records stated that a gas, which I believe was probably hydrogen, was manufactured in the Queen's Chamber. The gas rose through the well shaft into the Grand Gallery, and finally, into the King's Chamber. The King's Chamber acted as a powerful transducer. The gas resident in this chamber was subjected to a significant electromagnetic stimulant from the quartz crystals in the granite, resulting in the production of energy emissions. From what I know of modern physics (21st century), pumping the hydrogen atoms to higher energy states could have resulted in a masing effect, producing microwave energy at the wavelength of the hydrogen atom. The energy waves (probably microwaves) were directed into the northern ventilator shaft (wave guide) and were reflected back into the King's Chamber. The coffer inside the King's Chamber was designed as an optical cavity with concave surfaces at each end. It was apparently used to focus the reflected energy waves into an energy beam that was then projected out of the pyramid via the southern air shaft (wave guide).

The Great Pyramid (and others like it in Aztlan) was something of a Trojan horse; power generation was not their primary function. These giant pyramids could be modified into powerful weapons of stupendous mass destruction. It was written in the chambers of records that the Aztlaneans had planned to build these massive pyramids at strategic sites around the globe. They were to be used as sentinels, guarding not only from attack by the enemies of Aztlan, but also from the menace of comets and asteroids. In the end, these pyramids proved to be the downfall of Aztlan.

There were other methods of power generation utilised by the ancients. The Aztlaneans had electric generators, much as we have today, but vastly more efficient. They were driven by wind and hydro-energy. The systems of transmission and utilisation of electric energy were considerably in advance of anything that we have in the 21st century. Instead of employing the countless miles of expensive and vulnerable metal cables that we use to transport electricity, the Aztlaneans could transmit electricity through the air. A common method of transmission and reception of electricity involved the use of metal columns. These typically extended about seventy feet above the stone structures in which they were housed. The columns were from about 6-20 inches in diameter. At their top end, they were divided into a series of spokes, which were around 7 feet long. These were orientated in the directions of other transmitters/ receivers. The metal from which they were constructed was a special microcrystalline alloy that could conduct electricity beams of great intensity and power.

Electrical resonance was critical to power generation, transmission and reception. The energy beams oscillated at a frequency of millions of megacycles per second (hugely higher than the frequencies used today). A large red crystal (ruby?) was attached to the bottom end of the metal column. This was used to focus incoming or outgoing energy beams. In the case of an incoming energy beam, the red crystal focused the beam onto a large crystal prism. The prism was sited directly below the crystal. The air space between the two crystals varied, depending on the size of the metal column, but it could be as much as ten feet. The prism was mounted on top of a massive colourless and transparent hexagonal faced crystal (quartz?) that was cylindrical in shape. The energy beam was segmented by the prism to produce lower-intensity multiple beams, which were subsequently transmitted to smaller metal rods that were attached to receiver devices.

Electricity was frequently transmitted across the countryside, using networks of specially designed towers. The most enduring of these towers were crystalline granite blocks, tuned to the resonance of the power beams. These towers were the obelisks that were later adopted by the civilisations that succeeded Aztlan, such as Egypt. Essentially, electricity was transmitted as microwaves and subsequently modulated into a low-frequency electric current, using crystal-based resonance transformers coupled to electric resonance motors. It is clear that the Aztlaneans had electric-powered machinery for heating, cooling, cooking, communication and transport.

TRANSPORT

The public transport system was highly advanced. Various types of antigravity systems had been developed. Incredible as it may seem, the Aztlaneans had airships. This appeared to be the thing that amazed the baron the most. In his day, aviation was still embryonic. From footnotes in the journal, it is clear that he was greatly disappointed by the fact that the Aztlaneans had left no detailed instructions or schematics as to how their flying machines were constructed. The baron guessed that the twelve crystals that he had retrieved from the hidden chambers may well contain huge volumes of information, including instructions as to how to build these flying machines. It is clear that this information was not meant for the relatively primitive civilisations that followed them, but he was convinced that there was immense knowledge locked in the crystals that was ripe for the taking in his era of rapidly-advancing science and technology. The problem would be finding a way to unlock the secrets that the crystals most probably contained.

Two types of flying machines were illustrated on the metal walls of the chambers of knowledge. The smaller of the two crafts was saucer-shaped, with portholes and a dome. It had three hemispherical pods on the underside. According to the journal, this craft was propelled using a mechanical antigravity device system, based on the use of the liquid metal mercury. The larger craft was cigar-shaped and used similar propulsion technology to the saucer craft. The baron noted in the journal that these craft could take off vertically, were capable of hovering, and could fly very rapidly. Apparently the cigar-shaped craft could also travel underwater, and amazingly, also in outer space (but not beyond the limits of the solar system). This must have seemed utterly extraordinary to the baron. The nearest thing that the Victorians had to this technology was a hot air balloon.

THE WEAPONS OF AZTLAN

Just as is seen today, technological advancement brought with it the capacity to produce weapons capable of tremendous devastation. Although quite secretive about the mechanisms involved, the Elder scribes detailed a whole range of military hardware, but by far the most devastating weapon—a weapon of the most unimaginably terrible mass destruction—was the pyramid.

It was indicated in the journal that pyramids, built according to the design plan of the Great Pyramid, could be modified from a power plant to what was essentially a phase-conjugate mirror. This was the dreaded "Yin Yang Mirror" of legend. Again, the mechanism of action was based on a profound understanding of resonance and harmonics. Once the resonant frequency of a given target had been established, energy waves that were matched to that frequency were amplified in the pyramid. After amplification, these waves were projected to the target. In effect, harmonically synchronised energy was loaded into the target, resulting in the generation of an enormously powerful vibrational force that caused its complete disintegration.

Essentially, then, the pyramid could be changed from a power generator to a death beam weapon. This was achieved by removing the regular resonators from the Grand Gallery and replacing them with specially engineered crystals. These crystals were incredibly difficult and expensive to manufacture. The regular resonators used for power generation were hollow spheres of graded sizes, each with a small, round opening. Details of the material from which they were constructed were not given, but it could have been a metal alloy or a ceramic material. The crystals that replaced the regular resonators were meticulously engineered to be both optically and acoustically resonant. They were arranged in banks that were secured into slots on two side ramps, located in the Grand Gallery.

Situated inside the coffer in the King's Chamber was an enormous crystal that was about a foot and a half wide and over five feet in height. It was essentially a transparent cylindrical prism, with a hexagonal cross-section. The six sides of the crystal had been ground and polished with incredible precision. Indeed, it was indicated in the chambers of records that these power crystals were the crowning glory of Aztlanean crystal manufacturing technology. No other civilisation at that time (or probably even now) could achieve the incredibly tight tolerances needed for the manufacture of these crystals.

Energy rays, generated by the crystals in the Grand Gallery when incident on the great crystal, were reflected from each of its faces in turn—six reflections per revolution. The rays followed a helical path around the axis of the prism, undergoing thousands of revolutions. When the revolving energy rays reached the top of the crystal, a multifaceted prism located on the apex of the crystal refracted the energy rays back on themselves so that they pursued a helical path down the crystal. Eventually, this process resulted in an enormous build-up of energy in the crystal. When the energy reached a critical level, it was discharged out of the crystal in a massive burst that travelled up through the pyramid to the capstone. The capstone was made out of a gold-based alloy, a highly conductive metal. It was here that the final focusing of the beam took place, before it was projected from the pyramid. It was also indicated that a series of subterranean chambers and passageways had been carved into the limestone plateau under the pyramid. These housed instrumentation and machinery used in the control and targeting the weapon.

A feature that was absolutely unique to the Great Pyramid and its sister pyramids on Aztlan was that each of its four faces was indented slightly, but very precisely, at the centre. In other words, each face was shaped like a parabolic reflector. This was a design feature that allowed the pyramid to receive and amplify the harmonic signature of a given target. The Great Pyramid was essentially a death mirror, designed to collect energy emissions from a target; its function was to duplicate and greatly amplify these emissions and then send them back precisely in phase with the harmonics of the target. In theory, any target that could be detected by the pyramid could be hit, this included objects such as comets or asteroids travelling close to the Earth in outer space. When pulses of harmonised energy that had been fired from the pyramid reached the target, it was vaporised.

The plan had been to locate enough of these weapons around the planet so that any rogue asteroid or comet could be effectively detected, targeted and destroyed. In the end, these pyramids were used in the terrible war with the Rama Empire, destroying cities and huge swaths of countryside. They were ultimately neutralised by the forces of Rama and their allies, leaving the Earth defenceless from the approaching asteroid.

THE LEGACY OF AZTLAN

The Elder scribes concluded by stating that it was hoped that one day their records would be discovered by the

"Worthy," a civilisation advanced enough to learn from the tragic fate of Aztlan, and to profit from their vast knowledge.

Lifting his head from the paper, Frank rubbed his face thoughtfully, the day's growth of stubble grating against his hands. *Fascinating as all this is,* he thought, *it is probably only the tip of the iceberg. The amazing thing is that somewhere in Northgate Hall there exists real physical evidence of a lost civilisation; a civilisation that at its height appeared to be more advanced than our own civilisation, at least in some areas. Incredibly, we now also have in our possession the location of the fabled Lost Hall of Records. While there can be little doubt that the knowledge inscribed in the Hall of Records had a profound influence on the Egyptian civilisation at various points in its history, I would guess that the crystals are by far the greatest treasure of all. If there is indeed information stored in those crystals and it can be accessed, then the impact on modern civilisation could be nothing short of seismic.*

Frank's train of thought was brought to an abrupt halt by the ringing doorbell. Rising swiftly from the desk, his mouth watering, he headed into the hallway. "A man's got to eat," he purred.

CHAPTER 31
THE PRIESTESS

ഇ

They sat at the kitchen table, mopping up the last of the curry sauce with Naan bread. Two steaming mugs of coffee stood at the ready. "So, as I said," began Frank, reaching for one of the mugs, "the blue journals of Baron Northgate contain incredible information. We have much to discuss, young man. Let's deal with the most pressing issue first: the identity of that dreaded entity that means to do us mortal harm! It was a very beautiful ghost that tried to murder me on the way back to Oxford. Very beautiful indeed, I might say! But she is as lethal as she is beautiful! The question is, is she the spirit of the priestess mentioned in the baron's journals? My own view is that it is difficult to say without more evidence. Other than the baron finding the bracelet of the priestess, there appears to be no other link between them."

The Irishman paused and took a swig of his coffee. Alexander looked thoughtfully at the few remaining streaks of curry on his plate. "What you say is true, Dr. Malone," he said, "but it is clear from your recent encounter that the woman was in her late twenties or early thirties, and that she was dressed like an Egyptian of high status. She was wearing a distinctive hat that could probably be dated. Based on one of the books that I read from your collection on Egyptology, I would guess that it could be a style of hat that was prevalent in the New Kingdom. That would place the entity in the same era as the priestess mentioned in the journal. We know that the priestess was the wife of a prominent aristocrat in the court of Tutankhamen. She must have been a very senior figure in the cult of the Sphinx, because she had access to the Hall of Records. It is also clear that she removed something from the Hall of Records. The key item was probably the great crystal, but there could have been other artefacts as well. We also know that the baron continued to deploy his assistant on many digs after he found the Hall of Records. More than likely, he was trying to find the tomb of Nesmut in the hope of discovering clues as to the whereabouts of the giant crystal. Nesmut felt so strongly about this crystal and the ancient knowledge buried below Giza that she killed herself to protect their hidden locations."

The Irishman banged down his empty coffee cup. "By the saints, that could be it!" he exclaimed. "Much of the paranormal phenomena that has been documented over the years is associated with sites were people have died violently or have committed suicide. Many spiritual and religious philosophies assert that the spirits of the unfortunates that have taken their own lives can be bound to the Earth plane for centuries, perhaps even millennia. Nesmut probably committed suicide and she died with secrets of great value to protect. It could well be that she guards them even to this day. It is a fact that the baron was hunting for those secrets. Perhaps he found them. The massive obelisk that he built may well have been more than an extravagant monument. It could be an enormous machine. More than likely, it is a replica of an Aztlanean power tower. But to get it to work, he would probably have needed the giant crystal. So why build a hugely expensive structure without the crystal? It could be that Hall of Records contained a prophecy—a prophecy so terrible that the baron could not bring himself to record it in the journal. Perhaps the baron was building a weapon, a weapon that could destroy a comet—a comet or asteroid that is destined to hit the Earth." The Irishman sighed. "There are still more questions than answers."

"But we are getting closer to the truth, Dr. Malone," responded Alexander. "A prophecy could explain why the baron built the obelisk, or it could be that he just had more money than sense. Perhaps he was confident that he would eventually find the crystal, or maybe he was going to carry out his own experiments with a crystal, or crystals, made to specifications that he had discovered in the Hall of Records. If he had gotten the machine to work, he could have become one of the most powerful men on the planet. Maybe he felt that it was worth the financial risk, but putting two and two together, if the baron did find the great crystal, then it was Nesmut that he would have had to have dealt with. It could well be that it was her very mummy that the baron brought to Northgate Hall."

The chair creaked as Frank stretched himself. He needed a cigarette. "So if Nesmut is the culprit, I can understand her killing the baron, but why try and exterminate the Northgate Dynasty by mercilessly killing all the male heirs, generation after generation? Is that not taking things a bit too far?"

"Well, after everything that we have been through," replied Alexander, "there is no doubting that spirits are real! The baron appears to have been just as obsessed with the crystal and the ancient knowledge as Nesmut. No doubt when he died, that obsession lived on in his spirit. What we could be looking at is a battle in the astral world, with the baron trying to finish his work through his male descendants and the entity destroying them one by one. The baron was a ruthless man. It was clear that he was prepared to sacrifice lives if he had to. Anyway, what is the death of a human body to a spirit? To spirits, the body is just a shell. Life goes on after so-called death! To us, that is just a theory or belief, but to them it is a reality. It is pretty certain that my father was investigating Northgate Hall when he was killed. My mother just happened to be in the wrong place at the wrong time. I was lucky to escape with my life."

"But what exactly are they fighting for?" rumbled Frank. "In this day and age, we must have technologies that match anything that the baron was trying to put together, using primitive Victorian tools!"

Alexander nodded. "Maybe," he said. "Perhaps it has something to do with the twelve crystals. They may contain knowledge far in advance of our own; knowledge that could be very dangerous in the wrong hands. Agents of Ay may have been in hot pursuit of Nesmut, and she may not have had time to retrieve the crystals. Then again, she may have felt it best not to place all of her eggs in the one basket. In ancient times, they would have just been crystals to the uninitiated. Perhaps even the Priesthood of the Sphinx could not access their secrets; but maybe the baron found a way. As you say, Dr. Malone, there are still unanswered questions. While I am in no hurry to return to Northgate Hall, ultimately, it would appear to be the only way forward. The final answers may well lie in the great obelisk."

The Irishman groaned. "What you say is true," he said, "but for the love of God, let's give it a rest for a while." With that, he excused himself and headed for a cigarette.

CHAPTER 32
TO THE DEATH

Even though she had experienced quite a few of them, coincidences still surprised Zoe Watts. She was spending the day in London, looking at the latest high tech surveillance equipment, and pretty much anything else that took her fancy. As she admired a fetching pair of boots in an Oxford Street window, she caught sight of something out of the corner of her eye. Further down the road, standing outside a coffee shop, was an unmistakable figure. It was somebody that she had not seen in quite a while—Butch. The big woman, dressed in her black biker leathers was deep in conversation with a man. Zoe decided to stay put and observe.

From their body language, it was clear that they knew each other well. The man was around the same height as his female companion and was wearing an expensive brown leather jacket, blue jeans, and cowboy boots. His head was shaven and he wore a goatee-type beard.

Although no longer in uniform, Zoe—or more accurately Kathleen—still had the heart of a policewoman. The man suddenly broke off the conversation and headed down Oxford Street, raising a sudden dilemma. If she was going to follow him, she needed to cross the road, no easy feat on Oxford Street during shopping hours. Otherwise, she ran the risk of being recognised by Butch, who was still standing outside the coffee shop. She decided to risk it; it was too good an opportunity to miss. If she crossed the road, she could lose the target.

Zoe observed Butch as best she could through her peripheral vision as she walked briskly past her. The private detective had a very different look to the estate agent that Butch had encountered in the Firkin. Now she had short, aggressively-styled hair, an ankle-length coat, T-shirt and leather trousers—all black. The pavements were teeming, so the odds of her being recognised were extremely low. There were no sudden movements from the big woman as Zoe flashed past, so it was game on.

The target had reached the steps of the underground. Zoe picked up her pace and followed him down. Swiping a ticket, the target was soon through the barriers and descending the escalator, with Zoe close behind. Fortunately, she had a Tube day pass. Stepping off the escalator, the target headed in the direction of the Central Line. The place was thronging with travellers, so Zoe had to stay uncomfortably close to her quarry.

She found herself taking a passageway to a platform with Epping as the final destination. Walking onto the crowded platform, her hair was blown back. *Just in time*, she thought, as a train drew in. The doors slid open and people poured out. As soon as there was space, the crowds on the platform surged forward, pushing and jostling into the few available seats. Fortunately, Zoe managed to cram herself into the same carriage as the target. With so many people, it would be impossible to track him from another carriage. Twenty feet from her, he seemed oblivious to her pursuit.

The doors slid shut. Moving off, the train picked up speed rapidly, clattering noisily against the rails. It was like a sardine can in that carriage, bodies pressed one against the other, the air loaded with second-hand breath. After a while, there was a sudden jolt and the train started to slow. The doors opened. Tottenham Court Road. Release! Bodies surged out of the carriage. Personal space invasion—people hated that; and it does not get any worse than the Central Line. Relief was short-lived. A new influx of humanity filled the empty spaces, packing the carriage to its bursting point. Zoe found herself sandwiched between a pinstriped suit and a fat lady. Luckily, the target had maintained his position.

Slowly, with each passing station the pressure began to ease, and by Stratford there was even the odd free seat available. Zoe stayed standing, observing the target as best she could with her peripheral vision. By Snaresbrook she was becoming conspicuous as the carriage progressively emptied of people; she took a seat. *Looks like he's going all the way,* she thought, as he turned another page of his paperback.

Sure enough, the target was still reading as they pulled into Epping, the final station on the line. Zoe deliberately looked the other way as the doors opened and the remaining passengers rose from their seats. Stepping onto the platform, she stopped abruptly. Up ahead, the target had his ear to a mobile. Nodding once, he broke off suddenly and started to walk rapidly towards the exit. She followed, matching his pace.

Zoe knew only too well the value of surprise. A split second was all it took to gain the upper hand. In a single bound, the target jumped over the barriers and broke into a sprint. Moving surprisingly rapidly for a man in cowboy boots, he disappeared from view.

"Game over," hissed Zoe, now heading for the nearest cup of coffee. "Somebody must have called him and tipped him off—probably Butch. Shit!"

❧

It was dark in North Oxford as a hooded figure moved swiftly up a quiet side-road. Turning into a short driveway, he reached a door and pressed a bell. Moments later, a white van drew up and Butch, accompanied by the hooded figure, climbed inside. Soon the van had threaded its way out of

Oxford and onto the bypass. "What's this all about?" asked Butch in a low, angry voice. Looking across at her from the driver's seat, Douglas Flint smiled, but his eyes were cold.

"We need to have a chat, somewhere quiet where we won't be disturbed," he said. "Nothing to worry about, we just need to clear a few things up."

Butch was worried—very worried. "It's got something to do with that bloody woman—that private detective—hasn't it?"

"Not here," came the curt reply.

She knew better than to open her mouth again. Her companions were professional killers, and Flint was the most ruthless man she had ever met. The van joined the M40, heading in the direction of London. Butch's mood grew grimmer. They were going somewhere quiet, all right—too quiet. Thirty minutes later, the van crunched up a long deserted gravel drive. "I recognise this place," she mumbled. "It's where we brought that little prick from the university."

Her companions remained silent until the van had stopped. Pointing to the right, Flint said, "There's a clearing through those trees; we can talk there."

Leaving the van, they made their way towards the trees. Soon they reached the clearing. It was a cloudless night and the moon was almost full. Flint stopped and turned to face the big woman. He was lean and powerful, standing six-foot-three inches tall. Butch was scared now, but still defiant.

"What the fuck's this all about?" she growled.

Smiling icily, Flint unsheathed a large throwing knife and hurled it at a nearby tree.

"The hit at the station was our last job," he said. "It was a big payday for all of us. The assassination business is very lucrative, but not without its drawbacks. You've had it pretty easy—just the delivery boy. We've been ducking and diving in grotty bed-sits while you've been sitting pretty in the provinces. Bloody years of it, but now it's over, and I've got an awful lot of money to spend."

"So what's the problem? What's so frigging important that you have to drag me all the way out here?" asked Butch.

"Loose ends," said Flint. "Loose ends."

"What do you mean, loose ends?" growled Butch, growing angry now.

"Craig was followed yesterday," answered Flint.

"Are you certain?" asked Butch, her voice rising. "It was just a hunch, nothing definite."

"I got her on camera at Epping station," said Flint, his voice flat and controlled. "One of our associates did some checking; she's a private dick."

"So you're blaming me?"

"Well, we did you that favour. I told you it could be risky not killing him, but oh no, you just wanted to scare him. And now we've got issues... I reckon that private dick has been following you for some time, off and on. Yesterday she got lucky. And it ain't the first time, I'll warrant. That last drop in the parks...there was a chick there...bumped into a kid. I thought it was odd at the time, but I let it go. Now it clicks into place; she was following you. That little university bastard is trying to get even. He's using you to get to us. By now Craig and me will be sitting in a filing cabinet or on a hard drive—in full fucking colour."

"So what happens now?" asked Butch, her mind racing.

"It's time to clean up nice and tidy," said Flint.

Before Butch could say another word, he added, "You see that knife over there? I'm going to kill you with it."

Quickly, he stepped back three paces so she could not lash out at him. There were two sharp clicks as Craig, the man with the goatee beard, cocked a double-barrel shotgun. "Don't make a break for it!" barked Flint, "or Craig will blow you in half. If you get to the knife before me, use it. It's your only chance."

Butch did not wait. She turned and ran in the opposite direction to the knife. She knew that she did not have a prayer against Flint. "Don't shoot me, Craig!" she screamed as she ran. Craig held his fire as Flint sprinted after her. Moments later, a terrible crunching crack reverberated through the trees.

ꕥ

Zoe's eyes flickered open. She was in the back of a van. It had all happened so quickly. Just past midnight, when she had returned home after a job and was locking her car, the man with the goatee beard stepped out from behind a shrub—right in front of her. Next thing she knew, she was coming to—hands, feet and mouth bound with tape. Her aching neck told her that she had been hit from behind. Looking around with desperate eyes, she could see that she was not alone in the van. There were two very large barrels and a series of smaller barrels lashed to the front and sides of the vehicle.

The rear doors of the van creaked open and Craig climbed inside. Ripping the tape from Zoe's mouth, he said, "Dumb bitch! You've no idea who you've been messing with." He was a powerful man and picked her up easily. Flinging her over his shoulder, he stepped from the van. It did not take her long to realise that she was in a wooded area. He carried her to a clearing and dropped her to the ground.

"Scream if you like. Nobody's going to hear you out here," said a gruff voice. It was Flint. "If you want to live, then answer my questions—and don't piss me about!"

This is serious—couldn't be more fuckin serious, thought Zoe. Remaining silent, she looked straight into Flint's cold grey eyes.

"Listen, green eyes," he said. "Last chance! Start talking or die."

This is risky, but what've I got to lose?

"Come closer," she whispered.

As Flint bent over her, she spat at him straight in the face and said, "I don't do business with southern wankers!"

Straightening up, Flint wiped the saliva from his forehead. "Cut the bitch loose," he said calmly. "I'll have to beat it out of her."

Standing before the tall killer, Zoe flexed her hands and tried to shake some circulation back into her legs.

"You're cool under pressure, I'll give you that," said Flint, clenching both fists tight.

Bastard's probably a karate expert, thought Zoe.

"Let's see what you've got, little lady," sneered the big man.

Like Butch before her, she turned and ran, but her legs were stiff and she did not get far before Flint fell upon her. Grabbing her by the hair, he began to spin her around, intent on smashing a fist into her face, but as he stared incredulously, the top of her head peeled off in his hand. That was all that it took—one moment of shocked surprise.

Launching a snap kick, Zoe hit Flint straight in the groin. Falling to the ground, he writhed in agony. Jumping high in the air, she brought down her right foot with massive force, crashing it into the side of the killer's neck. Like him, she was no stranger to the martial arts, no stranger to deadly blows. He lay there, suddenly still.

Craig came charging through the trees, knife in hand. Getting to within five feet of Flint, he stopped. Zoe backed off slowly.

"Impressive," he said and grinned as he took aim with the knife.

Zoe faced him calmly, as the deadly blade sped towards her.

CHAPTER 33
WAYS OF THE ANCIENTS

ꚙ

Frank punched the buttons on his telephone a little nervously. He could hear the ringing at the other end of the line. Just as he thought the answering machine would kick in, a voice came through.

"Zoe Watts."

"Hi," said Frank, tentatively. "Good to catch you at home."

"Frank. Nice to hear from you," came the upbeat friendly response.

"It's been a while," said Frank. "How've you been keeping?"

Zoe cut straight to the chase. "You're ringing about Butch, I guess?"

"Sure," said Frank. "It's in all the local papers—disappeared without a trace."

"Very intriguing," said Zoe. "Up to no good that woman—probably dead!"

Frank was shocked. "What makes you say that?" he asked.

"Well, there's a good chance that she was mixed up with contract killers."

"What?" exclaimed Frank. "Where did you get that from?"

"Just a hunch," said Zoe.

"Do you think they'll come looking for me?" gasped Frank.

"You'd be dead by now if you were on their list," she said bluntly. "Pros don't hang about. They would have killed the two of you as a job lot!"

"So you think I'm in the clear?" he asked. Talking to this lady was starting to make him very nervous. He was sorry he'd rung her up.

"Trust me," said Zoe, "they won't be bothering you again."

Thanking her, Frank rang off.

Zoe had omitted to tell him that the two killers were now toxic soup, and probably Butch as well.

She cast her mind back to that terrible night last week. The knife had been on target when it had hit her, but she had shopped in New York, as well as London. She had learnt about body armour as a policewoman. In New York you could buy Kevlar jackets and coats. Expensive, even stylish, but more importantly, knife and bullet-proof. These days she always wore Kevlar on the job, and it had saved her life in those woods. The knife had bounced straight off her. Regrettably, she could not let Craig live. He was a killer, and sooner or later he would have hunted her down and liquidated her — him or his associates. Strong as he was, she had killed him with his own knife. Unfortunately, there was no way she could report the two killings to the police. At the very least she would lose her licence, and probably her liberty. As it happened, the barrels in the van proved to be very effective disposal units. Tip a body in, fill it with the fluids provided, leave it for a couple of days, and pour discretely down a drain or into a deep hole.

And why two barrels in the van? thought Zoe. *One was probably meant for Craig. After Flint had killed me he would have terminated Craig. Security had been compromised and in Flint's ruthless eyes, with retirement on his mind, Craig was just another loose end.* Anyway, what was done was done, and she had no regrets. Three less assholes walked the Earth.

ꕥ

"So," said Frank, continuing his conversation with Alexander, "finally it appears that someone has managed to unearth very solid evidence that the human race had a far more glorious past than the one that has been painted by mainstream academics. Part of the problem has always been, of course, the lack of evidence. Humanity has had a very sad and turbulent history. The great libraries of antiquity have been destroyed in wars and revolutions. The last great technological civilisations themselves seem to have been obliterated by a global catastrophe that pretty much wiped them from the face of the earth. Of course no self-respecting academic would believe a word that has been written in those journals without firm proof. Even the photographs and sketches of the baron would not be considered as conclusive evidence of the existence of the Hall of Records. People would have to travel out to Giza and have a look for themselves. And from what I have read, the water table has been rising there. The crypt in the Coptic Church would be flooded by now, and there is a good chance that the chambers themselves are now under water. Given the security on the Giza plateau these days, it is likely that the chambers of knowledge will remain hidden for a very long time."

"That may be no bad thing, Dr. Malone," said Alexander. "We need to establish exactly what knowledge is hidden in the crystals before world governments could be informed. In many ways, we still live on a pretty primitive planet. I wonder what happened to Salim?"

"I would like to think that he survived," responded Frank. "But who knows? The entity is a cold-hearted killer, that's for sure!"

"What about the location of Atlantis?" asked Alexander. "Most of the books that have been written speculate that it was situated in the middle of the Atlantic Ocean. The evidence that we now have contradicts this view."

"Well," said the Irishman, "some very interesting mapping and archaeological work has been carried out in Bolivia of late. In Plato's writings, the city of Atlantis was said to have been built on a rectangular-shaped plain that was located at a distance of fifty stades—five miles—from the sea, and midway along the longest side of the continent. The plain was described as being high above sea level, surrounded by mountains and fed by hot and cold underground springs. Just such a plain exists in Bolivia. The plain is called the "Bolivian Altiplano." It has a rectangular configuration, is enclosed by mountains, and is close to the sea. The Altiplano also has hot and cold springs. The mountains contain ores of copper, tin, silver, gold and Orichalcum—an alloy of copper and gold that occurs exclusively in the Andes mountain range. Indeed, Plato stated that Orichalcum was used to plate the walls of the circular city of Atlantis. The name "Atlantis" itself is of ancient South American origin and means the city of water and copper. Plato also stated that the city of Atlantis was built on a small volcanic island that was surrounded by circular belts of land and sea, some greater, some smaller—two being of land and three being of sea. Although the city has disappeared, remnants of the volcanic island still exist on the plain at a place now called "Pampa Aullagas." The island, or small mountain as it is today, is surrounded by circular depressions or belts filled with sand that once contained water."

"But I thought that Plato wrote that Atlantis sank under the ocean in a single day and night of rainfall?" interjected Alexander.

"Modern geologists have indicated that it is impossible for a continent to sink beneath the ocean in a single day. Indeed, there is no convincing geological evidence that a continent ever existed in the middle of the Atlantic Ocean, let alone sank beneath it. But it is certainly possible for a city to disappear under the waves due to earthquakes and floods. The Bolivian Altiplano has been subjected to earthquakes and floods in the past. In ancient times, Lake Poopo, which is situated close to Pampa Aullagas, was a large inland sea. That could have been the sea which inundated the city of Atlantis. The records from the hidden chambers certainly indicate that the fabled city was built near to this inland sea."

"So what about the famous canals?" asked Alexander.

"Well," replied Frank, rather pleased that he was managing to stay one step ahead of the boy, "Plato mentioned a large canal which was one stade wide and ran around the plain. The canal was fed by an underground spring. There is very clear evidence of such a canal on the Altiplano. It is also fed by an underground spring."

"What about ruins? Are there any ruins?" asked Alexander.

"Well, recent archaeological studies at the site indicate that there was once a city on and around the volcanic mountain, but the scattered remnants indicate that it was comprehensively destroyed. The area has yet to be subjected to detailed excavation."

"It will be facinating to see what they eventually unearth," said Alexander.

"So they had spaceships," continued the Irishman. "That is a difficult one to swallow!"

"I agree," said Alexander, "but there is evidence to support this. Actually, I've been reading a lot about ancient flying vehicles of late. A great deal has been written about such machines in ancient Indian texts. A news item a few years back reported that the Chinese had unearthed some ancient documents in Tibet. As they were written in the old language of Sanskrit, they were sent off to an Indian university for translation. It was revealed that the documents contained instructions for building spacecraft! An antigravity device was used as the main source of propulsion. The Chinese subsequently revealed that they were studying the information contained in the ancient documents carefully, with a view to incorporating some of the technology into their space program. I would guess that they were looking at the antigravity technology.

It is believed that the Indian flying machines were originally developed by the Rama Empire on the Indian subcontinent. There is evidence from recent archaeological studies that this civilisation was very ancient indeed. It was the Rama Empire that apparently went to war with the Atlanteans, or the Asvins, as the ancient Indian texts refer to them. The Indians had flying machines called 'Vimanas.' These were circular crafts with portholes and a dome much like a classic flying saucer, or they could be cigar-shaped. Many ancient Indian texts describe these crafts. There are even flight manuals still in existence. Apparently the crafts could take off vertically, could hover, and were capable of flying at great speed."

"Mother of Moses, that's amazing!" said the Irishman. "Is there any other evidence that these flying machines ever really existed?"

"Indeed there is," replied the boy. "Over three thousand years ago, a series of facinating hieroglyphs were carved into a ceiling beam of an Egyptian temple at Abydos. They depict what looks like a hover car—a spacecraft with portholes, an object that could possibly be a tank and a helicopter. The helicopter looks just like the modern state-of-the-art machines that we have today. There is no mistaking it. The image is of a helicopter and nothing else. The rotor blades, cockpit and tailfin are clearly visible!"

"Surely the Egyptians did not possess helicopters and spacecraft?" interjected Frank.

Alexander laughed. "Highly unlikely, Dr. Malone! But they obviously knew that such machines once existed. Perhaps the hieroglyphs were copies of the images on the metal walls in the chambers of records, or on the metal tablets."

"Humm," muttered Frank. "What about the Atlantean spacecraft? Any mention of them in the Indian texts?"
Alexander nodded. "Some of the texts mention a war that broke out between Rama and Atlantis. The Indians referred to the Atlantean flying machines as 'Vailixi.' The most common types of Vailixi were described as being cigar-shaped. Apparently they could fly in outer space, as well as travel underwater. They were used in warfare against the Rama Empire. The Atlantean flying machines were said to have been more technologically advanced than the Indian aircraft and could fire missiles and death rays."
The boy sighed. "It is no wonder the hidden records give few specific details on technologies that could be used to develop devastating weapons, given Man's predilection for war."

"I wonder what happened to the flying machines?" asked Frank. "They just seemed to disappear from history. There is loads of metal junk orbiting the Earth from our space programs. You would expect that if ancient civilisations had spacecraft, some of their junk would still be floating around out there."

"I think that is unlikely," responded Alexander. "A lot of our space debris is generated by the primitive rocket technology that is used to launch vehicles and satellites into orbit. With antigravity technology, the whole processes would be a lot cleaner and more efficient. Anyway, given a gap of eleven or twelve thousand years, much of our space-junk would have disappeared; pulled slowly back to Earth by the planet's powerful gravitational field and subsequently burnt up in the atmosphere. It's also not that surprising that little evidence of ancient flying machines has survived. Could our advanced civilisation withstand a major comet or asteroid impact, huge earthquakes, horrendous volcanic eruptions, massive tidal waves and enormous rises in sea level? All of these things happened at the end of the last Ice Age. More than likely, our civilisation would be obliterated, and it would be many, many thousands of years before man again reached the level of technological development that we have today. The only technology that would survive would have had to have been hidden in high altitude mountain caves or caverns and secret chambers. Perhaps that is what happened after the last global catastrophe. Maybe some of the flying crafts did survive. It is possible that a select few – priests, monks, or members of secret societies – have preserved these machines and other ancient technologies."

"What about this antigravity technology?" asked the Irishman. "Has anybody speculated on what that might entail?"

Enthusiastically, the boy said, "When I was researching designs for my electric bike I read a great deal about electromagnetic energy, power generation and electronics. A basic design for an antigravity engine has been given in a number of ancient Indian texts. The texts speak of mercury as being the critical component in the antigravity engine. An engineer who spent a great deal of time researching in this area was a man by the name of Bill Cledenon. He came up with a detailed design for a Vimana, based on the ancient texts, as well as his extensive knowledge of aeronautical engineering and electronics. The craft consisted of a circular air-frame, much like a classic flying saucer. Its primary component was an antigravity device. This was essentially a powerful electromagnetic field coil through which was passed a rapidly-pulsating direct electric current. The field coil was constructed from a closed circuit heat-exchange/ condenser unit that contained mercury. The coil was positioned vertically in the centre of the craft. It was inserted inside a ring conductor, which was essentially a giant flat metal hoop with three equally spaced gyroscopes embedded in it. When the field coil was energised, the ring conductor was instantly repelled from the Earth, propelling the craft into the air. In essence, electromagnetism was being used to generate an antigravity effect. Using a computer to control the flow of the electric current, the craft could be made to hover effortlessly in the air and accelerate up or down at enormous speeds. Forward propulsion was provided by an air-breathing turbo-pump propulsion system. Essentially, the system liquefied air that was stored in a series of tanks, which was then used as fuel by a gas turbine jet engine. Because the craft was weightless and almost frictionless in flight, it could travel at tremendous speeds."

"It all sounds surprisingly straightforward," said Frank. "It's amazing that there appears to be so little research and development in this area, given the enormous benefits antigravity aircraft would bring. They would be safer, quieter, and much faster than anything that we have now, not to mention far more environmentally friendly."

Alexander frowned. "I fear the technology has already become weaponised, Dr. Malone. In the United States, for example, it is believed that antigravity aircraft is one of the black projects run by the military. That effectively means that everything stays top- secret. We are basically dealing with the same mindset that ultimately doomed the Aztlaneans. Certain technologies must be kept secret so we can maintain an advantage over our enemies."

"Time for another coffee," said Frank.

ꙮ

After a short break, they resumed their discourse. "I have always been fascinated by the shape and structure of pyramids," said Frank. "Mainstream Egyptologists believe that they were originally used as tombs, but certainly in the case of the three big pyramids on the Giza plateau, there is no convincing evidence to support that view. A lot of people these days go along with the theory of them being temples where pharaohs were taken as part of the burial ritual. When the rituals had been completed, the body of the dead king was taken to a final resting place in the Valley of the Kings or other secret locations."

"I prefer the story written in the blue journal, Dr. Malone," responded Alexander. "It makes a great deal of sense to me. In the lost civilisation of Aztlan, the pyramid appears to have been a concept that originally evolved from standing stones used to channel the Earth's energies. Indeed, the great civilisation itself may have had its genesis from the energies flowing from these special stones. I have mentioned to you on a number of occasions that I need solid evidence before I can believe or be convinced of anything. Just such evidence was provided by the black boxes in Anita's lab. Having visited her lab, studied the data, and even witnessed the boxes in operation, I have become convinced that there is an 'Over-Mind' in existence on this planet. I believe that it permeates everything—living and inanimate. Currently, it is accessed unconsciously by every human mind, but I now believe that it can be contacted consciously. At this stage, it is just a hypothesis, but a hypothesis based on solid evidence from the black boxes."

"But surely the black boxes have not demonstrated conscious access to a world Over-Mind," said Frank.

"That is true, Dr. Malone," replied the boy, "but they have proven that the Over-Mind can be reached unconsciously, and I can see no reason why, under certain circumstances, it cannot be contacted consciously—but of course that has yet to definitively proven in the modern arena. The Aztlaneans claimed that they could do it by utilising the enormous geodetic energy channelled through the pyramid. Certainly there are many documented instances of people having powerful psychic experiences in pyramids, the most famous being the emperor Napoleon."

"That could explain how the Aztlaneans made such fantastic advances in so many different fields, and why they developed so many technologies that seemed to work in harmony with nature, rather than polluting and destroying it," added Frank.

"Yes," agreed Alexander. "It would appear that we have a great deal to learn from the Aztlaneans—both from their strengths and their weaknesses."

"But I find it difficult to believe that the Great Pyramid was once some sort of giant machine," said the Irishman. "That flies in the face of decades of research carried out by Egyptologists."

Alexander smiled. "If the pyramid was an ancient machine, Egyptologists would be the least qualified people to study it. Physics and engineering do not figure as part of a mainstream Egyptologist's training. They are no more qualified to evaluate the Great Pyramid in that context than they are a nuclear power plant! Since our initial discovery of the journals, I have been reading a number of relevant books written by alternative Egyptologists, some with strong scientific backgrounds. Of late, engineers and physicists have studied the pyramids, and some very interesting books have been written. For example, a detailed and well-researched book was published a few years ago by an engineer by the name of Christopher Dunn. He analysed the Great Pyramid in impressive detail and came to the conclusion that it was an ancient geo-mechanical power plant that responded sympathetically with the Earth's vibrations and converted that energy into electricity. A physicist named Joseph Farrell also studied the Great Pyramid in meticulous detail. He concluded that with the use of highly sophisticated crystal technology, it could have been used as a phase-conjugate howitzer. According to him, it could have been designed to collect, amplify and cohere energy emissions from a given target and send them back, exactly in phase harmonically, with that target. A rather simplistic analogy would be opera singers using their voices to smash glasses. To do this, all they have to do is produce a sound with their highly honed vocal cords that matches the fundamental harmonic vibration of the glass. The sound waves, which are both powerful and pure, cause an amplification of the glass's natural vibratory rate, causing it to shake itself until it cracks or disintegrates.

"The amplified energies emitted by the pyramid were enormously powerful, according to Farrell, and caused violent acoustic cavitation within the nuclei of the atoms, composing the target until it consumed itself in a violent nuclear reaction. In effect, then, the pyramid amplified, and then reflected back upon a target a powerful energy beam; it was a ray weapon of enormous destructive power. If the weapon had been fired at a military target, it would have neutralised all electronic equipment and detonated all explosive devices, including nuclear bombs. It would also have directly killed every living organism, even viruses. Unlike a nuclear bomb, the weapons' destructive power could be calibrated to selectively destroy both small and large targets, and there was no radioactive fallout after a strike. In many respects, it was an ideal weapon of mass destruction."

"That's thought provoking, to say the least," said the Irishman. "So, Alexander," he continued, "what is your final take on all of this?"

"We know who our enemy is now; it is Nesmut," the boy replied. "In my mind we have to track down her mummy and the crystals. Their destruction may be the only chance that we have to survive."

Closing his eyes, the Irishman sighed. "Sure. You may be right," he said. "If we could find and destroy all of the crystals, including the fire crystal, if it exists, then she would have nothing left to protect. But, of course, she may wish the crystals to survive and just kill us either way. In the right hands, the power and knowledge that they must contain could be of enormous benefit to mankind."

"It's a difficult one, Dr. Malone," replied Alexander, "but we have to at least find the crystals, and then, I guess, take it from there."

Frank decided to pour himself a large whisky. The boy had reminded him again of his own mortality. After a few comforting slurps, he asked Alexander to continue.

"In my opinion, the thing that was critical to the high civilisation of the Aztlaneans was the pyramid," said the boy. "I believe that the greatness of their civilisation lay in their ability to access the World Mind, even the Universal Mind, using the pyramid. The ancients had a profound understanding of harmonics, and their technologies worked in harmony with the Earth. They did not pollute and destroy the environment by burning fossil fuels for power, and yet they lived as well, if not better than we do. But due to a fatal error of judgement, they were destroyed by nature, nonetheless. We are on the brink of a similar fate, but their technology could save us."

Frank raised his eyebrows. He was not convinced. "Surely," he said, "we now have the technology to generate power just as well as the Aztlaneans. There is solar power, hydropower, wind power and even nuclear power, but the obsession with fossil fuels continues."

"Unfortunately, that's very true, Dr. Malone," said Alexander. "The problem is economics. At the moment it is much cheaper to burn oil, coal and gas. Things will eventually change as the reserves of these fuels start to dwindle, but that will be too late for the planet. We will have runaway global warming by then. Something needs to be done fast, and I believe the Aztlaneans had the answer; it is locked in one of those crystals. They knew how to transport electricity through the air and they knew how to utilise it very effectively. If we could discover how to do that, fossil fuels could be replaced quite quickly by cheap electricity that could be generated by clean power sources such as solar, wind and hydro power. Cars could run off electricity beamed through the air, and aircraft could fly using antigravity propulsion systems. The major problem that we now have is power utilisation. Electric-powered devices run extremely inefficiently, wasting a lot of the energy that is supplied to them. I now believe that resonance is the key to proper power generation, transmission and reception. I am convinced that the Aztlaneans had resonance-based electric power generators. A high-frequency resonance-based energy transformer would have been the main component in such a device. The employment of conductors with very low active resistance for their windings would have increased power output by many orders of magnitude relative to conventional electric power generators. Electric motors driving machines and vehicles would have operated along similar lines and would have been extremely energy efficient."

Pausing, the boy gazed into the distance. "It is clear, Dr. Malone, that there is much still to be resolved."

Grimacing, Frank excused himself and headed for another cigarette.

CHAPTER 34
BATTLE AT THE TOWER

ꕥ

Anita Gupta burst into the kitchen as Alexander stood, pouring hot water into a cup laced with instant coffee granules. She was wearing an olive-green Punjabi suit cut from the finest silk. It made her skin look even more radiant than usual. Her thick black hair was tied back in a bun, and except for her eyes, she was unadorned with makeup. A smile of familiar affection lit up her face.

What an attractive woman, thought Alexander, not for the first time. *I wonder who's the more beautiful, her or the priestess Nesmut?* And then a shudder stole through him as he remembered that terrible mummy and what it had tried to do to him.

Approaching the boy like an excited child, her big brown eyes gleaming, Anita said, "I just got a call from one of my post docs at the lab. The most amazing thing happened a few minutes ago. Do you remember me telling you about the Global Mind Project?"

Alexander nodded wryly; he never forgot anything.

"Well, the Random Generators have just gotten very excited. They have produced a huge spike—bigger than anything that we have seen so far. Something major is about to happen, that is for sure! If the pattern holds true, there will be a bigger time lag than any that we have previously recorded. This should give us some very useful new calibration data: spike size versus time interval to the detected event. Something big is about to happen! Mark my words, Alexander. Let's hope it is something good for a change!"

The blood drained from Alexander's face. *An asteroid ended the last great era of human civilisation, perhaps it was our turn now,* he thought. *Like the Aztlaneans, we have the means to defend ourselves, but what have we been doing? We continue to quarrel and war with each other in the time-honoured fashion. It seems nothing ever changes. There is no time to lose; I have to get back to Northgate Hall!*

Alexander was convinced that the obelisk was some kind of a machine. Perhaps it had been built to generate a death-beam capable of destroying a comet and other interplanetary bodies. He had to know. Countless lives could be at stake. If a comet or asteroid impacted close to the British Isles, there would be massive damage. The entire nation could be wiped from the face of the earth!

ꕥ

With a deep sigh of resignation, Dr. Frank Malone picked up the telephone. He could pretty much guess the identity of the caller. "Hello Alexander," he said, before the voice on the other end could speak.

"Yes, it's me," came the response.

"I have a tutorial in 30 minutes," growled the Irishman, "and you are supposed to be at it! I know about the black boxes. Anita just called me. But who knows what caused them to spike? It could be any number of things. The chances of it being an imminent comet or asteroid impact are minute."

"If only that were true, Dr. Malone!" blurted the boy. "I have been studying the literature on interplanetary bodies of late. My findings are really quite disturbing. The global detection system is patchy, to say the least. There have been two major near misses in the last five years, both undetected until it was too late to respond. Even a small comet or asteroid could kill millions if it hit the earth!"

Frank groaned. "But even if it is an asteroid, what can we really do? More than likely, the obelisk is just an extravagant garden ornament!"

"No!" shouted Alexander, almost pleading. "There is a mechanism in the pyramidion, and I believe that I activated it when I turned the key in the iris of the great eye. I heard a definite clunking sound."

"Listen, Alexander," retorted the Irishman. "My patience is at an end with this whole affair. I will accompany you to the house one last time. I cannot ignore the message from the black boxes. They have been one hundred percent accurate so far, but I have no faith in the obelisk being a death-beam generator. I will make one final attempt to bring this disturbing affair to a conclusion. After today, I'm washing my hands of the whole business, whatever the consequences! It is playing havoc with my sanity! I will pick you up at the Gupta's as soon as I have cancelled the tutorial, but I will need to collect some things from my house before we set off for the Hall."

"Thank you, Dr. Malone," said the boy.

Frank put down the phone. He had read carefully through both of the blue journals and had reached a similar conclusion to Alexander. Millions, if not billions, might be dead by the end of the day if there really was an interplanetary body on a collision course with the Earth. He had no choice but to do what he could, even if the odds of achieving anything were very long indeed. The black boxes had been chillingly accurate so far. Something terrible was going to happen soon, that was for sure.

ഇ

Alexander settled himself into the front seat of the Volvo. "Do you really think that it could be a comet?" asked Frank, as they sped off towards Northgate Hall.

The boy shivered at the thought of what lay ahead. "The more that we study the Universe with our increasingly sophisticated space probes and telescopes," he said, "the clearer it is becoming that it is a very dangerous place indeed. Impacts from comets and asteroids have had a profound effect on the destiny of the Earth. Some of these collisions have proved catastrophic. In the outer solar system beyond the planet Pluto there are billions of comets in a region called the "Oort cloud." These objects travel in very long orbits through the solar system and can appear unannounced. For one reason or another, comets can be deflected from their orbits and penetrate the inner solar system where the Earth orbits the sun. Comets travel at speeds in the region of 150,000 miles per hour and even a very small one would strike the Earth with the energy of a hydrogen bomb. And as we know, there is also the problem of asteroids!"

Frank shifted uncomfortably in his seat.

"Astronomers have calculated that there are more than one hundred thousand asteroids in the vicinity of the Earth that are large enough to cause massive damage, or even total extinction of the planet," continued Alexander. "Apparently there is a one-in- ten chance that an asteroid could hit the Earth in the next one hundred years. These are quite worrying odds."

"So when was the last time we were hit?" asked Frank.

"We received a major wake-up call in 1908, but that has only recently been recognised," replied Alexander. "Fortunately, it happened in a remote area of Siberia, known as Tunguska; otherwise, millions could have been killed. About four thousand square miles of forest was destroyed, along with a herd of nearly two thousand reindeer. The exploding object was believed to have been a meteor or small comet. Increasingly, the impact of extraterrestrial bodies is now being viewed as a major cause for the collapse of previous civilisations. For example, around 1200 BC, during the Bronze Age, numerous civilisations were destroyed or decimated simultaneously. These included the New

Kingdom of Egypt, the Hittites of Anatolia, the Palestinian civilisation, the Shang Dynasty of China, and the Mykenaens of Greece. Indeed, there is growing evidence that the Earth has been hit periodically. There are at least ten impact craters around the world that date from the last Ice Age. Based on current knowledge, major impacts of sufficient magnitude to cause ecological disaster on a continental or even global scale happen every two thousand to five thousand years."

The Irishman took one hand off the steering wheel and began to rummage in his overcrowded glove box for a packet of cigarettes. Frowning briefly at Alexander, he said, "The more you say, the more nervous I get. I think I will have a fag while I still have the chance!"

Alexander rolled down the window a tad, in advance of the impending smoke.

"But surely," said the Irishman, as the first soothing wave of nicotine hit his bloodstream, "they have state-of-the-art detection systems deployed now?"

Alexander shook his head. "Unfortunately, that is not the case, Dr. Malone. Our detection system is patchy. There have been numerous close calls of late where the Earth was nearly hit by asteroids. In 1996 an asteroid, about two hundred metres wide, passed within a quarter of a million miles of the Earth. A little closer and it would have been drawn onto a collision course by the planet's gravitational field. If it had hit the Earth, the destructive force would have been sufficient to wipe out an area the size of the British Isles. This asteroid was discovered only four days before it reached us. In 2002, two asteroids of similar dimensions also passed close to the Earth. One of them had been completely missed by the astronomers and was only discovered four days after the event! This was because it had come from the direction of the sun, obscuring it from the optical tracking telescopes. There was another near miss in 2004. Recently, a large asteroid over one mile wide has been detected. It could potentially hit the Earth in 2019. This asteroid is large enough to wipe out most of the planet."

The boy opened his window a little further. "What is urgently needed," he continued, "is a network of high-power optical and radio-telescopes around the Earth so that asteroids and comets can be accurately tracked. Indeed, it may already be too late! The space intercept technology is in its infancy and is incapable of effectively dealing with the threat unless it is detected many years in advance of a projected impact. This, of course, is due to lack of investment. We have all this tremendous technology at our fingertips, yet we choose to leave ourselves almost as defenceless as primitive man. It could be that history is about to repeat itself all over again! We may only have hours left!"

ꙮ

Bringing the big Volvo to a halt, Frank stubbed out his cigarette. "It seems that we are living on a planet run by ostriches." He sighed. "They either have their heads buried in the sand, or they are too busy searching the ground for worms to look up!"

The doors of the Volvo thunked closed and the two unlikely warriors began to make their way through the woods towards the gates of Northgate Hall. They both carried backpacks, containing the equipment they thought they would need for the job. The Irishman gasped as they approached the gates. They were exactly as Alexander had left them—smashed to pieces and strewn across blackened earth.

"What the hell happened here?" gasped Frank. "Do you know anything about this, young man?" he continued, fixing the boy with a stern gaze.

Swallowing hard, Alexander did his best to look innocent. "Well, there was a bit of a thunderstorm as I left the grounds," he said unconvincingly.

"Damn you, boy! I know you are lying," rumbled the Irishman, "but this is no time for harsh words. We need to stay fully focused now. Fortunately, it is a cloudless day and the weather forecast is good until tomorrow." Withdrawing his hip flask, he took a swig of the ferocious Irish spirit. "To the success of the mission," he toasted. Lighting another cigarette, he gestured to Alexander to move forward. It was time for the final reckoning and this might be the last cigarette he ever smoked, so he intended to make the most of it!

The air was crisp and quiet as they made their way through the old arboretum. "The still before the storm," muttered Frank, as he took a final drag on his cigarette.

It was not long before they had left the trees behind and entered an area of rough, desolate grass. Standing motionless in the distance was a single goat. As they got closer, they could see that it was a large ram with impressive horns. The ram looked straight at them, not the slightest bit intimidated by their presence.

"That's odd," said Alexander, studying the goat carefully. They were about forty metres from the animal now and the boy's sharp eyes could see its nostrils flaring. In the next instant it was charging at them. Taken aback by the sudden ferocity of the beast, the Irishman stopped dead in his tracks. He just stood there, looking incredulously at the furious ram as it rampaged towards them.

The boy had become quite battle-hardened now. He had taken on and defeated a homicidal suit of armour and a demon mummy. He was not going to be phased by an angry goat! Swiftly moving his right arm over his left shoulder, he grabbed the handle of the cricket bat protruding from his rucksack. He withdrew the bat in one seamless action, like a knight unsheathing his broadsword.

The Irishman stood rooted to the spot as the ram came on, its eyes wild and staring. Bat in hand, Alexander pivoted himself sharply as the animal thundered forward. Unfortunately, it was Frank who was wearing the bright red waterproof jacket, and it was Frank who would pay the price. The lethal horns of the rampaging beast were within a hair's breath of their target as the boy swung the heavy bat in an upward sweeping arc. With a sickening crunch, the bat hit home and the ram's jawbone shattered, but that did not stop it crashing with tremendous force into the Irishman. Flying backwards, he landed heavily, with the slaughtered animal straddled across him. The wind knocked from him, he lay there, spread-eagled and senseless.

As Alexander moved towards his fallen companion, something caught his eye. It was indistinct—a dark shape—but he could sense that it was getting closer. Turning again to his companion, he could see that he was still breathing, but stunned and helpless. The ram lay motionless on top of his body, blood trickling from its mouth.

Something made Alexander turn back in the direction of the shape. It was bigger now— a dog. He tracked it curiously, then with mounting concern. It was a powerful but compact dog. *The creature looks like a bull terrier.* The dog came on at full tilt like a speeding bullet. Tightening his grip on the cricket bat, the boy steadied himself.

The beast hurtled straight at him, its teeth bared and its eyes wild with fury. At the last moment, just before the ripping bite struck home, Alexander sidestepped the dog, smashing the bat into its ribcage. Screaming in agony, it fell to the ground. This was war now, and the boy would show no mercy. Eyes narrowing, he aimed the bat at the writhing dog and struck it with sickening ferocity on the back of the neck, just below the skull. Death came instantly.

Other dogs started to approach from the cover of the trees. They moved more cautiously than the first unfortunate brute. One by one, they stopped. Soon there were seven of them standing abreast in a line, about ten metres from Alexander. At the centre of the pack stood a large Alsatian, with a long shaggy coat. It gazed at him impassively, with cold, unblinking eyes. Next to it there was another big dog—a blond-haired Labrador-Alsatian crossbreed, by the looks of it. The rest of the dogs were mongrels of assorted sizes.

This is not good! thought the boy, his mind beginning to race. And then he saw the Mastiff! It was huge. The enormous beast trotted up casually to join the other dogs. *These dogs look like they have been trained, or worse still, are under some sort of control.*

The fear was growing in him fast, but he dare not show it. He was done for if he stood his ground, he knew. His friend lay there, defenceless, probably unconscious. There was only one thing to do. He would have to make a break for the trees in the hope that he could lead them away. It was a slim chance at best, but the only one he had.

Alexander's heart was thumping so hard now that he could feel his chest vibrating. Body tensing, he began to turn very slowly, his eyes scanning swiftly from side to side. He knew that the border of the arboretum was about twenty metres behind him. The trees were his only hope of escape. Poised to make his move, his leg muscles strained to aching point with pent-up tension.

A sudden low, menacing growl came from the big Mastiff as it fixed the boy with its small hazel-brown eyes. Alexander knew that these beasts had been bred as fighting dogs by the Romans. They were used like gladiators in the arenas and were lethal killers. Weighing as much as a large man, the brute stood on powerful legs and was nearly a metre high at the shoulder. The hair covering its muscular body was grey, except around the snout and eyes, where it was black.

Slowly, the dog started to stalk Alexander, its muzzle creased over large pointed teeth. They glistened horribly as saliva trickled down them. Turning quickly, Alexander fled. The dogs raced after him, barking savagely, as he bolted for the trees.

As if directed by an unseen force, the big Alsatian remained behind. Pouncing on the carcass of the ram, it sank its teeth deep into its flesh. It meant to drag the animal off the Irishman so that, dead or alive, it could tear his throat out.

Frank's eyes flickered open. He could feel that something was shaking him. Now he could sense the weight of the ram's body – even smell it. His eyes began to focus. He could see the shaggy fur and guessed what it was. The manic growl told him that the dog was not friendly. Gripping the ram tightly to himself, he used it like a shield. In a fury, the demented Alsatian ripped at the ram, shaking it violently from side to side. Anger surged through the Irishman like an avalanche. No dog was going to cower and intimidate him!

Roaring at the top of his titanic voice, Frank released his grip on the ram and pushed it from him. Momentarily stunned by the sonic blast and the sudden movement of the carcass, the dog fell backwards. Bellowing expletives, the Irishman rose rapidly to his feet and withdrew the metal baseball bat from his backpack. He may have been small, but he was strong and agile.

"Come on!" he bellowed.

As if driven by madness, the big dog growled, and then pounced forward, its massive mouth wide open. Frank swung the baseball bat, but it was too late. With lightening speed, the dog grabbed the bat in its powerful jaws. Frank lost his footing and fell backwards. He knew that if he relinquished his grip now he would be done for. Frantically, he searched a jacket pocket with his left hand, gripping the baseball bat tightly with his right. He could feel the weight of the dog pressing on his chest, smell its foul breath... Deranged and snarling, the animal tried to wrench his weapon from him. Pain began to tear down his wrist, but he would not let go. At the obelisk, hanging perilously above the abyss, he had given in to pain. But not now!

At last his fingers found their quarry! Pulling the stiletto from his pocket, he plunged the six-inch blade into the ribcage of the dog. Howling piteously, it released its grip and scuttled away.

ꕥ

Alexander sprinted through the trees, leaping over obstacles and pushing aside low- lying branches. His breath came in deep, bellowing gasps as he ran flat out, not daring to look back. He was getting close to the perimeter wall. Soon he would be cornered like a helpless rabbit. He needed to think fast! Coming to a sudden halt, he bent over, gasping, his mind desperately computing a plan of action. The dogs were close, very close. He could hear them crashing through the undergrowth; then came the sound of panting and the rumbling growls of the Mastiff.

He began to run again. Foolishly, he turned his head to see if they had caught him and slipped on a patch of wet leaves. He was fortunate not to fall; that would have been the end of him. Stumbling through some bushes, he ran on through a dense set of pine trees. Their branches whipped back at his face and hands, grabbing at his rucksack. Scrambling over a fallen tree trunk, he could see what he was looking for at last.

He stopped and listened. The sound of panting was unmistakable and he could make out dark shadows darting through the trees. It was clear now. They were circling round him. They meant to cut him off and then close in. Suddenly, his heart leapt. Something had moved out from between two trees up ahead. It was one of the dogs – a mongrel. With nowhere to run, there was nothing else to do. He would have to attack. Clenching both of his fists, he ran towards the dog. It stood its ground, growling menacingly. As the boy closed in, the dog leapt forward. Fortunately, it was not a big animal, and he caught it full in the face with a kick, knocking it to the ground.

Two more dogs hurtled at him from out of the trees. Jumping up, he grabbed a branch. It was a sturdy branch, growing horizontally from the trunk of an oak tree, about two and a half metres from the ground. He kicked, swinging his legs forward and hooking them around another branch. Jumping at him, the two mongrels snapped wildly. There were only centimetres in it, but his torso was too high for their jaws.

The blond Alsatian-cross loped into view. *That beast is big enough to get its teeth into me,* he thought, beginning to panic again. With his hands clawing against the bark of the trunk and using all the strength in his torso, he heaved himself into a sitting position. One of the mongrels leapt up, aiming its jaws at his ankles. Just in time, Alexander lifted his legs and scrambled up into the tree. He was standing on the branch now.

In a seamless movement, the blond dog jumped onto the trunk, its savage teeth bared. Narrowly missing its target, it fell away. Swiftly, the boy clambered up the tree until he was safely out of reach. Satisfied to have escaped, he would have let matters rest there, had it not been for his friend. Eventually, he guessed, the dogs would have given up and left, but he had to do something. Dr. Malone was still in mortal danger.

Carefully taking off his backpack, he removed a deadly weapon. He had hoped and prayed that he would never have to use it. It was a large powerful water pistol, the size of a rifle, with a big reservoir chamber. Replacing his backpack, he moved into position where he could see the dogs. There were six of them down there, growling and barking. He knew without a doubt that they would kill him without mercy, rip him to shreds, if they could get hold of him.

His heart sank as he realised that there was no sign of the Mastiff or the big Alsatian. His friend was probably already dead, torn to pieces. Well, they would pay a heavy price! Climbing down the tree, his feet met the branch that he had initially grabbed. This branch was low enough for him to bait the dogs. "Din dins," he shouted. "Come and get it!"

Within seconds, the blond dog was up and at him again, its powerful jaws snapping. Carefully aiming the water rifle, he squeezed the trigger. A jet of liquid burst from the nozzle and hit the animal straight in the face, burning its eyes. It fell back, yelping. Other dogs followed, sometimes in pairs, barking and snapping wildly. Eventually, all the dogs were wet from the jet spray.

"Eat this!" yelled Alexander as he threw the first burning flare amongst them. Instantly, two of the dogs exploded into flames. The deadly spray was a lethal cocktail of petrol, pure methanol and lighter fluid. Further flares followed and soon all of the dogs were ablaze. Yelping and screaming horribly, they ran in circles, blinded by the flames. Three of them charged off into the trees in a frantic search for water. Two other unfortunate brutes writhed in agony as the flames devoured them. In a last mad attempt to get at the boy, the blond dog leapt forward. With its head blazing like a torch, it looked like a demon from hell as it made its final lunge. Mercifully, a powerful blow from the cricket bat ended its life.

Dropping down from the tree, Alexander knew that at all costs he had to get back to his friend. Given the ferocity of these dogs, it was a slim hope that his tutor would still be alive, but he had to do what he could. Feeling very uneasy, he broke into a trot, and then a run. Instinctively, he sensed that something was stalking him.

Suddenly, an immense dog broke cover! It was the Mastiff, and it moved swiftly. Desperately, the boy began to sprint through the trees. The creature tore after him, gaining on him with every stride. Soon he could hear its heavy footfalls, hear its powerful panting, and then it was over. With a rumbling growl the beast sprang, knocking him rolling and sprawling to the ground.

The dog loomed over him as he lay helplessly on his back. Placing one of its massive paws upon his chest, it raised its terrifying head and howled triumphantly. Baring its enormous teeth, it looked at the boy with cold, killer eyes. Worse than that, it regarded him contemptuously with the malevolent mocking eyes of the entity. There was no mercy in those eyes – only certain death.

As the huge, terrible jaws moved towards his throat, Alexander aimed a desperate punch, but it bounced futilely off the beast's muscular flank. Raising his arms, he attempted to cover his throat, but the dog lunged forward, grabbing his left arm with its mighty teeth. Searing pain shot through him as the jaws tightened. The game was close to finished. Hopeless as a sacrificial lamb now, the dog put a second paw on the boy's chest, bracing itself for an almighty tearing tug.

The metal bat glinted as it arced rapidly towards the Mastiff's skull. It hit home with a clanking thud. Angered, rather than stunned by the blow, the beast let go of the boy and turned to face its attacker. Snarling, it tensed its muscles and then sprang forward. Another blow from the metal baseball bat impacted on the side of its skull, but that did not stop it. Pouncing on the Irishman, the huge dog forced him to the ground, but in that mortal moment it let out an agonised scream! A heavy blow had struck it from behind. Alexander had aimed his bat to cause the maximum amount of damage. The beast turned again, its left hind leg shattered at the knee joint. Eyes wild with agonised fury, it leapt at the boy, but he was too fast for the wounded monster. Roaring savagely, it went at him again, but the Irishman was behind it now and stuck its other hind leg a terrible blow. Falling to the ground, the dog writhed in pain. The man and the boy did not hesitate. They clubbed the stricken beast mercilessly until it lay dead.

ꙮ

Standing propped against a tree, Frank stared down at his blood-splattered trousers. *Mother of God, what a bloody awful business this is,* he thought sadly. *It was clear that the thing would stop at nothing to prevent them reaching the obelisk. The entity was more powerful than he could have imagined. Those poor deranged dogs were testimony to that. When it lived as a priestess, it must have mastered the high arts of magic, or the occult, as it is known today. What chance do we stand against a being such as that? I never would have believed that a spirit could possess such powers.*

Lifting his head, he looked over towards Alexander, who was calmly wiping the blood from his cricket bat. *Such an admirable boy in so many ways. Charmingly innocent, self-sacrificing and courageous, but there was something else there too – a cold, determined ruthlessness.*

Their eyes met and Alexander feared the worst. It seemed inevitable to him that his tutor would want to give up now. Who could expect any rational human being to continue on after partaking in that dreadful carnage? But his jaw fell as Frank Malone raised himself from the tree and said, "Let's finish this, son. There's no turning back now. By Christ, one way or another, it will end today!"

Withdrawing his hip flask, he took a deep gulp. "One for the road," he muttered as he strode forward resolutely. Alexander followed him, bat at the ready. They were soon walking down the gently rolling hill and into the shallow valley. The enormous house stood ominously in the distance. Soon they were skirting around it, their eyes darting left and right, searching for any new threat, but everything was quiet in the winter sunshine. Continuing on, they made for the Egyptian garden. Soon the obelisk came into view, more daunting than ever.

It did not take long before they were standing on the granite slabs in front of the mighty tower. Staring straight ahead, the Irishman did not dare to raise his gaze. The boy, however, craned his neck right back, trying to gauge how he could penetrate the pyramidion.

A stunningly beautiful woman walked majestically from behind the obelisk. Stopping about eight metres from them, she appeared as solid as the very granite on which she stood. Frank stared at her in fascinated horror. The boy was still oblivious to her presence. A dig in the ribs brought his eyes back down to ground level.

"It's Nesmut!" mumbled Frank. "She has come for us."

Alexander studied the woman calmly. Wearing her black hair straight and immaculately groomed in the Egyptian style, she was clothed in a flowing white silk gown and silver shoes. A magnificent gold necklace adorned her chest, and around each wrist, blue crystalline bracelets sparkled in the sunlight.

Dr. Malone was right, thought the boy. *She's the most attractive woman I've ever seen.*

But there was no warmth in that face, just a cold detachment. She looked at the boy, her gaze intense. In her right hand she held an ornate wooden staff, carved in the shape of a snake.

Suddenly her eyes lifted skyward and she began to chant in a hauntingly melodious voice.

"That must be ancient Egyptian," whispered Frank. "I've never heard it spoken before."

At first nothing happened, but then there was a rustling sound as dead leaves began to lift from the granite slabs and spiral upwards. Rapidly becoming a howling vortex, flashes of silver white lightening began to crackle from it. The man and the boy looked on, spellbound by the magic. Slowly, the priestess raised the snake-staff into the maelstrom and the horrible head opened its mouth. Before their very eyes, the lightening in the vortex was drawn into the staff and then, in an instant, the air was still again. Wrenching his mind from its fatal fascination, Frank threw his body in front of the boy as the priestess aimed her staff. A lightening bolt exploded from the snake-head and struck him with ferocious force, toppling him backwards like a falling tree. Catching his dear companion, Alexander broke his fall as best he could. He lay there, deathly still, and before his very eyes, Alexander could see the life-force draining from his body.

Within a fleeting moment, anger strangled sorrow and Alexander sprang to his feet, charging at the woman. "Bitch! Bitch!" he shouted. But she was gone. The boy ran on. He knew that his only chance was to find cover before she struck again. Frank was dead for sure. There was nothing that he could do for him now. *Nothing except avenge him!* he thought as he entered the Sphinx. Pausing, he ignited a flare, then ran through the tunnel towards the obelisk.

"I will avenge him!" he roared. It was a vow, not a promise. Charging up a flight of steps, he reached the chamber at the base of the obelisk. The concealed stone door lay ajar, just as he had left it. Light from the flare danced off the stone walls and the massive spiralling staircase. He guessed that if there was a way into the pyramidion, it would be at the top, rather than the bottom of the tower.

Once again, Alexander's feet pounded the stone stairway as he climbed the obelisk. Breathing hard, he took the final step and walked out onto the viewing platform. Hesitating momentarily, he could see no sign of the priestess. The shiny black stones gave no hint of a secret entrance; the joints between them were almost seamless. He could see now that it was polished granite, not marble. Reaching the area that corresponded with the position of the giant eye on the pyramidion above, he suddenly stiffened. A sound was drifting up from below him.

"Alexander! Alexander*!*" called the dreadful voice.

Fury raged within him. If there was any way he could, he would ram a flare down that wretched thing's throat; he would tear it limb from limb. It had murdered his family and killed his only friend.

Using the cricket bat, he began to bang the walls and the stone ceiling above him. And then the face appeared over the balustrade! It was the entity; still beautiful, but the smile upon its lips was malevolent. Hovering in the air, it aimed its staff at the boy's chest. He stood there, glaring at it fearlessly, making no attempt to run. A thunderbolt exploded towards him but fell away harmlessly, causing him no more injury than a torch beam. The rubber suit beneath his jacket had done its job.

Turning from the entity, Alexander continued to probe the ceiling with his bat. Suddenly, a big stone panel above gave way, moving slightly inwards and clicking. Then it hinged down slowly, like the trap door of a loft. He could see the black glistening metal. It was some sort of stepladder. Tugging at it, the ladder slid towards him effortlessly.

Looking up into the blackness, a powerful sense of trepidation began to grow in him. The very air seemed to tingle with strange energy. An urge, almost overwhelming, made him want to run, to escape, to stay in the daylight, to breathe the pure winter air, but then the anger surged again and he began to climb the steps, withdrawing a small torch from one of his jacket pockets.

Reaching the top of the steps, he found himself in an odd-looking chamber. He knew that it was pointless to pull up the ladder behind him and secure the trapdoor. The entity was a spirit and could pass through any physical barrier. Firing up the two diving lanterns that he had brought with him, he could see more clearly now. The view that greeted his eyes was not what he had expected. There were no signs of mysterious machinery—just an empty space. Or at least it initially appeared empty in the lantern light. As his eyes adapted, a number of objects came into view. The design of the room was very familiar. It was circular in shape, with a diameter of similar dimensions to those recorded in the journal. There was a series of twelve sturdy columns, equally spaced around the chamber; they had a rounded profile and looked metallic. The walls were white and very smooth, and there were twelve silver-yellow metal doors.

This is a duplicate of the central chamber of the Hall of Records! thought Alexander. Walking over to the nearest column, he began to examine it. He guessed that the engravings were exact copies. At the foot of each column, orientated towards the centre of the chamber, was a metal pedestal with a single gem embedded centrally in its top face. The gems were all of different colours. Positioned in the centre of the room there were three white columns. They were square in shape, about four feet high, and arranged in the form of a triangle. The columns supported a platform of similar dimensions to the one described in the journal.

Sighing heavily with disappointment, Alexander moved towards the centre of the chamber. The massive metal rod was missing from the ceiling and there was no sign of the great crystal. *This is just a work in progress,* he thought, his frustration growing. *It's obvious that the baron never got to finish the job.*

He was not sure, but he guessed that the obelisk was a security device, and not a weapon. It was a clever means of concealing and protecting the chamber. *But what is the function of the chamber?* he wondered. *Did the baron ever find out?*

Again, he sighed deeply. There was nothing he could do now. The planet would have to embrace its fate. He had failed, and his friend lay dead. *The baron must have owned half of England,* thought the boy as he examined one of the pedestals. *To get all this built in such a short time, he must have employed hundreds of craftsmen. In today's money, it must have cost many hundreds of millions. But the baron obviously considered the knowledge from the Hall of Records a priceless legacy. He probably had guessed that much of the ancient knowledge was locked in the crystals. It was unlikely, though, that he, or the Egyptians before him, had figured out how to use the crystals. They were probably the ancient equivalent of super microchips. More than likely, they were even more advanced technology than anything that we have in the modern world.*

Prodding a blue gemstone in one of the pedestals, the top popped open to reveal a magnificent crystal. Heartened a little, Alexander picked up the crystal, which was exactly as the baron had described it. About thirteen centimetres in diameter, it had been supremely crafted from what looked like quartz.

Flinching suddenly, the boy knew instantly that he was no longer alone. Replacing the crystal, he did not look around, but dove for cover behind the nearest pillar. The priestess stood in the centre of the chamber, her rod raised. It was clear that she had tried to kill him from behind by firing at his head. So why was he still alive? In the terrible excitement he had forgotten to pull up the rubber hood of the diving suit. The bolt from Nesmut's rod of death should have struck him dead.

The fabric of the chamber must be shielding me in some way, he guessed. Shouting in the ancient language, the priestess charged at him, wielding her staff. There was no fear left in him now, only naked hatred. Ducking just in time, a savage blow from the snake-staff narrowly missed his head and crashed into the pillar.

My God! That rod is solid! Stepping rapidly backwards, he unsheathed the cricket bat. Nesmut charged at him again. Many a brave man would have lost his mind to terror by now, but not Alexander. His hatred was all consuming. *Much of your power lies in fear,* he thought, *but you can't use that here.* She came at him again, but he stood ready. The snake-rod and the cricket bat crashed together as Alexander parried the powerful blow. Like Excalibur, the bat sliced through the rod and on into the body of the priestess. Disintegrating before his eyes, she vaporised into nothing.

Earlier that morning, Alexander had anointed the bat with sacred water from the Ganges. The bat had shed blood, it was true, but only in self-defence, only as a last resort, and only to grant a quick and merciful end to mortal suffering. It was clear to him that the wretched creature was still trying to stop him from finding something, or knowing something. *What lies behind those doors?* he wondered.

CHAPTER 35
MELTDOWN

The Irishman lay there, marble white in the winter sunlight. His face looked calm, but pinched, and his eyes were closed and slightly sunken. It was his lips, tinged blue, which confirmed the terrible truth. He was dead.

Far above, in the mighty obelisk, the boy pulled the first door open to find a small empty room. *That must be the stone face of the pyramidion,* he thought, looking at the sloping wall at the end of the room. Proceeding to the second door, he again found nothing. Methodically, he opened the next three doors. All of the rooms were empty. He tugged on the sixth door. At last, something! Before him stood two lines of the now- familiar glass cabinets, stuffed with packages.

These must be the photographs and sketches of the hidden chambers at Giza, he guessed. The next two rooms were similarly furnished. Pulling on the ninth door, it opened as effortlessly as the others. Instinctively, he shuddered at what lay before him: an open coffin—a coffin made for a child. Scattered around the coffin were strips of torn bandages, pieces of wood, and clumps of a fibrous woollen-looking material. And then he saw the head! It was a child's head, but fortunately it was made from wood, not ancient flesh and bone.

It struck him like a blinding flash! *There never was a child's mummy, just an effigy. The baron must have been searching for something. He must have torn the thing apart. I wonder if he found what he was looking for.*

The boy proceeded to the next door, anticipation mounting. Moving the door forward, he could see a staircase glinting in the lantern light. *Should I investigate these stairs, or proceed to the final two doors?* he wondered. On impulse, he walked towards the stairs. Feet clattering against the metal, he began to ascend. His anger had ebbed now, dampened by curiosity. Taking the last step cautiously, he walked out onto the roof of the chamber. His arm was stiff and sore, but he knew that he was fortunate to still be breathing. At first he could make out nothing other than the sloping roof of the pyramidion. And then he saw the figure sprawled on the floor!

The boy started to tremble as a feeling of terrible dread stole through him. Some long-forgotten horror began to surface in his mind. It was almost unbearable, but something deep inside him told him that he must move forward. Slowly, he edged towards the body. He could hardly bring himself to look at the thing, lying close by now. It was unquestionably a mummified corpse; and it did not take much imagination to guess whose corpse it was. It was the body of Algernon Northgate. Horrifying as the thing was, it was remarkably well-preserved.

The baron was lying face up in a position much like that of Frank Malone, with legs splayed apart and arms close into the torso. *More than likely he was killed in a similar manner to Dr. Malone,* he guessed. Grappling for the rubber hood of the sub-aqua suit, he quickly pulled it over his head. *Of course! There would be no shielding above the chamber. I guess the baron never realised that he would be in mortal danger here, but safe below!*

Glancing around him nervously, the boy could see no sign of the entity. Forcing himself to examine the corpse, he moved closer. Although the garments were dusty and moulded, the body was clearly dressed in the attire of a Victorian gentleman. It had a full head of black hair, but the skin was withered and rutted, like old wrinkled leather. The eyelids were closed and deeply sunken. Fortunately, the big black moustache was still in place. It softened the appearance of the lower face, which had been distorted into a ghastly expression of shock and horror.

He could look no more! It was too awful! Backing away, he noticed a package lying near to the body. Not wishing to get within another inch of the terrible corpse, he used his cricket bat to push the package to a safe distance. Grabbing it up, he walked briskly towards the stairwell. How he wished that he could take a swig from the Irishman's hipflask—anything to steady his nerves!

The boy squeezed the package into his rucksack. It was quite bulky, but surprisingly light. On an impulse, he retrieved one of the crystals and placed it with the package in the rucksack. Leaving the rucksack on the floor of the chamber and clutching his cricket bat, he marched forward towards the two final doors. Opening door number eleven, his eyes almost popped out of his head. Standing on a trolley was a giant crystal; it looked like quartz. The main body of the crystal was cylindrical in shape, cut with six equal sides. It was about a metre and a half in height and forty cm in diameter. On top of the crystal was a moveable capstone in the shape of a thirteen-faced prism.

This must be the great crystal that was missing from the chambers of records, thought Alexander. *At a guess, I would say that the baron found it in Nesmut's tomb. The missing red journal would probably confirm that.* And then he exclaimed out loud, "But of course! This is what she was protecting! And what of that package? I'll bet that also came from her tomb. It may have something to do with the twelve crystals. It could be the hardware needed to read them! There can be little doubt but that the baron was very close to putting all the pieces together when he died, or rather, when he was murdered by the priestess! He was the victim of his own success, and it was because of his actions that all the other Northgates have been murdered!"

Finally, he opened the twelfth door. It was only his hatred that saved his sanity as the hideous vision met his eyes. Lying in an open coffin, propped against the far wall of the room, was the body of Nesmut! The bandages had been cut from her mummified corpse and she appeared before him, withered and terrible. The flesh on the body had shrivelled and the bones beneath it were clearly visible, the ribcage in particular. Her black hair sprang from her head, coarse and matted, and the skin was tautly drawn across her skull-like face. Her nose was flattened and her lips were shrunken back from blackened teeth. The hideous face was contorted into a terrifying fiendish grin, but the worst thing was the glass eyes—large, black and staring. It was a gruesome vision, but the boy did not run. Fury surged through him like a raging torrent.

"Finally, I get to meet you in the flesh, so to speak!" he roared. "Well, I would just like to thank you personally for killing my mother and father, and my dear friend Dr. Malone. It's payback time, baby!"

Marching forward, he grabbed the awful thing by the hair. Remarkably, the ancient cadaver stayed in tact as he dragged it across the floor of the chamber. Reaching the trapdoor, he hurtled the awful corpse through the opening in the stone, sending it crashing down onto the viewing platform. As it hit the ground, the head broke away from the neck, rolling horribly. Coming to a sudden stop, it looked up at the boy with its terrible staring eyes, grinning mockingly.

Retrieving his rifle, Alexander refilled the reservoir from a large bottle that he carried in his backpack. Descending the metal ladder, he pressed the trigger furiously. Lethal liquid rained down on the corpse until the reservoir was empty. A flare burst to life and fell towards the headless monster. Soon its desiccated flesh was engulfed in an inferno of hungry flames.

Approaching the head, the boy looked down at it contemptuously. "Kill my family, would you!" he screamed, as he kicked the abominable thing into the flames. Soon all that remained of the body was a blackened head and a pile of ashes. Walking over to the abominable staring skull, he drove down the butt of his rifle, cracking it in two. Retreating from the terrible thing, he climbed back up the ladder and re-entered the chamber. It was time to leave Northgate Hall, but he vowed to return. A few minutes later he stood again over the skull of Nesmut. Using his cricket bat this time, he smashed the thing into tiny pieces.

As he turned to leave, something glistened through the ashes. Using the end of his bat, he poked at it. It looked like glass. He pushed it clear of the hot ashes. When the object had cooled, he picked it up. It was a natural, uncut translucent crystal about the size of a small orange. The crystal gave off a violet radiance.

This must have had a purpose, thought Alexander. *Perhaps it was used to replace the priestess's black heart during the mummification process. Maybe it had a symbolic role, or possibly it was part of some occult process. Perhaps the dark creature drew power from it. The giant crystal may have fed it. Then again, perhaps Nesmut drew her power from the great crystal directly.* He tossed the violet crystal over the balustrade and watched it fall. Crashing onto a huge granite slab with tremendous force, it disintegrated into tiny shards.

That's all I can do for the moment, thought the boy as he began to descend the obelisk. *If the creature still exists on the Earth plane and continues to stalk me, then the great crystal will suffer the same fate. I will smash it to pieces. Maybe that's the final solution; we will have to see – if the world survives another day, that is!*

Traversing the tunnel, he walked out through the base of the Sphinx. Nesmut was nowhere to be seen. He pushed the door in the pedestal until it clicked shut, disguising the small area of exposed stone with moss and dirt. Now the boy knew that he must face him. Walking to where the body lay, he stared down sadly. His poor dear friend looked like a man serenely sleeping, but not a mortal man, a man of wax—an empty shell. Strangely, there was not a mark on his cloths or skin—no signs of scorching.

A lump grew in Alexander's throat and his eyes began to burn. Taking a gasping breath, he tried not to weep. "Why, why, why?" he shouted. "Why did you have to die?" Chest heaving, red-hot tears began to pour from his eyes.

CHAPTER 36
MOMENT OF TRUTH

Anita Gupta sat in her lounge, flicking nervously through the TV news channels. It had been many hours since the black boxes had sprung to life, and still nothing major appeared to have happened. She had been at home all day, monitoring the networks. Her team at the lab was tracking the radio and Internet news services.

Anita jumped, startled by the sudden ringing of the telephone. "Gupta here," she said curtly, annoyed by the interruption. There was silence on the other end of the line.

"Is anybody there?" she asked.

The faltering voice of a boy responded. "It's me—Alexander."

"Alexander!" exclaimed Anita. "I didn't see you at breakfast so I thought you had left early for college. It's difficult, keeping track of your movements these days! Are you all right?" She thought she heard the boy sobbing.

"Are you all right?" she repeated more softly.

"Not really," replied Alexander. "I've something to tell you," he said, his voice faltering again.

"Where are you?" interjected Anita.

"I'm at home," responded Alexander.

"At home?" said Anita, her voice rising. "What on earth are you doing there?"

Silence again.

"What's going on?" Anita asked firmly.

"The police dropped me back there," came the reply.

"The police?" gasped Anita.

"I'm afraid I've something terrible to tell you," sobbed the boy. "Frank is dead."

"Dead?" cried Anita. "Was there an accident?"

Silence again.

Alexander knew that he would have to lie, that he would have to tell her the same lie that he had told the police. Who would believe him if he said that the poor man had been struck down by a thunderbolt—a thunderbolt that had been hurled by a homicidal three-thousand-year-old Egyptian priestess? He was having enough trouble explaining what he was doing in the grounds of Northgate Hall as it was. The police might even launch an investigation, if the results of the autopsy indicated death by electrocution.

Anita waited patiently for a response. Eventually it came.

"I think it must have been a heart attack. He just fell over and stopped breathing."

"That's terrible!" exclaimed Anita. "You poor, poor boy! What an awful shock."

She paused, trying to take it in. Dear Frank dead! "Where did it happen?" she asked.

She heard more sobbing, and then the line went dead.

The shock is too much for the child. Good thing that he is at home with his family. Anita put down the phone with a shaking hand. "Poor dear Frank," she sighed. "I warned him about all that smoking and drinking."

She poured herself a large brandy. "To you, Frank," she toasted. "Now you know, now you finally know! I hope you are at peace, wherever you are. Here's to you, Frank." Downing a large gulp of spirits, she put down her glass, tears streaming down her cheeks. Sad as she was, she returned to the TV screen.

It was evening when Anita slowly opened her eyes after dozing off. The TV stood out vividly in the darkness of the room. There was no mistaking the terrible words running across the bottom of the screen. "POWERFUL EARTHQUAKE HITS IRAN AND TURKEY. THOUSANDS FEARED DEAD."

Late into the night, the magnitude of the disaster became clearer. Initial estimates put the number of dead at two million. Concern was mounting that the nuclear facility had been badly damaged in Iran. Experts were predicting that when the final death toll was known, it could be the worst earthquake in living memory. The region was bracing itself for aftershocks.

Back in High Wycombe, Alexander also heard the news. Terrible though it was, he was hugely relieved. No comet, thank God! And then he began to wonder. Northern Pakistan in 2005, and now Iran. A fundamentalist Christian might stupidly say it was the hand of God smiting the harbourers of terrorists and the illicit makers of atom bombs. Given what he had learnt about death beams of late, he began to wonder if these disasters where truly the work of nature, or if there was not a more sinister force operating here.

CHAPTER 37
THE GUARDIAN

ꕥ

Alexander sat at home in High Wycombe. With the death of Frank Malone, he could not face the thought of college. Lady Margaret Hall would be unbearably empty without the tempestuous Irishman.

The boy had just finished assembling something. It was the contents of the package that he had retrieved from the obelisk. Anticipation, even excitement, was growing in him as he looked at the strange object standing on the desk. The lower portion of the device consisted of a four-sided pyramid with a base width of twenty centimetres and a height of twelve centimetres. It was made of a lightweight metal that looked similar to aluminium. Close to the apex, four short prongs projected from the pyramid. They were made of a glass-like material and were positioned equidistantly and at the same height. There was a second pyramid that mirrored the dimensions of the base pyramid. The apex of this pyramid had been cut away and there were four grooves that corresponded exactly with the position of the prongs in the base pyramid. Alexander had clipped the two pyramids together so they were joined apex-to-apex.

There was a hollow in the base of the second pyramid. Four little glass-like prongs were visible inside. The crystal that he had retrieved from the obelisk had been inserted into this hollow so it was in contact with all four prongs. A smaller crystal of identical shape to the larger crystal had been included in the package. It was about three centimetres in diameter.

Alexander studied the device and began to speculate. *I doubt that this object would have meant anything to the ancient Egyptians, or anybody else who was around at that time, for that matter,* he thought, *but the fact that it was preserved and protected so well indicated that somebody knew that it was a mechanism for seeing into the crystals. They must have believed that some day, in some future time, men would come who would understand the machine; the "Worthy."*

He stroked his chin pensively. He had learnt a lot about technology in the past couple of years. One thing was for sure—crystals were playing an increasingly important role in the modern world. The latest TV screens, for example, used liquid crystal technology. In the not-too-distant future, microchip based electronic computers would be obsolete. They would be replaced by vastly faster and more powerful optical computers that used photonic crystal technology.

"But of course!" he gasped. "This has to be an optical computer, and the crystal some sort of fantastic data storage device! Question is, how do you turn it on? And then what do you do? There is no keyboard or monitor!"

Picking up the device, Alexander examined it closely. *How could it be powered?* he wondered. *There are no wires, no holes. Perhaps brain waves are the key to its operation. Machines are being developed now that can detect and interpret brain waves. The ultimate objective is a direct mental interface between man and computer. Perhaps the Aztlaneans had achieved that.*

He grabbed the small crystal. *It may be some sort of transmitter,* he guessed. He pressed the crystal into his forehead. Nothing happened. Then he tried visualisation. Focusing his powerful mind, he created a mental picture of the device firing into life and projecting an image. He kept at it, persevering until his visualisation seemed almost real. Suddenly there was a clicking sound. He broke his concentration and checked the device. One of the panels on the top pyramid had loosened.

The mechanism may have stiffened up. It's been a long time since it was last used! Turning on his desk lamp to get a better look, he moved the light bulb as close as he could to the device. *String!* he thought, and left his desk. Eventually, with some fiddling around, he secured the crystal to his forehead using string and tape. "This'll do for now," he mumbled.

Undaunted, he began the procedure again. And then it happened! Slowly at first, the panel began to descend. After a minute or so it had dropped right down. Inside the device he could see row after row of small black panels, each about one centimetre square. *They look like some sort of semiconductor. The thing could be solar powered!*

He moved the device and positioned it next to a window. Leaving the room, he returned with two table-lamps, which he positioned close to the pyramids. After a short while the other three panels began to drop. He decided to leave the device for a while, and went off for a drink of water.

Later, he attempted the visualisation technique again. This time he could feel an odd, buzzing sensation from the crystal that was strapped to his forehead. Suddenly, an image flashed before his eyes. It looked like it had been projected into the space in front of him at eyelevel, but he guessed that it had been beamed directly into his brain. It was a picture of an enormous head—the head of a lion. *It almost looks like a screen-saver,* thought the boy. *This is going to take some getting used to!"*

He visualised a menu screen. A scroll suddenly appeared. It looked like a list, but unfortunately, it was not written in English. He knew now that he was going to have to learn to read the Aztlanean language if he was going to make any real headway. Fortunately, next to each line of writing in the list was an icon, or picture. There were different types of paintings, sculptures, books and musical instruments listed. Mentally, he pressed one of the icons.

Instantaneously, a magnificent painting passed before his eyes. Underneath it was text. He guessed that it was a short article on the artist, painting style, and so on.

After about an hour of experimentation, Alexander decided to take a break. He gave the device a mental instruction to shut down using visualisation, rather than words. Instantly, the images disappeared. The metal panels did not rise, though. The boy guessed that the power system was still charging. Pulling at one of the desk draws, he grabbed a bar of chocolate. This had been an amazing experience and a truly significant breakthrough. Now he had the technology to read the crystals. The problem was that the crystals that he really wanted to look at were still in the obelisk at Northgate Hall.

Is the priestess still there? he wondered. *Have I vanquished her, or is she waiting for me, lurking in the darkness?* He thought again about that once-beautiful woman, the priestess Nesmut. He tried to look at things from her perspective. In life, she had been an anointed guardian of the Chambers of Records. She had given her very life to protect the vast and profound knowledge of the Aztlaneans. For millennia she had rested, silently guarding the secrets of the crystals. Had it not been for the rapacious English aristocrat, Algernon Northgate, she would be resting still, hidden below the Egyptian sands. It was he who had violated the sacred sanctuary and desecrated her grave.

Standing, the boy began to pace the room. "But she became a killer," he said with a deep sigh. *She killed many times; both the guilty and the innocent*, he thought. *What knowledge could be worth the blood of so many? With humanity moving ever closer to global catastrophe, the information locked in those crystals could be of incalculable value. The ancients had no need of oil and coal to power their civilisation. Even from what was written on the walls of the hidden chambers, it was clear that they had a profound knowledge of crystals and energy generation, far in advance of our own, even to this day. Why does she still kill?*

Alexander bit into his chocolate bar. He needed something soothing. *For all their knowledge,* he thought, *the Aztlaneans were just as flawed as we are. Even as they watched the asteroid approach them, the massive rock that they knew would annihilate them, they chose to go to war. They could have saved their civilisation, but instead of sharing their technology to defeat the menace in the heavens, they chose war and conquest. They were destroyed by their own paranoid selfishness.*

Sinking his teeth into the chocolate bar, he took another bite. *Today we've raised ourselves high, in terms of our knowledge and technology, and we're becoming like the "gods" of old,* thought the boy. *Unfortunately, we're not working in harmony with the Earth; we're slowly but surely consuming and destroying it. We're poisoning the air, the water and the soil. We're moving closer and closer to the brink of climate collapse, to the point of no return. New cheap and self-sustainable energy generation systems need to be developed and deployed fast. Global warming is accelerating and will soon be unstoppable. Those ancient crystals at Northgate Hall hold the key to the survival of our civilisation. I'm sure of it!*

He raised his hands in the air in a gesture of despair. "Why does she still kill?" he shouted. *The Aztlanean crystal technology could be weaponised, there is no doubt. Such weapons could destroy the planet, it is true. But surely that can no longer be an issue. Thousands of nuclear weapons have been created, enough to annihilate the Earth many times over... Perhaps the priestess still awaits the chosen one, an initiate of the ancient mysteries worthy to take her place.*

And then another thought struck the boy. *Perhaps everything that I have been through has been a test. The other poor unfortunates had failed, but I have passed. Nesmut could have attacked me from behind as I stood transfixed in horror above the body of Algernon Northgate, but she did not. Perhaps she could even have killed me in the chamber in the pyramidion if she had really wanted to. My parents died, but I was allowed to live. Did she deliberately spare me? Maybe the cremation of her body and the destruction of the crystal that lay within her corpse was the final act in this terrible drama.* But there was no way of really knowing. He knew that he had no other option, that there was no other choice; live or die, one day he would have to return to Northgate Hall. That was his destiny.

CHAPTER 38
INFERNO

ꕤ

A body lay stiff and naked on a stainless steel trolley. It was Dr. Frank Malone. "Pronounced dead on arrival," said one of the mortuary attendants cheerfully. Death was a very routine business in this room. Another attendant produced a plastic body bag. Without further comment, they manoeuvred the body into the bag, zipped it closed and slid it unceremoniously into one of the many storage cabinets.

The following morning a body was retrieved from one of the cabinets and wheeled into the autopsy room. "This one's urgent," said the pathologist as a technician positioned the corpse. A scalpel blade sliced smoothly through the skin at the midline of the skull. The skin was carefully dissected back to reveal the bone. A surgical saw began to buzz, and it was not long before the brain had been removed—and placed like a grotesque grey jelly into a stark steel bowl.

The following day, in the afternoon, two sombre looking men in black suits arrived. They were regulars at the mortuary and were soon engaged in light-hearted banter with the attendants. A cabinet was slid open and a body retrieved. Five minutes later it had been boxed in a run-of-the-mill coffin and was on its way to Robinson's funeral parlour on the Abingdon Road, close to central Oxford.

ꕤ

Frank Malone found himself sitting in an unfamiliar room. It looked like a small chapel. There was a handful of people dotted around, none of whom he recognised. *Where the hell am I?* Everything seemed so hazy. He remembered throwing himself in front of the boy to shield him, but nothing after that. *The lightening strike must have given me amnesia.* Arising from his chair, he approached the nearest person—an elderly woman with blue-rinsed hair.

"Excuse me," he said, his voice as deep and melodious as ever. The woman ignored him. That annoyed the Irishman. "Excuse me," he said more loudly. There was no response. *Maybe the old biddy's deaf,* he thought. He moved forward so he was directly in the line of her vision. Still, she ignored him. "Excuse me!" he roared. Nothing! It was as if he was not there. Touching her arm, his hand passed straight through it! "My God!" he gasped, "She's a ghost!"

ᘓᘐ

A telephone rang and a plain but formidable-looking woman in her mid-thirties picked up the receiver.

"Dr. Snodgrass here," said the voice on the other end of the line.

"How can I help?" asked the woman.

"There has been a bit of a cock-up in the mortuary," continued the pathologist. "The Coroner's Office is involved, so we need to sort it out fast! To keep it brief, two bodies have been misidentified. A Frank Mallory died of cancer and should have been released for cremation yesterday afternoon. A Frank Malone should have been autopsied. In a nutshell, the wrong man got autopsied. We need to locate the body of Frank Malone with all due haste before it is incinerated!"

"Leave it to me," said the woman calmly.

ᘓᘐ

Frank was in a state of shock. The woman was a spirit entity! Walking rapidly, he approached another stranger—a well-groomed middle-aged man wearing an expensive camelhair coat. To his utter horror, as he touched the man's shoulder his hand passed effortlessly into his body. "A room is full of frigging ghosts!" hissed the Irishman. And then it hit him full on. It was he who was the ghost! It was he who was dead! The lightening strike must have killed him! In that instant of terrible realisation, everything disappeared.

ᘛᘚ

A big, burly, irreverent looking man in a donkey jacket pushed a coffin into one of a bank of ovens and clanked shut the sturdy metal door. Seconds later, row upon row of powerful flame jets began to eat into the wood of the coffin, consuming it ravenously, remorselessly. Soon the corpse was visible, bathed in a blanket of flames. Like a nightmare from Hades, it sat partially upright, the flesh falling from its face like melting wax. Soon it would be ashes.

ᘛᘚ

Frank felt a tingling sensation in his toes and a prickling in his fingers. A strange relaxation swept over him. It was almost as if he were floating. And then he felt his eyelids begin to flicker. Suddenly they sprang wide open, but everything was blackness—a terrible blackness!

"You are blind!" screamed a voice inside his head. He felt a sudden heaviness and then a coldness—a horrible coldness. Lying there motionless, he could now feel pain. And then in one awful instant it all became clear. He was still alive—alive, but trapped in blackness! Desperately trying to move, his limbs lay limp. Shrieking in utter panic, his lips and tongue were mute, still paralysed. The air grew warm, and then came the terrible roaring. His heart began to race, thumping the blood through his veins. He started to tremble, and then to shake violently as smoke began to fill his lungs. At last he knew! He was in a coffin! He was in a crematorium! Soon the flames would reach him! In searing agony, they would devour his living flesh!

CHAPTER 39
STRANGER THAN FICTION

The Irishman braced himself for death as blinding light exploded into the coffin. But there was no burning heat—just stillness and the distant sound of voices. He felt his body being lifted into the air—air that was soft and fresh. And then he heard the voices once again, but closer now.

"It's a bloody miracle!" said a deep gruff voice. "I've never seen the likes of it. This bloke should be dead!"

"It's lucky the police phoned through when they did," said a lighter, more measured voice. "We got the coffin out of the furnace just in time. Still, I was expecting to see a corpse lying there, not some poor unfortunate blighter seconds away from a terrible death!"

"Who'd av thought it in this day and age? You'd think by now they'd know if a bloke were dead or not!" said the burly voice.

"The human body's an amazing thing," said the second voice. "Apparently it can go into some sort of trance, where it can exist for many days in a state of suspended animation. Fortunately, it doesn't happen very often—but it does happen! Only last month I was reading about a chap who woke up in the nick of time on an autopsy table, just as a scalpel blade bit into his chest! That's a comforting thought.

I think we both need a drink. Finding this chap alive was a bit of a shock, to say the least!"

They were interrupted by the sound of violent coughing. "Make mine a treble!" spluttered a third voice.

Grinning broadly, the manager headed off in the direction of a brandy bottle. "Sometimes, mate," he said, looking at a dishevelled figure in a shroud, "life's stranger than fiction, stranger than bloody fiction!"

Swearing silently, Frank Malone closed his eyes and shuddered.

APPENDIX

What follows is the essay that Alexander wrote in answer to the question, "Discuss a phenomenon or event that is likely to have a significant global impact. Express a personal view on the likely response of world governments."

GLOBAL WARMING

The phenomenon

Most people in the developed world are familiar with the term "global-warming." Worryingly, though, many people remain oblivious to the rapidly approaching catastrophic consequences of this phenomenon. The activities of humanity are now starting to have a powerful impact on the climate of planet Earth. During the last 200 years of industrialisation, the atmospheric concentration of carbon dioxide (CO^2) has increased from 220 parts per million to around 370 parts per million. This is a massive 70 per cent increase.

CO^2 is one of the basic building blocks from which plants synthesise their food. At the present time, it is estimated that around six billion tonnes of carbon is pumped into the atmosphere every year, yet the relative concentration that is detectable in the atmosphere is only around 3 billion tonnes in a given year. This is because the oceans and huge rain forests, such as the 500 million hectares of trees in the Amazon basin, are acting as a massive carbon sponge, reabsorbing 50 percent of the carbon that is thrown into the atmosphere, thus slowing climate change. So climate change is being slowed, but not stopped.

Another factor that had been slowing the rate of global warming is air pollution with small particulates. The particles are 4 times smaller than most of the natural particles that make up clouds. These tiny particles become surrounded by small globules of water. Because the globules are so small, they do not form raindrops like the larger, natural occurring particles. They form clouds which, because of the shiny nature of the small water droplets, reflect the sun's rays and exert a cooling effect on the global weather. Ironically, due to more recent attempts to improve the air quality, particulate emissions from industrial processes and vehicles such as cars and trucks have dropped considerably, and the supply of the tiny particulates is drying up. It is due to this cleaning up of the air that these special reflective clouds are diminishing in number, thus accelerating the rate of global warming. Therefore, in a perverse twist of fate, measures designed to improve the atmosphere are actually speeding up the global warming phenomenon.

Many climate models now predict that as CO^2 concentrations rise, the El Niño weather phenomenon may become an annual event, resulting in an increase in the dry season. The sharp reduction of moisture in the air, and the loss of the heavy rains would cause massive devastation in the forests of the Amazon Basin. The trees would die, to be replaced by vast tracks of grassland or "savannah," as it is called. This disaster would greatly increase the amounts of CO^2 in the atmosphere, further elevating global temperatures and warming the oceans.

The oceans contain an even more potent greenhouse gas than CO^2. Methane is at least 20 times more powerful than CO^2 when acting as a global warming agent. Methane, formed from the decay of organic matter in the ocean floor, exists in vast amounts. It is held in a semi-solid form as a hydrate by the massive water pressure and by low temperatures. These methane hydrates are normally safely contained below the surface, kept solid by high pressures and low temperatures. However, as the seas begin to warm up, particularly in the shallower polar waters, methane will start to escape into the atmosphere, eventually reeking climate chaos on an enormous scale.

In view of this recent disturbing finding, it is critical that both the scientific community and governments wake up—and wake up fast. The general philosophy on this planet is this: do nothing until bad things start happening, then make the painful and politically unpopular decisions to fix them. The philosophy in relation to global warming is, let CO^2 gradually build up until the temperatures get uncomfortable, and damage due to severe weather conditions becomes a massive problem, then do something about it. However, few seem to recognise that once we exceed the critical threshold, climate change will be unstoppable. Given the present knowledge of the workings of the climate system, a concentration of 550 parts per million is an absolute limit which cannot be exceeded without catastrophic and irreversible alterations. At the current rate of growth in CO^2 emissions, if nothing is done, this level will be reached within the next 20 years.

Even now, massive glaciers are beginning to melt and sea levels are starting to rise. The incidence of severe weather events around the planet is also on the increase. So, the first effects of global warming are already with us.

The response

Now is the time for action—not next year or the year after. We are running out of time fast. While some nations recognise there *is a problem, and we have had initiatives such as the Kyoto Accord on Global Warming, key nations are not signing up to measures needed to reduce CO² emissions. Notable amongst these rouge nations is the United States. Their argument is that their industries are now under threat from emerging nations such as India and China, and that to remain competitive, they cannot adopt measures designed to reduce greenhouse emissions. Humanity seems to have lost the plot. There is nothing less than the fate of the planet at stake here! What is the good of economic competitiveness on a doomed planet!*

The cornerstone philosophy of the modern world is competition. Just about everything seems to revolve around competition, from economies to most forms of entertainment. We live in a world obsessed by competition. There is no real oneness or unity of purpose at the international level. Every nation puts its own interests first and foremost. Under these conditions, how can there be a unified strategy to combat climate change? Many seem to think that when things get bad, the scientists will sort it all out. "Surely science is the master of nature," they say. Well, in the modern era, even scientists have to compete to survive. The pure quest for truth, for knowledge, has become very rare. Scientists are now driven by the need for success and to meet near-sighted short-term goals. In academia, scientists must compete with other scientists for the limited funding available, and they are constrained by the dictates of that funding.

In industry, scientists must dance to the tune of their employers in the quest for products and technologies that generate money. Indeed, the catastrophe which we now face is due to industrialisation and the insatiable need for energy. Most of this energy is, of course, produced by burning oil, coal and gas, which floods countless tons of CO^2 into the atmosphere.

The global climate is like a juggernaut, slowly starting to run out of control. Soon it will be impossible to stop, even by the best efforts of science. If too little is done too late, what are the likely consequences for the human race? They are grim, very grim indeed. Sea levels will continue to rise as the global temperature increases, with the eventual inundation and submersion of all of the world's coastal cities and much of the land at lower altitudes. There will be death on a massive scale due to starvation, as many areas of the world are reduced to deserts by the relentlessly escalating temperatures.

There is also the unthinkable scenario of a massive ice mass, the size of Texas, splitting from the melting ice sheets of the north or south poles, and drifting into the ocean. Such a sudden and monumental shifting in weight could destabilise the earth's spin, causing the planet to tilt on its axis. Only a minor tilt would be needed to destroy most, if not all, of the human race in a series of enormous tidal waves, huge earthquakes and terrifying volcanic *eruptions. Black dust clouds from the eruptions would block out the light from the sun for years.*

There is only one solution. The world must act, and the world must act now! But who will rally the nations? Who will give the clarion call? And most worrying of all, will any of them listen—really listen?

LaVergne, TN USA
11 December 2009

166682LV00003B/65/A